"From page one, *The Journey Ho*
me never wanting the book to enu. ... .
span this book touched on was both inspiring and touching, leaving me
with the indescribable words at how brilliant this read was for me. Sometimes the path is winding and filled with unexpected detours, but fate rights
the path, bringing us...home."

– KRISTIN MAYER, author of *Ripple Effect* and The *Trust Series*

"Kelly Elliott knocks it out of the park again! Cale and Maddie's story was
an angst-filled roller coaster I loved from the very first page."

– KAHLEN AYMES, *USA TODAY* Bestselling author of
The Remembrance Trilogy and *The After Dark Series*

"*The Journey Home* is a heartbreaking tale of how love can shatter into a
million pieces at night, only to rise again into the most brilliant of sunrises
in the morning."

– BECCA MANUEL, Becca the Bibliophile

WHAT THE READERS ARE SAYING –

"Kelly Elliott takes us places she's never gone before. *The Journey Home* will take you on a roller coaster of emotions. Cale and Maddie will go through lies, heartache, and deceit. You will love and hate their journey. Love is not always easy, but when it is true you always find your way home."

– KAREN BELL

"This amazing story is unlike anything I've read before by Kelly! She has spun together a web of love, loss, lies, suspense, drama, and twists which caught and held me captive from the beginning. *The Journey Home* will make you experience every emotion possible through the eyes of Maddie and Cale. Kelly shows us how, with fate being on your side, home and love, and new beginnings are possible."

– LISA WAUGH

"OMG, this book was amazing. Although I loved the *Wanted* series, this has been my all-time favorite book! It's so real to life, it's relatable and the story lines makes you not want to put the book down."

– JESSICA BAYRON

"Kelly has done it again. *The Journey Home* is a sexy story about two people that have an indescribable instant connection that they have to learn to adjust to in their everyday lives. Drama, suspense, and the feeling of love and loss are only a few emotions Kelly will bring out of you through Maddie and Cale. 10 golden stars for *The Journey Home.*"

– CHRISTINA STEVENSON

The Journey Home

Kelly Elliott

Copyright © 2014 by Kelly Elliott
Published by K. Elliott Enterprises
Cover design by Lisa J Wilson with Design by Blink
Editing by Emily Anderson with Yellow Bird Editors
Interior design and formatting by JT Formatting

First Edition: October 2014
Library of Congress Cataloging-in-Publication Data
The Journey Home – 1st ed
ISBN-13: 978-0-9903210-3-3

www.kellyelliottauthor.com

For exclusive releases and giveaways signup for Kelly's newsletter at
http://eepurl.com/JoKyL

PROLOGUE

Cale

T HE MOMENT HER green eyes looked into mine, I knew I was in trouble. Then she smiled at me and I knew I was screwed for sure.

"Cale, dude, we just graduated from college. I didn't have this damn party for you to pussy-ass around. Find someone and screw her. Tonight's mission is to get laid by the first willing girl. Not stare for two hours at some girl who is clearly out of your league.

I looked at my best friend, Jack, and laughed. "Is that so? Then why are you still standing here?"

Jack shrugged. "I just haven't found the one yet. That's all."

I rolled my eyes and chuckled. "Uh huh. I'm going outside for some fresh air."

Jack was about to say something when a blonde walked by. Her breasts were falling out of her shirt. As she walked by, she licked her lips and winked at Jack.

"And there she is," Jack said.

He slapped my back and smiled as he turned and followed the blonde. I shook my head and walked around to the back deck that led down to the beach. I wasn't surprised that Jack was hooking up with someone tonight. We'd been friends since first grade and, even back then, his blue eyes and blond hair seemed to attract the girls. Jack was more into one-night stands, but I at least wanted to find someone who made me feel something.

I stepped off the back deck and made my way down to the water. I couldn't get those green eyes out of my mind. I walked to the water's edge and looked out at the black ocean. *I wonder if she goes to the University. Who did she come here with?*

I shook my head and laughed. "Snap the hell out of it Blackwood."

"Do you make a habit of talking to yourself?"

I smiled and turned around to see her standing there, giving me a smile that forced me to fight to keep my knees from shaking.

"Only when I'm alone, standing on a beach in the middle of the night," I said.

The girl laughed and it pulsed through my body like nothing I'd ever experienced. I swallowed hard and tried to come back to my senses.

She walked up to me and tilted her head as she bit down on her lower lip. "Or when your best friend just ditched you to hook up with someone?"

"The blonde?"

She nodded. "Monica has been after your buddy all night."

"Have we met?" I asked her, looking her up and down. I'd definitely remember this girl if I'd seen her before. She was beautiful. Her brown hair fell just below her shoulders. She had a perfect body with breasts that were begging to be held in my hands and hips that gave her the prefect hourglass figure. I'd never cared for stick figures or girls who wanted to be rail thin.

She laughed and began walking along the beach. "No, but I've been admiring you from afar." She said as she wiggled her eyebrows. "At least for the last two hours."

I smiled and followed her. "I guess that makes two of us then."

"To think I didn't even want to come this party. I guess we're both lucky that I got dragged along."

I glanced at her as she looked away and bit her lower lip. I had the feeling she didn't put herself out there like this very often.

"Do I get your name, at least?"

She stopped and looked at me. "Maddison, but I go by Maddie. Yours?"

"Cale."

She reached out her hand and I took it in mine. In that moment, I felt it. With the way she sucked in a breath, I knew she'd felt it too.

"Maddie, may I ask you something?"

She smiled slowly. Now it was my turn to suck in a breath.

"Depends on what you're gonna ask me, I guess."

I lifted my mouth and gave her a half-smile as I thought, *What is it about this girl?*

"Would you think it was too forward of me to kiss you? I mean, we *literally* just met, but you take my breath away."

Her lips parted slightly. The moonlight was shining on her face, lighting it up in such a way that I could see her eyes searching my face.

"Do you often find yourself on alone a beach, propositioning a stranger for a kiss?" She asked with a smirk.

I shook my head. "This would be a first for me."

She looked down the beach and giggled. "Me too."

She looked back at me. "I can't explain it, but you...you make me..." She laughed and shook her head, looking away. "This is crazy insane. I can't even believe I followed you out here."

I placed my finger under her chin and brought her eyes back to mine.

"I make you what?"

Her smile faded as she said, "You make me want more than just a kiss, Cale. And I've never in my life done something like this."

I'd never had my heart beat so hard in my chest before. "Maddie..." I shook my head as I leaned down and brushed my lips against hers. She placed her hands on my chest and slowly moved them up, wrapping them behind my neck as I deepened the kiss.

I'd kissed plenty of girls, but I'd never felt anything like this before. She let out a little moan as I pulled her closer to me. She ran her hand through my hair, slightly tugging.

I pulled my lips back, attempting to get my erratic breathing under control.

"Tell me how far you want to go with this, Maddie."

Her chest was moving up and down so fast as she eased herself down onto the ground. I followed her as she laid back on the sand and I brought my lips back to hers.

The kiss started out slow and soft. She wrapped her legs around me and pulled me closer. As I pushed my hard dick into her, she let out a moan. I began grinding my dick against her.

"Touch me," she whispered, as she began unbuttoning her shorts. "Please touch me."

Briefly, I felt like I should stop us from making a mistake. But didn't feel like it could possibly be a mistake. It felt as if we had been waiting a lifetime for each other.

Maddie

I COULDN'T BELIEVE the words that were coming from my lips—asking a complete stranger to touch me. On a beach. Where anyone could walk up at any moment.

The second he looked at me with his piercing, green eyes, something happened. I'd felt him watching me all night as I moved around the room. Earlier, when Monica told me about the party, and how she desperately needed a night out, I knew my best friend wasn't going let me get out of going.

Then I saw him. *Cale.* It was as if we had been searching for each other. The moment we looked into each other's eyes, we found destiny.

I'd watched him make his way down to the beach with a blanket. I stood there for a few seconds, contemplating whether or not I should follow him. Maybe he wanted to sit on the beach alone and unbothered.

Now I was lying on the beach, Cale slipping my shorts and panties off as he laid his blanket underneath me. *What the hell am I doing? I don't do this sort of thing. Ever.*

His lips grazed across my neck and I let out a moan, thrusting my hips toward him. I needed to feel his touch and it was driving me crazy that he was taking so long to touch me. He pushed my shirt up, pulling my bra down and exposing my hard nipples. When he leaned down and began sucking on one, I let out a gasp.

"Oh God, yes."

Who is this girl? My mother would disown me if she saw me right now. Did I remember to take my birth control pill? God, I feel so easy. But this feels so right.

Cale sat up and ran his hand through his beautiful, wavy hair. It fell back in his eyes, light brown in the moonlight. I could feel the wetness between my legs. "Maddie, I've never been so turned on in my life. But I'm not sure I should...I mean we...God, I mean I want to like you wouldn't believe. I just..."

If I didn't do something soon, he would get up and revert to being a gentleman. But I didn't need a gentleman. What I needed at that moment was to feel him inside of me. I quickly began undoing his pants and, as I pushed them down, I watched his erection spring out. I licked my lips and looked up at him as I wrapped my hand around his dick. I'd never been so brazen, but I had to have him. I was leaving in the morning for Europe, and I needed Cale to make love to me *now.*

I lay back and spread my legs open as his eyes followed every curve of my body. He reached for his pants and pulled a condom from his wallet. I couldn't believe how my body was shaking with the anticipation of him being inside me.

He set the condom to the side and leaned down again, capturing my lips with his. The kiss was soft and gentle as Cale moved his hand down my body. He lightly touched my thigh as I let out a moan. *Touch me.* I needed him to touch me.

"Fuck me…" he whispered as he slipped his fingers inside me. I could feel my body pulling him in. I needed more. His fingers massaged inside of me as he kissed and sucked on my nipple. His other hand pulled and twisted my other nipple and I felt my build-up begin. *Oh God, This is going to be a huge orgasm.*

"Maddie, you feel so damn amazing," he said.

"Cale!" I shouted as he pushed his mouth to mine and began rubbing my clit with his thumb. I fell apart hard and fast. I moaned into his mouth as he rubbed out my orgasm. Other guys had given me an orgasm before, but none of them had worked their fingers like Cale did.

"I want to bury myself deep inside you, Maddie."

I looked into his eyes and smiled. "What are you waiting for?"

He sat up and grabbed the condom, slipping it over his dick. He looked back into my eyes. "I've never in my life wanted someone like I want you." He slowly began to push in when he stopped.

"Are you sure?" he asked.

I smiled as I nodded and wrapped my legs around his body, pulling his body closer to mine.

"I've never been so sure of anything in my life." I said as I placed my hands on his face and brought his lips to mine. "Cale, don't be so gentle. Please, I need you."

He closed his eyes and impaled me. I let out a gasp as my body adjusted to him. He was bigger than any guy I'd ever been with. Not that there had been a ton—I'd slept with two other boyfriends. Neither of them ever made me feel the way Cale did—and I'd only known him for thirty minutes.

Cale took me to heaven and back. Not once, but three times. He hovered over my body as we tried to catch our breath and calm our beating hearts. Then he leaned down and kissed me. "Maddie," he whispered against my lips before he deepened our kiss. I'd never experienced a moment in time like I just had with Cale. My heart still raced, overwhelmed with the emotions that were overtaking my body.

Could it really be possible to fall in love with someone so quickly?

1

Cale

TWO YEARS LATER

"**C**ALE. CALE, DID you even hear a word I said? Jesus... Cale!"

I turned my head to Jack. "What did you say?"

"I was asking when you're leaving town, you ass," he said. "What the hell are you looking at?"

I shook my head and quickly turned back to check out the girl across the street. I could have sworn it was her.

"Nothing. I thought I saw Maddie."

Jack let out a laugh. "Jesus Christ, dude. Maddie? Really? It's been two years and that ship sailed the moment she left you after fucking you on the beach. Without so much as a goodbye, even!"

I gave Jack a dirty look. "She said goodbye."

Jack rolled his eyes. "That's right. You asked for her number and said you wanted to see her again. She freaked and said she was leaving the country the next day to start a new job. Sorry dude, that's code for 'you were a terrible fuck and I never want to see you again.'"

I shook my head and held back the urge to hit my best friend. Jack was like a brother to me. Otherwise, maybe I would have thrown that punch.

My phone pinged and I took it out of my pocket. I let out a sigh as I read the text from my mother.

Mom: *Darling, dinner tonight. Don't be late. And please bring a date for Pete's sake!*
Me: *Can't tonight, mom. Plans.*
Mom: *Cancel them. Your father needs you there. It's a very important business contact. Don't disappoint him, Cale.*
Me: *Mom, I really can't and you have to give me better notice. Besides, I'm not dating anyone.*
Mom: *I'm giving you notice. Dinner tonight at 7:30 sharp. I'll expect two. I have to run, getting my nails done.*

I shoved my phone back into my pocket. "Fuck."

"Let me guess," Jack said. "That was Mommy and she's hosting a dinner party for one of Daddy's big, important friends."

I smirked at Jack and nodded. We'd been friends long enough that he knew better than anyone how damn controlling my mother could be. She was going to shit her pants when she found out I was moving to Beaver Lake, far away from them in Fayetteville. Granted, I would only be an hour away by car, but my mother would still say that I was abandoning the family.

Jack laughed as his coffee was called out. He slapped me on the back and said, "I'll meet you outside."

When my caramel macchiato was finally called out I walked up to the counter and smiled at Dee.

"Hey there, Cale. How are you today?" she asked with a wink.

I grinned back and nodded my head slightly. "I'm doing well, Dee. I'll see you tomorrow morning."

"Okay! See you then!" Dee shouted out.

I walked outside, inhaling the crisp, fall air. I loved fall. It was my favorite time of year.

Looking over, I saw Jack talking to some redhead. He pulled out her hand and wrote his phone number on her wrist. I chuckled as I watched her blush and nod. Probably agreeing to call him later this evening.

I sat at the table and looked at him, shaking my head.

He walked up to me, smirking. "What the hell are you looking at?" he asked.

I rolled my eyes as I took a sip of my coffee. Setting it down, I turned around and watched the redhead walk away. I glanced back at Jack and said, "Don't you ever get tired of playing this game?"

He pulled his head back and looked at me like he had no clue what I was talking about.

"What game?"

I raised my eyebrow. "Jack, don't you ever think about settling down? Aren't you tired of the dating scene?"

You'd have thought I'd just asked him to solve world hunger or something.

"No, I never get tired of it. I like my life. Hell, you'd like your life a hell of a lot more if you stopped looking for goddamn one-night-stand-Maddie. The chances of you ever finding her, Cale, are slim. Very, very, *very* slim. You've got to let it go. Let *her* go." Jack shook his head. "Cale, you've walked away from so many girls because you're comparing them to her. I get that it was earth-shaking, mind-boggling sex, and you felt a connection with her. But Cale, it's time to move on."

I took another sip of coffee and looked away from Jack as I nodded. "Yeah, I know." I let out a sigh and said, "Looks like I'll be telling my parents tonight about moving to Beaver Lake."

"That's more like it. That's the old Cale I know. Now go flirt with that blonde who keeps hitting on you at the bar. She looks like she is begging to be fucked."

I almost spit out my coffee as I looked around to make sure no one had heard him. He stood up and shook my hand before saying, "Good luck with Mom and Dad tonight. Take a picture of your mother when you tell her you're moving away."

He started laughing as he grabbed his coffee and took off toward his BMW—but not before he stopped to talk to yet another girl. I stood and grabbed my coffee and headed to my own car. I had to leave for London in two days. Another thing my mother wasn't pleased with, even though my father asked me to go. She hated my job, since I'd sometimes be gone for weeks working. But I loved it and had no intentions of getting off the road anytime soon.

Another reason not to settle down with just anyone who came along. I stopped and turned to look back at Starbucks when the strangest feeling came over me. But I saw nothing. Shaking my head to clear my thoughts, I continued toward my car.

Cale, it's time to move on.

2

Maddie

"**I** DON'T KNOW why you stay friends with her, Maddie. She's a jealous bitch. Why you can't see that she actually wants to be you is beyond me."

I laughed as I made my way to the entrance of Starbucks. I pulled the door open to step inside. I stopped and Monica slammed into my back as she let a very loud "Shit!" escape her mouth.

"Way to stop in the middle of the damn doorway, Maddie. Jesus, I swear!"

I looked around the Starbucks. The weirdest feeling came over me. Like there was someone here that I knew. A quick look around revealed that there was no one. I shrugged and made my way up to the counter.

"One tall caramel macchiato please," I said with a smile.

I waited for Monica to order before I started talking. "Monica you don't understand. Zoey is sick. She needs friends, and I'm the only friend she's got."

Monica rolled her eyes. "There's a reason she only has you as a friend. She's a bitch! Plus, I don't trust her as far as I can throw her."

I let out a small giggle. Zoey *was* a bitch. I couldn't argue with that. But she needed me and I couldn't abandon her.

"Hey how was the date last night?" Monica asked, wiggling her eyebrows. "You get laid?"

My mouth dropped open as I looked around the coffee shop. "Holy crap. Can you be any louder?"

Both of our drinks were called out and Monica laughed as she walked up to retrieve her iced green tea. "Yes. Yes, I could be much, much louder."

I grabbed my drink and smiled at the laughing young girl behind the counter. We made our way out of Starbucks and started to head to one of the shops I worked for.

"The date, Maddie? You can't get out of answering me, bitch."

I sucked in a deep breath and let it out quickly. The smell of fall was in the air. I loved fall. "It sucked."

"Oh Jesus. Why? And don't say you 'just didn't feel a connection.'"

I looked away, taking a sip of my coffee. "Okay, I won't."

We walked in silence only about thirty seconds before Monica grabbed my arm. "Are you going to spill it, or what?"

"You just told me not to tell you."

"No. I said don't tell me the same damn thing you always tell me. Tell me he had gross, yellow, crooked teeth or that he pissed the bed or that he stunk."

I let out a giggle. "Nope. He had perfect teeth, almost too perfect. I'm going to guess that, since he workouts regularly, he has amazing self-control therefore has a decent control of his bladder. He *did* come on to me and invited me back to his place, but I turned him down."

"Ugh! Maddie, why?"

I shrugged. "He wasn't…him."

Monica stopped walking and hung her head.

"What's wrong?" I asked.

"*Him.* Him is what's wrong. This guy, this one-night stand you had two years ago – a guy who, I might add, you pushed away after getting spooked by your intense feelings. This guy, Maddie, has probably moved on. I saw him that night when he walked us to the car. He was good looking, *really* good looking. I doubt he's sitting at home hoping to run into your ass on the beach again."

I took a sip of my coffee and then sighed. "I know, Monica. Believe me, I know."

I thought back to that night. Cale was indeed handsome with a body that, to this day, made me burn with desire. He was tall and built, but not so built that he looked fake. His messy brown hair and green eyes would be burned into my memory forever.

"The fact that you went to Jack's house six months after your night with Cale only to be told that Cale was in a relationship, that should have snapped you out of it."

I rolled my eyes, thinking back to that day. "Yeah, I know. God, I still can't believe his friend tried to get me to sleep with him. What a prick." I said, giggling.

Monica rolled her eyes. "I'm not. The guy was a class-A prick but, man oh man, was he good in the sack. I'd totally do him again." She wiggled her eyebrows as I let out a chuckle.

My phone beeped as I pulled it out of my pocket.

Mom: *Maddison. Dinner this evening. I'll send the car.*

I rolled my eyes and let out a long, drawn-out sigh.

"What's wrong?" Monica asked as she sipped of her coffee.

I bit on my lip, trying to think of an excuse not to go this evening.

"Give it up. You've never been able to tell her no, so don't bother trying to now," Monica said as she raised one eyebrow at me.

"Shit," I whispered. I hit reply.

Me: *Mom, I have plans this evening. I'm so sorry.*
Mom: *Break them. The car will be there at 7:30.*

I saw her reply and wanted to scream. "Ugh! She treats me like a child and I'm so damn sick of it."

Monica stood up and looked down at me. "Do something about it, then. Don't go tonight. Show her she can't boss you around."

I looked up at her and smiled. "I think I'll do that."

Monica let out a gruff laugh. "Uh huh. Let me know how that works out for you, darlin'. I've gotta run. Got a date tonight with that guy. You know, the one that knows how to make dates end rather nicely. He's got a cock ring too!"

I rolled my eyes and waved goodbye to Monica. I loved my best friend but, I swear, she'd screw any guy who was good looking, blond, and blue-eyed.

I stood and made my way to my car. As much as I wanted to blow off my parents' dinner tonight, I knew I wouldn't. I got in my car and turned toward the cleaners as I attempted to psych myself up for an evening of hearing my mother ask me over and over why I was single, then following up with telling all of her friends about my bizarre singleness. In my mother's eyes, I was a failure, and she reminded me of this every single time I saw her.

"This is going to be one hell of a long evening," I said to myself.

3

Cale

I APPROACHED MY parents' front door and jumped when it flew open. I smiled at my mother, who stood before me, dressed to the nines.

"Mom, you look lovely this evening," I said as I took her hand and kissed it.

"You're late, Cale," she hissed through her teeth.

I noted the empty driveway. "Doesn't look like the party's started yet, Mom."

She shot me a dirty look and turned to walk back into the house. "Mitchel," she called. "Your son is here. The party is not here, Cale."

I rolled my eyes as my mother walked into my father's office. When she was pissed at me, I was my father's son. But when I did well, I was her darling baby boy.

I followed her into the office. My father was sitting behind his giant, dark walnut desk. The smell of the office instantly brought me back to my childhood. I'd loved to play in here, hiding from my mother under the desk. My father would laugh and tell me that she'd never find me, since she'd declared the office forbidden to me. But, according to my father, I was a breath of fresh air—I was always

9

welcome.

"Evening, Dad," I said with a smile, reaching across the desk to shake his hand.

"Cale, it's good to see you, son. Let me just finish up this one thing and then we'll head to the goddamn party your mother is forcing us both to attend."

I attempted to hide my smile as my mother shoved her hands on her hips and glared.

"Do you know how important this man is to your career, Mitchel?" she asked in a shocked tone.

My father closed his laptop, stood up, and gave my mother a fake smile. "Do you know how badly I want to retire and travel the world? I can't, though because my wife demands the world of me and, in order to keep up with her high maintenance lifestyle, I have to work my ass off and socialize with arrogant, stuck-up assholes."

My mother gasped as my father winked at me and left the room.

My mother muttered a few words under her breath and grabbed her shawl and a clutch. She gave me a dirty look and shook her head as she walked out of the office, ordering me to follow her.

"Come on, Cale. Maybe we can find you a nice, young lady tonight."

"Oh, God, Mom. Please don't start that again."

She threw her hand up, brushing me off. I followed my parents out and slipped into the back seat of a Bentley Mulsanne. "New car?" I asked as I settled into the seat.

"Your father's new car." My mother said as she powdered her nose.

"Nice," I said, my voice dripping with sarcasm.

My mother sighed. "You'd have all of this, Cale, if you weren't so damn stubborn. All you had to do was work for your father's company. But, no, you had to go after some silly job."

I shook my head and looked out the window. I had a degree in civil engineering with a minor in mathematics. I loved my job as a surveyor, and I loved traveling. It meant I could be hundreds of miles away from my mother, for weeks at a time.

"I don't want to work for Dad, Mom. I like my job."

She chuckled. "You live in a flat! You could have so much more. *That's* why you're single."

My father had inherited a shit-ton of money from his father. My granddad was originally from London, England—some hotshot duke of something. He owned an English newspaper and lived half the year in the UK and the other half in America. We'd gone to England at least a half dozen times to see family before I was even sixteen. I always loved visiting their country estate.

"Mary, please," my father said. "Leave the boy alone. I admire his ambition to make it on his own."

My mother lowered her voice. "Psh, he'd have a wife by now if he would just do things my way."

"You know, Mom," I said, "I'm still in the car and can hear you."

"Let's just get there and pray that this evening is beneficial." She said as she pulled out her phone and began texting someone.

TWO AND HALF hours later, I was standing in the corner, drinking another glass of wine while my mother moved from person to person. She was attempting to kiss up to some guy who owned a communications company. Every now and then, she'd walk a young girl up to me to introduce her, and I'd have to stand there and make small talk. I just wanted to get the fuck out of there and get home so I could pack my bags and prep to leave for London. I was making the trip to take care of something for my father regarding Gramps'

newspaper.

I was just about to find my father and tell him that I'd had enough when the hair on my arms began to stand on end. Something about the air in the room changed. It felt electrified. I caught a glimpse of a girl walking by, heading toward the exit of the hotel ballroom. Her light brown hair was piled on top of her head. She walked up to the guy my mother had been brown-nosing all night and kissed him on each cheek. He brought her in for a hug, then whispered something in her ear.

Something about her was very familiar. I started to head in her direction.

"Cale? Cale, darling, I'd like you to meet someone." My mother grabbed my arm and pulled me to a stop. I turned to see a young girl standing there, smiling. She couldn't have been more than eighteen.

"Ashley Jackson, This is my son Cale. Cale, this is Ashley. Her daddy owns a condominium housing development on Beaver Lake."

I glanced at my mother and smiled before turning to Ashley.

"Really? I just bought a house on Beaver Lake."

Lucy smiled. My mother didn't.

"What? You bought a house? By yourself?"

I slowly looked down at my mother. "Yes, Mommy Dearest. I bought a house, by myself. I have this thing called a job. I work for my money."

Ashley covered her mouth with one hand in an attempt to hide her laughter. My mother's mouth fell open, and she stood there, stunned into silence. I downed the rest of my wine and set the glass on the tray of a passing waiter. I glanced back and saw the brown-haired girl leaving the room.

"Ashley, if you'll excuse me. I really have to run. Mother, it was good seeing you again."

"Cale, you're being rude, darling."

Glancing over to Ashley I smiled. "Ashley, excuse my rudeness. I really have to get going. Tell Dad I said goodnight, Mom."

I turned and quickly made my way to the exit. When I pushed

open the doors, I started jogging toward the elevators. The doors were shutting, but not before I caught a glimpse at her. She was staring down at her phone, her face hidden in shadow. She appeared to be crying.

The doors shut and, just like that, she was gone.

"Fuck," I whispered.

I pulled out my cell. I had the photo I was looking for saved in a specific folder. I tapped the screen and pulled up the picture.

There she was with her light brown hair and the most beautiful green eyes I'd ever seen. I studied her face as I stood in front of the elevator. When the doors opened, I stepped in and pushed the button for the ground floor.

I was tired of feeling like this. Empty. Alone. Searching for someone I'd never see again.

I headed out to the front of the hotel and hailed a taxi. When it stopped, I opened the back door and slipped inside.

"Twenty-seven Downing Court, please," I said to the driver.

Ten minutes later, I was walking into my apartment and throwing my keys on the side table. I grabbed a beer and I headed for the sofa. As I sank into the cushions, I let out a sigh.

I turned on the TV and channel surfed as I drank. After a few minutes, I texted Jack.

Me: *What are you doing?*

Jack: *Just got done fucking my date in the ally outside her apartment. You done hobnobbing?*

Me: *Yep.*

Jack: *Want to meet for a few beers?*

I stared at Jack's text. If we went out, I'd end up getting drunk. I was too pissed off at my mother not to. It was always like this. Every time I saw her, I ended up going out and drowning my sorrows in beer. Way too much beer.

Me: *Nah. I'm gonna head to bed.*
Jack: *Pussy.*

I laughed as I got up and set my phone on the table next to my empty beer bottle. I walked into my bedroom, stripped out of my clothes and crawled into bed.

Another night all alone. I thought.

I closed my eyes and all I could see were green eyes.

Maddie...

4

Maddie

"COME ON, MADDIE. Stop being such a drama queen." Zoey said as we walked through the airport.

I attempted to hold my frustration back. The *one* time I really wanted to bitch about my mother, Zoey wouldn't hear it. Zoey complained *constantly* about her parents. Her mother was always on her back to find someone and settle down. Zoey, on the other hand, wanted to live life on the edge. Her rare autoimmune disease had led her to live her life each day like it was her last. In a way, I envied her for that. I think almost dying last year had really thrown her for a loop.

I stopped and looked at Zoey. Before I could say anything, she opened her mouth.

"Listen, I'm not trying to be a bitch, Maddie," She said. "I'm really not. But that party was two days ago. So your mother humiliated you and made you leave the party in tears. So you broke down in an elevator and cried. Who gives a shit? Next time, tell the bat off!"

I was about to respond when the announcer came on. Zoey put her finger up to my mouth and said, "Shh, hush up."

I closed my eyes and prayed for strength. If she weren't my

friend, and sick, I'd have knocked the hell out of her.

"That's my plane boarding! Gotta go! Have fun in London while I'm in Jamaica!" She quickly kissed me on the cheek and skipped off toward her plane. I watched her as she walked away. She had on tight jeans and a blouse that you could practically see through. Her body was to die for, not soft like mine. I could stand to drop about ten pounds, but Monica said it made me look sexy with the added curves.

I was about to turn around when Zoey yelled, "Maddie! No fish and chips. Your ass is already getting bigger."

My mouth dropped open as she laughed and waved to me before disappearing into the crowd.

"Bitch," I whispered before turning to head for my gate. I just wanted to get this stupid trip out of the way and get back home.

THE GUY SITTING next to me at the bar had been eying me for a while when he asked, "What do you do for a living sweetheart?"

I smiled and replied, "I'm an import manager."

"Nice. What brings you to London?"

I laughed. "Chocolate."

He took a sip of his beer and said, "Chocolate huh? I'm pretty sure you have chocolate in the States."

I took a sip of my wine and nodded. "Our supplier asked me to come with them to London. We were trend shopping. I'm helping them with their packaging before visiting the factory we ship from."

He looked at me like I'd just spoken in another language.

He was from the States, too, and the wedding ring on his finger wasn't lost on me. He turned to me and said, "Listen, babe, do you want to come up to my room or what? This small talk is getting old."

What?

I glanced at his ring before looking him in the eye. I smiled as I drank the last of my wine. Grabbing my purse, I slipped off the barstool and faced him.

"Why don't you think about this for a bit?" I said. "You have a wife back home, maybe a child or two, but I sure hope not. What do you think your wife is doing while you're sitting here trying to pick up a lay? I bet she's taking care of your house, the bills, the kid, the dog…all that shit a wife does. If you're not happy, leave her. Don't fuck around behind her back you asshole."

I turned and headed for the elevator.

I am so over men, I thought. *They are nothing but pricks. No one will ever hold a candle to Cale. None of them.*

Once in the elevator, I said a quick thanks to God that tonight was my last night in London. Three days in this town and I was ready to get back home. I hit the button for the tenth floor and leaned against the wall, closing my eyes.

"Wait! Hold the elevator."

I know that voice. I was instantly taken back to two years ago, to a beach with the most beautiful green eyes I'd ever seen.

I opened my eyes just as the doors closed. I quickly reached for the button to open them again, but the elevator began moving up.

"No! No, no, no!" I yelled as I hit the button for the ground floor. The elevator continued to whisk me up to my floor. The doors opened and I hit the ground floor button again causing them to close as the elevator begin its descent to the ground floor.

"Hurry, you damn thing," I shouted. The doors opened and I ran out of the elevator. I looked around frantically. *Where is he? I know it was him. It was Cale. I know it!*

I quickly walked over to the reception desk. The young lady working there looked up and smiled. "May I help you with something?"

"Do you have a Cale…?" *Oh. My. God. I don't know his last name.* "Um, do you have anyone with the first name of Cale staying here?" I asked as anticipation sped through my veins. The front desk clerk looked at me like I was insane.

I know it was him. I'd know that voice anywhere.

She smiled politely and began typing. "I, um…let me see if I can…uh…" I looked at her with pleading eyes before she smiled and looked back down at the computer screen. "Hmm, I'm so sorry. There is not anyone with the first name of Cale staying at this hotel."

My whole body sank with disappointment. I closed my eyes and shook my head. "Miss Powers? Are you okay?"

I opened my eyes and smiled, nodding. "Yes, I'm just…stuck in the past. Thank you for checking."

She gave me a confused look before smiling the way people do when they feel sorry for you. Or think you're a lunatic.

I headed back to the elevator. I needed to snap out of it. *Why the hell would he be in England?* I was never going to find him. Two years ago, I walked away from him, and now I had to live with that regret for the rest of my life.

I walked into the elevator and took in a deep breath. I could almost smell him.

"Jesus, Maddie. You seriously need to move on." I said to myself. I pulled out my phone and sent Monica and Zoey a text.

Me: *Hey, girls. Coming home tomorrow. I need to get wasted and find a guy. Anyone up for a night out tomorrow?*

Zoey: *Hell yeah I am! I know just the place to go!*

Monica: *I'm down for a little bit of fun. Does this mean you're finally letting him go?*

Zoey: *Oh, the mystery man, Cale! Jesus Maddie. You need to get screwed and forget about him.*

Me: *Monica…yes and Zoey…I know. Tomorrow night is the night.*

I PULLED THE covers over my head and sighed. "Oh mother eff-er. I'm never drinking again," I whispered. Last night's events hit me like a brick wall.

After getting back from London last night, I met with Monica and Zoey at a club. Zoey made me a bet that I wouldn't ask a guy to dance. And not just dance, but dirty dance with him. I also had to make out with him before the night was over. Before I knew it, I was in the corner of the club with some guy feeling me up. I must have needed it, though. The feel of his erection grinding against me caused me to have a full-blown orgasm as he pushed against me and squeezed my breasts. When he whispered in my ear that he wanted to fuck me against the wall, I knew it had gone too far. I pushed him away, apologized for my behavior, and made my way back to Zoey and Monica who were sitting at the bar laughing.

My phone rang and I jumped. I reached for it and somehow managed to speak, even though my mouth felt like it was packed with cotton.

"Hello?"

"Why, good morning! Do you remember your orgasm last night?"

I rolled my eyes and let out a moan. "God, Zoey. Are you ever going to learn that if you dare me I'm gonna do it? It was a mistake, and I feel like a whore."

She laughed. "Please. When was the last time you had an orgasm?"

I slowly sat up and leaned against my headboard as I tried to remember my last orgasm.

"Umm…"

"Yeah. See, if it takes you that long to think of the last time, you *for sure* needed it. Besides, he was hot and I'm kind of pissed that you got off as easily as you did."

"Change of subject. I did my part, now you have to up hold your end of the bargain."

I slowly dragged my ass out of bed and dragged my feet along the floor as I made my way to my bathroom.

"What was it again?" Zoey asked with a chortle.

"I believe I said you had to find a guy and date him for a month straight. No one else. Just him."

"That's right. Has my mother been talking to you? She has been on my ass lately."

I smiled as I hit the speakerphone button on my phone and set it down on the sink. I turned on the water and splashed my face. "No, I haven't been talking to your mother. She's right though, Zoey. This lifestyle of yours is dangerous. You need to find someone."

I heard her sigh. "I'm fine! I can't even remember the last time I was sick."

I turned off the water and headed to the kitchen.

Coffee. I need coffee.

"What are you doing right now?" I asked.

"I'm about to walk into Starbucks. Why?"

I smiled as an idea came to my head. "Are you outside of it? You haven't gone in yet, have you?"

"Nope, but I'm about to."

I giggled. "Okay, I'm calling in my bet now. Walk into the Starbucks. Go up to the first cute guy you see, take out your phone and tell him your friend has dared you to ask a stranger to dance."

Silence.

I'd always wanted to do something like that, but I'd never had the nerve.

"You want me to do what?"

I finished pouring the water into my coffee maker as I smiled and sat down at the bar. "You heard me, Zoey Jones. Now do it. I'll expect a full report."

She let out a sigh. "Come on, Maddie. That is something *your* bubbly little ass would do."

I laughed. "Listen, you and Monica made me push Cale out of my head last night by having a random orgasm with some stranger. It's payback time, bitch."

"Fine. I see a very handsome guy sitting down inside. Maybe I'll at least get a one-night stand out of this thing. I'll call back later."

She hung up and I chuckled. No way in hell she'd do it. She was too shy. Besides, she would never be able to date just one guy for a month. I had this bet in the bag.

5

Cale

I SAT IN Starbucks as I read the text from my mother. She was insisting that I join her and my father for some cousin's wedding next weekend. I let out the breath I'd been holding and tried to figure out which of my friends' sisters I could bribe to pretend we were dating, and then take to the wedding.

I heard a woman clear her throat. I looked up to find a blonde girl, maybe five foot two looking down at me.

"I never do this kind of thing, but my friend bet me and, honestly, I'm tired of the brat always winning. She bet me I couldn't walk into a Starbucks and ask a hot guy to dance with me. So here I am. Asking you, said hot guy, to dance with me."

I looked around and then looked back up at her. "You want me to dance with you? Here? In Starbucks?"

She made a funny face and nodded her head. I checked out her body.

You need to move on, Cale.

She was dressed to the nines and carried a Louis Vuitton handbag. My mother would like that. She was thin—too thin, really—but had nice tits. She chewed on her lip before she noticed me staring. She ran her tongue along her teeth and, for the first time in a long time, my dick jumped with anticipation.

I stood up and, putting her hand on my chest, she said, "Listen, I'm not looking for anything else but a dance."

Too bad, I thought. *She'd be a perfect date to the wedding.*

I smiled, but she was blankly staring back at me. "Do I get to know what your name is before we dance?" I asked.

She smiled and winked. "Zoey Jones. And you?"

I reached for her hand. "Cale. Cale Blackwood."

Something on her face changed. It was if she was trying to remember me from somewhere. The smile that spread across her face made me think she'd just figured something out—and that it made her entire day.

"Cale? Your name is Cale?" She asked, smiling bigger.

I nodded. "Yes ma'am. Do we know each other?"

She tilted her head and ran her eyes over my body. "Did you graduate from the University of Florida two years ago?"

I laughed and said, "Nope. University of Arkansas. But you're right about when I graduated."

Her mouth fell slightly open. "Holy shit," she said. "I'm finally going to win one," she whispered.

I pulled my head back and looked at her and was about to ask her what was wrong. "Listen, I didn't want to say this before, because this whole thing is so crazy, but I have to admit that I'm super attracted to you. So here's the rest of the deal: I'm also supposed to date the guy I dance with for one month, exclusively, to prove to my friend that I can be monogamous. I don't suppose you'd be interested in helping a girl out?"

I gazed at her lips as she slowly ran her tongue over them. I smiled, focusing in on that soft mouth. I met her eyes. She looked nothing like Maddie. Maybe this was the girl that could help me finally push that one night out of my head—and heart.

"I need a date for a wedding this weekend." I said. "Looks like we can both help each other out, Zoey."

She pulled me toward her. We started to dance to the sounds of

Lily Allen playing across the speaker of her phone as she pushed herself into my growing erection. "Oh, trust me, Cale. I have a feeling we're going to help each other out in more than one way." She laughed and, for second, it truly sounded evil.

IT DIDN'T TAKE long for me to figure out that Zoey wanted me as much as I wanted her. The way she flirted was giving my neglected dick a sliver of hope. I'd never met a girl and just taken her home to have sex, but all these crazy sightings of maybe-Maddie were pushing me over the edge. I needed to get her out of my head. I needed to move on.

I'd given Zoey my address and told her to follow me back to my place. She pulled up, left her car, and began walking to the elevator, unbuttoning her shirt as she went. That's when I knew it wouldn't take long to wipe Maddie from my memory.

The elevator doors opened and we stepped in. As soon as the doors shut, she threw herself at me and reached for my dick. She moaned into my mouth as I pulled her lips to mine and slammed her against the elevator wall.

"Yes," she said. "I like it rough. Fuck me. Fuck me hard, Cale. And no damn foreplay. I want it all, and I want it now."

Oh Jesus. I'd never been with a girl who'd said anything like that to me before. I reached up her shirt and pushed her bra up and over her tits. I pinched her nipple as she pulled her lips from mine.

"Yes," she hissed through her teeth.

When the door opened she jumped up into my arms and wrapped her legs around me. I carried her to my apartment and fumbled with opening the door as she pulled my hair.

"Hurry," she said. "I need to be fucked. I'm so wet for you, Cale."

"Jesus," I mumbled.

I pushed the door open, and threw my keys on the table. I put Zoey down and she quickly pulled off her panties and tossed them to the side. She looked around my apartment, then walked over to my sofa and smiled.

She slid her skirt down and pulled her shirt over her head. She undid her bra and began playing with her nipples. "Fuck me from behind," she said. "Hard and fast."

Holy fucking shit.

I unzipped my pants as I walked over to her. I pulled them down and stepped out of them. She pushed my boxer briefs off and my dick sprung out. Licking her lips, she dropped to her knees and took me in her mouth before I could even stop her.

"Holy shit," I said as I grabbed onto the back of the sofa. She moved her mouth up and down my shaft and moaned as she began playing with my balls.

I grabbed her head and began fucking her mouth. I'd never done anything like this, with the exception of the night with Maddie. This was the type of shit Jack did, but there was something about this girl. It was like she knew exactly what I needed. I pushed her back when I felt my build-up.

"Zoey, I don't want to come yet."

She licked her lips as she stood up and turned around. She leaned over the back of the sofa and looked over her shoulder.

"Hard. And fast. Make it so I can finally say I've outdone her!" she said as she winked at me.

"What? Who?"

"Cale. Fuck. Me. Now."

I quickly grabbed a condom from my bedroom. I rolled it on and returned to Zoey. With my hands on her hips, I began teasing her entrance with my tip. She wasn't lying. She was soaking wet.

She pushed her ass against me and whined: "I need this. Please, Cale. Give this to me. I *need* you to give this to me."

I dug my fingers into her hips and slammed my dick into her. She threw her head back and yelled out. "Oh God, yes! Fucking finally!"

I began pumping as she kept repeating, "Finally! Finally! Fucking yes!"

I wasn't sure if she just hadn't had sex in a while or what.

"Does that feel good, Zoey?" I asked as I pounded into her over and over.

"Yes! Harder! I want to feel that you were here! I want to remember this moment!"

Soon, she was shouting. "I'm going to come! Yes! Oh fucking hell. Yes!"

She moaned as I felt her pussy clamp down on my dick. As she pulled herself away, she turned to face me and smiled.

"I want more," she said. "I want to be fucked against the wall," she said, jumping into my arms.

I picked her up and pushed her up against the wall in my hallway. I rammed myself into her again and began moving.

"Cale, faster. Jesus, do it harder. Harder!"

Holy shit, this girl was crazy! She wanted to be fucked senseless. Jack was going to flip when I told him this shit.

I gave her what she asked for. I could feel my build-up. "Oh God. Zoey. I'm so close."

She snapped her head forward and moved along with me. "Yes! Cale yes! I'm going to come again. Oh God, give it to me."

I grabbed her ass as I pushed in harder. "Zoey, I'm coming,"

She smiled as she let out a scream. "Yes! Fucking yes. Oh God, this is perfect! I totally fucking won!"

I held on to her as she dropped her head back against the wall. I had to put my hand out and lean against the wall. I hadn't ever screwed anyone like that. It felt fucking amazing. It felt freeing. But it also felt like I was just used by Zoey in some strange way.

I didn't care.

I pulled out and slowly put her down. When she began laughing I looked at her and tilted my head.

"Oh, baby. That was fucking amazing. I've never done anything like that before. I can't wait to tell my friend how you fucked me senseless. She's going to be so damn jealous. I've overheard her saying how she's always wanted hot wall sex with some mystery man."

I laughed and shook my head. "I'm glad I was able to help with that. I think."

Zoey smiled and ran her hands through my hair. "You know, I wasn't looking for anything other than a quick fuck. But you, Cale Blackwood, you just became a game changer."

I smiled as I pulled her to me. "I could say the very same thing, Zoey Jones."

She took a step away before walking over to the sofa where she laid down.

"I think we should slow it down now," she said. "Don't you?"

I wasn't surprised when my dick came back to life so quickly. I made one more detour to the bedroom for a condom. What I thought would be lovemaking turned into another fuck-fest on the sofa. When I came, she ran her hands through my hair, and I pushed away the uneasy feeling I had, wrapping Zoey up in my arms.

I began to doze off, but not before she grabbed her phone from her purse and sent off a text message. I closed my eyes and she snuggled back into my arms and let out a sigh.

Something still felt wrong about what had just happened, but I pushed it out of my head and let myself sleep.

6

Maddie

I WAS JUST returning from a run with Monica when my phone buzzed. Picking it up, I saw I had a text message from Zoey.

Zoey: *I flipping won! I not only danced with him, but we have plans to go out tomorrow night AND he asked me to be his date at a wedding. AND...he just fucked me senseless...against a wall and from behind.*

I sat there with my mouth hanging open. Monica came over and bumped my shoulder. "What's wrong?" she asked as she as she sat down on my sofa, attempting to catch her breath.

I looked up at her and shook my head. "Zoey. She danced with a guy at Starbucks, has two dates planned with him. And, apparently, he just fucked her against a wall and from behind."

Monica sat up. "No fucking way. I hate her. I'm telling you, I hate her. Do you believe her?"

I turned my phone and showed Monica the picture Zoey had sent. It was a selfie of her in the arms of a guy...naked.

"Ewww! Oh my God my eyes!" Monica said as she jumped up. "I can't un-see that Maddie! Ever."

I shook my head and put the phone on the counter. "Too bad she didn't get his face. Who knows if he was even worthy?"

Monica laughed. "Right? Who cares? She'll keep him around for a bit and then toss him to the side, just to piss her mother off. What a whore."

I sat down next to Monica. "That's mean," I said.

But you're probably right."

I suddenly had a strange feeling. Like I'd just lost something.

Monica sat up and looked at me. "What is it?"

I shrugged, shaking my head. "I don't know. I just all of a sudden feel kind of sad." I glanced back at my phone.

"You need to find someone, Maddie. Please. It's time to move on."

I smiled and nodded. "Want to go out tonight?" I asked. "I need a drink."

"Hell yeah, girl. What time should I be ready?"

I smiled, pushing Zoey completely from my mind.

I LOOKED AT my phone and rolled my eyes as I sighed in frustration.

"She sent you another one?" Monica asked.

I showed Monica yet another text message from Zoey. She rolled her eyes. "My God. You'd think the bitch had never been with a guy before. What is her damn deal?"

I shook my head. "I have no clue. But this morning she sent a text to tell me that she rode this guy all night. She's been with this guy for almost a month and I already can't stand him."

"What's his name, anyway? She only calls him "Mr. Hot Pants" with me."

I shrugged. "I have no clue. I think it pisses her off I haven't asked. Honestly, I'm tired of hearing about him. He sounds like an ass who just likes to fuck all day and night. No, thank you."

"Okay, well, who the hell cares about Zoey?" Monica said. "When do you close on the house?"

I smiled and jumped a little. "Tomorrow! Can you believe it? I'm buying a house!"

"And a waterfront property, no less, on Beaver Lake. With a dock! How in the hell did you pull *that* off without Mommy and Daddy's help?"

I pushed Monica's shoulder, she stumbled and laughed. My mother was *not* happy with me—I still refused to work for my father at his telecommunications company, Powers Communications. My mother couldn't understand why I wanted to work and earn my own way. According to her I struggled to make ends meet. Truth be told, I made decent money. And I loved my job. I didn't want to take a dime from my parents—if I did, my mother would take it as permission to control my life. *No thank you*, I thought. *I did that for eighteen years.*

"The dock isn't going to do me any good without a boat." I said, making my way to the kitchen.

"Maybe you'll have a hot neighbor with a boat." Monica said, wiggling her eyebrows.

I threw my head back and laughed. "That would be nice. To be honest, I wouldn't mind a guy pushing me against a wall and having his way with me."

Monica picked up an apple and took a bite. "Just get Zoey's guy to do it," she said.

"I swear, if she tells me one more time about him fucking her against a wall, I'll scream."

I shook my head. Zoey had dated plenty of guys, but she'd never once shared like this about her sex life. Why she felt like she needed to share now was beyond me.

"Why do you think Zoey is so fixated on telling me about her sex life?"

Monica shrugged. "Who knows? I'm telling you, I don't trust her. That night we were talking about Cale, I *swear* she was listening in. I wouldn't be surprised if she tracked him down and fucked him just to get one up on you."

I looked at Monica and frowned. "She would *never* do something like that, Monica."

Monica rolled her eyes. "She's evil. Pure evil."

I giggled and shook my head. "She's sick. Be nice."

"Shit, she could live another fifty years. I don't care if she's sick. I don't trust her and I think you need to be careful with her."

"Okay. Let's forget about sex-crazed Zoey. Tonight is *our* night. Maybe we'll even get fucked against a wall."

We both started laughing as we made plans to head out for drinks and dancing.

7

Cale

"THAT'S THE LAST box," Jack said, out of breath, as he dropped the box on the floor.

I looked out the giant window that over looked Beaver Lake and smiled. *I can't believe I own a house.*

Jack slapped me on the back. "Now you just need a boat to fill that empty spot on the dock."

I laughed and shook my head. "Let me get my mortgage under control first."

"Shit, just ask your dad for one. He'll buy it for you in a heartbeat."

"Not an option."

My phone buzzed and I pulled it out.

Zoey: *Hey handsome. How is the move coming along? I can't wait for you to fuck me on every surface of the house. I'll be there soon!*

I sighed and sat down on the sofa. I'd been dating Zoey for over a month and wasn't sure how much more of her I could take. I liked her, but something was off.

"Zoey?" Jack asked, shooting me that all-knowing look.

I nodded.

"You have a hotter than hot girlfriend, and she's kinky as fuck. She'd probably do anything you asked her to do. Why are you pouting?"

I sucked in a deep breath. "That's just it, Jack. That's *all* it is for her. Fucking. There's no real connection between us. I mean, she's great in bed. But something is missing. For once I'd like for her to come over, sit, and have a glass of wine with me. Talk to me. The moment she walks in the door she strips out of her clothes and either drops to her knees to suck me off or goes to the bedroom and tells me she's had a hard day and needs to be fucked."

Jack smiled. "Sounds like my dream woman. What's the problem?"

"I don't know. Something feels off. I feel like she's hiding something from me. I plan on talking to her about it tonight."

Jack stood up. "Dude, honestly?" he said. "There's something about her that doesn't sit right with me. It never has. She has that look in her eye."

I tilted my head and looked at him. "What do you mean?"

"She's a liar."

I stared at Jack. I could feel anger building in my veins and I wasn't sure why. "How the hell do you know that?"

Jack shook his head and looked away. As he turned back toward me, the look on his face was sad. Regretful, even.

"Because when I look in her eyes, I see my own."

He turned and headed out the front door. I stood there stunned. "What the hell does that mean?" I whispered to myself.

I followed Jack back out to the truck we'd rented. I grabbed his arm pulling him to a stop. "Is there something you want to tell me, Jack?"

He stared at the ground, then out toward the lake. "About six months after you and Maddie hooked up, she came to my house."

My heart slammed in my chest. "What? Why didn't you tell me? What did you say to her?"

Jack kept staring out over the lake. "When I opened the door and saw her standing there…I don't know if I was jealous that she'd come back for you, or the fact that I'd wanted to hook up with her that night, or just that I'm a dick." He gave me a weak smile as I stood there, waiting to hear what he was going to say.

"She said she'd just gotten back home from her internship in London and was looking for you. I told her you had a girlfriend. That it hadn't taken you long to move on. I invited her in and was ready to put a move on her, but she turned me down—flat. I'll never forget the look in her eyes, though. She was crushed. When she turned to leave I almost called out for her to tell her it was all a lie, but I couldn't. I let her walk away."

I'd never hated Jack in my entire life. I don't think I'd ever really been mad at him, until right now. Hurt and anger built up inside me.

Jack looked at me. "Sometimes, as I'm falling asleep at night, all I can see is her eyes. The hurt in her eyes keeps me awake for hours."

I swallowed and took in a slow, deep breath. "Is that why you pushed me so hard to find someone? To move on? Because you pushed her away from me?"

Jack gazed out at the lake and slowly nodded his head. "I saw her again."

Maddie. He saw Maddie.

"What? Where? Where did you see her, Jack?" I wanted to grab him by the neck and shake him.

"About two months ago. I saw her walking out of my lawyer's office. She didn't recognize me, and I was going to call out to her, but I couldn't open my damn mouth. I watched as she walked up to some guy and gave him a kiss on the cheek. I figured it was her boyfriend. I didn't want to tell you because, if she had a boyfriend, you'd just fall right back to where you were two years ago. I didn't want to see you hurt again."

I pushed my hand through my hair and leaned against the truck. I felt sick to my stomach.

"You saw Maddie here? I mean, in Fayetteville? Two months ago, in the same goddamn town where I live, and you didn't say *anything* to me? What the fuck, Jack? How the hell could you do that to me?"

"Shit, Cale, I don't know. I really don't. Jealousy?"

"What were you jealous of, for Christ's sake? The girl I slept with two years ago who may or may not have a boyfriend? You knew how much I wanted to find her. You had no right to make that decision for me. You knew she's all I've ever wanted, Jack. You had no right. No right at all." I pushed my hand through my hair again, trying to calm down. "Fuck!"

I turned to walk back into the house and stopped dead in my tracks. Zoey was standing there, stunned. I couldn't tell if it was hurt in her eyes or anger.

Oh shit.

She smiled a little, and whispered, "I had to talk to you, I'll um…I'll be in the house."

I closed my eyes and dropped my head. *Son of a bitch.* I glared at Jack.

"I didn't even see her walk up, Cale," he said. "Dude, I'm really sorry. I should have just kept my damn mouth shut."

I let out a breath and shook my head. "I can't stay with Zoey now. No fucking way. Not knowing that Maddie is out there, so damn close."

Jack looked at me, shocked. "What? Wait a second, Cale." Jack lowered his voice and continued talking. "I know you said you weren't feeling it with Zoey, but do you really think breaking up with her to go look for Maddie is a smart thing to do? This is a girl who might have a boyfriend or even be married."

I felt my insides being pulled in two different directions. "I don't love her," I said. "At least I don't right now. It's not fair for her to be with someone who isn't able to give her one hundred percent."

Jack kicked a rock and then looked at me. "Just don't do something you're going to regret. Maddie could be gone. She might have just been in town visiting family or a friend. Maybe that girl Monica. She might still live in the city."

"I need to talk to Zoey," I said. "Can you return the truck?"

Jack nodded his head. "Yeah, yeah. Of course."

I started toward the house.

"Hey Cale?" Jack said.

I was so mad that I could hardly think straight.

"I really am sorry for being a dick and a shitty friend."

I gave him a weak smile and nodded. I continued up the driveway. I really liked Zoey, and I enjoyed our time together, but I needed to be honest with her. I couldn't wait another minute to do it.

Around the corner, I bumped into Zoey.

"Oh God, sorry!" she said. She looked flushed.

"Zoey were you out here the whole time?"

She blushed like she'd just been caught eavesdropping. Looking everywhere but my eyes, she said, "Um, no. I was coming out to talk to you because…well…Cale I really need to tell you something. It's important."

I nodded, following her inside. She sat down on the sofa and stared at the floor.

"I've been keeping something from you."

I sat in the chair opposite her.

I knew it. I knew she had been keeping something from me.

She took a deep breath. "I have to be completely honest with you."

I nodded. "Okay. Honesty would be great. It's apparently been lacking around here lately."

She smiled weakly. "When I first meet you, Cale, I didn't think anything would come of this relationship. I thought you were hot, and I came on to you because of a dare and, honestly, I thought maybe we'd hook up and that would be it. That's kind of how I live my life. I don't get attached to anyone, but you forced me to break that rule. Cale, I'm falling in love with you, hard."

I sucked in a breath. *Shit*. I needed to nip this in the bud and fast.

I was about to speak, but Zoey did what she always did—she cut me off, taking the lead.

"Let me get this all out first, Cale. It's important, please."

I nodded.

"Cale, I don't really know how to say this, but…I'm sick. Actually, I'm slowly dying."

I sat there, stunned. "What?"

She swallowed hard, and I watched as a tear rolled down her cheek. "I'm really sick, and I know it wasn't fair of me to keep this from you. I had *no* idea I was going to fall in love with you. I thought we'd have fun and move on."

I shook my head to clear my thoughts. "Wait. Zoey, what's wrong with you?"

She took in another deep breath and blew it out. "I have an auto-immune disease. Put simply, my body is attacking my kidneys and liver. My doctor said I could have twenty years or five years. They don't really know. I've been taking some experimental drugs and I haven't been sick in a long time."

"Can't they…I mean…can you get a new kidney or liver?"

She let out a throaty laugh. "I'm not a candidate for a transplant. My doctors told my parents that if I follow their directions, eat right, and stay stress free, then I'll live longer. My mother has been on me for the last few years to settle down and find someone who will make me happy…make me give up my hectic life."

My head was pounding. I stood up and began pacing.

I turned and looked at her. "Zoey, I'm so sorry this is happening to you. I wish…I mean…"

She smiled and tilted her head. "I'm sorry I didn't tell you in the first place, Cale. It was selfish of me."

I raked my hands down my face. This didn't change anything. I didn't love her. I wasn't ready to settle down. Then there was the small fact that I loved someone else.

Someone I would probably never be able to hold in my arms, let alone see again. I couldn't let Zoey live out the rest of her life with a man who didn't feel the way she did.

"Zoey, I…I don't really know how to say this without now seeming like a dick. I don't…I mean you said you loved me, but I don't love—"

Her smiled dropped and her eyes turned from sadness to anger.

She stood up. "I wasn't done, Cale. I have other news. Bigger news."

I raised my eyebrows. "What the hell could be bigger than you're sick and dying?"

She gave me the same smile she flashed when I first told her my name. There was something evil behind it.

"I'm pregnant."

8

Maddie

I PULLED UP to JJ's Bar and Grill and parked. Monica had been talking non-stop since we left the title company, and I had the keys to my new lake house in my hand. We'd stopped by and toasted to a new life with a bottle of champagne in the living room. I was ready to put the past behind me and start a new life. I looked at Monica and smiled.

"Ready?" She asked.

I let out a giggle. "More than ready!"

We headed down the boat ramp to the restaurant. I'd gotten a text from Zoey earlier and hadn't bothered to read it before the closing. I was sick of hearing about her Prince Charming and what a great screw he was. Still, I pulled my phone out and read her text.

Zoey: *Hey Maddie. I feel like we haven't seen each other in months. I want to introduce you to my guy. I've got some big news to share with you!*

Me: *Sorry for the late reply, Zoey. I closed on a house today.*

Zoey: *OMG! You bought a house? Why didn't you tell me?*

I'd been finding myself keeping more and more things from Zoey. Ever since Monica and I had walked around a corner to see Zoey standing there, on that day when we were talking about Cale. Zoey claimed she'd just walked up, but Monica still swears that Zoey was eavesdropping.

Me: *I wanted to make sure it all turned out okay before I said anything to anyone.*
Zoey: *Did Monica know?*

I rolled my eyes and sighed.

Monica was smiling big as she scoped out the restaurant. "Holy shit!" she said "There are some good looking guys in here." She turned to me. "What? What's wrong? You looked stressed."

"Zoey. She just asked if you knew about me buying a house. I didn't tell her until today—I don't want to hurt her feelings."

Monica made a face and shook her head. "Who gives a fuck? I don't trust that girl. I'm telling you, Maddie. Something's up with her."

I looked at my phone and decided I wasn't going to lie to her.

Me: *Yes, Monica knew. What are you up to this evening? You could stop by and we could have a little toast!*
Zoey: *Figures she knew and I didn't. I'm always the last to know. Not sure what I'm doing. Let me check with Mr. Hot Pants! I'm about to meet him for lunch.*

I groaned and shoved my phone back into my purse. I couldn't believe how pushy Zoey was being about her relationship with this jerk. I dreaded the day I'd meet him.

"Ladies, would you like to sit out on the deck?" the hostess asked.

"Inside would be great," I replied with a smile.

As we walked to our table, I felt like someone was watching me. It was so strong that I looked over my shoulder.

Monica sat down, grabbing my arm to pull me into my seat. "What's wrong with you?"

I shook my head as I continued looking. "I don't know. I feel like someone is watching me."

"Nice, Maddie. Freak yourself out, why don't you?"

I chuckled at Monica. "I know, right? I'm going to be all alone in a giant house soon, and here I am talking about being watched."

We both started laughing. But, when I looked up, I instantly recognized the eyes staring at me. I sucked in a breath.

"Oh…my…God," I whispered.

"I know," Monica said. "I have no damn clue what to order. Everything sounds so good."

I couldn't pull my eyes away. He and I just stared at each other; neither of us could look away.

"What are you going to order, Maddie?"

His eyes were just as beautiful as I remembered. I could almost feel his lips on my skin as I smiled.

"It's him," I said.

"What? Maddie, what are you talking about?"

The way his lips curved into a smile had me pressing my legs together, longing for his touch. It didn't seem like it could have been two years ago. It seemed like it had been only moments.

"Maddie? Hello? Earth to Maddison!" Monica waved a hand in front of my face.

"It's Cale," I said. "Cale's here."

Monica turned her gaze to where I was anchored. "What? No freaking way!"

When Monica gasped and jumped up, I wanted to follow. I wanted to run into his arms, but something was holding me back. And something was holding him back, too.

"Oh perfect! He's with his little friend. And by little I mean the guy with the little—"

"Monica!" I gasped, teeth clenched. I stood up and grabbed her arm as she laughed. I turned back and noticed Jack sitting with Cale.

Jack looked stunned. Almost panicky.

Cale stood, smiling wider. I couldn't hear anything other than my heart pounding.

"I knew you buying that house was a good sign," Monica whispered.

Cale was about to head our way when I saw a blonde walk up to him. His smile vanished as his gaze drifted toward her. Instantly, the warmth disappeared from his eyes.

Monica began cursing under her breath. "Oh no, she *didn't*," she said.

I couldn't stop watching Cale. He pulled a chair out for the girl, but kept his eyes on me.

"That little fucking bitch. I'm gonna pound her head into the ground and…"

Monica's rage pulled me out of my trance. "What?" I asked. "Who?"

"Maddie," Monica said, her eyes turning serious. "That girl with Cale is *Zoey*."

I gave Monica a look like she was crazy. Turning my head slowly, I finally noticed Zoey. I held onto my stomach as I sat back down. I felt like I was going to be sick.

"No. Oh, God, no," I whispered. Cale's eyes seemed so sad as he looked back at me. "I can't…I can't do this."

I pushed my chair back, reached for my purse and made for the door. Monica was right behind me.

I was breaking into a run by the time I pushed the door open. When the fresh air hit my face, I gasped for breath. My lungs felt tight. Monica placed her hand on my back, rubbing in circles.

"Take a deep breath, Maddie," she said. "In through your nose and out your mouth."

I felt tears in my eyes. Was Cale the guy Zoey couldn't shut up about?

"No," I said. "No, this is not happening. Zoey's with Cale?"

Monica's eyes were filled with pity. I couldn't stand it. "I'm going to kick her damn ass," she said. "She *knew* how you felt about him."

I began shaking my head. "No, she didn't know about Cale. I mean she knew, but she couldn't have known how strong my feelings were."

Monica laughed gruffly. "Please! I'm telling you she overheard us talking about him." She looked back toward the door. "You *have* to confront her, Maddie."

"What? Confront her with what? Tell her she's dating the guy I had a one night stand with? The guy I blew off, and then obsessed about for two years?"

Monica reached for my purse. Grabbing my phone, she pulled up Zoey's name.

"What are you doing?"

"Asking her sorry little ass."

I pulled the phone from her hand. "No!" I said. "No, I need to get out of here. I need time to think."

I'd started walking down the dock ramp to the parking lot when I heard her voice.

"Maddie? Monica? Oh my gosh!"

I stopped in my tracks.

"Aw, hell. Here we go." Monica said. I gave her a look.

"Don't say a word," I whispered, looking at Zoey.

"Hey stranger," I said, my voice cracking.

Zoey sauntered toward us. She didn't look good at all. Her face was pale and she looked like she'd lost more weight. "Zoey, are you feeling okay?" I asked.

She smiled slightly and nodded. "What are you two doing here?" Her body was tense. She didn't seem at all happy to see us.

"Oh, um…we just left the title company and were heading here for lunch and…"

Her smile faded before she forced it back onto her face. "Wait, you bought a house *here*? On Beaver Lake?"

I smiled and nodded. "Yeah, I did."

"I see. Well, nothing like being the last to know," Zoey said, glaring at Monica.

Monica grinned. "Oh, you're not the last. Her parents don't know yet."

I closed my eyes and attempted to regulate my breathing before opening them again.

Zoey gave Monica a dirty look before grabbing my hands. "I'm so happy for you, sweetheart!" she said, plastering on that fake smile. "Anyway, my boyfriend is here and I'd love for you to meet him. I have some rather big news myself!"

Panic set in. "Well, um...we were just leaving. I forgot I had to...I um...I need to go buy..."

Monica yelled out, "Laundry detergent!"

I snapped my head over to give Monica a wide-eyed glare.

Zoey laughed. "Laundry can wait. Come on, I want to introduce you both to my guy."

She pulled me back into the restaurant. I looked over my shoulder and mouthed, "Laundry soap?" at Monica. She just shrugged.

Before I knew it I was walking up to Zoey's table. Cale leapt up to greet me.

Zoey stopped and gave me a smile I'd never seen before. She almost seemed...pleased with herself. "Cale," she said, "this is my dearest friend, Maddie Powers. Maddie, this is my *boyfriend*, Cale Blackwood."

Zoey's stress on the word *boyfriend* didn't go unnoticed. Cale glanced at her quickly before returning his gaze to me.

A million thoughts raced through my head. *Do I let her know I know him? Do I tell her Cale is my mystery guy? The guy I'd been desperately in love with for the last two years?*

Then it hit me: *This* was the guy she met in Starbucks. The guy who's fucked her every which way but loose. My stomach clenched and my heart broke into a million pieces. He'd moved on. And, in that moment, I knew what I had to do. I stuck out my hand and attempted to smile. "Hello, it's a pleasure to meet you, Cale."

Cale looked down at my hand, then back into my eyes. I couldn't quite tell what he was feeling. He eventually reached out and took my hand in his. I gasped slightly when our fingers touched and everything from that night two years ago zipped through my body. I quickly pulled my hand from his and looked away.

Cale cleared his throat. "It's, um…my pleasure, Maddie."

We both just stood there, attempting not to look at each other. Cale's friend, Jack, stood up and reached out his hand. "I'm Jack Rembrandt, it's nice to, uh, meet you." He turned to Monica and smiled. "And you are?"

Zoey chuckled. "Where are my manners? This is Monica Price, Maddie's friend."

Both Cale and Jack shook Monica's hand as she attempted to politely follow my lead.

"Waiter! Can you please bring us two more chairs?" Zoey asked, winking at me.

Monica and I both panicked and shouted, "No!"

Startled, Zoey jumped. "Nonsense," she said, giggling. "You're staying for lunch."

Before I knew it, I was sitting directly across from Cale. I looked away and smiled at Zoey as she gazed back and forth between Cale and me.

Zoey gave me a sly smile. "Is everything okay, Maddie?" she asked "You look like you've seen a ghost."

Monica hit me on the leg under the table. I grinned and shook my head. "I'm fine. Totally fine."

We spent the next fifteen minutes listening to Zoey describe how her and Cale met, how wonderful the last month had been, and how she couldn't believe both Cale and I had bought houses on Beaver Lake. When Cale heard that, he stared at me, shocked.

The waitress set down my Caesar salad as I attempted not to look at Cale. I glanced up to see Jack and Monica glaring at each other. This was turning into a nightmare. *I need to get out of here.*

"Zoey, I really need to go," I said as I reached into my purse to take out money. I could ask the waitress for a to-go box.

"Oh no!" Zoey said. "Not yet. I haven't even told you the best news!"

Cale dropped his fork onto his plate. He leaned over and whispered, "Zoey, what are you doing? I don't think this is a good idea. We need to wait and…"

She swatted her hand toward him as if she was shushing him up. "Nonsense, Maddie is my best friend. I can't wait to tell her!"

"Tell me what?"

Cale had a panicked look on his face as his eyes darted between Zoey and me. "Zoey," he said, "please! We still have to talk more about this and…"

Zoey glared at Cale and he stopped talking.

She turned back to me and sucked in a breath of air. Letting it out, she said, "I have some wonderful news to share."

Cale seemed sick to his stomach as he looked at Jack. Jack was glaring at Zoey. Clearly Jack didn't care for her.

I forced myself to smile at Zoey. "Well, I can't wait to hear it," I said, my voice cracking.

Zoey sat up taller and gave me a hair-raisingly creepy smile. "I'm pregnant," she said.

Monica choked on her food and Jack jumped up. "Are you all right?" he asked

Monica grabbed her water and waved her hand at him, indicating that she was okay.

I was stunned. All I could say was, "What?" Zoey couldn't have kids. If she did it would be dangerous for both her and the child. "How? I mean, who's the father?" I asked.

Zoey's smile vanished and Jack started laughing. Zoey glared at Jack before giving Cale an adoring look.

Oh God, please, no. This is not happening. Please don't do this to me.

Zoey reached for Cale's hand. "Cale and I are expecting a baby in about eight months. I'm only just a few weeks along."

Monica cleared her throat. "Are you sure it's Cale's baby?"

Zoey gave Monica a look that should have dropped her to the ground. "Yes, I'm sure," she hissed.

Monica took a sip of her wine and raised an eyebrow. "Well, one can never be too sure with girls like you."

Jack started laughing again as he looked at Monica. "I like you," he said. "A lot."

Monica smiled and winked at Jack.

I kicked Monica under the table and was pretty sure Cale had done the same thing to Jack with how they both jumped and then shut up. My heart was beating at a crazy pace.

"Zoey, does your mother know?" I blurted. "What about the doctor? That kind of stress on your body can't be good for you or the baby." I wasn't even sure if Cale knew Zoey was sick.

Zoey picked up her glass of water and took a sip. "This was supposed to be a happy announcement, and you're ruining my moment. I wish you could just be happy for me, Maddison. There is no need to be jealous."

I wanted to reach across the table and slap her. I looked at Cale and his eyes were filled with sadness. No, worse—they looked completely empty. He clearly wasn't happy to be expecting a child. Without taking my eyes from Cale I managed to smile and say, "I'm thrilled for you, Zoey. I'm happy if you're happy."

She grinned from ear to ear. "I've never been happier."

Monica cleared her throat and asked, "Cale, what about you? Are you happy about becoming a daddy?"

Zoey sighed and rolled her eyes. "Of course he is, Monica."

Cale smiled, but I could sense it wasn't genuine. "It was a shock when Zoey told me," he said. "Not expected at all. I wasn't really ready for parenthood."

Zoey laughed. "Well, with the incredible sex we have, I'm not surprised."

I couldn't breathe. I needed to get out—now. I pushed my chair back, startling everyone at the table, and pulled some cash from my wallet.

"I um…I need to go. It was a pleasure meeting you both."

Zoey was sitting there with what seemed to be a very satisfied smirk on her face. As if she felt that she'd won a game that I hadn't even realized we were playing.

Cale stood up, "Maddie, wait."

The look I gave him sent him right back to his seat.

I smiled weakly at Zoey. "Have a wonderful afternoon."

She chuckled softly and said, "Oh, I will."

As I walked away, I sensed Monica right behind me.

I stormed out of the restaurant and practically ran down the boat ramp and into my car. As I turned the key in the ignition, I leaned my head against the back seat and started to cry. Monica took my hand in hers.

"I know you don't want to hear this," she said, "but I swear to God, Maddie. It was like Zoey *knew* you and Cale had a history."

I didn't want to believe it. My head was telling me that Zoey knew, but my heart didn't want to believe she would be so cruel.

I wiped my eyes, pulled out of the parking lot, and began driving toward my new house. "We're going out tonight," I said. "I need to forget this entire day."

9

Cale

I WALKED INTO the house and threw my keys down on the table. I still couldn't believe I'd just seen Maddie. She'd been right fucking there…and then Zoey had to walk in. Sighing, I grabbed a beer from the refrigerator. I walked into the living room and sank into the sofa.

"Cale?" Zoey said. "You're upset. Why, baby?"

I rolled my eyes. I knew it wasn't Zoey's fault, but what were the damn odds that she'd be friends with Maddie? And it almost seemed like she got some thrill from telling Maddie she was pregnant.

"I'm not upset, Zoey," I said as I downed my beer.

She sat next to me and sighed. "I told my parents today, about being pregnant. My mother is so excited. Thrilled, I should say, but she was a downer at first, like Maddie. Maddie was just jealous, though. She always wants what I have. It's kind of sad, really."

"Don't you think you should wait and talk to your doctor? You said yourself that he's going to tell you that this is a high-risk pregnancy. I mean, you're telling everyone. You're not even that far along and you're telling your friends."

She glared at me. "You want me to have an abortion? Is that

49

what you want, Cale?"

For a brief moment I wanted to tell her yes. I didn't want to have a baby yet, let alone with Zoey. I wanted to be in love—madly in love. And married. More than anything, I wanted to be with Maddie.

Shit. I need to stop thinking like this.

I knew it wouldn't be long before Zoey picked up on the fact that Maddie and I knew each other. I had to admit, I was shocked when Maddie pretended not to know me. Then again, I couldn't blame her either.

My head was spinning. I was pissed at Jack for lying to Maddie, I was pissed at Zoey for not telling me she was sick, and I was pissed at myself for not going after Maddie when she walked out of JJ's. Or when she walked away from me two years ago.

I glanced at Zoey. "No, Zoey, I don't want you to have an abortion. This is all just hard for me. I mean, I travel so much and I'm probably going to be gone for most of your pregnancy. What if you get sick or something happens? And when the baby is born I'm never gonna be around. How do you see this working out?"

She smiled and took my hand in her hand. "Cale, I know this is hard. It is for me too. I mean, this is *my* life we're talking about. But I want this baby."

"Zoey, you told me that the doctors said you might have as few as five years. Are you thinking about this child? Do you really want her to grow up without a mother?"

Zoey stood and squared her shoulders. "I'm going to be okay. I haven't been sick in over a year. I'm going to be fine. *We're* going to be fine."

I laughed, cynically. "I'm not even going to know my own child, Zoey. Does that matter to you?"

"You will, babe. I promise, you'll be very much involved in this pregnancy. I'll make sure of it. Let me fix you a drink before I leave." Barely stopping for a breath, she continued. "Oh, and my parents are insisting on meeting you now, of course." She stood up and walked over to the bar where she poured scotch into a glass.

This is not happening.

I went into the kitchen and grabbed another beer. I downed the whole damn bottle right there in less than a minute. I was going to get drunk and forget this day ever happened.

"Here baby," Zoey said, handing me the scotch. "Drink this."

I grabbed the drink and downed it in one gulp. She poured another glass and handed it to me. Leaning against the kitchen island, she looked at her watch. "I'm going to pack a bag and start moving in, bit by bit."

"What?" I gasped. My heart dropped into my stomach. "What do you mean?"

She turned to me and placed her hand on my chest. "Cale, I'm having your baby."

I blinked slowly and nodded. "I know, you keep reminding me."

She seemed angry, but her eyes soon softened. "I'm going to let that comment slide, babe. I know you're stressed out." She grabbed my glass and poured me another scotch.

I looked at her and laughed as she walked back up to me and handed me the drink. "Yeah, I'm a bit more than stressed out," I said as I downed the drink. The room started to spin.

Shit. I never could hold my damn alcohol.

Zoey dropped to the ground and before I could stop her she was sucking my dick.

"Zoey, stop. This isn't what I want right now." My words were beginning to slur.

She stopped and looked up at me. "Close your eyes and just relax babe. Just let me make you feel good. Think about nothing but feeling good."

I closed my eyes and green eyes popped into my head. *Maddie.*

I went back to the night Maddie and I had spent together. I could hear every sound she made, see every smile, every time she looked into my eyes. I could feel my build up as I heard Maddie calling out my name as she came. *Oh God, Maddie.*

"Oh, God yes," I whispered as I felt myself explode.

It wasn't Maddie's moans that pulled out of my fantasy, but Zoey's. We were in bed and Zoey was riding me fast and hard. "Yes. Oh God, yes. Baby, I'm coming with you!"

She arched her head back and screamed.

"Zoey…" I quickly grabbed her and tried to stop her. I didn't even remember coming to the bedroom. *Did I put a condom on? Fuck! How in the hell do I not remember coming in here?* My damn head was pounding and I could feel the buzz of the alcohol.

"Zoey, shit! I don't have a damn condom on!" I shouted as she snapped her head forward and laughed.

She leaned down and kissed me on the nose. "Silly, I'm already pregnant! No reason to have a barrier between us now," she said. "That was amazing. Your dick felt so good without a condom on. Besides, you were the one who started it, babe. You were so buzzed that you fucked me on the floor in the living room and twice more in here before passing out. Then you played with your dick in your sleep. I had to get on and ride it."

She got off of me and walked into the bathroom. I sat up and instantly felt sick to my stomach. The damn room was spinning.

Jack's words raced through my head. "You don't know for sure that she's pregnant." he'd warned. "She could be lying. Don't have sex with her without something on."

I ran my hand through my hair and looked down at my dick. It was covered in cum.

Son. Of. A. Bitch. How many damn scotches did I drink?

My cell started ringing as Zoey walked by, already dressed. "Here ya go babe," she said, handing me my phone. "I've got to run, but I'll see you before you leave town. Love you!"

I didn't say a word to her as she walked out the door. I looked at the missed call.

Jack.

I hit his number as I got out of the bed and headed to the bathroom.

"Jesus, Cale. I've been trying to fucking call you. Where have you been?"

I shook my head, attempting to clear my mind. "I've been home."

"I've tried like ten times."

"Really?"

"Yes, really. I found out something you might be interested in. I pulled the recent sales in the Beaver Lake area. Guess who just purchased a house across the lake from you?"

I reached for the Tylenol and took out three. *Jesus, I need to not drink so damn much.*

Sighing, I said, "I give, dude. My head hurts too much to play this game. Plus, I'm somewhat drunk."

Back in my bedroom, I glanced at the clock.

What the hell? It had been over six hours since we'd gotten home from JJ's. I sat on the bed and tried to think back to my conversation with Zoey. Had we talked that long? And how many drinks had I had?

"Maddison Powers."

Hearing her name from Jack made me totally forget everything else. "What about Maddie?"

"Dude, where you even listening to what I was saying? Maddie, she bought the house across the lake from you. You're fucking neighbors."

I swallowed hard. "Holy shit," I whispered.

"Holy shit is right. Now, what the hell are you going to do about that Zoey bitch?"

I walked to my window and looked out across the lake. It was one of the houses I'd looked before buying mine. It was tucked back into the trees, like this one, but smaller. *Maddie's house.* I'd wanted this girl for two years and now she was practically under my nose and I couldn't have her.

"I got drunk after we came home. Zoey started coming on to me," I took a deep breath. "I closed my eyes and started day dreaming about Maddie. Before I knew it, Zoey was moaning and I was coming…without a condom."

"No. *No.* Why in the hell where you drinking?" Jack yelled. "Dude, you had three beers at lunch and then you went home and drank? I told you I didn't trust her, Cale. I told you not to screw her until you saw a damn test!"

I shook my head. "I don't think Zoey would lie about this, Jack. She isn't evil."

Jack laughed. "I call bullshit. I saw the way she looked at you and Maddie when you shook her hand. I'm telling you, she knows your past. She got way too much satisfaction out of telling Maddie she was pregnant."

I didn't want to believe Zoey could do something like that. I *wouldn't* believe it.

"Jack, what the hell am I going to do?"

There was silence for a couple of seconds before I heard Jack let out a breath. He mumbled a few curse words.

"The right and honorable thing, if she really is pregnant. You're going to stand by Zoey."

I nodded in silent agreement. I knew Jack was right. There was no way I could dump my pregnant, dying girlfriend for someone who might not even be interested in me.

"Jack, do me a favor. Keep your ears and eyes open, and let me know when Maddie moves into her house."

I could hear Jack moving papers around. "The offer still stands if you want to use my friend, the private detective. Let me have him poke around a bit."

Jack had offered a dozen times to search out Maddie for me. It just never felt right. Like, if it was meant to be, it *would* be. But things were different now. I knew I shouldn't do it, but I had to know. I had to know everything about Maddison Powers.

"Okay. Do it. Get him to find out as much as he can."

10

Maddie

ONCE I WAS on the plane, I found my seat and sighed in relief as I sat down. I was flying home from Seattle after meeting with suppliers. My boss was nice enough to upgrade my ticket to first class, and I was going to give her the biggest hug and kiss when I got home.

I felt my phone vibrate in my pocket and pulled it out. When I saw I had a text from Zoey, I rolled my eyes.

Zoey: *When are you headed back home? I'd love to go out and have a drink.*

Me: *Today. And did you forget that you're pregnant?*

Zoey: *Ugh. No, I didn't forget it. I'm starting to have to buy those nasty clothes.*

Me: *Maternity? Is that what you mean?*

Zoey: *You're snippy! If you don't want to meet up that's fine. It's just that Cale's been gone for three months. He left pretty much immediately after I told him I was pregnant. I hate his house and I've been staying at my place in the city.*

Me: *Why did you move in with him if you don't like his place?*

Zoey: *One reason would be that I'm pregnant.*

Me: *I know, Zoey. I have to go. The plane is about to take off.*

I hate her. I felt guilty for feeling that way. The last three months had been hell. Cale had pretty much left town the day after we "met" at JJ's. Monica had somehow hooked back up with Jack and the two of them had come to the conclusion that Zoey had always known about Cale and me. Jack *swore* she planned the pregnancy because she'd sensed that Cale was about to dump her. The only part of this whole crazy thing that kept me somewhat sane was that I knew Cale didn't truly want to be with Zoey.

I sighed. I didn't really want to believe that Zoey, someone I called my friend, would be so evil. Bitchy, yes. But not evil.

Then there was the sex thing. All I could think about was Zoey talking about Mr. Hot Pants fucking her all over the place. That wasn't the Cale I remembered. Even though it was a one-night stand, he'd been sweet, romantic, tender. His words echoed in my ear as I closed my eyes. I could almost feel his lips on my skin.

"Ugh, oh my God. Stop this, you idiot!" I said to myself, trying to think of anything other than Cale Blackwood.

I heard a laugh and felt my heart begin to beat harder in my chest. "Do you always talk to yourself while you're alone on a plane, Maddie?"

My eyes snapped open. I couldn't believe what I saw: Cale. Standing in the aisle.

Great, two years of wishing him to appear and nothing. Now he's going to start showing up everywhere.

"What are you doing here?" I asked. My words came out ruder than I meant.

His smile faded slightly. "I'm flying back home from Alaska."

The image of him screwing Zoey against a wall popped into my head.

"I'm sure Zoey will be happy to have you home. She's been sex starved."

Cale's smile completely vanished as he turned and started to sit in the seat opposite of me. "Yeah, I'm sure she'll be happy."

I watched him take the seat across the aisle from me. "Are you kidding me? You're sitting *there*?"

He looked all around him, then down at his ticket. "It appears I am. Do you have a problem that, Maddie?"

His smug smile made me even madder. Now I'm mad that I was mad for no real reason. I rolled my eyes and looked away.

We didn't speak the rest of the trip. I tried to read a book, but I could feel his eyes on me. I hated the way it made my body feel.

When the plane landed and had finally taxied in, I leapt to exit the plane as fast possible. But I felt a tug at my wrist. I let out a gasp. It felt like a million bolts of lightning rushing through my arm where his hand touched me. I looked down at his hand on my arm.

"Why did you leave me that night, Maddie? Why did you walk away?"

My chest started heaving as I looked into his beautiful, emerald eyes. The crowded plane seemed to fade away. I swallowed hard and closed my eyes briefly before opening them to stare up at him.

"Because I was scared to death."

He tilted his head and looked at me with a questioning look. "Scared of what?"

I gazed quickly at his lips before looking back into his eyes. "Of how quickly I fell in love with you."

Cale's eyes lit up with fire and I pulled my arm from his and began walking away. Again.

I was starting to get good at walking away.

MONICA AND I sat on the deck drinking mimosas.

"Aren't you glad you took me up on the morning drinking?" she asked with a smile.

I nodded my head. "Yes I am."

Monica glanced across the lake. "Have you seen him lately?"

"I don't really want to talk about Cale."

She snickered and said, "I'll take that as a yes."

I sat back in my seat and sighed. "He's everywhere. I swear. I go to the store and there he is. I go to the car wash, there he is. JJ's to grab a burger and, bam! There. He. Is. And next to him, always, is *Zoey*."

"Did I tell you that I ran into her at Mulligan's a few weeks ago?" Monica said. "Jack told me that every time Cale leaves town, Zoey goes out, pregnant or not. I wouldn't be surprised if she was screwing around on Cale."

I looked at Monica, disgusted. "Oh God, don't say that. She's pregnant!"

My cell rang and Zoey's name flashed on the screen. I knew I was her only friend, and it killed me to feel the way I did about her. I took a deep breath and answered.

"Hey, Zoey. How are you?"

Monica rolled her eyes as she picked up her phone and sent someone a text.

"Hello there, stranger," Zoey said. "It sure would be nice to see you, especially since you live practically next door."

Guilt ripped through my body. "I know. I've been so busy with traveling lately. I'm headed to Florence, Italy in the next few days."

Zoey let out a pathetic sigh. "Jesus, it must be nice to jet off around the world like you do. I hate my life right now."

My mouth dropped open and I hit the speaker button, signaling Monica to listen in. "Zoey, you're pregnant. You should be reveling in this."

"Really? You think so? I feel like shit, Cale doesn't want to marry me at all, this baby is slowly killing me, and all of this bullshit just to—" Zoey cut herself off.

I sat there stunned. Monica didn't flinch. It was like she wasn't surprised at all.

"Just to what?" I asked. It was silent on the other end of the line. "Zoey? Are you okay?"

"I'm just tired. Cale had me up all night with one orgasm after another. God, he just never stops. I mean, do you know how hard it is to have sex with your belly swollen at seven months pregnant? On the kitchen island, because your boyfriend wants you *now*?"

I felt sick to my stomach. "No, I suppose I don't."

Zoey laughed. "Or course you wouldn't. If Cale wasn't such a good fuck, I swear I'd probably tell him that I need a break from sex."

"Zoey, is there anything else you and Cale do other than have sex? I mean...can you not talk about anything but screwing?"

Zoey giggled. "Why, Maddie Powers! Are you jealous of my relationship with Cale? It's too bad you can't find someone like him."

Monica stood up and was about to grab the phone, but I quickly picked it up and took it off speaker.

"Anywho, darling, my mother is coming for lunch today. I *really* need you here with me for support."

I shook my head and laughed nervously. "You need me where?"

"Here, at the house. My mother and father will be here for lunch, and I can't face them all alone. They just started talking to me again and I don't want to ruin things. Please say you'll come over for lunch."

"Um...to Cale's house?" I asked.

"No," Zoey said. "To *our* house."

I bit down on my lip as Monica asked over and over what was wrong.

"Uh, I don't think I'm going to be able to make it."

Then I heard her start crying. *Aw, shit.* Guilt raced through my body yet again.

"Don't do it," Monica said, pointing at me.

"Maddie, please! Please don't abandon me. I feel so alone. All Cale wants is sex, my parents are treating me like I've sentenced myself to death…you're all I have left."

I rolled my eyes and dropped my head, defeated. "What time do you want me there?"

"Damn it, Maddie," Monica said as she walked into the house.

"Oh, Maddie you're the best! They'll be here in a few hours. I'm getting more and more tired the further along I get. Can you come over soon and help me get ready?"

Cale must be out of town I thought. *That's why Zoey needs me there.*

"Let me change really quick and I'll be right over," I said.

Zoey thanked me again and hung up. I slowly walked back into my house to face one very pissed-off Monica.

"Why do you let her do this to you?" she asked.

I shook my head and tried to push past her. "I don't know what you mean."

"You let her torture you. You and Cale are the only fools who don't see what she's doing." Monica grabbed my arm. "She's playing you. She's always been jealous of you, Maddie. And when she found out Cale's name that day in Starbucks, she *must* have put two and two together. I mean come on—Cale isn't a very common name. She planned all of this. Cale was going to leave her. Especially after Jack admitted he'd lied to you."

I turned and looked at Monica. "What? When did Jack lie to me?"

"The day you went to his house. He wanted to hook up with you, so he lied and said Cale had a girlfriend. He didn't, and Jack has felt like shit ever since. He told me that since that night, Cale has been stopping on the street, going up to girls to see if they were you. He never got over you. He told Jack he didn't have any feelings for Zoey. He was leaving her. And that's when she showed up and overheard them. Jack thinks she lied about the pregnancy, then got Cale to have unprotected sex so she could get pregnant."

I started massaging my temples. "Monica, stop. This is all just nuts. No one goes through all that trouble, out of jealously, to upset someone. No one." I turned to walk away but stopped and glanced back to Monica. "If Cale doesn't want to be with her, why did he let her move into his house? Why are they always having sex? You don't fuck someone you don't care about. It's just a strange coincidence. That's all."

Monica sighed. "You're right. You don't fuck someone you care about. You fuck someone to fuck them. She's lying about how much sex they are having, Maddie. She's lying about everything."

"Monica, I don't want to talk about it anymore. Zoey can't possibly be that evil." My head was telling me one thing, but my heart was telling me another. I was beginning to think that maybe Zoey *did* plan this whole thing.

I started to head up the stairs when Monica called out, "You keep telling yourself that, Maddie. Every time she sticks the knife in further, you keep telling yourself it was just a coincidence."

I shut the door to my bedroom and leaned against it. My breathing picked up and I had to settle my nerves. I didn't want to believe Jack and Monica's theories. I really didn't. But the more I thought about it, the more it seemed to be possible.

11

Cale

I SURPRISED ZOEY by taking a late flight home, since we finished work early. I found her in our bedroom sleeping peacefully,
and I realized I was no longer attracted to her. It ripped my world
in two. She was carrying my child, risking so much, and I felt nothing for her. I hated it. I needed to try. So after not having touched
her months, I woke her up and made love to her. But Zoey wasn't
much for making love. She wanted to be fucked, not loved. After we
finished, she came out of the bathroom and gave me a smirk. "Why
did that feel like you were making love to someone other than me?"

"What are you talking about?" I asked. "I just wanted to surprise
you. You're always complaining that I don't touch you anymore. I
wanted to make love to you, and now you're turning it around on
me?"

She glared at me before crawling into bed and telling me to
sleep in the guest room. I was too tired to argue with her, be honest I
was glad she kicked me out. I crawled into the guestroom bed, getting the space I needed away from her. She was right, anyway—the
whole time I made love to her I imagined I was with Maddie.

On the way home from the airport I'd told my parents about Zoey. My mother was furious that I'd waited until Zoey was seven

months along before telling them. And, of course, she was livid that I'd gotten a girl pregnant out of wedlock. Worse yet, that girl who would most likely be dead before our child was even ten.

"I can't even believe you would be so selfish, getting a girl pregnant like this," she'd screamed. "Do you know what this is going to do to your father's reputation?"

With those words ringing in my ears, I closed my eyes and tried to sleep.

MY MOTHER'S WORDS were still running through my mind the next day as I walked down the stairs and headed to the kitchen. I stopped in my tracks when I heard her voice.

What the hell is Maddie doing in my house? Why is she here? How often does she come over here?

I walked into the kitchen and stared at Maddie. I wasn't sure why, but guilt for sleeping with Zoey last night hit me like a brick wall. I knew Maddie wasn't seeing anyone—the private detective had confirmed it. She pretty much worked and stayed home. On occasion, she'd go out with Monica. She traveled a lot for her job and seemed happy.

I cleared my throat and Maddie spun around. "What are you doing here?" she asked. She was holding a knife and stood by the kitchen island, where she appeared to be making finger sandwiches.

It wasn't just the knife in her hand that made me think she was upset. In fact, the more she ran into me, the more she seemed to despise me. In a way, I couldn't blame her. "I live here," I said.

Looking at Zoey, Maddie said, "You told me you had to face

your parents alone. You told me he wouldn't be here."

Zoey smiled that snarky smile of hers. It seemed she saved that smile only for Maddie. "Did I say I was going to be alone?"

Maddie raised her voice. "Yes," she said, "you did. Specifically. It's why I came over. You *lied*."

Zoey's smile faded. "I didn't lie! How dare you say I did! I told you that I was *tired*, that I could use your help. I'm exhausted."

Maddie zeroed in on me. "Do you do anything else but fuck her?" she asked.

I reeled back in shock. "Excuse me?"

"You know, Cale. Do you help out around here? Seems to me that all Zoey does is complain about how tired she is and how you're always wanting to have sex with her. If you stopped thinking with your damn dick and started helping her out, then maybe she wouldn't be so tired."

I stood there stunned. Where would Maddie get the idea that we were having so much sex? "First off, as far as our sex life is concerned, it's none of your damn business. Second, I help around here plenty when I'm home. But, like I said, it's none of your business."

"It's hard to stay out of it when all Zoey does is talk about it."

I caught myself glaring at Zoey.

"Okay, okay," she said, seemingly oblivious to my frustration. "Let's all play nice before my parents get here." She paused, then startled. "Oh! Wow. The baby just kicked."

I moved closer to her and placed my hand on her pregnant belly. Indeed, I could feel the baby kicking. I smiled at Zoey. But when her smile faded, I knew something was wrong.

"What is it?" I asked.

Zoey nodded and said, "I think Maddie's outburst really rattled me. I feel faint."

"My *what*? I didn't—"

I looked back over my shoulder at Maddie. "Just stop. You're upsetting her and she doesn't need the stress."

I helped Zoey into a kitchen chair.

Maddie squared her shoulders and nodded. "I'm sorry, Zoey. I'll head home now, especially since I know you have help now with Cale here."

Zoey held out her hand for Maddie, "No! Please no don't go, Maddie."

Maddie smiled and said, "I think it's best if I leave." She put the little knife she'd been holding down on the counter.

I looked into Maddie's eyes. "Let her go, Zoey. That's what she does best. Walks away."

As soon as it came out of my mouth I regretted it. I'm not even sure why I said it. But I saw the hurt on her face immediately. I wanted to apologize, but I was so tired of being treated like the enemy. But, when I saw the tears in her eyes, I about dropped to my knees. I went to tell her I was sorry, but Maddie looked away from both of us as she turned back to work on the sandwiches.

"I uh," she stammered. "I'll finish up the sandwiches while Zoey rests. Zoey, Don't worry, I'll make sure things are ready for your parents."

Zoey stood up and smiled. She looked pale, and I could tell that she truly wasn't well today. "Thank you, Maddie. I think I'll go lay down. Cale, will you walk me to our room please?"

Maddie dove back into the sandwiches. A part of me wanted to stay in the kitchen. Instead I took Zoey by the arm and smiled as I lead her to the bedroom.

Once we were in the bedroom Zoey walked over and took a bottle out of her purse and took a pill out.

"Zoey are you okay?" I asked. She smiled briefly and then crawled into bed.

"I'm just so tired all of sudden. Just *so* tired. Please call my parents and tell them I need to cancel lunch."

I sat down next to Zoey on the bed. I placed my hand on her forehead and was relieved when she didn't feel feverish.

"Okay." I said. "I'll do whatever you'd like."

She went to say something else but all that came out was a

whisper. "So. Tired."

I sat there for a few minutes watching her as she fell asleep. I wanted to make myself love her, but I couldn't. At the same time, I knew I'd never leave. Not now, when she was sick and carrying my child.

Back in the kitchen, small finger sandwiches where all laid out on a plate, along with some fresh fruit. I picked up my phone and called Zoey's parents. After telling them Zoey was tired and needed to rest, her mother informed me they were calling Zoey's doctor tomorrow and we were all going to go. I agreed. It was yet another quick conversation – her parents still hated me.

I sighed as I ran a hand through my hair. Something caught my eye on the deck. Maddie was standing there, looking out over the lake. I took in a deep breath and made my way out to where she was. The closer I got, the more I felt it—the connection between us was so strong, and I knew the only reason we bickered so much was to mask our feelings. Maybe keep each other at bay. If Zoey ever found out, she'd be devastated.

I stopped just short of her and stood there. The sun was high in the sky and reflected against the water. Maddie's brown hair was softly blowing in the wind.

"I can't do this anymore," she said, sensing me behind her. "I can't keep pretending that I'm okay, standing by and watching you with her. Hearing about the two of you together...I just can't do it. My heart is slowly breaking."

When she turned and looked at me, I sucked in a breath. The tears on her face did something unexplainable to me. I never wanted to see tears on her face again.

I approached her and gently placed my hands on Maddie's face and wiped her tears away with my thumbs. Moving my hands to the back of her neck, all I could focus on was her breathing. Her chest was heaving, and she kept flicking her eyes across my face. I leaned down and gently brushed my lips across hers. She moaned sweetly and closed her eyes. I wanted her more than I'd ever wanted anyone.

I kissed her soft lips and I whispered her name before pulling away.

I wanted to deepen the kiss, but I knew that this was unfair to both her *and* Zoey.

Maddie placed her hands on my chest and began to cry harder. She looked up, locking eyes with me. She was filled with sadness. I leaned down again, barely kissing her.

"I'm so sorry, Maddie." I gently kissed around her lips, whispering my apology over and over.

She shook her head and looked away. I placed my finger on her chin, pulling her eyes back to mine. "If I could go back to that night on the beach," I said, "I'd have never let you walk away."

She let out another sob and took a step away from me. "I...I have to go."

I nodded and knew I had to let her go. She turned and walked away, never once looking back. I turned and looked out over the lake. I'd just let the only woman I'd ever loved walk away from me. Again.

12

Maddie

I TRIED TO seem interested in Andre's story, but my mind was a million miles away. This morning, Zoey slipped and said something that had been weighing on my mind all day. I don't think she'd even realized she'd said it:

"All I had to do to get him to forget was let him fuck me."

We hadn't even been talking about Cale. When I mentioned it to Monica, she pulled out her handy dandy "Zoey notebook" and wrote it down. She and Jack had been spending more and more time attempting to take Zoey down.

"Maddison? Are you even listening to me?"

I snapped my head back to Andre and smiled. He smiled back, slightly melting my insides. He was so handsome. I'd meet Andre on a business trip in Florence. The moment we bumped into each other, I felt something awaken in me. He was tall and broad-chested, with dark brown hair, blue eyes, and muscles to make a girl squirm. His family was from Florence and he said he flew to Italy a couple times a year. Since returning from Florence, he'd already flown in to Northwest Arkansas six times from his home in New York just to see me. Last weekend, I'd finally decided to move on by flying to New York City. Of course, Monica was dying to know how Andre was in bed, and I couldn't complain. He always made sure I had at least one orgasm before he did, and he showed amazing attention to detail. Unfortunately, I just wasn't feeling it. He wasn't Cale.

"I'm listening," I said. "I think I'm just tired."

Andre licked his lips and I could feel pressure building between my legs. "I know how to relax you, Bella," he said.

I bit down on my lip. I needed to forget, and Andre always made me forget. At least for a little while.

"My place, or your hotel?" I asked as I raised my eyebrow.

"Your place. I want to wake up to the sounds of the lake, then hear you moan as I make you come."

I inhaled sharply, nodding. I stood and Andre led me out of the restaurant and to the car he'd hired. I slipped into the back seat of the BMW as he settled next to my side.

"We're going to Maddison's."

The driver nodded and took off for my house. But it wasn't long before I was on Andre's lap. He slipped his fingers inside me and I dropped my head back and moaned.

"Yes..." I whispered. I closed my eyes but, when green eyes appeared, I opened mine to see Andre. I leaned down and kissed him.

"Jesus, Bella, you feel so good. I want to take you right here."

I laughed and rubbed against his hard dick. "I'm okay with that. I'd say you were more than ready."

He laughed that deep, throaty laugh of his and looked into my eyes. "You know my last name, Gallo, means cock in Italian."

I rubbed against him again and moaned.

The driver cleared his throat. "Mr. Gallo, we've arrived at Miss Powers' house."

I pouted and moved off of him. Andre smacked my ass. "Next time, Bella."

Stepping out of the car, I headed for my door. But Andre grabbed me from behind. I turned around and he picked me up. I wrapped my legs around him as he pushed me into the door. Still outside, he shoved my shirt and bra up and sucked on my nipples.

"Oh, Andre," I moaned.

I heard what sounded like someone saying excuse me.

"Bella, are you still wet for me?" Andre asked.

"Um…Maddie?"

Cale? I was hearing Cale's voice. I hadn't seen or spoken to him since that kiss on his deck over a month ago.

Andre quickly pulled my shirt down and eased me back onto my feet.

I attempted to compose myself. Why I cared that he'd caught me making out with another man, I had no clue. Zoey had texted me just yesterday to tell me that Cale had asked her to marry him. It was official: He'd never be mine.

"Cale? Is everything all right?" I asked. "Is Zoey okay?"

Cale and Andre glared at each other. As if they were both trying to lay claim to me.

"Cale? Why are you here?" I said, more sternly this time.

Keeping his eyes on Andre, Cale said, "I needed to talk to you."

Andre smiled, "Well sorry, *signore*. You're going to have to talk to her tomorrow. We were in the middle of something."

My heart dropped to the floor when Cale turned his gaze to me. He shook his head, disappointed. "Some guy you picked up for the evening?"

My mouth dropped open and Andre grabbed Cale by the shirt. "Don't you ever talk to her like that again, you prick!"

Cale looked at me with something in his eyes I'd never seen before. "Answer me, Maddie," he said.

Andre pushed Cale back and slammed him into the side of my house. "Her name is Maddison."

Cale broke Andre's grip with a few quick moves. I didn't even have time to let out a scream before Cale had Andre pinned up against the house. "Her name is *Maddie*."

I approached Cale to pull him away, and that's when I smelled the alcohol. "Stop this," I said. "Now."

"I just wanted to talk to you," Cale said.

I nodded. "Let go of him, Cale. If you let go of him, I'll talk to you."

"What?" Andre said. "The hell you will, Bella."

I turned to Andre. "I know him, Andre. He's an old friend and I'm close with his fiancée who is going to have a baby soon. Let me just talk to him. He's clearly upset."

Andre's eyes flicked back and forth between me and Cale. He shook his head and said, "Bella, he interrupted us."

I could feel my cheeks burning as Cale rolled his eyes and walked up to my door.

I walked Andre back out to the curb. His driver always waited for him, no matter how long he stayed with me. "I promise to make it up to you. I swear," I whispered against Andre's ear as I kissed him goodbye. He looked pissed, but kissed me again before getting into the BMW and driving off. I rushed back to check on Cale.

I unlocked my door and pulled Cale inside. "If Zoey sees you here, she's going to freak." I said as he stumbled over to my sofa.

"She lied."

"Who?" I asked as I took off my jacket. My nipples were still hard from all of Andre's foreplay.

Cale checked out my breasts. "Does he turn you on, *Bella?*"

I shot Cale a dirty look. "Stop it. You have no right to judge me."

He held up his hands in surrender.

I sat down and took off my heels. "Now, who lied to you?"

"Zoey," he sighed. "I found out today from the doctor that she's not as far along as she'd claimed to be."

I leaned back into the sofa. "What do you mean?"

He laughed and shook his head. "I mean, she wasn't fucking pregnant when she told me she was. She lied because she knew I was going to break up with her."

I sat up, leaning closer to him. "Well, do you know for sure, Cale? I mean these dates aren't always completely accurate, you know?"

Cale stood up and walked into my kitchen. "Do you have a beer?"

I let out a long, deep breath. He wasn't going to be able to make it back home at this rate. The last thing he needed was beer.

"Cale, why don't I make you a cup of coffee? Do you want me to call Zoey to come pick you up?"

"No!" He shook his head. "Maddie, I confronted her this afternoon. She broke down and told me she overheard Jack and me talking about how I wasn't feeling it with her. She said she panicked and that's when she told me she was sick. When it still seemed like I was going to break up with her, she lied about being pregnant."

I covered my mouth in shock. "What? She admitted this to you?"

He stumbled, and I ran over and caught him before he could fall.

"Yep," he said. "And I just fucking asked her to marry me because her fucking mother and my fucking mother both guilted me with all this 'Zoey is sick and deserves to be properly married' bullshit," he said. Then he laughed. "Nothing like being forced into a fucking fake marriage."

I stood there, stunned. None of this made any sense.

He leaned against the kitchen counter and grabbed my arms. "Don't you see, Maddie? She lied. If she hadn't lied, I'd have found you. We would be together, and that would be me holding you like that and me sucking on your nipples. It would be me asking if I turned you on...not some asshole."

The heat between my legs was unreal. Cale just talking about touching me turned me on more than anything. I fought back the urge to tell him to touch me. I stepped away and he smiled at me.

"You feel it, don't ya, Maddie? Tell me you feel it."

I wanted to tell him I felt it. I wanted to run into his arms and beg him to make love to me. But I knew he was drunk. I knew that, sober, he'd be thinking about Zoey and the baby. Even if he was angry, he wouldn't have run to me if he weren't intoxicated.

"Cale, you need to go home."

He closed his eyes and shook his head. "You're doing it again. You're pushing me away. I'm tired of it, Maddie. I'm so tired of it."

I swallowed hard and turned to find my phone. I needed Jack to come pick up Cale.

I was about to dial my phone when Cale grabbed me. He turned me around and backed me up until I hit the living room wall.

His eyes were filled with lust. That look had my panties soaked in seconds.

He lifted up my dress and, in one quick movement, he ripped my panties from my body. I wanted to cry out *yes*. I wanted to let him take me, but I couldn't.

"Cale," I said. "Don't do this."

He kissed my neck and I started to give in. When his hand touched my inner thigh, I startled. His lips moved to mine and I moaned, desperately, into his mouth. He brushed his fingers against my lips. Slowly, he pulled up my leg and sank his fingers inside me.

"Oh God," I whispered. I tried to come to my senses. "Cale, please don't do this. We can't do this."

He moved his lips to my jaw line as he kissed around to my ear. "You're so wet," he said. "Are you turned on by me? Or by him?"

The moment he asked, I felt like a whore. I dropped my leg and pushed him back. He lost his balance, falling over my coffee table and onto the sofa.

I wiped the tears from my eyes.

Cale managed to stand up and shake his head. "Jesus. I didn't mean that Maddie. I just—"

"Get out," I said. "Get out of my house and don't you dare set foot near me again. I hate you, Cale."

He shook his head. "No, please don't say that. I didn't mean it—"

"Get. Out!" I screamed.

He came closer and reached out to me. "Don't touch me!" I yelled.

"Fuck, Maddie, I didn't mean to say that to you. I was jealous and angry. Please."

As he took another step closer, Monica and Jack walked in.

"What the hell is going on here?" Monica asked, looking between Cale and me.

"Get him out," I said. "I never want to see him again. Please, just get him out and take him home to his *fiancée*!"

Jack put his arm around Cale's shoulders and began guiding him out the door. Cale was still begging.

"Maddie, please wait," he said. "I didn't mean it. I don't love her. I didn't want to ask her to marry me. I did it for the baby. Please, God, just…please. *I'm so sorry.*" Then he started crying.

With tears streaming down my face, I turned to Jack and whispered, "Get him out of here."

"Maddie…*please.*" Cale slurred. "God, please don't say that. I love you, Maddie. I've always loved you. I'll always love you."

I slammed my hands over my ears and began crying harder. I turned and ran up to my bedroom and slammed the door. Stripping out of my clothes, I took a long, hot shower.

I finally surrendered to my tears and sank to the shower floor, sobbing. I'd never cried so hard. It was as if my entire world had stopped and I didn't know how to get it moving again.

As I sat there, wet, rocking back and forth, I whispered, "I hate you, Cale. I hate you…"

13

Cale

THE KNOCK ON the door startled me, pulling me out of my daydream. I'd been trying to reach Maddie for two weeks, but she wouldn't return my calls or text messages. Zoey was getting moodier as she got closer to her due date. She interrogated me the night I showed up at the house drunk. She asked me if I'd run to Maddie to cry on her shoulder. She has to know there's something between us. She has to. She is so insanely jealous of Maddie it is unreal.

The knock on my door grew louder. "Blackwood. Boss wants to see you."

I got up and made my way to Chuck's hotel room. Chuck had been my boss since my first day with the company. I loved my job, even though we traveled a good portion of the year. We all lived out of hotel rooms, and I found myself longing to be on the road rather than home. Especially after my last fight with Zoey.

The scene played out in my head.

"YOU'RE NEVER HOME!" Zoey yelled at me.

"It's my job, Zoey. You knew this when we started dating. I travel. A lot. It's never going to change. Ever."

"You have me now, Cale. The baby. Your mother said that if you really wanted to, you'd stay home and take care of me."

"My mother? You talked to my mother about this?" I yelled.

She smiled and nodded. "Yes. She said all you have to do is go to work for your father. They'd make sure you got paid three times what you're getting now. We could take vacations together, if you still wanted to travel."

I just stared at her. I couldn't believe the words that were coming out of her mouth. "We're getting ready to have a baby. We can't travel. And you're getting weaker, Zoey."

She put her hand on her stomach. "Fuck. I can't wait to have this kid. Damn it. This is not what was supposed to happen. Stupid-ass Maddie is dating that hot, rich guy and I'm stuck home alone, pregnant."

"Why did you get yourself pregnant if this is not what you wanted, Zoey?"

She put her hands on her hips. "I had to! Don't you understand, she—"

Zoey cut herself off. She was hiding even more than she'd admitted. I knew it. Things hadn't been the same with us since she'd confessed to getting pregnant on purpose. We hadn't made love in weeks. The last time I touched her was the night of our wedding, and it was classic Zoey. It was rushed, our parents where the only people in attendance, and the honeymoon wasn't much different. It was spent with Zoey on top, fucking me. Once she came, she crawled off of me and told me to finish myself off.

My life was miserable. I glared at her.

She shook her head. "Cale, I feel like I'm losing you, baby. Please. Just touch me once. Cale, please!"

The moment she began crying, I knew I was done for. I didn't want to hurt Zoey. I cared about her. We were having a baby together and, after talking to her doctor, Zoey was going to have a long recovery. Her parents were still angry and wouldn't give us their blessing, even though her mother had insisted we get married. My mother had pretended that the baby wasn't real until we were wed, and my father just sat back, behind the scenes.

I pulled Zoey into my arms. I started to kiss her, showering her body with attention. It didn't take her long to get on her hands and knees and tell me to fuck her hard and fast. There was no lovemaking with Zoey. Only fucking.

I SHOOK MYSELF out of the memory and walked into Chuck's hotel room, where I sat down at the desk.

He cleared his throat and then spoke. "Don't you think you should start putting in for some time off for your kid's birth?"

I stared at him. "What?"

He threw his head back and laughed. "Time off. You know, when the baby is born, you usually take a few weeks to be with the mom and the baby. Bond and all that shit."

"Oh yeah. Right. Well, her due date is in three weeks. They are talking about doing a C-section to lessen the stress on her body. I'd have to ask Zoey for the specifics."

Chuck tilted his head. "Blackwood, are you the least bit excited for this?"

I gave Chuck a puzzled look. "Of course I am."

He raised an eyebrow at me. "Really?"

I took a deep breath and slowly blew it out. "Shit, I don't know anymore. I'm excited, but I just wish...I mean I wish it was...aw, shit. If I answer this I'm going to sound like a real dick."

"You wish it was with another girl."

My eyes widened as I looked at my boss. "Yes! That is exactly it."

"She trapped you?"

I nodded my head. "You could say."

He nodded. "Doesn't matter. Your dick was working and you knew what you were doing. It's your responsibility to be the best damn father you can be."

I nodded. "I know, sir."

"So go do it. Help your wife prepare for the birth of your child."

I was about to say something when my phone vibrated in my pocket. It was a text from Jack that said *911*.

"Um...I need to see what this is about. Sounds urgent. Do you mind?"

Chuck motioned for me to go ahead and I started to read my messages.

Jack: *The private detective found something you really need to know about.*

Me: *Is Maddie okay?*

Jack: *Dude, this is about Zoey.*

Me: *Zoey? What is he doing with information about Zoey?*

Jack: *You've known I haven't trusted her from the very beginning. I needed to know what she was hiding and I just found out.*

Me: *Can it wait until I get home?*

Jack: *No.*

I looked up at Chuck. "It's about Zoey. Do you mind if I step outside and make a call?"

"Of course, go ahead. You know where to find me when you're ready to request that time off."

I nodded and walked outside. I hit Jack's number.

"Cale?" he answered.

"Yeah, what's going on?"

"I knew something was off with Zoey the moment I met her. I told you something was wrong."

I let out a frustrated sigh. "Yes, I know and it was her being secretive about being sick. Dude, we've been over this a million times."

"No, Cale that's not it. That's not it at all. Zoey *knew* about you."

I waited for him to follow up. He didn't. "What do you mean, she knew about me?"

"Cale…she knew you were the "mystery guy" Maddie talked about all the time. She overheard Maddie and Monica talking about how much Maddie was still hung up on you. That day in the Starbucks, she wasn't the least bit interested in you. She was trying to prove a point to Maddie, who had dared her to ask a stranger to dance. Once you said your name, Zoey figured it out and set out to get with you and make Maddie jealous."

My heartbeat began to speed up as I tried to make sense out of everything Jack was telling me.

"Wait, how do you know all of this?"

"Did you know Zoey had a cousin?"

I shook my head. "No. She's never mentioned anyone close to her other than her parents and Maddie."

"Well, the private detective found her. Zoey meet up with her cousin at least once a week and, up until two months ago, they had been going out to clubs every time you went out of town. Apparently, about a month or so ago, the PI's mother passed away suddenly, and he had to fly home to take care of her estate. He called me yesterday morning and said with everything going on he'd forgotten to tell me about this cousin. Said she was a player and screwed anything with a working dick. I found her at her favorite hangout last night and, once I got her talking, dude, she didn't shut up. Zoey used you like a pawn in some twisted game to mess with Maddie. Her cousin said that the moment Zoey met, Maddie she became crazy obsessed with her and wanted to have her life. I mean, Cale, Zoey wants *everything* Maddie has. She even told her cousin that after she has the baby, she's going after Andre, Maddie's boyfriend."

I couldn't breathe. It felt like I was in a tiny room with walls closing in on me.

"I need a second...I can't...I can't breathe."

"Sure. Shit, I'm sorry, Cale. I just unloaded all this shit on you about your wife."

I sat down on a bench. "I'll call you right back." I hung up on Jack and thought back to the day I met Zoey. All if it began making sense. The little comments she would make here and there. The way she forced Maddie to come to the table that day, then dropped the bomb that she was pregnant, even though she wasn't even pregnant at the time.

I dropped my head in my hands and groaned. I'd played right into her twisted game. She'd used me, and I'd let her. I'd let her destroy my life and Maddie's.

I looked down at my phone. After a moment's pause, I pulled up Maddie's number and hit dial. When a recorded message came up saying that I'd dialed a non-working number, I jumped to my feet. She changed her number. *Fuck!*

I called Jack. "Hey dude, are you okay?"

"No. Do you know if Maddie is still seeing Andre?" I asked. I knew Jack and Monica had been hooking up recently, and she told him everything.

Silence.

"Jack, please I have to know."

"What good does it do, Cale? Why beat yourself up about it?"

"Jack! Just tell me."

He let out a breath and said, "Yes. She's seeing him still. They're...um...well—"

"Jesus, just spit it the hell out."

"They're together in Florence right now. Maddie told Monica she had to get out of town for a bit after Zoey told her about the wedding."

"What? She's in Italy with this guy? How serious are they?"

Jack let out a sigh. "I don't know dude. I mean, she went to Italy to meet his family."

I swallowed hard. "They've only been dating a few months."

"Cale, you *married* Zoey. What was Maddie supposed to do?"

It felt like my whole world had stopped.

I lost her.

I've lost her forever.

14

Maddie

NDRE AND I strolled the streets of Florence in a peaceful si‐
lence. That was one of the things I loved about him. He could
leave me alone in my thoughts and not ask me things like
What's wrong? What are you thinking about? Are you okay? Every
five seconds.

As we walked into the Piazza della Repubblica, Andre held my
hand and hummed an Italian song. I smiled when I saw all the chil‐
dren running in an attempt to pop the giant bubbles that a street per‐
former was making. We walked up to an older gentleman who was
sketching a portrait on the ground. He had an old, worn-out, black
and white picture that he was working from, but the portrait he drew
was full of color. I sucked in a breath as my eyes took in the girl's
beautiful, young face.

"Who is she?" I asked.

Andre asked the older gentleman, who was sitting, drawing the
young girl's lips using a ruby red chalk. The man looked up at Andre
and me, sadness in his eyes. His rapid response in Italian caught me
off-guard. His words were pure passion. Andre nodded.

"What did he say?" I asked, almost holding my breath in antici‐
pation. I wasn't sure why my heart felt so heavy. It was as if I felt

the same thing as this elderly artist felt.

Andre smiled weakly. "He said she is the love of his life. He left for the war and, when he returned, she was nowhere to be found. He's been drawing her picture all over Florence, hoping she will return to him."

I sucked in a breath.

Cale.

I wanted to fall to my knees, take the man's hands in mine and tell him I knew how his heart felt. Tears welled in my eyes as I looked away from him.

"So sad," I whispered as Andre placed his hand on the small of back and led me on, silent again.

Church bells began ringing and my heart soared as I saw a young couple snuggle up in a horse-drawn carriage pulling away from the church. She was dressed in a beautiful white gown, he in a black tux. The love pouring off of each other was almost tangible.

The aroma of the food from the surrounding restaurants filled my senses and, for some reason, I was longing for home.

"Ciao, Bella,"

I pulled my eyes from the young couple to see Andre's mother standing in front of us. She placed her hands on the sides of my face and pulled me in for a kiss on my right cheek, then my left.

"Ciao," I said as I smiled at her.

She looked at Andre. "Are we ready to head to the *vigneto*, Andre?"

Andre pulled me close to him and nodded his head. "Yes, *Mamma*."

Andre's grandparents owned a vineyard in the hills of Tuscany, and his mother couldn't wait to get there. Andre had insisted we stay in Florence for one night before heading out to the country. Andre's mother had been upset that we'd stayed in Florence, in a hotel room together, alone. She had moved to America as a young girl, but still held onto the old-fashioned ways of her Italian family.

A few hours later, we were making our way down a long driveway. Either side of the driveway was flanked by nothing but vine-yards. The driver parked in the front of a massive, beautiful home. I was walking up granite stairs to a house that would turn my mother green with envy. The front doors were large and wooden. They looked like you would need five men to push them open.

"Oh my," I whispered.

Andre chuckled. "It's just a house, Maddison."

I turned and looked at him. Andre had more money than he had sense. He showered me with gifts, which made my mother fall in love with him immediately. Of course, my father didn't trust him, and I struggled with my feelings as well. I wasn't a girl who needed to be bought, and it bothered me that Andre thought I was.

The wooden doors opened just as we reached the top step. An-dre's mother pushed past us, practically running into the house. As I stepped into the foyer, the sounds of my heels walking on the marble floors echoed across the large entryway. A grand staircase stood in front of me and I gasped at the size of the place.

"Andre, as much as I disagree with your...ways, I've arranged for you and Maddison to stay in the west wing. Your grandparents won't be back from Paris until tomorrow. I have you set up in two adjoining rooms, but, as far as they are concerned, you are behaving like a gentleman." She turned and shot me a distrusting look. "And a *lady*."

Andre threw his head back in laughter as my eyes widened in disbelief. "Yes, *Mamma*. When they return, I promise to keep my hands to myself. Come, Bella. Let's play before we are thrown back to the old days when men respected a woman's virtue."

He grabbed my hand and pulled me along the long, massive hallway. When he pushed open the doors to one of the bedrooms, I gasped yet again. The massive headboard was leather, and the room dwarfed the giant, king-size bed. There was also a desk, two dress-ers, a wardrobe and a lounge chair.

The doors shut and Andre took me in his arms and spun me around.

"Fucking hell, your scent has been driving me mad all day."

He began to undress as I stood there and smiled. I truly enjoyed being with Andre. He took care of my needs and gave me anything I asked for. He was an okay lover, always putting me first—but he lacked something I couldn't put my finger on.

"We're taking a bath, Bella," he whispered as he reached behind me and unzipped my dress. The fabric pooled at my feet and I stood before him dressed only in a cream-colored lace bra and matching panties.

I felt the tightness in my core as his eyes raked over my body. "You're perfect. Your curves could drive a man insane."

I smiled and looked away, my cheeks burning from embarrassment. The last time I'd seen Zoey, she'd made sure to tell me I was at least ten pounds overweight.

Andre took my hand and led me into the massive bathroom. The shower was in the middle of the bathroom and wide open. To the right was a smaller room that held the toilet and bidet. To my left was a giant spa-style tub. I moaned ever so slightly as I thought about soaking in a hot bath.

Andre dropped my hand and walked over to the tub, turned it on, and adjusted the water temperature. I stayed silent. I wasn't sure how I felt about doing this with Andre's mother in the house. She could walk in any time she wanted to.

"Andre, your mother?"

He smiled. "Is a pain in my ass. She won't be bothering us, Bella. I promise."

He approached me and placed his hands on my shoulders, turning me around. He unhooked my bra, letting it fall. As he reached around me, he cupped both of my breasts and moaned as I arched my head back and rested it on his chest. He ran his hands all over my body before he moved them down to my panties. He slid my panties off as he placed soft kisses along my body. There was no doubt that Andre knew how to turn me on.

"Turn around, Bella."

I turned as he crouched down and pushed his face into my folds as he threw my leg over his shoulder. I closed my eyes and leaned against the tub, trying to enjoy the feel of Andre's tongue as it dipped into me. I opened my eyes and watched him.

What the hell is wrong with me? Why do I have the urge to tell him to stop?

Andre pulled away and stood up. He helped me into the tub and sat across from me, positioning my legs to where I was spread wide open to him.

"Your pussy is my one of my favorite things to look at on your body. I want to bury myself so deep inside you that you forget everything but us."

I smiled as I felt the heat between my legs. *Finally. Time to forget.*

"Maddison, no one can hear you in here. I'm going to make you come so fucking hard, you'll be screaming for me."

I licked my lips. I needed this. Images of Cale had been running through my mind since we saw the old man drawing in the square. I needed to erase him from my thoughts, and the only way to do that was with Andre.

"I'm ready," I whispered.

Andre grabbed the removable showerhead and turned it on. The moment the water hit my clit, I dropped my head back and touched my breasts.

"Does this feel good, Maddison?"

"Yes," I said, barely able to whisper.

The warm water hitting my sensitive nub was pushing me to the edge. "Fucking hell, you look good," Andre said.

"Andre," I whimpered as my build up began.

"That's it, Bella, let go and come for me."

My orgasm hit fast and I let out a scream. I closed my eyes and called out Andre's name over and over again as my insides pulsed again and again. When I finally came down from the orgasm, I closed my eyes and focused on controlling my breathing.

Cale making love to me on the beach popped into my head. I snapped open my eyes and looked at Andre. *I need more. I need to forget him.*

I climbed on top of him and sank down onto him. "Bella, I need a condom."

"Hurry," I panted lifting off him.

Andre reached for a condom and stood up to quickly roll it on.

I'd never been so brazen in my life with how I was acting, expect for the night with Cale.

Andre pushed his fingers inside me and worked my body up again. I sank down on him and moaned, hungrily.

"I need to fuck you, Andre. Then I need you to fuck me. I need it rough, and I need it hard."

He smiled as he grabbed me and held onto my hips as I began to ride him. Water sloshed around us as I came again. This orgasm had my whole body quivering. I called out Andre's name and rode him as hard and fast as I could. Andre pulled me off of him and jumped out of the tub. He picked me up and carried me out the room where he took my wet body and placed it over the back of the chair.

He pushed my legs apart and slammed his dick inside me. I screamed, just a little. He didn't bother to ask if I was okay, which kind of bothered me. He grabbed my hips and gave me exactly what I asked for: a rough, hard fucking. Andre had never been so rough with me before—he was more of a gentle lover. This was exactly what I needed, though.

"You turn me on so fucking much, Maddison," he said. "I like this side of you."

I dropped my head back. "Harder," I pleaded. "I need it harder."

As soon as my orgasm hit, Andre let out a moan and we came together. He slowed down, but kept his dick inside me as he began kissing my back.

"Bella," he said, "that was amazing. I'm falling in love with you, baby."

I closed my eyes as he pulled out. I stood up and faced him.

Smiling, I tried to think of something to say back. If only I could tell him I was falling in love with him, too. I cared for him very much, but love him? No. I didn't love him…at least not yet.

If only my heart didn't belong to another man.

"Come, Bella. Let's rest for a bit." Andre wrapped a towel around me and dried himself off. I rubbed myself down with the towel and followed him over to the giant bed. I crawled in and faced away from him. He wrapped his arms around me, pulling me close. When his breathing finally steadied out and he fell asleep, I allowed my tears to silently fall. Nothing would ever push Cale from my thoughts. No matter how hard I tried, he wouldn't leave my memory…or my heart.

Images of Cale and Zoey together ran through my mind. I hadn't spoken to Zoey since changing my phone number, and the guilt of ignoring her was beginning to eat away at me. But I just couldn't take listening to her talk about her and Cale anymore.

With no tears left to cry, I felt my body relax. I settled in for a few minutes of sleep.

15

Cale

I WALKED INTO the house and looked around. Zoey wasn't waiting for me in the living room like I'd expected her to be. I'd driven around for a few hours after my plane landed, because if I'd come home knowing what I know, I'd have unleashed it on Zoey.

Jack was calling Monica to tell her everything he had found out from Zoey's cousin.

I walked into the den and found Zoey sitting there. She looked up at me and smiled. When I didn't smile back she placed her hand on her stomach. She didn't look good. Her face was pale, and she seemed weak. As much as I wanted to scream at her, I had to think about her health and the baby. My mind flashed back to the last doctor's appointment I'd been to with Zoey.

"YOU BOTH KNOW how incredibly hard this pregnancy is on Zoey's body," Dr. Richards had said. "And on the baby. I need you to start taking it easy, Zoey."

Zoey had glared at her doctor as she fumbled with her purse. "I am taking it easy."

Doctor Richards sighed then, raising an eyebrow at Zoey. "Do you have someone coming in to help her around the house?"

"Yes, of course I do," I'd said. "Especially when I'm out of town."

He'd shaken his head. "Zoey, we may have to start thinking about bed rest soon."

"What? I already have no life. No. Not an option."

I'd wanted to grab her and shake some sense into her. Instead, I'd calmly listened to Doctor Richards as he explained—again— why this pregnancy was so dangerous.

"Zoey, your heart is growing weaker the further along you get. I need you to think about what is happening to your body and be mindful of it. You will be on bed rest, and if that means admitting you to the hospital, then that is what we'll do."

At that point, Zoey had looked away and stared out the window. She didn't utter a single word for the rest of that day.

"ARE YOU OKAY?" I asked.

She nodded. "I hate being pregnant."

I walked over sat across from her. "You wanted this."

She looked away. "I'm so sorry I did this to you." She shook her head, then looked back at me. "I wanted you, but for all the wrong reasons."

I inhaled deeply. *Was she finally going to tell me the truth?*

"What were your reasons?" I asked.

She looked into my eyes and grinned. "It doesn't really matter anymore. I thought I would finally win. But, in the end, I lost everything and she still won."

I knew in that moment she was talking about Maddie. She took in a shaky breath and slowly let it out. "May I ask you something, Cale?"

"Of course you can."

She began chewing on her lip. "Do you love me? I mean, at one point during this relationship, have you ever loved me?"

My heart dropped. *Do I lie to her? Do I keep living this lie or finally put it all to an end?*

I let out a breath and decided to end this now. "Zoey, I know the truth."

She tilted her head and looked at me. "What do you mean?"

"I know the only reason you went after me was because you knew about the night Maddie and I spent together. You did all of this to make Maddie jealous didn't you?"

Zoey slowly shook her head. "How did you...how did you find out?"

I was about to answer when the phone rang. Zoey attempted to get up and answer it but I beat her to it. "I got it, Zoey."

I took a deep breath in and let it out quickly before answering. "Hello?"

"Hello, Mr. Blackwood?"

"Yes,"

The female on the other end of the line cleared her throat. "Mr. Blackwood, this is Doctor Richards' office. Zoey was supposed to come in this morning, but she never did. Doctor Richards told Mrs. Blackwood that she needed to be admitted to the hospital for the rest of her pregnancy. She's to be on mandatory bed rest. She said she would go home to pack and would return this morning to be admitted. Did she tell you this?"

I closed my eyes and shook my head. "No. I wasn't aware of this." I turned to Zoey. "Zoey? Zoey!"

"Mr. Blackwood, is everything okay?"

I ran over to where Zoey was now slumped on the ground. "She's fainted or something. Oh God! Zoey?"

"Mr. Blackwood, I'm calling 911 right now."

My hands shook as I checked for a pulse. "Okay. Please tell them to hurry." I couldn't find her heartbeat. "I can't find her heartbeat. Oh God. Please tell them to hurry up." I dropped the phone and cried.

"Please don't do this to me, Zoey. Please...oh God! *Zoey please!*"

I SENT A text to Jack to let him know I was on the way to Mercy Hospital with Zoey. I wasn't sure what was going on. All I knew was they were barely getting a heartbeat.

"The baby? What about the baby?" I asked.

The paramedic smiled weakly at me. "We're doing everything we can, sir."

Minutes later, I was standing alone in a waiting room, pacing back and forth. I'd called and left a message with Zoey's parents and my own. Every time the door opened, my heart would drop.

I sat down in a chair and buried my face into my hands.

"Cale?"

I looked up and saw my mother and father standing over me. I jumped up and I prayed that, for once in my life, my mother would act like a mother.

"Mom," I swallowed hard "Zoey's heart wasn't beating very strong and I don't…I mean…no one has told me…" I attempted to hold back my tears, but terror shot through me.

My mother opened her arms and reached out. I walked into her embrace and sobbed. She held me close, and I felt my father put his hand on my back.

"Shh, darling," my mother said. "Take a deep breath. They'll both be fine."

I let out sob after sob as I pictured them trying to get Zoey's heartbeat going.

"I overheard them say that the baby was in distress and they would have to get her out as soon as possible. They said to prep for an emergency C-section. Oh, God. Why didn't I just lie to her? Why didn't I just tell her I loved her? *I* did this. I brought it all up and caused her to…"

My mother held me even tighter. "Cale, stop this. Calm down, darling." She sat down in a chair, and I sat next to her. My father sat on the other side of me. He grabbed my hand and held it tight.

We sat there in silence. My parents didn't even ask me what I'd had been talking about earlier. They both knew I didn't love Zoey. I'd told them both about Maddie, I'd told them about the night we shared together. My mother had even put two and two together and figured out that Maddie's father was Mr. Powers of Powers Communication, but she'd still agreed that I needed to "do the right thing" and marry Zoey.

The doors opened and a doctor came striding out. He looked straight at me. "Mr. Blackwood?"

I jumped up along with my mother and father. "Yes. That's me."

He came over to me and extended his hand. "I'm Dr. Philips. I was the OB on call when your wife came in. You have a very healthy baby girl."

My mother placed her hand over her chest and began to cry. My father let out a deep breath.

I closed my eyes and whispered, "Thank you, God." I opened my eyes and asked Dr. Philips, "Zoey? Is she okay?"

Dr. Philips swallowed hard but turned as Dr. Richards walked through the doors.

I reached out and shook Doctor Richards's hand. "Dr. Richards. How is Zoey? Is she okay? Does she know about the baby yet?"

Taking a deep breath, he looked into my eyes. "I'm so sorry, Cale. The pregnancy put a terrible strain on Zoey's body as it fought to keep her kidneys and liver working. Along with the pregnancy, her heart just couldn't keep up anymore. We tried everything we could, but...Zoey's gone."

My legs felt like they were about to give out on me. I shook my head and whispered, "No. No. Oh, God, no…"

My father grabbed me and led me back to the chair. "Cale, sit down. Breathe, son. You have to breathe."

I closed my eyes. All she'd wanted to know was if I loved her. Why hadn't I just lied? *Oh God. I did this,*

I did this.

16

Maddie

I WRAPPED THE sweater tightly around myself as I walked along the path. It was early June, and the temperatures in Tuscany were still chilly—especially in the morning.

"*Buongiorno*, Maddison."

I turned to see Jessica standing there with a huge grin on her face. She was a beautiful girl who'd just started working for Andre's grandparents. Her strawberry blonde hair fought for attention in the glow of the morning sun. Her smiled made me giggle. Andre had told her to make sure I had everything I needed, which meant that Jessica was following me around like a puppy, constantly asking me what I needed.

"*Buongiorno*, Jessica. I don't need anything, but thank you."

She shook her head. "No, *telefonata importante*."

My heart started beating harder in my chest. I'd made sure to text Andre's cell phone number to Monica, along with the number to his grandparents' house.

"An important phone call?" I wasn't sure why I was asking. I knew that was what she'd said.

"*Sì, es* Monica."

I quickly walked toward her. "Show me where the phone is, Jessica. Please."

She nodded and turned on her heels, walking back into the house. She pointed to the phone on the table. I ran over and picked it up.

"Hello? Monica? Are you okay? My parents?"

"Maddie, your parents are fine, I'm fine. I have…um…can you come home?"

I felt my heart start to race. "Why? What's wrong?"

Was Monica crying?

"Cale needs you, Maddie."

"What's happened? Monica, you're scaring me."

Monica let out a sob and said, "I can't tell her."

I shook my head as I yelled, "Can't tell me what?"

A male voice came over the line. "Maddie, it's Jack."

I felt my legs giving out on me. *Cale. What's happened to Cale?*

"Sweetheart, I don't know any other way to tell you this, but to just blurt it out. Zoey's passed away."

The air left my body in one quick breath. "What? Wait…what do you mean? Jack, what do you mean?" I covered my mouth with my hand, trying to hold back my sob.

"Maddie, I'm so sorry to tell you over the phone. Zoey had a heart attack. Her heart just couldn't take any more stress and…she's gone, Maddie. They were able to get Lily out okay. She's okay, the baby is okay."

My thoughts raced. *Baby? Lily? Cale had a girl? Zoey's gone…*

I let out the sobs I'd been holding in as I sank to the floor. Andre came around the corner and took one look at me before running over.

"Maddison!" He fell to the floor and held my face. He tried to wipe my tears away. I shook my head, trying to calm myself.

"Cale? Is… Cale… okay?"

Jack sighed. "No. He hasn't even seen the baby yet, Maddie. His mother and Monica have been taking care of her."

I gasped. "What? Why?"

"He's blaming himself. He thinks Zoey had the heart attack because he confronted her about her knowing about the two of you all along."

What? My head was spinning. I looked at Andre and nodded as he helped me into a chair. "What do you mean, Jack?" I asked.

"Listen, Maddie, I'll explain it all when you get back. Can you come home? Zoey's parents want *nothing* to do with the baby. Zoey's mother said that Lily will remind her too much of Zoey."

I nodded. "Yes. Yes, I'll try to get the next flight back to the States."

Andre grabbed my hands. "Bella, I have my family's private plane. I'll bring you anywhere you want to go."

I smiled at Andre. "I'm on my way now. Andre's private plane is here. I'm on my way."

I hung up and ran down the long hallway to the room Andre and I were sharing. I hadn't even unpacked, since we'd just arrived the previous evening.

I grabbed my suitcase and began throwing the few things I'd taken out back in.

"Maddison, please tell me what's happening."

"Oh God I'm so sorry, Andre," I said. "You remember my friend, Zoey, the one who was pregnant?"

He nodded and said, "Yes. Cale is her husband?"

I felt a stab in my stomach as I remembered the night that I sent Andre home after Cale showed up drunk.

"Yes. Well, she had a heart attack and…and…she died. The baby is okay, but Cale hasn't even touched his daughter. Hasn't even held her. Zoey's parents want nothing to do with the baby. I have to get back home. I'm so sorry."

Andre ran his hand through his hair. "Bella, I'm so sorry about your friend, but I don't see why you need to rush back home."

I stopped moving and stared at him. "*What?* My friend just died, her husband, who is also a friend, now has no one."

Andre looked at me funny. "I thought you said you couldn't

stand Cale. Why are you rushing back for him? Do you have feelings for him, Bella?"

I couldn't believe my ears. "Are you for real? You're really asking me this, Andre? His wife just fucking died. My friend. I was her only friend, and you're standing here asking me such stupid-ass questions?" I grabbed my suitcase and pushed past him. "I'll find my own way back to the States. I don't have time to play games."

He grabbed my arm. "Maddison, wait. Please forgive me. I didn't mean to sound so cold-hearted. Of course you should be rushing back. She was your friend. I'm being so insensitive. Let me grab my suitcase and I'll meet you out front. I'll call the airport and have the plane ready to go by the time we get to Pisa."

I dropped my suitcase and wrapped my arms around Andre's neck, pulling his lips down to mine. "Thank you," I whispered against his lips as I pulled them away.

"Anything for you, Bella."

"MADDISON, ARE YOU sure you don't want me to bring you home?" Andre said. "I can stay a few days, work from your house. You know I can work from anywhere."

I smiled, placing my hand on Andre's cheek. "I love that you want to do this for me. But let me get a handle on things. You know you're welcome anytime. I'll miss you."

He pulled me to him and I could feel his hard-on. "I'll miss you, Bella. I'll fly home and take care of some things, then fly back in about a week. You'll let me know if you need anything, yes?"

I grinned and reached up to kiss him. "Yes. I promise. Have a safe trip to New York."

He tucked my hair behind my ears and gazed at me, longingly. "I meant it when I said I was falling in love with you, Bella. I won't push you into saying it back, but I want you to know how I feel."

My heart tightened in my chest as I smiled and chewed on my lip. He turned and headed back to his plane. I watched him until he rounded the corner, out of sight.

I pulled out my phone and hit Monica's number. "I'm here," I said as I walked toward the airports nearest exit.

I sat in Monica's car in silence as she drove us to my house. I wanted to stop and shower and change my clothes before heading to Cale's. The baby came home yesterday, and Monica and Jack had stayed with Cale last night and most of today.

"He won't even look at her," Monica said, her voice cracking.

"Why? I don't understand?"

"It's simple—he blames himself for Zoey's death."

I shook my head. "Why?"

Monica gripped the steering wheel and sighed. "Jack found out from Zoey's cousin that Zoey knew all along about you and Cale."

"How in the world would Zoey know?"

"I told you! You know, that day when we were talking about Cale and your feelings for him? I always thought that Zoey was listening in on our conversation. You didn't believe me. Well, she was, and the moment Cale told her his name, she realized who he was and set out to win him over. That's why she just went full force on him. It was Zoey who was always bragging about how much Cale loved to fuck. It was *her*. She wanted it that way. Cale barely touched her since he saw you again. Then, when he found out she'd tricked him into the pregnancy, things really changed. He told Jack he wanted to have feelings for Zoey, but couldn't, because of his feelings for you."

I looked away and tried to let everything sink in. I shook my head. "If he didn't have feelings for her, why would he marry her?"

"Pressure from both their parents. He was trying to do the honorable thing, Maddie."

I held back my tears. "You're on Cale's side now?"

Her eyes widened as she gave me a look at a stoplight. "I didn't realize we had sides, Maddie."

I stared out the window in silence.

"You and Andre had sex while in Italy, right? I mean, you've been sleeping with him for a while now."

"Excuse me?"

Monica raised an eyebrow at me. "You heard me."

"What the hell does that have to do with any of this?"

Monica pulled into my driveway, parked, and looked at me. "It has a *lot* to do with it, Maddie. You sit here and act pissed off because Zoey and Cale had sex. He was having a baby with her. They dated. They were together. He had no idea that Zoey even knew about you guys. He had no idea she was playing him. He tried to do the right thing. Did they sleep together? Yes. Did Zoey exaggerate their sex life? Very much so. But don't sit there and judge Cale when you're fucking Andre while your heart belongs to someone else."

She got out of the car, slamming the door behind her and heading for my front door.

I sat there in a stupor. Zoey had played all of us. Somehow, I think I knew it when she told me she was pregnant. It was in her smile. I dropped my head back against the seat.

"This just sucks," I whispered, pushing the door open. I didn't want to admit that Monica was right. So I did what I always do.

I pushed my feelings aside.

17

Cale

I SAT ON the deck and looked out over the dark water. I hadn't heard any voices in about an hour. I still hadn't seen my daughter yet. I let my mother name her when the hospital said they needed a name for her birth certificate. I didn't deserve to name her. I didn't deserve to be her father.

I took another swig of beer.

I could feel it the moment she stepped onto the deck. The energy in the air changed and goose bumps moved across my skin. I closed my eyes. The last time I'd seen her was the night I'd had my fingers buried inside her warm body—then insulted her in a drunken rage. I wasn't drunk this time. Yet.

"Cale?"

"I thought you were in Italy?" I heard her suck in a breath.

"You knew I was in Italy?" she asked.

I laughed. "Well, when my best friend is dating your best friend, I find things like that out. But we don't have anything to talk about, Maddie. You made yourself clear the last time we talked. You remember that night, don't you, Maddie?"

She approached me. "Fuck you, Cale. Stop acting like a prick and get in there and bond with your daughter."

I let out a gruff laugh. "She doesn't need me."

Maddie pulled a second chair over, scraping it against the deck. She sat down directly across from me and gave me a once-over.

"You look like hell."

My eyes locked with hers. Those beautiful green eyes—I always found myself getting lost in them.

I tipped my beer back and drank the last of it. I sat it down on the table and said, "Well, I guess I would, since the mother of my child died and left me alone to raise our baby. Plus, you know, I'm the one who probably caused her death in the first place."

I reached for another beer. I had ten of them all lined across the table. Maddie grabbed it from my hand then gathered up all the full beers, dumping them all in the porch garbage can before sitting back down. I glared at her as I held my hand out.

"Give me my beer back."

She shook her head. "No."

I laughed. "It's my fucking house. Get the hell out and leave me alone."

"Again, fuck you, Cale."

I gave her a smug look. "What do you want from me?"

She folded her arms across her chest. It caused her breasts to ride up a little further in her shirt. Her nipples were hard and pressed against the light fabric of her top. What I wouldn't give to come home every night and make love to her.

I shook my head to clear my thoughts. "Leave me alone, Maddie."

She stood up and looked down at me. She turned on her heels and walked away. "There ya go, *Bella*. Doing what you do best," I called out after her. I hadn't noticed that she was carrying the trashcan full of my beers with her.

Fuck.

I was about to stand up when I felt cold water all over my body.

"Jesus Christ! What the hell?" I jumped up and stumbled backward. I turned and looked to see Maddie standing there with a smile on her face holding a bucket.

"You're done. This ends right now. Stop moping. Zoey died because she did something she shouldn't have. She got pregnant. Her fate was sealed the day she decided to trap you with the pregnancy. There was nothing you could have done for her. The doctor told her that her heart was too weak to take the additional stress of a pregnancy. Her *whole body* was too weak. She knew, Cale. She knew she wasn't going to make it. Her jealousy consumed her and it clouded her judgment. Why do you think she always said she hated being pregnant? You didn't kill her. Her own actions sealed her fate."

I stood there, soaking wet. I could only tell that I was crying when the heat of my tears warmed my face.

Maddie set the bucket down and placed her hands on her hips. "Go shower and change. We are going to meet Lily together for the first time."

My heart slammed in my chest. What I wouldn't give to have Lily be Maddie's baby. *Our baby.* As I walked by, I stopped next to her. We locked eyes, and I knew she felt the same way.

MY MOTHER AND Maddie chatted for a bit after I introduced them. Maddie smiled that sweet smile of hers and I could tell that my mother loved her immediately. It had nothing to do with who Maddie's father was.

"Are you sure?" My mother asked Maddie.

Nodding, Maddie smiled. "Yes. Go home and rest. Cale and I will be fine. I've taken care of plenty of babies. I promise I know what I'm doing."

My mother's shoulders relaxed. "Oh Maddie. Thank you, honey." It was then that I saw how tired my mother looked. I took her into my arms.

"Thank you, Mom. I'm so sorry I abandoned you with the baby." I pulled back and tried to smile. "I love you, Mom."

She sucked in her bottom lip and wiped away a tear. "I'm sorry, Cale. For everything." She turned to Maddie and grabbed her purse. "Now, if you need anything, call me. I'll write my cell number in the kitchen in case Cale falls asleep and you need something darling." My mother kissed Maddie on the cheek as she smiled. "Okay. Thank you, Maddie."

We watched as my mother walked down the stairs. The front door shut and I met Maddie's gaze. She gave me a weak smile. "Are you ready to see your daughter?" she asked.

I swallowed hard and nodded. Maddie turned and opened the door to the nursery. It wasn't even decorated. I kept asking Zoey when she wanted to decorate, and she kept putting it off. She said she wanted to wait and meet the baby first. I wasn't sure now if she just didn't care, or if she'd somehow figured out that she wasn't going to make it. If maybe she thought the baby wouldn't, either.

I took a deep breath and held it in. Maddie reached for my hand and the shock I felt caused me to let out my breath.

We entered the nursery. I took in the bare walls. There was a rocking chair in the corner and a crib against the wall. Jack had gone out and purchased the crib and chair yesterday before my parents brought Lily home. That's when it hit me. Zoey had done nothing to prepare for the baby. It was all a blur. I remembered Monica and my mother making a list of all the things they needed:

"Cale? Did Zoey not even have a baby shower?"

"No. She didn't want one."

She knew. Zoey knew she wasn't going to make it. But she was wrong about one thing. Our daughter was much stronger than Zoey gave her credit for. I looked over to Maddie when I heard her let out a sob.

"Oh my God," she whispered.

I stopped walking. I was frozen. The guilt began to set in and I wanted to run. Maddie reached into the crib and picked up my daughter.

Maddie brought the baby up to her face and smelled her head, then kissed her. I felt tears burning my eyes as I watched Maddie hold my daughter. *This should be her child. This should be our daughter. Our moment.*

She turned and looked at me. "Cale, come meet your daughter, Lily. She needs her daddy."

I took a slow first step. My feet felt like lead. It took all my energy to walk the five more steps I needed to walk to get to my child. When I finally looked down at Lily, I couldn't believe what I saw. She was gazing into Maddie's eyes.

Maddie was talking to Lily. When she looked over at me and smiled, a tear rolled down her face. I couldn't help but wonder what Maddie was thinking, whether she was thinking and dreaming the same thing I was.

She held the baby out for me and whispered, "Lily Rose, meet your daddy."

I took Lily in my arms and, when our eyes met, something in me changed. It was as if everything I'd done wrong in the last three days was wiped away. I was starting with a clean slate.

My daughter looked into my eyes as if she was trying to tell me how much she needed me. I smiled as I took in her breathtaking face. "I've never seen anyone so beautiful in my life," I said.

Maddie laughed, and then hiccupped. I glanced up at her and she crinkled her nose. "Sorry," she said. "That happens when I'm trying not to cry and then laugh. It's like the laugh and cry come out at the same time as a hiccup."

I walked around the room holding Lily. I had no idea how I was going to make this work on my own. I was scared shitless but, somehow, in this moment, I wasn't worried. I'd figure it all out sooner or later. Right now, I wanted to enjoy this moment with my daughter. I walked out onto the balcony and showed Lily the lake.

"This is where you are going to grow up, Lily," I said. "I'm going to teach you everything I know. How to swim, ski, and fish. You'll be a better fishermen than daddy."

I felt Maddie come up next to me. I turned and she smiled at me before looking down to Lily and touching the side of her face. My heart pounded. I wanted this forever. Just the three of us, forever.

Glancing back down, I smiled at my baby girl. "I'm going to show you the world, Lily. You and me, together."

18

Maddie

I TRIED TO focus on the report I held in my hand, but all I could hear was Cale talking to Lily on the balcony. Cale sharing his dreams with his daughter had pulled hard on my heartstrings, and I wanted more than anything to stand next to him and be a part of it.

I tossed my pen down and sighed in frustration. Cale was sitting on the back deck holding Lily as she slept. He'd hardly put her down all day.

"He's spoiling her," Monica said as she set a glass of wine down in front of me.

I picked up the glass and took a sip. "No, he isn't. He's bonding with her."

"Uh huh. What was your excuse last night?"

"What?"

She grinned. "Yeah, I got up to pee last night and I heard you humming as you rocked Lily for God knows how long last night."

I looked away quickly to hide my red cheeks. I'd packed a small bag that first day, but I'd been staying with Cale for almost a week. Andre wasn't so thrilled with my decision, but I didn't care. Every night I snuck into Lily's room and held her for at least two hours before she woke up for her feeding. Then I'd feed her and hold her for another hour before slipping her back into her crib and sneaking back to the guest room. I was pretty sure Cale knew, despite my attempts at being stealth.

Cale and I had hardly spoken to each other. Other than helping each other give Lily a bath together, we pretty much just took turns with her. I lay in bed almost every night and fought to hold back my tears. I longed for something more with Cale and Lily. But I felt so guilty for the things that were running through my mind. I closed my eyes and pictured us walking along a path, each holding one of Lily's hands as she begged us to swing her again.

My phone vibrating on the table pulled me out of my daydream. I picked it up and saw it was a text from Andre.

Andre: *Ciao, Bella. Have you missed me? I've missed your touch, your smell...me buried deep inside of you. I'm leaving first thing tomorrow morning.*

I put my phone down and tried to push the panic down.

"Are you okay?" Monica asked me. I smiled and nodded my head.

"Yep, just my boss."

Oh God. Why did I just lie?

Cale stood and began dancing with Lily as he sang to her. My insides melted instantly as I tried to ignore the pulsing sensation between my thighs. I wanted him. I wanted to share this life with him so bad.

Andre. I cared about Andre. Thinking like this was wrong. It was just wrong.

I cleared my throat as I pulled my eyes from Cale. "Andre's flying in tomorrow."

Monica spun around. "Why is he coming here? What about Cale? What about Lily?"

Her outburst caught me off-guard. "What about Cale and Lily?"

Her eyes flicked between Cale and me. She almost seemed panicked. "You're just going to leave them?"

My mouth gaped open. "Um…considering the fact that I'm not Lily's mother, or Cale's wife, I don't think it's my place to stay here any longer."

My hands shook as I fought the battles taking place in my heart. I could easily text Andre and tell him to wait another week. I know he wouldn't argue with me. Or I could walk away, leaving Lily and Cale on their own. I was so tired of walking away.

Monica sat down next to me. "Listen, Maddie, I'm not trying to tell you how to live your life. But your being here is really helping Cale."

I laughed. "We don't even talk to each other."

"You know what I mean. It's like, with you here, he feels like he can do this. You were the only person who could snap him out of it after Zoey's death. Can't you just give it another week?"

I looked back out at Cale and Lily. My heart exploded with something I had been trying to fight for months.

I texted Andre back.

Me: *Ciao! Things are crazy here. I'm trying, along with Monica and Cale's mom, to help him and Lily get settled. Zoey didn't pre-pare at all for the baby. This week's task is to get the nursery ready. I'd hate for you to come now when we wouldn't get to spend any time together. Do you think you could hold off a week? P.S. I've missed you too.*

I set my phone down and waited. Since Andre had questioned my feelings for Cale in Italy, I was worried he would think there was more going on then there was.

Andre: *Wow. That has to be really hard for Cale that Zoey didn't have any plans. I'm so sorry, babe. I don't mind waiting an-other week if needed. I promise to completely relax you when I get there, though. I have plans for endless massages and orgasms.*

My stomach clenched at the thought of what Andre would do to relax me. I bit my lip and felt my cheeks flush.

"Damn, girl. Is that boy sexting you?"

I giggled as I rolled my eyes at Monica.

Me: *You have no idea how wonderful that sounds. I'll text you later this evening or tomorrow. Maybe you can help me…relax.*

Andre: *Son of a bitch, Maddison. I'm in a meeting fighting to keep my dick from growing.*

Me: *Haha! Talk to ya soon!*

Andre: *Arrivederci, Bella.*

I set my phone down and picked up the report I'd been working on earlier. The main perk of my job was I worked mostly from home, except for when I had to travel. I sighed as I tried to concentrate.

I heard the door to the deck slide open. I looked up to see Cale walking in with Lily. He was grinning down at her, and I couldn't help but smile at the love on his face.

Monica laughed. "Jesus, Cale. You're going to spoil her by carrying her around all the time."

He didn't even look up at Monica. "I don't care. She likes being in daddy's arms."

My stomach dropped and I had felt a slight pinch of jealousy.

Monica stood and walked over to kiss Lily on the head. "I'm going to miss you my sweet, little peanut."

I snapped my head over. Both Cale and I blurted, "What do you mean?"

Jack came into the room. "Oh, shit. Didn't we tell you? Monica and I are going to Texas to visit my grandparents. You know, introduce my bitch to the rest of the family and all that shit."

I stood so fast that my chair flew backward and crashed onto the floor. Lily instantly started crying.

Cale shot me a dirty look. "Good going, Maddie. You scared

her."

I gave him a dirty look back. "I didn't do it on purpose. Besides, she needs to get used to loud noises or she'll react that way all the time. Just like at naptime—you have to stop tiptoeing around. She needs to learn to sleep through noise."

Cale laughed as he put Lily in her swing. "Like you're an expert."

"Fuck you, Cale."

He winked at me and said, "You wish you could."

"Well, now that I know the two of you are going to play nice and not act like twelve year olds, Jack and I can leave with the confidence that Lily is in good hands."

I glanced back at Monica. "Wait. You two can't leave us."

Jack looked at me like I'd grown two heads. "Maddie, you know more about taking care of Lily than any of us. You'll be fine."

I shook my head. "I'm not worried about, Lily. You can't leave me here with Cale."

I felt his hot breath up against my neck as he came up behind me. "Don't worry, *Bella*...I promise to behave."

I spun around and punched him on the arm. "Stop calling me that, you asshole."

Cale laughed as he turned and walked into the kitchen. I looked back at Monica with pleading eyes. "Please," I begged.

She kissed me on the cheek. "Sorry, Maddie. We've had this trip planned for weeks. You'll be fine. Stop trying so hard to hate each other. If you put as much effort into being his friend as you do trying push him away, you'd probably both be so much happier. You can't push love away forever. Fate has a way of stepping in, one way or another."

I stood there, staring at my best friend. I wasn't sure if I loved or hated her right now.

I reached for my inner strength and pushed aside my true feelings. "Pssh, please. I don't even know what you're talking about. I have a boyfriend, and we're very happy, thank you. I care about him, and he fulfills me in more than one way."

Monica's eyes changed. The way she looked at me, I couldn't tell if she was feeling sorry for me or if she was pissed off. She rolled her eyes and sighed.

"Whatever, Maddie. I'm glad you're enjoying your boyfriend." Monica looked over my shoulder, and I was guessing Cale had come back into the living room. She shot me an evil smile. "Too bad you pushed Andre's arrival back for a week. Hope you packed your handy, dandy vibrator. You need a serious orgasm, sweetheart. I know how bitchy you get when you need to...*relax*."

My mouth dropped open as Jack busted out laughing. Monica turned and headed for the door. She waved, saying, "Have fun guys. Take care of my peanut for me."

Jack slapped Cale on the back, then kissed me on the cheek. I stood there stunned. I was going to kill her. *Kill. Her.* She did that on purpose.

I wasn't sure how long Cale and I stared at the door before he finally spoke. "I can't believe they left us," he whispered.

I closed my eyes and tried to push it all out. I turned to Cale and was about to say something when my whole world came to a stop.

Oh Fuck. I'm so screwed.

He stood there, having the nerve to look amazing, with his toned body and messy, brown hair. His green eyes pierced mine, holding my stare longer than they should have. My eyes moved down his body. He had on a muscle tee that looked like it was two sizes too small, jeans that hung just barely on his hips, bare feet...and he was carrying a damn bottle full of milk and a bib.

Sexiest. Thing. Ever.

A soft moan escaped from my mouth. We were alone. For the first time we were *truly* alone. I licked my bottom lip back and forth and then bit down on it as I stared at him.

Maddison Powers what the hell is wrong with you? Turn away. Look. Away.

The smile that spread across his damn face told me he could see how turned on I was just by looking at him. The idea of him making love to me pushed itself into my mind. I placed my hand on my stomach and fought like hell to keep my fingers from slipping into my panties, relieving my ache.

I could almost feel his hands on my body. I kept telling myself: *You have a boyfriend.*

He tilted his head slightly, as if he was trying to read my mind.

The thought of his lips moving gently across my body as he slowly showered me with his attention did crazy things to my body. *You. Have. A. Boyfriend.*

I took a step closer to him. His smile faded for a brief second.

I wanted him, and I was having a hard time fighting it. Damn him for being so sexy.

I took another step, but stopped there.

"Do you, um…do you want me to feed her while you go work-out?" I asked.

I somehow managed to push my feelings down, back into that part of my heart that was forbidden.

Cale's smile vanished, and his eyes filled with something I hadn't seen in a while. Loneliness.

He came closer to me and looked down at my lips. I sucked in my lip and looked up into his eyes. "Is that what you want?" he barely whispered.

I knew what he wanted to hear. But my phone vibrated and I looked down to see Andre's name flash across the screen.

I looked back up at Cale with a fake smile across my lips. "Yep. I think it would do you good to get out of the house."

He looked down at my phone, shook his head, and then glanced back at me. He shoved the bottle and bib into my hands, turned, grabbed his keys, and left.

19

Cale

I'D BEEN SITTING at the bar for almost four hours. My phone went off again with yet another text message from Maddie.

Maddie: *Okay, asshole. No one works out for four hours! Where the hell are you?*

I set the phone down, ignoring the text. The dark-haired brunette down the bar had been eye-fucking me for an hour. With each beer I drank, and each shot I downed, she moved closer. I smiled as I caught her looking, again. She winked and I turned to Louie.

"Give me another shot, Lou, will ya?"

He shook his head. "Cale, do you have a ride home?"

I felt a hand slide down my back. "Yes, he does."

I turned to see the brunette sitting down next to me. "My name's Jackie. What's your name, good looking?"

I smiled my crooked smile at her and replied, "Horny as fuck."

She let out a fake laugh, making sure her tits bounced in just the right way. My dick jumped a little.

She ran her tongue along her teeth and hissed, "I bet I can take care of that for you, handsome."

I placed my hand on the back of her neck and pulled her closer. "I bet you could."

The memory of Maddie staring at me earlier popped into my head. I knew she'd been turned on. Her continuing to fight it did nothing but piss me off. I'd heard her in the guest room the other night, and I thought she was just getting herself off until I heard her whisper fucking Andre's name. I heard his voice and realized that she had his ass on speakerphone—they were having phone sex. I'd stormed down the hallway and locked myself in Lily's room. An hour later, I heard Maddie trying to get into the room. I knew she went to see Lily every night around two in the morning. There was no way I was going to let her into my daughter's room.

Jackie ran her fingers though my hair. "Your place or mine, baby?"

I smiled. "Mine."

JACKIE LAUGHED AS she pushed the door to my house open and we both stumbled in. I was so shit-faced that I knocked over a lamp, resulting in a loud crash. Jackie and I had stayed at the bar another couple hours and, after a few more drinks, we'd taken a taxi to my place.

I pushed her against the wall and kissed her hard as she moaned into my mouth. Then a light came on.

I heard Maddie gasp before she said, "What the hell?"

Jackie pushed me away. She looked at Maddie,—who happened to be holding Lily—then glared at me.

"Oh my God," Jackie said. "You're married? And you have a

baby?"

Maddie was so pissed that I could almost see her whole body shaking. I threw my head back and laughed. "Hell, no. You see, Jackie, Maddie here thinks I'm not good enough for her. I've *never* been good enough for her. All she does is push me away."

I saw the hurt flash in Maddie's eyes.

Jackie stared. "Um, the baby?"

I smiled. "Oh, yeah…she's mine."

Jackie grabbed her purse. "She can't be more than a week old, Cale."

"Um…she's almost three weeks," I said.

Jackie pushed me and I fell over the back of the sofa, crashing onto the coffee table.

Lily started crying as Jackie approached Maddie. "I'm so sorry. I'd have never …oh God, I'm so sorry."

She turned and made her way out the door. "Wait! Jackie, it's not what you think!"

The door slammed and I just stood there, staring. I was too afraid to turn and face the wrath of Maddie. But I could feel her— I was pretty sure her eyes were shooting daggers.

"I'm going to go put Lily down in her crib once I get her back to sleep. Then you and I are going to talk."

She spun around and walked up the stairs. I let out a breath and stumbled into the kitchen. I somehow managed to get coffee going and had almost drank a whole cup when Maddie came in.

"So, is that something Lily should expect often from her father? Bringing home a stray whore every now and then to fuck?"

I closed my eyes. "Go to hell, Maddie."

"I'm already there, Cale."

I turned and looked at her. "If you hate it here so much—hate *me* so much—there's the door, sweetheart. Don't let it hit your ass on the way out."

She laughed as she came closer and poked me in the chest. "There is no way in hell you could do this without my help."

I knocked her hand away. "I could, and I will...until I have to go back to work."

"What? What do you mean?"

I turned and poured another cup of coffee. "I have to go back to work, Maddie. How the hell do you think I pay for all of this?"

I heard her sit down. "But...what about Lily? Who's going to take care of her when you're gone for weeks at a time?"

I shrugged. "I'll hire a nanny I guess."

"No," she whispered. "Cale, why are you doing this?"

I slammed my mug down so hard that it broke into pieces. I turned and looked at the only girl I'd ever loved. The one I'd never be able to have.

"Because, Maddie," I said. "I have a fucking job that takes me out of town for weeks at a time. I didn't sign up for this shit. I didn't ask for her! I didn't ask for my life to be turned upside down."

She jumped up. "You have a child now. You're going to have to make changes. You're all she has, Cale. You're going to have to take another job. Work for your father or something."

I took a step close to her. "I'm not working for my father. I *have* a fucking job! I want my old life back!" I yelled.

Maddie was startled, but she held firm. "Oh, boohoo for you. Your old life is gone. The only thing that matters is Lily. She's all you have."

I took a step back. Tears filled my eyes. "I know, Maddie. You don't have to remind me. I know."

I was walking away when she grabbed my arm. "What do you want from me?" she asked "I can't say anything without you turning it against me. So I walked away from you. It was the biggest mistake of my life, but I can't change the past. What do you want me to do?"

I grabbed her arms and shook her. "I want you to fucking admit you love me. I want you to admit that you want me as much as I want you."

She stared at me. Her eyes said that she loved me, but her body stiffened as she looked away from me. "I can't tell you that. I...I have a boyfriend and—"

I pulled her to me and slammed my lips against hers. I moved my tongue along her bottom lip, praying she'd open her mouth to me. She moaned and pushed her hands through my hair as her lips parted. Our tongues began to dance, gently at first, but soon becoming more heated. I pulled her body to mine and pushed my hard dick against her.

"Cale," she whispered as she pulled her lips from mine.

I picked her up as she wrapped her legs around my body. I pushed her against the wall. I slipped my hand under her shirt and I moaned when I realized she wasn't wearing a bra. Her hard nipples begged to be sucked.

"Jesus, Maddie. I want you."

I pushed up her shirt and moved my lips down to her nipple and began sucking on it as she called out my name. I slipped my hand into her pants and then into her panties where my fingers teased her. She began pushing against my hand and I couldn't wait another second. I pushed two fingers inside of her and was met with nothing but pure heat and wetness. She clamped down on my fingers and pulled them further in.

"You're so fucking wet, Maddie."

"Wait, Cale…we can't…oh, God."

The doorbell rang. It seemed to pull Maddie to her senses. I set her down as she pushed me away, pulling her shirt down. Her chest was heaving as she attempted to slow her breathing. The doorbell rang again. I turned away and headed to the door as I adjusted my rock-hard dick.

The second I opened the door, I recognized him. I stood there staring at the bastard.

I heard Maddie behind me. "Andre? What are you…? How did you know I was here?"

Andre gazed between me and Maddie. "I have my ways." He said, giving me a wink.

Fucker.

Maddie pushed past me, walked into his arms.

"I've missed you, Bella," he said.

I rolled my eyes, turned and walked away as she told him how much she'd missed him, too. She wasn't missing him two minutes ago when I had her against the wall.

"Actually, you told me you were staying here with Monica. I looked up Cale's name, and when I stopped by your house and found it empty, I figured you were here."

Maddie let out a nervous giggle. "Wow, you could be a detective."

Andre laughed. "Well, now that I'm here, gather your things, Bella. Let's go home."

I sat down on the sofa and turned on the TV, waiting to hear her response.

"Um, Andre? We talked about this. I need another week to help get things settled."

I glanced over at them. Andre was glaring. "Well, from the smell of alcohol on his breath, I'd say some things haven't changed."

I stood and began to approach him. "Listen here, you prick. You can't just show up on my doorstep and—"

Maddie stepped in front of me. "Cale, please go sit down."

I smiled at her. Her cheeks were still flushed. I lifted my fingers to my mouth and her eyes grew wide. I dropped my hand and walked back to the sofa.

"Andre, you can't just show up and expect me to leave. I can't to do that to Lily."

He leaned in close and whispered to Maddie. "Is this for Lily, or for him?"

"I'm not even going to answer that. I've never pegged you as the jealous type, Andre. I asked you for one more week. After Saturday, you'll have me all to yourself."

My stomach turned—I felt sick.

"Bella, this is *not* your responsibility."

I heard Maddie sigh as the front door opened. They stepped outside, the door closing behind them. I smiled.

If Maddie did what I was hoping she'd do, I'd have six more days with her. Six more days to show her how much we were meant to be together. Six more days to show her she didn't have to be afraid of her feelings for me.

20

Maddie

I SHUT THE door and turned to Andre. I glared at him. I was so pissed that I couldn't think straight. I was almost madder at myself, for being pissed that Andre interrupted what was happening between Cale and me. In a moment of weakness I'd let my guard down. As much as I claimed I didn't want to sleep with Cale, I was shaking mad that I'd lost my opportunity.

"How dare you! How dare you show up here and pull this stunt after I told you I needed more time? I'm so pissed off right now, Andre, I don't even know what to do."

Andre grabbed me and pulled me to him. He pressed his lips to mine. What once got me hot and bothered now seemed flat and boring. I attempted to show interest, moaning a little and tugging his hair. When he pulled his lips from mine he was panting. Clearly the kiss had affected him more than me.

I closed my eyes, feeling like a tramp. I'd been letting Cale kiss me and finger-fuck me while my boyfriend stood on the other side of the door.

"I've missed you, Bella," Andre breathed. "I've missed you so much. Please forgive me. I do have a jealous streak, and I'm so very sorry."

I smiled, placing my hand on his cheek. "You have to trust me." Guilt swept over me as I made a silent vow to resist Cale as much as possible for the next week.

"I'm staying here until Saturday. Cale needs my help."

Andre sighed and nodded. "Okay, Bella. I'll leave you be. But, come Saturday, I'll be waiting for you at your house. I'm going to take you to heaven and back. Multiple times."

I smiled and nodded. "Deal. I'm sorry you flew all the way down here for nothing."

He raised his eyebrows and my heart pounded. "We could go back to your house, Bella. A quick fuck from behind, like in Italy. You look like you could use one."

I swallowed hard, trying to push my mixed feelings away. There was no way I was going back to my house to have sex with Andre after what had just happened between Cale and me.

I pouted and shook my head. "I can't, Andre. I'm so sorry."

A look of disappointment washed over his face, but he quickly smiled and pulled me closer. The feeling of his hard dick against my stomach excited me, but I was so confused. Was I turned on because of Cale or Andre?

"Something to think about during the next six days," Andre said. He kissed me lightly and let me go as he walked away. I watched as he got into his car and drove off.

"Oh, Jesus. What is happening to me?"

I sat on the porch swing and tried to gather my thoughts. I'd never felt like I did when I was with Cale. It was so powerful and so strong—it scared me to death. Wanting and needing someone as much as I did Cale had me thinking back to our first night together.

I'd been so scared when it hit me, when I'd realized that I loved Cale. I'd only been with him for a few hours, but we talked like we'd known each other for years. The instant bond we'd shared scared the piss out of me. The easiest thing for me had been to run.

Like I'm doing now, I thought.

The door opened and I looked up at the only man I'd ever loved.

I was beginning to think he'd ruined me for all other men. He looked into my eyes and smiled. "I'm sorry. I'll be sure to keep my hands to myself."

I sat there, stunned. I wanted to jump up and beg Cale to make love to me, but all these things were running through my head. I opened my mouth, but Cale started talking again.

"Good night, Maddie."

He shut the door, leaving me alone on the porch. I leaned back against the swing and let the tears fall.

21

Cale

I WALKED INTO the kitchen and started the coffee maker with one hand as I held Lily in my other arm. I smiled as she looked up at me. "We got this, don't we, baby girl?" She yawned and I laughed—my charm clearly wasn't going to work on her. I took out a coffee cup and set it down as I retrieved one of her bottles and heated it on the bottle warmer. My baby girl waited patiently as I made my coffee and her breakfast.

"Daddy's getting pretty good at this stuff, isn't he sweetheart?" Lily made a bubble with her mouth and cooed. "I'll take that as a yes."

I took a sip of coffee and set it on the table, then tested her milk on my wrist. "You know it's coming, don't you?"

I put the nipple up to her mouth and waited for the normal pattern. The feel of it on her lips made her start kicking her feet until you placed it into her mouth. She did it every single time.

Her feet started moving as she opened her mouth and waited. "There's my morning show! Enjoy, Lily Rose. Daddy made it just for you." She closed her eyes as if she wasn't the least bit interested in what I had to say right now.

"Hmm…my charming skills clearly need to be honed."

"Do you make a habit of talking to yourself in the kitchen?"

I looked up to see Maddie leaning against the doorjamb, smiling. Her smiled faded as she raked her eyes over my body. I was only wearing a pair of linen pajama pants. No shirt. I liked holding Lily close to my chest in the mornings. It felt like we bonded more. I only did it when we were alone, though, since Maddie had made it very clear she was not interested in anything but friendship.

"Holy shit," she whispered.

I tried not to pay attention to her as I reached for my coffee and skillfully took a sip while holding my daughter and balancing her bottle at the same time.

"What's wrong?" I asked.

She walked slowly into the kitchen, she reached up to get a coffee cup. I'd purposely put them up higher, just so I could watch her reach with all her might. Usually it gave me a peak at her midriff.

I grabbed a cup for her, making sure I kept my body away. I could see the disappointment in her eyes.

"Um…what are your plans for today?" she asked.

My heart sunk as I thought about my to-do list. "I'm interviewing nannies today."

She spun around and looked at me. "What?"

I checked out Maddie's body. She was wearing a pencil skirt, a white blouse that was dangerously close to showing too much cleavage, and red pumps. She looked hot as hell. I wanted nothing more than to push up her skirt and take her right here in the kitchen.

"Maddie, I have no choice. You're going back to your real life tomorrow, and I believe you said you were traveling to Seattle on Monday. I have a job that I have to take care of, too."

"We can't leave her alone with a stranger, Cale. That breaks my heart."

Anger boiled in my veins. She enjoyed playing house with me, and had gotten damn good at it. I, on the other hand, was tired of it. Tired of hearing her every night on the phone with Andre, telling him she couldn't wait to see him, to be in his arms. Though she hadn't had any sexual encounters with him all week, which I thought was interesting.

"Well, I'm sorry that breaks your heart, Maddie. Tomorrow you'll be done playing house and can move on with your life. I need to think about Lily's future. And mine."

She slammed the coffee cup down and jetted out her hip in that sexy ass way she does when she's mad. "Playing house? Excuse me? I've worked my ass off this week helping you. We painted Lily's nursery and decorated it together. We set up the toy room with all the toys and made sure everything in this whole damn house was ba-by-proofed. What about the shopping we did for her clothes? She's the best-dressed baby on Beaver Lake! How dare you say I've been..."

She stopped talking and scrunched up her nose as she took a minute to think. She looked away and didn't say a word.

To Lily I whispered, "I wish it didn't have to end."

Walking out of the kitchen, I heard Maddie whisper, "Me too."

I ignored the tightening feeling in my heart. She wasn't going to change her mind. She'd seemingly avoided feelings this week as we'd concentrated on all things Lily.

I burped Lily and rocked her to sleep. After placing her in her crib, I walked to my office and called my boss. I knew what I had to do.

After telling my boss I was resigning, something amazing hap-pened. A huge weight was lifted from my shoulders. "I'll be on the first flight Monday to Seattle," I said. "I understand, and I'm sorry as well, Chuck. But this is something I have to do."

I hung up and took a deep breath. Then I made my next phone call. "Yes, may I speak with Mr. Powers? Cale Blackwood calling."

"Yes, of course. Mr. Powers has been expecting your call."

I closed my eyes and got ready to do the one thing I knew was right for both Lily and me. It was time for me to make serious changes in my life.

I SAT DOWN at the meeting table in the hotel conference room. All I could think about was Lily. What was she doing? Was she eating well? Were they taking care of her? Did she miss me?

I pulled out my phone and sent my mother a text.

Me: *How is Lily?*

Mom: *Why hello there, Cale. I'm doing well, thank you for asking.*

Me: *Sorry, mom. I just hate being away from her. She's not even a month old, and I've left her.*

Mom: *For one day. Maria is amazing. Although, I'm having a hell of a time understanding her damn accent. You had to hire a nanny from Spain?*

Me: *She used to nanny for a damn prince, Mom. I figured she would work for my princess. She's wonderful. Just tell her to talk slowly. You understand Spanish.*

Mom: *You can't see me, but I'm giving you the finger.*

I laughed as I put my phone back in my pocket. I couldn't believe how having Lily had changed both my mother and me. We were closer than we'd ever been. Even her and Dad seemed to be getting along better. She no longer cared if her hair and nails were perfect. She cared about Lily. With all her heart. In a way, I think she looked at this as her second chance at doing it right.

Chuck walked in with another guy from HR. They reached out to shake my hand and each gave me their condolences. I thanked them and slid my letter of resignation across the table. Chuck's face fell.

"Cale, you were moving up in the company. I can promote you so you're at a desk all day. Shit, you can bring Lily with you to work."

I smiled and shook my head. "I don't want her living out of hotel after hotel, Chuck. I want her to have a stable home."

He nodded. "I understand. Something about when they look into your eyes that first time—you're done for. That's the reason I took off for so many years."

I stood and reached to shake their hands. "Thank you for taking a chance on me," I said. "I really did love my job. I'll miss it."

Chuck got up and pulled me into a hug. "Good luck, son, in whatever you end up doing. You're always welcome back here."

I slapped his back, then headed out the door and to the airport. One day away from Lily was one day too many.

As I got in my rental car, a feeling came over me that I couldn't really explain. I was starting a new life, and I wasn't sure how it would go. The road was bumpy as hell but, as long as I had Lily, that was all that mattered. We'd eventually find our way home.

22

Maddie

I WALKED INTO Starbucks and smiled the moment I saw Monica. It had been two weeks since I'd left Lily and Cale after helping them get settled. I walked right into her arms and hugged her. "God I've missed you!"

She laughed and said, "I've missed you, too. I can't believe you were in Seattle for two whole weeks. What the hell?"

I rolled my eyes. "I know. It was like my boss was coming up with every excuse under the sun to keep me there. Then she wanted to send me to Milan. I told her I needed a couple of days to recuperate. Plus, I needed to see my Lily. I've tried calling Cale to talk to him, but he always just texts back and says they're both fine. I know he's upset with me."

Monica made a funny face and took a sip of her coffee. "How's Andre?"

I attempted to smile, even though she was clearly changing the subject. "He's fantastic. He's waiting for me at the house. Last I talked to him he was sitting outside, enjoying the weather."

Monica smiled politely and took another sip of coffee. I knew Monica didn't like Andre at all. It was time for me to change the subject again. "How was the trip to Texas? How are you and Jack?"

Her smile widened as she held out her hand. An oval-cut diamond sparkled on her ring finger.

"Oh my God!" I gasped, grabbing her hand. "Jack proposed?"

She nodded, excited like a kid on Christmas morning. "Yes! It was so romantic. He did it in front of his grandparents while we were celebrating their fiftieth wedding anniversary at this nice restaurant. In his proposal, he said he wanted to wake up every morning and see my face, and that he wanted to sit in the same restaurant fifty years from now. I'm not gonna lie—I swooned. The little man-whore took my breath away!

I sat back in my chair as my best friend talked about her engagement and how happy she was. "I can't believe you tamed Jack," I said. "I can't believe Jack tamed *you*. I thought you said you'd never get married because of your parents' divorce."

She looked directly into my eyes, serious now. "I guess I figured that I had to stop being so afraid and take a leap of faith. Sometimes, I think, we have to learn to let go of the control we think we need in order to find what fate has in store for us."

I could feel myself starting to frown, but I kept it together. I could tell that Monica was no longer talking about herself—she was talking about me.

I was happy. I had a boyfriend who wasn't expecting anything from me. I had good sex and a wonderful job. I was able to travel and see the world. I had exactly everything I wanted—or so I pretended.

I took a sip of coffee as I eyeballed Monica's ring.

My heart began to hurt as I admitted to myself that I longed for something else. Something I'd been pushing away for so long.

I SAT IN my car and took a deep breath. I'd hadn't seen Lily in almost a month. She was now two months old, and I was sure she wouldn't know me anymore. After returning from Seattle, I'd found out that Cale had taken Lily to his grandfather's place in Colorado. I was only home two days before I'd had to travel for almost another two more weeks to see clients in Milan. Now I was finally back home on Beaver Lake, and couldn't wait to see her. Lily.

My hands were shaking. I couldn't kid myself—I was dying to see Cale, too. My phone buzzed and I quickly pulled it out to see a text from Andre.

Andre: *I'm pulling up to your house. Can't wait to see you.*

I sighed and hit Reply.

Me: *I'm just pulling up to Cale's. I wanted to see Lily.*
Andre: *Wait for me there, I'll be right over.*
Me: *Okay.*

I sat and waited. Andre wasn't even supposed to be here for another two days. He'd flown to Milan and spent almost the entire trip with me. Which turned out to be okay, since I didn't even need to be there. Why my boss sent me there was beyond me.

I smiled as I saw the driver pull up and let Andre out. I opened my car door, got out, and practically slammed it. Andre was starting to smother me.

He came up to me and kissed me on the mouth. "Ciao, Bella."

"Ciao," I whispered back.

I turned to make my way toward the door. My hands were still shaking, so I dug deep inside myself to find the strength I needed to get through this. I rang the doorbell.

"One minute!" A female's voice rang out. An instant pang of jealousy raced through my blood before I realized the voice belonged to the nanny. Cale must have been out of town, working. *My poor Lily*, I thought. *She must be heartbroken with both Cale and me leaving her.*

When the door flew open, I was standing face to face with someone I knew. At least I *thought* I knew her.

"Oh my gosh! Maddison, how are you?"

I stared at the tall blonde before me. She was dressed in a business suit that hugged her in all the right places. Her pumps made her even taller, and she stood about two inches over than me, even though I was wearing heels, too. Her skin was perfectly tanned, and her hair was done up in a perfect chignon. She was flawless.

I smiled politely. "I'm sorry. Do we know each other?"

She giggled and waved us to come in. "I sure hope so. I've been working for your father, Mr. Powers, for three years now."

That's where I know her from! "Cassidy?"

She nodded. "That would be me."

I looked around the house for Cale, and finally found him walking into the living room with two glasses of wine. Lily was in her bouncy chair, sound asleep.

Cale called out, "How about red? That's all I've got."

Cassidy cleared her throat. "Cale, Maddison is here."

He stopped dead in his tracks when he saw me. He smiled, but then saw Andre and began to scowl. "Back from Italy, I see."

I swallowed hard. *He's moved on.*

I nodded. "I didn't mean to interrupt anything. I was so excited to be home. I rushed straight from the airport here to see Lily."

Cassidy laughed. "Oh, no. This is not..."

"It's no problem at all," Cale said. "Would the two of you like to join us for a glass of wine?"

"Of course," Andre replied.

At the same time, I nearly shouted, "No!"

I flicked my eyes between Andre and Cale. Cassidy reached down and scooped up my baby like Lily was her own.

I placed my hand on my stomach as she spoke gently to my Lily. My other hand went to my mouth. *My baby. My Lily.* I began to feel sick.

"Hey there, little princess," Cassidy said. "Aunt Maddison is here to visit you."

The horror in my eyes must have been seen by both Andre and Cale as they both asked me at once, "Are you all right?"

I shook my head and ran to the restroom. I slammed the door shut and slid down to the floor, tears streaming from my eyes.

Oh my God, what have I done? I've lost them both.

I wanted to control every single thing, but this was the one thing I couldn't. I crawled over to the toilet and threw up.

23

Cale

I KNOCKED ON the bathroom door. I was positive I heard Maddie crying before she started puking.

"I'm fine," she said. "Please, I just need a moment, Andre."

It felt like I had a knife in my heart. That asshole couldn't tear his eyes away from Cassidy long enough to come check on his girlfriend.

I cleared my throat. "Maddie, it's me."

I heard her sob. "Cale."

I rested my head on the door and whispered, "Please let me in, sweetheart. Please."

The door slowly opened and she stood in front of me, mascara running down her face. I wanted nothing more than to pull her into my arms and I tell her how much I missed her. How much I loved her.

"I'm sorry. I guess I just missed Lily more than I thought." She spun around to the sink and splashed her face with cold water, attempting to clean up. I watched her intently. I knew that wasn't why she was really upset. She obviously thought Cassidy and I were together. Cassidy calling her "Aunt Maddie" must have pushed her over the edge. I wasn't even sure why Cassidy said that.

"Lily's missed you too," I said.

She shook her head. "How could you leave her alone?" she asked. "Don't you miss her? Don't you feel bad that a stranger is raising your daughter?"

I was so pissed that my hands shook. She was accusing me of being a bad father. She had no idea I was working for her father's company. Then it hit me—Maddie was doing what she always did. When she felt herself getting too close, she pushed me away by fighting.

I took a deep, calming breath and slowly blew it out. "I quit my job, Maddie. I flew out that Monday, gave my notice, and flew right back home. I work from home mostly, with my new job, but Maria still comes and helps me with Lily during the day so I can work. I haven't been away from her for more than twenty-four hours. I can't say the same thing about you."

Horror struck her face again and tears were building in her eyes. I shook my head. "I'm sorry," I said. "That wasn't fair of me to say. Lily isn't your daughter and I know you have your own life, with Andre."

She looked up into my eyes. She opened her mouth to say something, but stopped herself. Finally, she looked away as she asked, "May I spend some time with Lily later? After...after..."

"After Cassidy leaves?"

She nodded.

I placed my hands on her shoulders and turned her body to face mine. "I'm glad you're back. Will you be home for a while?"

Her beautiful green eyes were filled with sadness. Something was missing in them. They weren't only sad—they were empty.

"I hope so. I'd like to bond with Lily again, if you don't mind. I mean, I'm not asking to move back in or anything. But..."

Andre walked up to Maddie. "Maddison? Maybe we should head back to your place, you must be tired. Cassidy just put Lily down, so you can't really spend time with her right now."

I saw the same look of shock move across her face—the same as when Cassidy had called her "Aunt Maddie." I could clear up the confusion. I could easily tell Maddie that Cassidy was married and only here because of work. Her husband had left not fifteen minutes before Maddie showed up.

But I didn't. And my heart ached knowing that I was purposely hurting her. Then again, when she walked around me, straight into Andre's arms I was just as hurt.

I walked them to the door to see them out. Glancing into the living room, I saw Cassidy looking over the project we were working on. I opened the door and gave Andre a polite smile. He didn't return it. He looked at me like he wanted to take me out. I was clearly a threat to his ass.

But my heart leapt at the way Maddie looked at me. I smiled gently at her.

"I'll call you about Lily?" Maddie asked with a weak grin.

"You never have to call, Maddie. You're always welcome here...always."

Her eyes lit up and I saw something there. A spark. A spark of life that she was so desperately triying to hide. She stood on her toes and kissed me on the cheek. I closed my eyes briefly. Her lips on my face had my heart soaring.

Why can't she see how much I love her? How much Lily and I need her.

The door shut and I headed back into the living room. Cassidy stood and tilted her head at me. "Why are you allowing this to go on?"

I jerked my head back and gave her a look. "What are you talking about?"

She put her hands on her hips and shook her head. "You'd have to be a damn fool not to see that the two of you are head over heels in love. That asshole boyfriend of hers actually *flirted* with me while Maddie was upset in the bathroom. He doesn't love her, Cale. He has control over her. Why do you allow it? Why aren't you fighting for her?"

I sat down and downed my glass of wine. "You don't under-stand, Cassidy. There's a long history between Maddie and me."

She grabbed her purse and gave me that all-knowing look that most women have. "Well, if I were you, I'd sure as hell be figuring out how to fix this." She pointed at the door. "Because that girl, whether she wants to believe it or not, is madly in love with you and Lily. It's only once in a lifetime, Cale, that someone looks at you like that."

I ran my hand through my hair. "I don't know what to do, Cas-sidy."

She smiled and gave me a pat on the arm. "Love is a journey, Cale. Sometimes we get lost along the way, but love always brings us home."

I nodded and smiled.

"I can show myself out," Cassidy said. "We'll work on this on Monday. It's been a long week—I'm going home to a hot bath and an even hotter husband."

I laughed as Cassidy made her way to the front door.

"Ciao!" She called over her shoulder.

I laughed and shook my head. I sat back down and worked for a little bit more before heading upstairs to Lily's room. In the nursery, I looked down at my daughter. After all the hell Zoey put me through, she'd left me with the most precious gift of all.

I gazed down at Lily, watching her little stomach rise and fall with each breath. Her light brown hair curled up in the back just a bit. She was still so tiny, but strong and healthy. She was stubborn like her old man, but I could feel sensitivity in her, too. I wished I could look into her beautiful, blue eyes. She deserved everything I could give her. Every ounce of happiness. Every opportunity to ex-cel. She deserved love. Not only my love, or my parents' love, but a woman's love. Someone who would teach her the things I couldn't.

She needed a mother. She needed Maddie. I needed Maddie.

I placed my hand on Lily. No one had ever made my heart swell with such love as she did. She'd forever changed me. My love. My life. My daughter.

24

Maddie

I WALKED INTO my house and sighed. I was home and *so* relieved. I was tired of traveling. Tired of being away from Cale and Lily. But I had to stop thinking that way.

I tossed my purse onto the sofa and walked into the kitchen, where Monica had set up a small bar. I grabbed a bottle of scotch. I didn't even drink scotch—Jack did. But I poured a glass and downed it.

Yuck. There's a reason I don't drink scotch.

Andre called out to me over his shoulder. "Bella, I'm taking a shower. Would you like to join me?"

My stomach turned. For the first time since meeting Andre, I didn't want to be near him. I didn't want him to even touch me.

"I have to take care of a few things," I said. "I'll meet you in the bedroom in a few minutes."

He mumbled something and took off toward the master bedroom. I sat down at my computer and found an email from my boss. Silently, I prayed that she wasn't sending me out of town again.

The subject line was, "Call me. ASAP."

Dear Maddison,

I need to speak with you. It's urgent.

Carol.

I stared at the short email. "She's sending me out to town again. Fuck."

I stood and spun around to see Andre standing there. He smiled, shaking his head. "You love him don't you?"

Swallowing hard I asked, "I beg your pardon?"

He laughed as he shook his head. "I see the way you look at him, Bella. I long for you to look at me that way. Your eyes light up in his presence. They dance with a desire I've never been blessed to see."

I sat down as he walked into my office and sat on the sofa. "I've tried everything I could think of to push him from your heart, Bella. *Everything.* I even bribed your boss to send you to Seattle and Milan."

I gasped and covered my mouth with my hand. "What?" I whispered.

He looked away. "You were pushing me away after little Lily was born. I wasn't going to be bested. I thought once we were back in Italy, I would be able to show you everything you need. It appears I underestimated your love for Cale. I saw it this evening. I saw what my interfering did to you."

Everything hit me at once. What I wanted in this life was the one thing I'd been trying to ignore. I took in a deep breath and stood up. "I'm glad you told me this. It makes my decision to leave my job all that much easier."

Now he was stunned. "You're leaving your job? Maddison, you love your job."

I shook my head. "No. I love something far more important than my job."

His body jerked back as if he'd been struck. He nodded and picked up his cell phone and wallet. "This is what is in your heart, Maddison?" he asked.

I nodded. "He's been in my heart since the moment I met him."

Andre placed his hands on my shoulders. He leaned down and

gently kissed me on my right cheek and then my left. When he went to kiss my lips I turned slightly away and whispered, "I can't."

"I hope you find your happiness, Bella. You deserve it."

With that, he walked out my front door, gently closing it behind him. I let out the breath I'd been holding and walked into my bedroom. I stripped out of my clothes and stepped into a hot shower.

After getting dressed in Victoria's Secret sweat pants, a University of Arkansas T-shirt, and a pair of flip-flops I looked at myself in the mirror. I smiled.

This is me. This is the girl who has been missing for the last three years.

I TOOK A deep breath and knocked on his door. I prayed that Cassidy was not there still. If they were dating, I was about to make a fool out of myself. The door opened and I moaned ever so slightly.

He looked like a god. A Greek god. No, better.

My eyes fell first on his bare chest. Then I nearly swooned at the sight of his perfect abs and that damn V that dipped into the linen pants that hung just barely on his hips.

I told myself not to look down. But I couldn't help myself. His bare feet were so damn sexy. Finally, I looked him in the eye. "Um, are you alone?" I asked.

His eyes pierced mine as I held my breath and waited for his answer.

"No."

I closed my eyes. My heart broke all over again as I nodded. I was the only one to blame for this. I was the one who'd pushed him away. "I see. I'll just talk to you tomorrow, then."

"Maddie, wait. I'm not alone because *Lily* is here."

That bastard. I wanted to turn around and start screaming at him. He did that on purpose. Stupid jerk. I knew I deserved it, showing up here earlier with Andre. I counted to ten, spun around and pushed past him. I looked around. The house was a bit of a mess. Not dirty, just messy. Cale was terrible about putting things away. I'd learned so much about him when I'd lived with him for two weeks.

"I have a proposition for you," I said as I sat down on the sofa. I peeked up at him and watched as he sauntered across the room, looking all hot. I could hardly stand it.

He leaned against the entrance to the hallway. "Sounds interesting."

I raised an eyebrow at him. "It isn't anything sexual, so stop looking at me like that."

He smiled that damn crooked smile of his. The same smile that I'd seen across the room three years ago. The one that's haunted my dreams ever since.

"I'm listening."

I sucked in a breath, sat up taller, and blurted out, "I need a job."

His smile vanished. "Wait. What?"

Damn it. I didn't want to sound like I was begging. "I quit my job just now. I need a new one."

He pushed off the wall and looked at me, his mouth hanging open in that oh-so-sexy way. How I wanted his lips on my body. I could almost feel the heat as I imagined him kissing my inner thigh and...

I shook my head. "Ugh. Will you please put a shirt on?"

He looked down and then looked back at me with a smirk. "Why?"

I glared at him. "It's distracting."

He smiled bigger. Oh he was enjoying this. "Why is it distracting, Maddie?"

I slapped my hands down on my legs and jumped up. "Fine.

Have it your way. Stand there in nothing but a pair of pants, you won't distract me."

He raised his eyebrows. Then he stared back at me. I watched as his stomach muscles flexed with each little movement he made. I wanted to run my tongue along his abs. I wanted to remember what being wrapped in his arms again felt like. I wanted...to stop acting like a silly teenager.

"If you're not distracted, why are you not talking?"

I gave him a dirty look. "I love Lily, and when I saw Cassidy with her today, something happened. I'm not really sure what it was, but it made my heart hurt like never before. I'm tired of being gone. So, I'd like to take over as Lily's nanny. No one knows her like I do. Well, I mean besides you. I was a huge part of her life and I hate that I missed the last month. I don't want to miss anything. I can...um...I can move in and...um...well...take care of her while you work. I'll take care of the meals, your laundry, grocery shopping, and any other things you might need or that the nanny would do." I paused. "So, do you accept my proposition?"

I stood firmly in my spot as I tried to calm my pounding heart and keep my hands from shaking. Cale was trying to not be affected by the fact that I'd basically just told him I wanted to help raise his daughter...and move in with him.

He let out a breath and looked around as if he was trying to think. "Let me see if I have your *proposition* right. You no longer have a job."

I nodded my head. "Correct. I'm...jobless."

"Uh huh. You want to move in here. And be Lily's nanny."

I began to chew on my lip. "I don't want to be her Aunt Maddie, Cale. I want to be more."

"More?"

Tears burned my eyes and I blinked to hold them back. "Yes," I said, my voice cracking.

Cale opened his mouth, but nothing came out. He cleared his throat. "Like, a mother figure?"

I felt a tear slip down my cheek. I whispered, "Yes."

He took a step toward me. "If you move in, what happens when you want to have your boyfriend over? Or I want to bring a date home?"

A small sob escaped my mouth, but it had nothing to do with Lily. It had more to do with the idea of Cale talking about dating. Him moving on.

I swallowed and wiped my tears away. "I don't have a boy-friend. We broke up."

Cale's eyes lit up as he attempted to hide a smile. "Why did you break up?"

I began wringing my hands. *Don't push your feelings away, Maddie. Let go of the control.* Monica's words popped into my head.

"Sometimes, I think, we have to learn to let go of the control we think we need in order to find what fate has in store for us."

I sucked in a shaky breath. "We didn't want the same things."

Cale took a step closer to me. "Is that right? What did he want?"

I looked Cale in the eyes. "He wanted me to look at him…like I look at you."

Cale's green eyes widened as he stopped in front of me. He placed his finger on my chin and lifted my face to his. He leaned down and got closer to my lips. "Why do you look at me differently, Maddie?"

I moaned a little, knowing his lips were mere inches from mine. I'd never, in all my life, wanted to be kissed as much as I wanted to be kissed in this moment, by this man I loved with all my heart.

"I look at you differently because…" My eyes searched his face like I was trying to memorize it. I stared at his mouth and I ran my tongue across my bottom lip. Finally, I looked into his eyes and smiled. "Because I love you."

Cale closed his eyes and whispered, "Finally." When he opened them, he pulled me closer and was about to kiss me when Lily began crying.

I let out a giggle, "So it begins."

"Shit. Let me go check on her, Don't move."

I smiled softly. "I promise, I'm not going anywhere."

As he walked backward, Cale had a huge smile on his face. I wanted to tell him to watch out, but it was too late. He fell over the ottoman and did a pretty impressive roll. I slammed my hands to my mouth to cover my laugh.

"Are you okay?" I asked

He jumped up. "Yes! I'm more than okay. Just hold on. Don't move." He turned and began running up stairs, but he tripped and fell. "Shit! I'll be right back!" He yelled as he continued running to the nursery.

I dropped my head back and hugged myself, reminding myself that I needed to take this slow. I knew I shouldn't jump into bed with him, no matter what I felt.

"Oh, God!" Cale shouted. "Oh my God. What the hell?" he continued as he walked down the stairs, his arms outstretched, holding Lily.

"What's wrong?" I asked as I started to walk toward them. Then I smelled it. I placed my hand over my nose. "Oh my God! What's that smell?"

"Bath! Maddie get the bath out!"

That's when I saw it. Lily had shit all the way up her back. I ran over to the cabinet and grabbed the bath before racing into the kitchen. I began frantically taking dirty dishes out of the sink.

"Jesus, Cale. When did you last do dishes?" I asked as I tossed them all on the counter.

"I'm gonna throw up. Oh God!" Cale cried out as he began to gag.

I turned on the water and looked around for the damn rubber duck thermometer Monica had insisted we buy, to make sure we got the water temperature just right. "Where's the rubber duck? Shit! Where's the rubber duck?"

Cale was gagging as he tried to take off Lily's clothes. "Right. There. Oh God, I'm gonna throw up...it's in her hair! How the hell did she get shit in her hair?"

I found the rubber ducky and pushed it under the running water. "Cale! We can't swear in front of her."

Perfect water temperature. I went back to the cabinet and grabbed a washcloth and baby soap, then ran back into the kitchen where I slipped on something and went down. Hard.

I jumped back up and yelled, "I'm okay! I just slipped on…" I looked down to see Lily's shitty clothes on the floor.

Cale pushed Lily toward me. "Take her! Oh, God, take her, I'm gonna throw up."

I took her and felt my hands touch something warm. *No. Nope. I didn't just touch shit. Nope. I didn't.* Then I looked.

"Oh God oh God oh God! Eww! Oh my God, it's all over her." Cale grabbed the sprayer and began spraying Lily.

"Stop! It's spraying in my mouth! Cale, stop!"

I turned and placed Lily in the tub. When I looked at her she had the biggest smile I'd ever seen on her face. My heart soared as I noticed how big my baby girl had gotten in just a month. I smiled back at her and grabbed the washcloth and poured soap on it.

"We can't let her sit in this water," I said. "Grab the back-up tub!"

Cale was still gagging as he jumped over the mess on the floor and ran upstairs to Lily's room.

"You little stinker. What did you do?" I asked as I attempted to clean her off. Cale came running back into the kitchen and put three towels down. I handed Lily to him as I said, "Here, take her for right now. I think I got most of it off. Let me dump this and fill the other tub up with clean water."

Cale wrapped her up in a towel. "Baby girl, what are you trying to do?" he asked. "Daddy can deal with a little bit of poo…but not that much."

I giggled as I filled up the new tub. I turned and held my hands out for Lily. Cale gave her to me and I slipped her down into the clean water to give her a proper bath.

"I'll take all this into the laundry room," Cale said as he started picking up the clothes on the floor.

I watched him walk out of the kitchen attempting to hold his nose as he brought the dirty clothes and tub to the laundry room. I glanced back at Lily and shook my head to get the naughty thoughts out.

"Your daddy is the hottest man ever," I said, fanning myself. She smiled. "Yeah, you know he is, don't you? Only he could make gagging look sexy as hell."

Once I had her all cleaned up and wrapped in a towel, I stood and held her. I took in a deep breath and sighed. "I missed you so much."

"Um…Maddie. You might want to give me Lily now."

I glared at Cale. "No! I haven't seen her in a month and she's all clean-smelling. She's mine."

He walked up to me and smiled as he ran his finger along Lily's face. His love for his daughter had my stomach clenching with desire. He looked up and placed his hand on the side of my face. "Maddie, you have shit all over your pants from where you fell on her pajamas."

I grimaced. "Oh, gross."

"Here, give her to me and I'll give her a bottle and get her back to sleep. Go take a shower."

"What should I do with my clothes?" I asked.

He gave me a look that made me take a sharp breath. "Put them in the laundry room with Lily's. You can put on one of my T-shirts if you want."

I bit down on my lip and slipped off my favorite pair of comfy pants. I watched Cale as his mouth opened slightly and his eyes traveled to my lacey, white thong. I pulled my shirt up and over my head, silently thanking God that I'd decided to wear the matching push-up bra. I winked at Cale as I walked out of the kitchen and into the laundry room. I grabbed Lily's clothes and threw hers and mine into the washer and put it on hot. In the living room I glanced over my shoulder to find Cale staring at me.

"Do you mind if I use your shower?" I asked in my sexiest voice.

"Um…uh…"

I turned away from him and kept walking, making sure to swing my hips just a little bit more than necessary. "I'll take that as a no."

The hot water felt amazing. I must have stood under it for at least ten minutes. I grabbed the shampoo and was about to put some in my hand when I felt his touch on my shoulder. The feeling that zipped through my body was unbelievable. I spun around to find him standing in the shower with me. Naked.

I gazed down his body and then met his eyes. They were filled with desire.

"Maddie, I'm going to make love to you now."

I smiled as I dropped the shampoo bottle and wrapped my arms around his neck.

"Screw taking it slow," I whispered. He grinned back and pulled my lips to his.

Finally.

25

Cale

I'D STOOD OUTSIDE the bathroom door for a couple of minutes and debated my reasons for not going in. Finally, I thought, *fuck it*. I stripped out of my pants and headed into the bathroom and saw her standing in my shower. I threw out the idea of taking things slow. I wanted her. I needed her.

When our lips finally connected, she pushed her hands into my hair and moaned. I pushed her back against the shower wall and kissed her like I was never going to kiss her again.

"Cale," she whispered. "Oh, God. I've missed you."

My heart slammed in my chest. I moved my lips down her neck as I lifted her leg and she hooked it around me. My hand moved down and cupped her perfect breast. I leaned down and sucked on her nipple.

She moaned and said, "Feels. So. Good."

I moved my lips to her other breasts as she reached down and began to stroke my dick. "Maddie, I won't last if you keep touching me."

She pulled her hand away and placed both hands on my shoulders. "More. Cale. Please. I've waited so long."

I lightly traced my fingers down the side of her body as I moved my lips back up to her neck, along her jaw and to her ear lobe, which I began to kiss and nibble.

She sucked in a breath as my fingers made their way between her legs. She pushed into my hand and I couldn't help but smile.

"Do you need to come, baby?" I whispered in her ear.

She thrashed her head back and forth. "I need you, Cale. I only need you."

I pushed my fingers into her and moaned when I felt her clamp down. I closed my eyes and moaned against her sensitive neck. I began to massage her insides, slow at first and then faster. Her hips began a rhythm as I pulled back to see her face. Her head was leaned back against the wall and she was biting on her lower lip.

Fuck. I could come right now, watching her fall apart because of my fingers.

"Yes," she said. "I'm so close."

I knew one touch of my thumb to her clit would send her over the edge. I pulled my lips from hers and pushed my thumb against her clit, moving it in a circle. Her eyes snapped open and her head jerked forward as her eyes captured mine.

"I'm going to come, Cale. I'm going to come." I slammed my lips back against hers and swallowed her screams of pleasure. I kept on massaging out her orgasm until she went limp in my arms.

I held her in my arms as her breathing slowly returned to normal. She had wrapped her arms around my neck and buried her face as she rode out the last waves of her orgasm. When she pulled back, she was crying. My entire world stopped.

I placed my hands on the side of her face. "Baby, what's wrong?"

She sucked on her lower lip as she shook her head. "Please tell me I'm not dreaming. Please, Cale. Tell me this is real."

In that moment I knew nothing would ever be the same. I reached over and turned off the water, then grabbed a towel and began drying her off. Once she was completely dry, I wrapped the towel around her. Grabbing another towel, I quickly dried off. I stepped out of the shower and threw my towel to the floor. I reached down and picked her up and carried her to the bedroom. Gently, I put her down and pulled the towel off of her body. She acted as if she wanted to cover up.

"You're so damn beautiful. The most beautiful and perfect woman I've ever seen."

She blushed and looked away for a second before she said, "You take my breath away, Cale."

I picked her up again and laid her on the bed. I climbed onto the bed and over her. "How far do you want to take this, Maddie? I'll do whatever you want, baby."

She smiled that sweet smile of hers. She placed her hand on the side of my face. "I want to know I'm not dreaming. I want to wake up in the morning wrapped in your arms. I want you to make love to me."

I smiled as I leaned down and kissed her gently. "I want that, too." I reached over and pulled out the side drawer. She grabbed my arm.

"Have you been tested recently? I mean since…Zoey."

I swallowed hard. "Before I married Zoey, the first thing I did was get tested. Then again after she…after she died I was re-tested. Jack suggested it."

Maddie gave me a weak smile. "I've been tested, too. I don't want there to be anything between us, Cale. I'm on the pill."

I pulled back and looked at her. "Maddie, are you sure?"

A look of horror crossed her face. "I mean…if you'd rather not. I didn't mean…"

I quickly moved and placed my hands on her cheeks and kissed her. I spread her legs open wider and teased her entrance with my tip, pushing in a little bit further each time.

"Please don't make me beg, Cale," she said. "Please just take me as yours."

Jesus.

I closed my eyes and moaned as I pushed myself into her. She whimpered and I stopped. "Did I hurt you?" I asked.

She smiled and wrapped her legs around me. "No. Everything feels amazing."

I moved in and out of her. The way we kissed each other was like nothing I'd never experienced. Something was happening between us, and we both felt it. Her fingers traced up and down my back as I pushed deeper into her. I couldn't get deep enough.

"I want to crawl inside your body," I said, "and stay there forever."

I took her hand and intertwined our fingers. I pushed our hands above her head as I pushed deeper into her with each thrust.

She moaned as she arched her back. "Cale, don't stop. I'm going to come."

I placed my lips to her ear as I pushed in as deep as I could and she began to whisper my name. As I felt my own release build, I spoke into her ear, "Maddie, I love you. I love you so much."

"I love you, Cale," she said as she wrapped her legs around me tighter, holding onto me as I poured into her. As I came, I moved my lips to hers and kissed her as we whispered each other's names in this unbelievable moment of passion.

I didn't want to pull out of her. I held her and she held me and we stayed as one.

I moved so that I could look into her eyes. "I love you, Maddie."

A tear rolled down her face and I kissed it away as she blinked slowly. "I love you, too, Cale. I finally feel like I'm home."

My heart dropped and I stared into her eyes. I slowly smiled before kissing her again. "We're both home. Forever."

26

Maddie

I WOKE UP to the sun shining through the bedroom window. I didn't even have to move to know that Cale and I were wrapped in a tangled mess of hotness. He had his arms around me and his legs were over mine. It was as if he was afraid I would sneak away while he was sleeping.

I closed my eyes, remembering our night together. My body was going to feel it today. After making love, Cale and I had fallen asleep. But then Lily woke up. I threw on a T-shirt, and fed her while Cale slept. When I crawled back into bed, he climbed onto me and made love to me again. Of course, not before first giving me the most amazing orgasm with his lips.

I opened my eyes as I touched my swollen lips. Closing them again I was taken back to just two hours ago when I'd woken up to hear him breathing. Turning over to watch him sleep, I couldn't take it another second. I'd crawled on top of him and taken my turn at making love to him.

The night was amazing. Magical. Incredibly romantic. I'd never experienced anything like it before.

Cale moaned as he rolled over. I missed his warmth as soon as he let me go. Rolling over, I rested my head on my hand and watched him sleep. Everything about him was perfect. I reached down, pinched my arm, and smiled. *Nope. Not a dream.*

Lily was making little sounds through the baby monitor, so I crawled out of bed and reached for the T-shirt I'd left on the floor. I slipped it on and made my way upstairs to the nursery. When I walked in and looked down at Lily in her crib, she smiled the biggest smile I'd ever seen.

"Good morning, baby girl. How did you sleep last night? You were such a good girl and only woke up once."

I scooped her up and brought her over to the changing table. After a quick diaper change and dressing her in a pretty little new outfit, I picked Lily back up and headed downstairs to heat up a bottle. I stopped dead in my tracks when I saw a woman standing in the kitchen.

"Um…you startled me," I said as I gave her a polite smile.

She gave Lily and me a once-over before saying, "I could say the same, señorita."

This must be the nanny, I thought. *Maria. Shit.*

I started to flush, realizing I was wearing only Cale's shirt—with no panties.

She tilted her head and stared. "You um…what do you say…spent the night?"

I felt the heat move through my cheeks. "Ah. Yes I did."

"You sleep in guest room? You're a friend, *si*?"

The way she was looking at me like she was ready to stomp on me told me Maria had feelings for Cale.

"No, Maria. She's more than a friend. Did you forget that I told you I didn't need you on Saturdays anymore?"

When Maria saw Cale, her eyes lit up. "You need me, Mr. Blackwood, you just don't know it."

I attempted to hide my smile as I glanced over to Cale. He looked shocked.

"Um," he said, "can I speak with you in my office please?"

"After I feed the baby," Maria said as she held out her arms for me to give Lily to her. I held on tighter.

"Maddie will feed her. I'd like to talk to you now, please," Cale said as he turned and walked to his office.

Poor Maria's face dropped as she followed him. I peeked over my shoulder and watched them both walk away.

To Lily, I whispered, "I think Maria is about to have a bad day little one."

Lily smiled and I couldn't help but giggle as I put her in her swing. I took a bottle out of the refrigerator and heated it up. "Shall we have breakfast on the deck, sweet girl?" I headed into the laundry and quickly pulled my pants from the dryer and slipped them on before getting Lily and heading out the deck.

I stared out over the lake as Lily drank her bottle. Every now and then I looked down at her and grinned. My heart filled with so much love for this little girl. I'd never in my life felt so content.

"I love you and your daddy, Lily," I said. "I love you both so much and I've been so stubborn and silly. Not anymore, though! I'm going to shower you both with lots of kisses and hugs. Oh, and long walks. I love long walks. Especially in the fall. Something about fall and the leaves when they change colors—I just love it. When you get older, we'll make those silly little leaf collection things."

She cooed as she grabbed onto my finger. I gently traced a pattern on her cheek as she drank her bottle.

"Oh, God. Please don't let me wake up to find this is all just a dream. I want nothing more than to be here. Right here where I am." Gazing back at Lily, I continued, "Your daddy is an amazing man. I knew from the first moment I spoke to him. He charmed me and, before I knew it, I was in love. But I was so scared. I'd never experienced those feelings before, and the way I felt with him..." I chuckled. "I just didn't know what to do with those feelings. I was starting a new job that was going to have me gone for six months. After meeting your dad, I didn't want to leave. I wanted to stay with him forever and, let me tell you, that scared me. So I did what I did best when faced with something I didn't want to deal with. I ignored it. It was the hardest thing I'd ever done, the moment I told your daddy I wasn't interested in a relationship." Lily stopped drinking, as if she was trying to focus on the story. I laughed and set the bottle down, before burping her.

"None of that matters now. It was a very long journey for me and your daddy. But we got you out of the deal, so that's a big positive."

Lily let out a burp that would put any man to shame.

"Good one."

My skin felt like it was on fire. I must have had at least a dozen butterflies dancing in my stomach when Cale touched me on the arm.

I smiled at him. "Just spending some girl time together."

He laughed and sat down across from me. "What a beautiful morning," he said. "Want to take Lily on a walk before it gets too warm?"

I nearly jumped up as I said, "Yes!"

Cale must have known how much I'd missed Lily—he was totally letting me hog his daughter.

"May I give her a good morning kiss?" he asked as he pouted.

I giggled and handed Lily to him as I said, "If you must take her from me."

Cale scooped Lily up into his arms and began walking across the deck. I pulled my legs up and tucked my knees under my chin as I watched the two of them together. I'd never seen a man so in love before. The way he looked at Lily made my heart soar. My eyes burned with tears. I wanted to share that with him—that bond. I looked away when I realized that I couldn't. Lily wasn't mine. As much as I wanted her to be mine, she was *Zoey's* daughter. Zoey and Cale's. *What would I be to her? Would I ever be given the chance to give Cale a child of our own?*

I quickly wiped a tear away as I looked out over the water. When I realized that Cale was standing in front of me, I tried to pull myself together. I didn't want him to know I was upset so I jumped up and began to walk back into the house.

"I'll go get her a jacket."

Cale gently took hold of my arm and stopped me. "Maddie, look at me."

I closed my eyes and fought like hell to stop my silly crying. "I…I can't."

Cale turned me around and I stared at my feet.

"Maddie, please look at me," he begged. "Please don't push me away. Tell me what you're thinking. What you're feeling."

I looked into his eyes. "I wish it had been me."

He tilted his head, confused. "What had been you?"

I glanced down at Lily, who was now sleeping peacefully in her father's arms.

"I wish I had been the one to give you…to…" A sob escaped me as I tried to control my emotions.

Cale placed his hand on my cheek. "Tell me. Please."

"I wish Lily was mine. I wish I'd been the one to give you your first child. I want so much to be…to be…" I finally just let it go and started crying. "I'm so sorry I pushed you away. I wanted it to be me. Oh, God, how I wanted it to be me."

Cale gently pulled me into his arms and kissed the top of my head. "Baby, please don't cry. It tears my heart out to see you cry. You and Lily are my whole life now. It's just the three of us."

I pulled back and met his eyes. "How can you forgive me? How can you just let me walk back into your life?"

He smiled. "Because I love you. And Lily loves you. Because I need you and she…" he looked down at Lily and smiled bigger. "She needs you, Maddie. When I think of my future, I can only imagine it with you. Don't you know by now? You're my everything."

I sucked in a breath. "I think I'd better go home and pack a suitcase."

Cale laughed. "I think you'd better pack more than a suitcase. I just got you back—I have no intentions of letting you go.

27

Cale

THE MINUTE I opened the door and walked into the house, I smiled. Maddie was in the kitchen singing to Lily. I'd been coming home from the office to this same scene for the last month.

I set down my briefcase and inhaled what smelled like lasagna...and cake. "Maddie? I'm home, baby."

Maddie peeked around the corner and smiled. "Welcome home, Daddy. We have big plans for Miss Lily's three-month birthday party this evening."

I laughed, shaking my head. "Oh yeah?"

When she stepped around the corner I about dropped to my knees. "Oh, yeah. Daddy gets his gift first though."

My eyes took in every inch of her body. She was dressed in a red corset, thigh-high stockings, and white heels. I moved my eyes back up to her beautiful face. Her hair was piled on top of her head in a messy bun.

"Um...I wasn't aware that it was my birthday today, too," I said as I discarded my jacket and began loosening my tie.

Maddie bit her lip and shook her head. "It isn't."

"Why the gift then?" I stood in front of her, immediately drawn to her emerald eyes.

"Because both our parents are coming over this evening for the party, and with your parents staying the night, I thought we might…play before everyone gets here."

I closed my eyes and moaned before opening them again. "Have I told you today how much I love you?"

The smile that played across her face had my dick rock hard. She put a chocolate-covered spatula in her mouth and moaned before pulling it out and pouting. "Not in at least six hours, but you should probably give Lily some loving before I ask you to make love to me in the kitchen."

I swallowed hard and looked over to Lily sitting in her swing with a huge smile on her face. My mother said Lily could sense the love between Maddie and me. I was starting to think my mother was right.

I cupped Maddie's face in my hands as I leaned down to kiss her. "I love you," I whispered against her lips.

I winked at her and made my way over to my princess. Lily was kicking as fast as she could. "Hello there, princess. Daddy missed you so much today."

I unbuckled her and scooped her up into my arms. She laughed when I kissed her on the cheek. "I love that she is laughing now," I said.

"Oh my gosh," Maddie said. "You have to see what she does when you put the plastic mirror in her crib. I swear she was talking to herself. Oh! Then, I swear, she tried to pull herself up. I mean, wait until you see how strong she is, Cale."

I turned to Maddie. My heart soared and I couldn't believe how incredibly lucky I was to have her.

She crinkled up her nose in that cute way she does and asked, "Why are you staring at me like that?"

I let out a soft laugh. "Because you're standing there, looking sexy as hell, with a spatula in one hand, and you're talking about our daughter. It's a dream come true."

Her eyes filled with tears and I knew it was because I'd said *our daughter.* "Cale," she whispered.

I gave Lily another kiss. "Princess, your mommy has me all kinds of crazy right now. Daddy-daughter time will be in a few minutes." I placed her back into the swing and buckled her in. When I stood up, Maddie had tears running down her face. I'd never unbuttoned my shirt so fast in my life. I threw it to the floor and unbuckled my belt as Maddie stared.

She dropped the spatula when I pulled her close. I ran my hand up her backside to her neck and grabbed a handful of hair as I pressed my lips against hers.

"I'm going to need that gift now, Maddie."

I kissed her as she ran her hands through my hair.

"The baby..." she whispered.

I turned and saw Lily staring at us. I jogged over to the swing and turned it just a little, then wound up the mobile. Lily's eyes were fixed on the pink horses.

"She won't ever remember even if she does see," I said as I grabbed Maddie and picked her up, pulling her corset down—it pushed her breasts up beautifully.

I began sucking on her nipple as she moaned. "But..."

I pulled my lips from her nipple but not before gently biting down, making her hiss. "Maddie," I said, "let me make love to you."

She looked into my eyes. "Okay," she whispered, slamming her lips to mine.

I pulled away from her lips slightly. "Do you like these panties?" I asked as I moved my hands down to the lacey fabric.

"Kind of...I just bought them."

I set her back down and dropped to my knees. I caressed her legs, slowly moving my hands up. "I'm going to leave the stockings on, along with your beautiful shoes." I said, smiling at her as she bit down on her finger. "But these panties have to go."

I pulled them once and watched them fall apart in my hand.

"Oh God," Maddie said as she grabbed the counter.

I stood back up and smiled. "I'm going to pick you up and I

want you to put your legs over my shoulders, baby."

Her eyes widened. "Um…okay," she said, licking her lips. When I lifted her and got her where I wanted her I told her to lean against the wall.

"Oh God, Cale…I'm…it's not going to…"

I licked across her clit and she yelled out my name. I loved having her so exposed to me like this. She ran her hands through my hair and pulled my face closer to her.

"More…"

I pushed my face into her and began sucking and licking her. It didn't take long for her to say my name over and over as she rocked her hips into me.

"Oh God…I can't take anymore…Cale!" she panted as I continued my assault on her clit.

I pulled my face away and grabbed her and lifted her off of me. I slowly slid her back down my body as she smiled. "Jesus, Cale. That was the hottest damn thing ever."

"I'm not done yet."

Maddie smiled as I picked her up and she wrapped her legs around me. I set Maddie down on the island.

"Lay down, Maddie."

I pushed my pants and boxer briefs down and kicked them to the side. I jumped onto the island and positioned myself over her. "I love you, Maddie. I love you so much."

I pushed my dick slowly into her as she arched her back and grabbed my shoulders.

"Cale…I love you. I love you," she breathed.

I kissed her neck as she wrapped her arms around me. Moving to her ear, I whispered, "I'll love you forever and always, Maddison. I swear to God, I'll love you forever."

When she wrapped her legs around me and started calling out my name, I pushed in harder and released everything into her. I could feel myself pouring into her body. I loved making love to Maddie, and being together as one. We would always end our lovemaking by kissing each other as my dick twitched back to life inside her. It was as if neither one of us wanted to be apart from the other.

I rested my elbows on either side of her face and used my thumbs to wipe away her tears. "Please tell me those are happy tears, baby."

She closed her eyes and nodded before opening her eyes again. "I love being with you. I love seeing you with Lily and I love—" her voice cracked and a small sob escaped her.

"Tell me Maddie," I whispered as I gently kissed her tears away.

"I love you calling me mommy. And I really love you calling Lily *our* daughter."

Maddie cried harder as I quickly moved off of her and jumped down. I put my boxers back, then picked her up and held her in my arms as I placed her back down.

"You are her mother, Maddie. Please don't ever doubt that. And some day, we'll give Lily a brother or sister."

Maddie buried her face in my neck and cried. "I don't deserve your love, Cale."

I pulled her closer. "Tell me you love me."

She pulled back and looked into my eyes. "I've never loved anyone like I love you, Cale Blackwood. I love you more than I love the air I breathe."

Lily made a few loud noises, as if she was letting us know she was still there.

"I better go shower and change before our parents get here." Maddie said as she kissed me. She sucked in my lower lip and nibbled it.

"Jesus, Maddie. Do you know how you drive me crazy?"

She stood up and winked before she walked over to Lily and kissed her. "Enjoy your time with Daddy, baby girl."

I got up and reached back down for my pants. I watched Maddie walk through the living room, toward the hallway that led to our bedroom.

I washed my hands and face before I turned and looked at my

little princess. "You, my dear, are one good little girl. To let mommy and daddy have time together like that." I shook my head and unbuckled her. "Let's go have a dance outside shall we?"

I walked outside and took in a deep breath of the cool, fall air. Lily loved being outside. Anytime she was fussy, all we had to do was walk out to the deck—she was instantly calmed.

I didn't want to stay outside too long, since it was chilly out. I held Lily close to my chest and sang to her as we danced. I had been doing the same routine since starting work. Every night when I was done working I brought Lily out onto the deck and danced with her.

"You know, she's going to have you wrapped around her little finger," Maddie said with a giggle.

I smiled and turned to her. I stopped moving as I saw the breathtaking woman before me. She had changed into a tan dress that fell just above her knees. It flared out at the bottom, but fit her curves in the most amazing way. She had on light tan heels and she'd put her hair up, but with a few curls framing her delicate face.

"Maddie, you look…you're stunning."

She blushed and looked away briefly before turning back to me. "Thank you. Your mom and dad will be here in a few minutes. I'll go change the birthday girl and put her in a new outfit I bought today."

I walked over and handed Lily to her. I rolled my eyes as I watched her head upstairs with our daughter. "I think that child has an outfit for every day of the year."

"Not yet, but we're getting close," Maddie called back. I laughed as I made my way to our bedroom.

I'd never felt so happy in my entire life.

28

Maddie

"**O**H MADDIE! IT'S beautiful," Mary said as she admired the three-tiered cake on the kitchen island. It was covered in adorable, pink teddy bears. I'd almost forgotten to clean and sanitize the kitchen before everyone arrived for the party. I felt my face blush at the memory of Cale and I making love on the island.

I smiled and said, "I guess it's a little overboard for just three months, but I was so excited."

Mary waved her hand. "Nonsense. Nothing is too much for Lily."

Monica laughed and shook her head. "Cale's mom is just being polite, aren't you, Mary?" Monica winked at Mary as they both laughed quietly. "I can't wait to see what you do for her one year birthday," Monica said. "Will there be a circus there?"

I glared at her. "Ha-ha."

My mother came into the kitchen holding Lily. I smiled at her, but didn't receive a smile in return. Our relationship was still sour, even with Cale working for my father.

"I remember when you were this age, Maddie. I wonder what Lily's mom looked like at this age." My smile faded and my heart instantly hurt. My mother had to rub in the fact that Lily was not my biological daughter.

I felt a hand on my arm. I turned to see Mary. She seemed understanding of my struggle, unlike my own mother.

"Nancy," she said. "I'd love to get coffee together sometime."

My mother's eyes lit up. "I'd love that, Mary. Maybe we can invite Maddie along, see what she plans on doing with her life now. Perhaps she'll pursue a new career with her father's company."

I turned away and rolled my eyes. I opened the drawer and pulled out the cake slicer.

"Actually, *Mother*," I said, "I've found a little part-time job."

"Really? Where?" My mother asked.

She handed Lily to Mary, who swayed back and forth as she hummed to the baby.

I took in a slow, deep breath. "Crystal Bridges. I'm working in the library, assisting one of the librarians."

Mary smiled, as did Monica. My mother, though, had a look of horror on her face.

"What? You're working at an art museum?" she asked.

I smiled and nodded my head. "Yep."

She pursed her lips in distaste and squinted down with one eye, looking like she wanted to throw up. "What do you do in this *assistant* position?"

I shrugged and reached into another draw for three candles and a book of matches. "I shelve books, answer emails. Oh! And she's showing me how to order books for our branch. I check out books, help people find materials…things like that."

My mother put her hand to her chest and gasped. "Maddison Powers! If you'd wanted to be a file clerk, you could have just skipped college and gone to work in the mailroom at Powers Communications. It would have saved us money."

Monica turned to my mother, a nasty look on her face. "Has anyone every told you that you're a—"

"Well, let's see about getting that cake out to the gentlemen, shall we?" Mary said, quickly putting out the fire that was just getting started.

My mother spun on her heels and stormed out of the kitchen. I felt tears threaten my eyes as Monica gave me a hug.

"Don't listen to her, Maddie," she whispered. "She's just an old bitch with a crusty vagina."

I nodded and giggled as Monica made her way out to the living room.

I took a deep breath as I attempted to get my shaking hands under control. I was never inviting my mother here again.

Mary walked up to me and smiled. "To think I used to be that kind of a bitch."

I looked at her, shocked. Then I busted out laughing. "Mary, you will never know how much of a breath of fresh air you are."

She winked. "I wasn't always like this. I used to care more about how my nails looked than whether my son had his dinner."

"Really?" I asked, surprised.

She nodded. "The moment I laid my eyes on Lily, it was like I'd been given a second chance. In a way, Lily brought Cale and me back together. In fact, we've been closer in the last three months than we have been in his entire life."

I looked down at my baby girl in her grandmother's arms and smiled.

"Let's get this ridiculous cake out there and eat it, shall we?"

Mary grinned and said, "Yes, let's. Come on, Lily! Let's go show them how we celebrate Princess Lily's three-month birthday!"

CALE SHUT THE door and leaned against it. I sat down on the bed and sighed.

"Maddie, I hate to say this, but your mother is a bitch. And she's my boss's wife!"

I chuckled. "You're not the only one who thinks that. I don't honestly know how my father puts up with her."

Cale slowly nodded. "I thought Monica was going to jump across the table and bitch-slap her when your mom said the lasagna wasn't cooked properly."

I laughed and dropped back onto the bed, kicking my heels off and groaning. "Oh God," I said. "Why did I invite her? Oh, yeah— she's my evil mother and would never let me live it down if she'd been left out."

I felt the bed move and looked to see Cale lying next to me. "I'm glad my parents decided to head home and not stay the night.

I smiled and nodded my head.

Cale smiled and said, "So that cake."

I covered my face with my hands and groaned again. "I know, I know. I got carried away. I promise, no more month birthdays. I'll stick to the years, and I promise not to go crazy with the cakes."

He rolled onto his side and pulled me to face him. "I loved it. I loved how you made Lily's third, um, month so special."

I giggled and bit my lip. "This is what happens when a girl goes from a full-time high-stress job to being a stay-at-home mom with a part time job."

"How are things at Crystal Bridges?"

I smiled. "I love it. I really do, Cale. It's amazing to go to a job and love what you're doing. And to be able to leave the job at work when you walk out the door. I mean, I love being home with Lily, but spending just two days a week at the library and talking to people is wonderful. Plus, it gives your mom an excuse to spend time with Lily."

Cale smiled. "Yeah, she loves it."

I sat up and turned. "Will you unzip me?"

Cale sat up and ran his hand up my arm, making me shudder. His touch did the most amazing things to me. He moved his hand along the nape of my neck, pulling me closer.

"You looked beautiful tonight, Maddie."

I closed my eyes as he moved his lips to my neck and began gently kissing me.

"Mmm, feels so good," I said.

"I want to make love to you, Maddie," Cale whispered against my skin.

He moved his hand to my zipper and began unzipping my dress, then stood, pulling me up along with him. He pushed my dress off my shoulders and let it fall to the floor, letting his eyes wander slowly over my body, as if he was memorizing every detail.

I unclipped my bra and pulled it off, dropping it next to my dress. Cale licked his lips, hunger filling his eyes. I slowly pulled off my panties while looking into his eyes.

I took a few steps back and lay on the bed. I watched as Cale stripped out of his clothes and quickly joined me.

"There is nothing I desire more than making love with you," I said against his lips.

His hand started on my cheek, then moved down to my chest, slowly making it's descent to my upper thigh. My stomach clenched in anticipation. I'd been dreaming of this since Cale had whispered that he wanted me, earlier tonight, while my father was telling Monica and me about a charity project he was starting.

Right as his fingers found my need, Lily started crying.

"No! Oh, no not now," I whimpered.

I closed my eyes and attempted to pull my libido back into check, but I felt Cale's hot breath blowing on my clit. My eyes sprung open and before I could even say a word he was licking and sucking on me.

My back arched and I let out a moan. "Cale! Lily...crying...Oh God..."

It didn't take long before I was grabbing the pillow and moaning into it as Cale managed to give me an incredible orgasm. I'd never had an orgasm like that before. I wasn't sure what he did, but it was amazing.

I lay there attempting to catch my breath while Cale got up and walked into the bathroom. I could hear the faucet running, so I sat up and looked toward the bathroom.

"Wow. Just…wow. Cale, that was…oh wow."

He walked out dressed in those damn sexy-ass linen pants of his. The smile on his face melted my heart.

"How did you make me come so fast?"

He smiled bigger as he made his way to the bedroom door. He looked over his shoulder as he said, "I gave you a little ass action. I've always wanted to do that. Seemed like a good time to try it out."

With that, he left the room. My mouth dropped open as I heard him run up the stairs.

I heard Lily's door open over the baby monitor. Then I heard Cale talking to her.

"Hey, Princess. Are you hungry, baby girl? We're gonna let mommy rest while you and I have a serious talk about how boys are to stay as far away from my princess as possible."

I covered my mouth and chuckled. I looked at the monitor only to see Cale laying Lily down on the changing table and smiling. There was nothing sexier than him with his daughter.

I fell back onto the bed and smiled, thinking about how wonderful my life was. I bit down on my lip and rolled over to grab my phone off of the side table. I texted Monica.

Me: *Hey are you up?*
Monica: *Yep. Just got home. I'm going to have to talk Jack into moving to Beaver Lake.*
Me: *Oh my gosh, I would LOVE that!*
Monica: *HAHA! Me, too! What's up?*
Me: *Um…I have to ask you something.*
Monica: *Okay, ask away.*

Me: *It's kind of sexual and embarrassing.*

Monica: *As long as you don't ask me to make out with you, I think I can handle it.*

Me: *Have you...I mean...well...have you ever let Jack or any-one play with your...you know... Ugh this is so weird.*

Monica: *Back door action?*

Me: *OMG yes! How did you know that's what I saying?*

Monica: *'Cause I'm good like that. Jack has been the only one to ever take that plunge.*

Me: *Jesus, I shouldn't have asked. Officially taking back my question. Goodnight.*

Monica: *Oh, HELL no. You can't ask me that and then not give me the chance to ask you about the same thing.*

Me: *Okay, well, Cale did something while giving me oral sex and I had the most powerful orgasm ever. I asked him how he was able to make me...you know...so fast.*

Monica: *What are we in high school? COME? How he made you COME so fast?*

Me: *Bitch! Yes. I asked how he made me come so fast and he said he did a little back door action, but I didn't feel it. Or I was too caught up in the intense orgasm to notice.*

Monica: *Dayum. Go Cale! Gettin' some double-hole action.*

Me: *All right, I'm done talking to you about this.*

Monica: *Oh my. I'm laughing so hard right now and Jack wants to know why!*

Me: *NO! You wouldn't.*

Monica: *Oh. I would. Night darling.*

I sighed as I set my phone back down on the side table. I heard Cale singing to Lily as I crawled under the covers. I'll never be able to look at Jack again. Still, I felt my eyes getting heavier. I was going to have to tell Cale how much I enjoyed this part of the evening. I couldn't help but smile at the way my body seemed to still be humming.

I drifted off to sleep to the sounds of the man I loved humming to Lily. Our daughter. My baby girl.

29

Cale

"I HEARD YOU got some back door action the other night," Jack said as he threw the basketball, missing the hoop. "Damn."

I stopped and looked at him. "What?"

Jack laughed. "Seems you were the first to do that to Maddie. She texted Monica about it."

I smiled. "Really?"

Something about knowing Maddie had never played like that before had my dick jumping at the thought of doing it again tonight.

"Dude," Jack said. "Are you seriously standing there thinking about it?"

I grabbed my towel from the bench and wiped my face. "You brought it up."

Jack dribbled the ball, then jumped and threw it, this time making a basket. "Yeah," he said, "well, I take back this conversation. Moving on. Monica and I are talking about getting married on December 23rd."

I smiled and made a beeline for the basketball. I knocked it out of his hands and turned and shot for the hoop. When it swooshed in, I whooped and turned to Jack. "I do believe that was the winning shot."

Jack rolled his eyes and grabbed his towel and bottled water from the bench before heading to the locker room.

"Oh, come on. Don't be such a poor sport," I said, jogging over to grab my stuff. "So December, huh? That's a quick engagement."

"No, it's not," Jack, said.

"Dude, y'all haven't even been dating a year, and you're engaged and planning a wedding."

Jack stood there, staring. "What's your point?"

I shrugged. "I don't know. I mean, a year ago, you were hooking up with two girls a week. Now you're talking about settling down and getting married. It's just...weird."

Jack shot me a dirty look. He pushed the locker room doors open and headed straight to the showers.

Fifteen minutes later Jack sat down next to me. "I've never felt the way I feel when I'm with Monica. She changed me. I mean, I can't imagine my life with anyone but her. I want things with her that I never dreamed I'd want with anyone."

I smiled as I shoved my workout clothes into my duffle bag. I stood and placed my hand on Jack's shoulder. "I'm really happy for both of you, Jack. I truly am."

"I know you are," he said. "You want to be my best man?"

Grinning I said, "I'd be honored."

Jack laughed. "Good, 'cause I expect a kick-ass bachelor party, and I know you won't let me down."

He headed out the door. I chuckled and followed him. "No strippers though, right?"

"Fuck yeah, there'd better be strippers."

I shook my head and rolled my eyes. "I'm already regretting this decision."

TWO MONTHS LATER

I WATCHED AS Jack paced back and forth in front of the window. He must have run to the bathroom to throw up at least three times in the last hour.

"I didn't even fucking drink last night. I mean, we sat around and watched movies all night. What the hell is wrong with me?" Jack asked, surveying the room.

I attempted to hold back my laughter. Jack had talked and talked about a kick-ass bachelor party but, three weeks ago, he'd finally broken down and told me he wanted a low-key night with just a few friends at my place. So Maddie and Lily went and stayed at Monica's parents' house and had a girls' night in while we stayed at my place and listened to Jack's father and my father tell fishing stories.

Jack's father, Craig, placed his hand on Jack's shoulder. "Son, just calm down. Take a deep breath and relax."

Jack looked at his dad like he'd grown two heads. "Relax? I'm getting married,

Dad. *Married.*"

His father raised an eyebrow, then looked to my father. "Should we tell him?"

I sat up straighter, my interest piqued.

"Tell me what?" Jack asked.

My father nonchalantly shrugged and said, "If you want. Not sure what good it'll do now."

I smiled and shook my head. Our dads lived to torment us. They've been doing this sort of thing as long as I can remember.

"What are y'all talking about?" Jack asked.

Craig placed both hands on Jack's shoulders. "Son, because I love you, I'm going to tell you this."

Someone knocked on the door and yelled, "Showtime! Take your places, gentlemen."

Craig frowned and said, "Well, looks like it's time, son. Let's go."

He turned for the door while Jack stood there, his mouth gaping open.

My father walked by and hit Jack on the back. "Let's do this thing!"

Everyone followed Craig out the door except for Jack and me.

I snapped my fingers in front of Jack's face to break his trance. "Dude," I said. "They're screwing with you. You know they've always done this sort of shit."

Jack nodded, looking into my eyes. "I'm scared shitless. What if I'm not good enough for her, Cale? What if she gets tired of me? What if…"

"Jack, stop this. Do you love Monica?"

He nodded, smiling. "More than anything."

"Do you want to spend the rest of your life with her, and only her?"

Smiling he said, "Yeah, I do."

I slapped his back and said, "Then you've got this. Monica is *crazy* in love with you. You guys are perfect together. You make each other happy. Dude, just relax."

Jack nodded. "Right! I mean, you're right. Jesus, what's wrong with me? Monica is probably cool as a cucumber right now and here I'm acting like a pussy."

I swallowed and nodded my head. "Yeah, you know Monica. She's got this."

"Shit! I've got this, too!" He stood up taller, cracked his neck, and started for the door. "Let's do this shit!"

I chuckled as I followed him. I pulled out my phone and saw Maddie's last text to me.

Maddie: *Monica looks like she's about to pass out. If she makes it through this, I'll be impressed. She keeps doing these breathing exercises to calm down. It's starting to freak me out!*

Me: *Jack is pacing back and forth. I find it rather amusing.*

As we walked down the aisle to where the pastor was waiting, Jack stopped a few times to welcome friends and family. That's when I saw the small soldier girl—the wedding planner—coming. She was terrifying.

"Mr. Rambrandt, you need to get into position please." She barked. Jack turned to me and swallowed hard. "I've got this."

I nodded and said, "You've got this."

Jack turned and approached the altar where he greeted the pastor.

Tommy Harding, an usher and one of our college buddies, slipped a twenty into my hand. He was tall and thin with white-blond hair that stood out even more in the black tux.

Tommy narrowed his green eyes at me and said, "Shit, you win."

Tommy and I had placed a bet back in college. I'd said Jack would get married eventually, but he'd said there was no way in hell Jack would ever settle down.

I smiled, pocketing my cash and taking my place next to Jack.

30

Maddie

"**I** NEED THE bride! It's time."

I rolled my eyes at Monica's wedding planner as I looked at Monica in the mirror. "You look beautiful," I said, my voice cracking.

"Don't make me cry, Maddison Nicole Powers. I'm about to walk down the aisle."

I laughed, shaking my head. "You? Cry? I don't think I've ever seen you cry."

"I've cried before," she said. "I've cried plenty of times."

I raised an eyebrow. "Really?"

She shook her head and looked away. "I can't believe I'm getting married, Maddie."

I sat down. "Are you scared?" I asked with a slight smile.

She began chewing on her lip. "I'm so scared it's not even funny. I mean...what if Jack changes his mind? What if I go to start walking down the aisle and he realizes he doesn't want this? What if we moved too fast?" She attempted to hold back the sob, but it was too late. She fanned her eyes as she took deeps breaths.

I grabbed her hands. "Monica. Do you love Jack?"

Her eyes lit up. "Yes. More than I could ever imagine."

"Does your heart feel like you've rushed this?" I asked. "Not your head, your heart."

She shook her head and a single tear escaped and slid down her cheek. I wiped it away. "Then don't be scared," I said. "Trust your heart, Monica."

Another tear slid down her cheek and she pulled me closer and held me tight as she did the one thing I'd never seen her do before. Cry.

"Oh, no. That is not what the maid of honor is supposed to do," the wedding planner chastised. "You're supposed to keep her happy, not make her cry! We have fewer than two minutes to get your makeup touched up and get you down the aisle. They are walking down right now. Maddie, go get your flowers and get into position!"

I jumped up and saluted to the young girl Monica had hired to help plan the wedding. Both of Monica's parents were in France, and when they'd told her they wouldn't be coming back to the States for her wedding, it had nearly broken my heart. Monica hadn't been surprised. That was just what they did. Even in high school, Monica had spent more time at my house than her own. I knew it had hurt, but she would never admit it.

I winked at Monica and made my way to my position. As the music started, I stood and waited for my turn to walk down the aisle. We were all dressed in light teal gowns with white shawls. It had taken Monica all of thirty minutes to choose our dresses. Her only request was that they be the most expensive light teal dresses in the store. For her dress, we'd flown to New York. I was almost positive she'd bought the most expensive dress just to stick it to her parents—especially after her father told her to just bill him for all of the expenses. Her first stop after the news that they wouldn't be attending was to Pinnacle Country Club. Two hours later, the wedding date had been set and Monica had a smile plastered across her face. I swear, her wedding was fit for royalty. I had made a round through the private room where the reception would be held and I'd never seen so much crystal and silver. And she must have found every kind of flower known to man.

Fingers snapping in my face pulled me back. "Maid of honor! You're up."

Ugh. I hate this wedding planner. I shot the planner a look and said, "I have a name. It's Maddie, not maid of honor."

I was feeling pretty good about myself for standing up to the Wicked Witch of the West—until she glared at me, making a strange noise.

"Walking now," I said as I made my way to where I would start heading down the aisle. While I was walking, I smiled and nodded, saying hello to complete strangers. I didn't know most of these people, and I was pretty sure Jack and Monica didn't either.

That's when I saw Cale. I sucked in a breath and attempted to keep my jaw from dropping to the ground and drool escaping. *Holy shit. I need a new pair of panties.*

He was dressed in a black tux, white dress shirt and a light teal tie. His messy brown hair was tamed, but not too much. The smile on his face made me slow my pace, until I heard a whispered, "Speed it up maid of honor!" I looked behind me, but the evil wedding planner was nowhere to be seen. Maybe I'd imagined it. Or she had something planted in my flowers so she could boss me around remotely.

As I came to the front, I saw Cale's parents, Mary and Mitchel, sitting with Jack's parents, Craig and Diane. My heart hurt for Monica, knowing that her parents weren't here. Mary was holding Lily, who was also dressed in a light teal dress. She was five months old and just the sweetest little thing. I felt tears building in my eyes, and I looked away. I glanced back at Cale and his smile faded briefly before I gave him a slight grin. When I got to my position, he caught my eye and mouthed, "Happy tears?" I nodded and winked. I wasn't sure why, but I was suddenly overcome with sadness.

The wedding march began and everyone turned to watch Monica. My heart leapt with awe. She was stunning. I smiled when it looked like Jack's knees were going weak. His smile was huge as he watched her walk toward him. When she finally arrived at his side, he held his hands out for her. He leaned in and I could hear him say, "You look beautiful, Monica. More beautiful than what I dreamed."

That's when it happened. My best friend, a woman I'd known since middle school, publicly broke down in tears. Rachel, me and Monica's college roommate, leaned over and whispered in my ear, "I'll give you the fifty bucks after the reception."

I smiled and nodded.

I TOOK IN a deep breath, inhaling Cale's heavenly scent. I closed my eyes, moaning just slightly.

"Maddie," Cale said, "keep making noises like that and I'm going to sneak you out to my car and have my wicked way with you."

I looked into his eyes and giggled. "I'd totally be okay with that."

Cale looked around. "Shit, I wish we could."

I followed his gaze. My eyes caught Jack and Monica dancing.

"They really are so good for each other. I'm so happy for them," I whispered as Cale pulled me closer.

"We're going to be next," he said with a grin.

My heart slammed in my chest and I swallowed the lump in my throat. He turned and captured my eyes with his intense stare. His lips curled into that crooked smile that melted my heart.

"That's not a very romantic way to ask me to marry you, Mr. Blackwood."

Cale let out a chuckle. "No it wasn't was it?"

I slowly shook my head.

He leaned down and lightly brushed his lips against mine. "I love the way your lips taste." His eyes searched my face. "I love the way your eyes reveal how much you love me." His hands moved up and cupped my face. "And I love how you are mine."

I closed my eyes and barely spoke the words, "Yes. Yours."

His lips met mine again and soon we were lost in our kiss. Cale's want pushed up against my abdomen and had my fingers digging deeper into is arms.

"Cale, I love you so much," I said. "You're all I've ever wanted. All I'll ever need."

He moved his hand down to my neck and pulled me back into a kiss. It was as if we were the only two people in the room. I was lost in his passion, engulfed in his love.

"Excuse me, maid of honor and best man? It's time for the toasts so break it up and follow me."

Cale glared at the wedding planner. "I hate that woman," he hissed through his teeth.

I giggled and turned to follow her. I didn't even know what her name was. I was starting to think that Monica didn't either. The lady only referred to herself as "the wedding planner." So everyone called her that.

"I don't think she believes in names. I don't even know if *she* has a name," I said.

Cale grabbed my hand and kissed the back of it as he laughed. "She has a name all right. It's 'bitch.'"

I covered my mouth and laughed as the wedding planner turned and glared at us. I hit Cale in the side. "Great, now you've got her mad at us."

"After the toast, let's make a run for it. Just for our own safety, no other reason."

I nodded. "I think that's a good idea. Purely for our own safety, we should skip out on our best friends' wedding before *they* even leave."

"No one will even notice we're gone." Cale said, pulling me

closer to him and wrapping his arm around my waist.

"Nope, no one. I don't even know these people," I said looking around. We stopped at the wedding party table and the planner handed us each a glass of champagne.

"Since I never did get those speeches ahead of time like I asked, keep it short and sweet. No one wants to be bored by your toasts. Make it personal but not about you." She gave me a once-over, and I made a face, slightly offended. Cale started laughing but quickly stopped when the evil witch turned to him. "Don't say anything about his past girlfriends, sex life or any of that bullshit. Him. Monica. That's it. Got it?"

Cale chuckled. "Um…yep. I got it, Your Evilness."

She shot Cale a dirty look and said, "You're on first, smart ass. Thirty seconds."

Cale winked at me before he stepped up to the microphone.

It took everything out of me to stand there with a straight faced as Cale started from kindergarten and moved his way through college, with stories of him and Jack. The wedding planner finally took the mic from Cale, thanked him for his toast, and handed the mic to me. I smiled at Jack and then Monica.

"I've never in my life met two people so in love with each other," I said. "Your courtship was an amazing whirlwind, your wedding a breathtaking adventure, but your union…" I smiled as I watched Monica wipe away her tears. "Your union is a journey that will lead you to your happily ever after. I love you both so much, and I'm so happy for both of you. Congratulations Mr. and Mrs. Rembrandt."

Monica looked at me and mouthed, "I love you," as Jack kissed her on the cheek.

Cale walked up next to me and leaned down. His hot breath on my neck had me placing my hand on my stomach to calm the butterflies.

"You're so afraid of the wedding planner aren't you?" he said.

I smiled and nodded. "Yep."

31

Cale

I SLOWLY ROLLED over and pulled Maddie closer. The moment she let out a soft moan, my dick hardened. I smiled and turned her over.

"Good morning, beautiful." I said as I kissed the tip of her nose. She stretched and smiled back. "Good morning, handsome."

"It's our first Christmas Eve together as a family."

The tears in her eyes made my heartbeat pick up. I loved Maddie so much, and I wanted to scream it from the tallest mountain.

"I know," she said. "I'm so excited. I feel like a little girl."

I teased her entrance as I cupped her face with my hands and gently kissed her cheeks. "Do you want your first present?"

She thrusted her hips toward me and giggled. "If my first present is you making love to me, then, yes. I want it very much."

I slowly pushed into her as we both moaned. "God, Maddie. It's like the first time every time with you." She wrapped her legs around me and pulled me closer.

"Mmm…nothing is better than this. Best. Present. Ever." She whispered against my lips.

I slowly made love to her as we kissed. We couldn't get enough of each other, but we needed it to be slow. Gentle.

"Dada…"

I stopped moving and looked at the monitor. I pulled out of Maddie, stood up, and pointed to the monitor. "Oh my God!"

Maddie quickly sat up and looked. "What? What's wrong with her? Oh, God!"

She stood up next to me and looked at the monitor. Then gasped and started jumping up and down. "She's sitting up. Cale! She's sitting up!"

"Dadadada."

My mouth dropped open. "She said, 'Dada,'" I breathed. "She said, 'Dada!'"

Maddie tilted her head. "Yeah, I didn't hear 'Dada.'"

"What? She clearly said, Dada.'"

"Mamamama…"

Maddie punched me in the arm. "Oh! My! God! She said, "Mama!'"

My shoulders dropped and I stared at Maddie as she jumped up and down, grinning like a fool. "She is sitting up and saying, 'Mama!'"

I shook my head. "Uh, no. She's sitting up, but she said, 'Dada,' then rambled off and said nothing but jumbled baby talk."

"Dada…Dada…." Maddie and I both looked at the monitor again.

"Damn it. She said, 'Dada.'" Maddie said as I ran toward the dresser. "Wait! Cale, where are you going?"

I grabbed my phone off the dresser and headed upstairs. I opened the door and looked at my little princess sitting up all by herself. She looked up at me and smiled as she started to tip over. I quickly reached for her and sat her back up.

"Good morning, Princess," I said as I took a picture of her sitting up. "Were you calling for me? Dada? Say it again baby girl."

She smiled bigger and my heart about burst from my chest. "Mama," she said.

I shook my head. I put my finger up to my lips and whispered,

"No, *Dada*."

She giggled. "Mama…Mama…Mamamama." I picked her up and smiled.

"Dada," I whispered.

She looked over my shoulder and I sucked a breath as I watched her smile. I swear, her eyes filled with something I'd never seen before.

"Mama!" she said.

I turned to see Maddie standing there. Tears were sliding down her beautiful cheeks. She placed her hand over her mouth and cried harder. I pulled her to me, and the three of us stood there together. *Our little family.*

Maddie sniffled and pulled back as she wiped her nose with her robe. "Cale?"

"Yeah, baby?"

"Do you realize that you're holding our daughter…and you're naked?"

I looked down and then looked back up. I handed Lily to Maddie and ran back down stairs to get dressed.

Maddie walked into the kitchen with Lily and laughed. I poured both of us a cup of coffee and shook my head as I set Maddie's cup of coffee down on the table. "Thank God she's still too young to be affected by her father walking around butt-ass naked.

Maddie laughed harder and set Lily down in her highchair, then kissed me. "Thank you," she whispered against my lips.

"For?"

"Loving me," she said. "I think the greatest gift I've ever received is you and Lily."

I swallowed hard and shook my head. "Do you know what I want more than anything, though?"

I pulled her closer. She raised her eyebrow at my hard-on pressing into her.

Chuckling, she asked, "What do you want more than anything?"

I locked eyes with her. "I love Lily with my whole heart. You are both my whole world. But I want to see your stomach growing with our child, Maddie. I want to have a baby, you and me."

Maddie sucked in a breath and blinked rapidly, trying not to cry. She closed her eyes and whispered, "Cale…"

I placed my finger under her chin and lifted her face so I could search her eyes. "The only thing our little family is missing," I said, "is a piece of me and you."

Maddie placed her hand behind my neck and pulled me to her. We lost ourselves in the kiss. Before I knew it, I was taking Maddie right there on the kitchen floor.

"Yes. Cale. Oh God, yes," Maddie panted as I pounded her. What started out as a sweet and tender moment had quickly turned into heated passion. Maddie called out my name as I released myself into her.

I buried my face in her neck and controlled my breathing. "Maddie," I whispered as I felt my dick twitching inside of her. "I love you so much."

She was about to say something when I heard one of the kitchen chairs being pulled out. Maddie and I both stood and saw Monica sitting and pulling Lily's high chair over to her. "Oh, peanut. Are these nasty adults teaching you about sex?"

I quickly pulled up my pants as Maddie dropped to the floor and grabbed her panties.

"Jesus, Monica. Did you just walk in here?" I asked. Maddie pulled her robe tighter and turned to Monica. Next thing I knew, Jack was walking into the kitchen.

Jack kissed Maddie on the cheek and then turned to me. "Damn! When you gave us a key to your place, I didn't think we would be getting porn with the deal."

Maddie swatted at Jack. "I'm gonna go get dressed," she told me. "Please strip Jack and Monica of our house key." Her cheeks were beautifully flushed, and I winked at her.

Maddie made her way out of the kitchen, and I glared at Monica and Jack. "Really, you guys? You couldn't have made yourself known when you let yourselves in?"

Jack laughed. "Sorry dude, we rang the doorbell and figured y'all were outside."

"Dadadada…"

Jack jumped and Monica gasped.

"Holy shit! She talked!" Monica yelled. "She talked!"

I chuckled. "She's sitting up on her own, too."

Jack gave me a shocked look. "What? No way."

I nodded and took a sip of coffee. "You want coffee?" I asked.

"Nah, we had Starbucks on our way over." Jack said as he watched Monica.

She was trying to get Lily to say, "Monica." In this moment, I could see it in Jack's eyes—he was ready for a baby.

"Oh my gosh! Oh my gosh!" Maddie shouted as she came running into the kitchen clapping her hands. Lily jumped around in her high chair, excited.

I had to adjust myself as I watched Maddie jumping up and down. I couldn't believe my guy was at attention already.

"What the hell are you freaking about over there? Late orgasm?" Monica asked.

Maddie stopped and glared at Monica. "Don't talk like that in front of Lily."

Monica laughed. "Excuse me! You were just having *sex* in front of her."

Maddie rolled her eyes and turned to me. "Cereal!"

"Oh my gosh!" I said. "Cereal?"

Maddie grabbed my hands and jumped again. She threw herself into my arms. "Cereal!"

I spun her around and set her down. "I'll get out the formula and you get the bowl."

She skipped a little and squeaked as she said, "I'm on it."

32

Maddie

A S I RAN by Jack and Monica, I couldn't help but notice how they were looking between Cale and me.

"Is there some new cereal out that we should know about it?" Jack asked.

I grabbed the bowl and a small baby spoon, then hurried back over to Cale.

Monica laughed and then she jumped up. "Oh my God! Cereal? It's time for cereal?"

I looked at her and nodded as we both started jumping in our excitement.

Jack's mouth gaped. "Will someone please tell me about this amazing cereal?"

"It's for Lily, Jack. She's old enough to have cereal now," I said as I stood there and watched Cale mix the cereal with Lily's formula.

Monica grabbed my arm and said, "This. Is. So. Exciting!"

"Why?"

We all turned and looked at Jack. I shook my head and said, "Don't you get it, Jack? Lily is having solid food...for the first time. Ever."

"And...this is why we are all acting like lunatics?" Jack asked.

"No, wait—you're the ones acting like lunatics."

Monica grunted and said, "Don't pay attention to him. He doesn't get it. I thought y'all were going to give her some cereal in her formula last month when she wasn't sleeping very good."

Cale shook his head. "Nah, she ended up sleeping fine and Maddie and I decided to wait until she was five months. I can't believe we totally forgot!"

I sighed. "Epic failure moment as parents."

Cale held out the bowl of cereal and smiled. "Are we ready?"

I skipped and squeaked a little, making Lily squeal and giggle. "Yes!" I said. "Let's do this!"

Cale and I sat on either side of Lily. I pulled her highchair back out so the others could watch. Jack went to leave when all three of us asked, "Where are you going?"

He seemed to be able to read all of our faces before he slowly sat down and said, "Um…nowhere."

Cale took in a deep breath and said, "Okay, Princess. Here is your first bite of cereal."

Lily was doing her favorite thing—making spit bubbles. My hands shook as I recorded Lily eating cereal for the first time on my phone. I held my breath as the spoon went in. Lily made a funny face and tried pushing the cereal out with her tongue.

"Smart kid. Tastes like shit and she knows it." Jack mumbled.

I glared at Jack as Monica smacked him. "Don't say that in front of her."

"Jack's mouth dropped open. "Holy crap…they were just fucking in front of her and I can't say the word shit?"

Cale shot Jack a dirty look before giving Lily another bite. This time she took it.

"Look at her little tongue! She doesn't know what to think." I said, giggling.

I watched as our baby girl took her first bites of cereal. She looked so much like Cale. Her hair was coming in more and more and it was a very light brown. She now had enough hair that I could put a little Velcro bow in it. Her bright blue eyes sparkled as she lifted her eyebrows with each bite Cale gave her.

"She is so precious. I can't wait until y'all give her veggies. I *have* to be here when you do." Monica glanced over to Jack and smiled. "I'm so glad we didn't leave for our honeymoon until tomorrow!" Jack looked at Maddie like she had grown two heads.

Cale pushed the bowl toward me. "You want to feed her some now?"

"Yes!" I nodded in excitement as I handed him my phone. I put a small amount of cereal on the spoon and gave it to Lily. She was loving it. She started mouthing for more. "Look, she wants more!"

I gave her another spoonful and she started talking again. "Dadadada…" I peeked over to Cale and my heart soared as he dabbed the corner of his eye.

Jack sighed and stood up. "Oh for the love of God. I liked the porn show better."

"MADDISON! MADDISON!"

I turned to see who'd been calling out my name. When I saw that it was my mother, I took a deep breath and slowly let it out. She walked through the library at Crystal Bridges as she called out my name, clearly not caring that she was in a library. I hadn't spoken to her since Lily's party when she was three months old.

I plastered a fake smile on my face and waited for her to come up to me. She kissed me on both cheeks. "Did your father let you know I was back from Greece? I just flew in this morning."

I nodded. My mother had gone to Greece two months ago and

I'd never seen my father so happy. He'd been coming over at least three times a week to spend time with Lily and us. He'd fallen head over heels in love with our daughter. He also informed me he was going to be divorcing my mother.

"He did tell me, yes," I said.

She smiled weakly. "I thought so, since he had dinner with you and Cale last night."

"What are you doing here?" I asked.

She looked around. "I heard you were still working here…part time."

I gave her a fake grin. "Yep, I'm working here at the library. I absolutely love it."

She waved her hand in the air as she looked around. "You don't find this type of work to be a waste of your college education, Maddison?"

I sighed. "No, Mother, I don't. I enjoy it and it allows me to spend time with Lily."

She raised her eyebrow. "The child who is not yours."

I swallowed hard and looked directly into her eyes, scowling. "She *is* mine," I said. "I'm her mother, and she is my daughter. We are a family. She and Cale are my life."

"I don't see a ring on your finger." She said coldly.

I glanced down at her hand. Her wedding band was missing. "I don't see one on your finger either."

She snapped her eyes down to her hand, then back up to my eyes. "That's because your father made a grave mistake this morning when he picked me up from the airport. He is seeking a divorce. I was hoping for some support and understanding from my daughter, but all I get is…this" She gestured with her hands. "Disrespect. Like always."

I rolled my eyes and turned to walk away, but she followed me. "Please, Mother. The last thing you came here for was support from me. You want information as to why Daddy is asking for a divorce."

"Does he have a lover?" She asked.

I laughed lightly. "If he's smart, he's had one for a few years."

She grabbed my arm and pulled me to a stop. "Excuse me?"

"I'm tired of this. I'm tired of being treated like I'm some damn mistake that you made years ago. If you didn't love Daddy, why didn't you just leave him? Stop acting like you're the victim here, Mother. You are far from it. Daddy knows about your affair. He's known for the last year."

She brought her hand up to her mouth. "What? How? I mean..." She looked away.

I nodded and pulled my arm from her grip. My mother had been having an affair with one of my father's business associates. They'd meet at a hotel or at my parents' own home after my father would leave for work or when he was out of town.

"Karma is a bitch, Mom. Good luck living without Daddy's money."

I turned and walked toward the elevator. I was expecting her to follow, but when I looked back, she was just standing there, stunned. I stepped onto the elevator and leaned on the wall as I tried to calm down. I'd never stood up to my mother before, and I wasn't sure if I was relieved or if the reality of having the worst mother in the world had just showed up on my doorstep.

I walked out to my car and decided that I would be the mother to Lily that I'd always wanted. This nonsense about me not being Lily's biological mother was now behind me. Regardless of our situation, I was going to be the best mother for her, and I would always be there for both her and Cale. As I walked through the endless trail of flowers, I took a moment to look around. I loved Crystal Bridges. Even in the winter, they had flowers planted. I loved the quietness of it. It had a way of calming my nerves. I closed my eyes and could hear the water running along the creek that flowed through the property.

I stopped at my car and placed my hand on my stomach. Cale's words replayed in my head:

I want to have a baby...you and me.

I pulled out my phone and texted Cale.

Me: *Dinner at JJ's tonight?*
Cale: *Sounds good to me.*
Me: *I think Lily will love feeding the fish and turtles.*
Cale: *Oh man, she will. I came home earlier and was talking to Mom. She's heading out the door now. You may or may not have a surprise waiting for you when you get home.*
Me: *I'm on my way! I need something to cheer me up. My mom came by to see me.*
Cale: *Oh man. I'll cheer you up. I got this, baby. I got this.*

I walked into the house and looked around. "Cale?"

I walked into the kitchen, dining room, Cale's office, and finally walked outside onto the deck. I looked down and saw him on the dock. Taking off my pumps, I made my way down the stone steps. It was mid-January and unusually warm. I looked around at the bare trees. There was a slight wind blowing, and I could smell the fire from a nearby fireplace. We hadn't had much snow this year but, when we did, I loved sitting on the deck, wrapped up in warm blanket, looking out over the white landscape.

As I made my way down, I noticed Cale didn't have Lily. I panicked for a moment and thought about turning around. "Cale? Where's Lily?"

When he turned, the way he looked at me stopped me in my tracks. I sucked in a breath and my heart dropped to my stomach. He was so handsome and his smile drove me mad with desire.

He began walking toward me, and that was when I noticed his bare feet. *Oh Lord help me.* I wanted to strip out of my clothes and beg him to take me then and there.

"Lily is spending the night with her Grammy and Grampa." Cale said, his voice laced with seduction as he sauntered my way. I smiled and tilted my head.

"Is that right?" I asked as I slowly ran my tongue along my

teeth. He stopped just short of me and placed his hand on my cheek. My stomach took an immediate dive and my hands trembled as I thought about all the things I wanted him to do to me.

"I need you to go change."

I looked at him, confused. "Change into what? I would think you'd be asking me to undress."

One side of Cale's mouth moved up into a grin and I was ready to drop to the ground and beg him to take me right that second. I felt my face flush at my wayward thoughts.

"Why are you blushing, baby?" He asked as he moved his lips to mine. I moaned and placed my hands on his chest.

"Cale, please, I want you," I said, almost panting with desire. I looked up into his eyes and saw nothing but passion. I knew he wanted me, too.

"I have somewhere I need to take you first."

I smiled. "If it's to JJ's, I think I'll pass."

Cale laughed and shook his head. "No. Dress warm, we'll be outside this evening."

I scrunched up my nose. "Outside? For dinner?"

He turned me around and slapped my ass. "Yep! Come on, we need to get going."

33

Cale

"HOW WAS WORK?" I asked as Maddie got into the car. I grabbed her hand and gave it a kiss.

"Good," she said, grinning. "We closed early today, though, because someone was renting out the whole restaurant." She wiggled her eyebrows. "It was being kept on the down-low. I'm guessing someone big must be using it."

I was looking back at the road as I shrugged. I headed into Bentonville and Maddie talked about Lily the whole time.

"Can you believe she's six months old, Cale? The time is just flying by." She shook her head, smiling.

I laughed. "I still can't believe her poop turned orange. Scared the piss out of me."

Maddie laughed and squeezed my hand. "I can't wait to give her something sweet. Can we do that tomorrow, do you think?" Maddie asked. I quickly glanced at her, then back at the road.

"Sure we can! I don't see why not. We've pretty much introduced her to all the veggies. Should we invite Jack and Monica over?"

Maddie chuckled. "We totally should. Tell them we're having a small dinner party." Maddie put her hand to her mouth, trying to hold back a laugh. "I'm texting Monica right now!" she said, grabbing her phone.

I was glad she was distracted, because I was driving straight to where she worked—Crystal Bridges. Crystal Bridges was an amazing place. Lily loved being in her stroller as we walked the trails.

I pulled up to the front while Maddie texted Monica. I'd hired a few people to work that night, and originally had planned on using the restaurant. But when the weather turned out to be so nice, I made other arrangements.

Maddie laughed, "Monica and Jack are a go for..." she started, then, seeing where we were, she said, "Wait. Why are we at Crystal Bridges?"

I smiled and got out of the car. I walked around to the front of my car and up to a young lady standing there. "Mr. Blackwood, everything is ready. It looks beautiful. Thank you again for your generous donation, sir."

I nodded and said, "Thank you for taking care of all of this for me."

She nodded and smiled. "It was our pleasure."

I opened Maddie's door. She sat there, stunned. I held out my hand and helped her out of the car.

"Cale, what are we doing here? They have a private event tonight!"

I chuckled. "We're just going to go for a walk on the trails, baby. I just want to spend some time with you at a place that is dear to your heart."

She smiled and shook her head. "I thought...what about dinner?"

I grabbed her hand and started for the trail. "Dinner is still on."

We walked along the trail in silence. I knew how much Maddie loved it here. The gardens were breathtaking, even during the middle of winter. The pansies and evergreens set against the barren trees were exactly what I wanted for this moment. As we made our way to the spot I'd had set up, I began talking to Maddie.

"The first moment I saw you, I knew there was something special about you."

She grinned and began chewing on her lip.

"I couldn't take my eyes off of you. It was if all the air had been sucked out of the room when you smiled. Then, when you followed me to the beach…" I slowly shook my head. "That night, Maddie, I will forever be the best night of my life."

I stopped right before we turned the corner and took both her hands in mine. "I think I loved you the moment I first saw you."

Maddie swallowed hard and tried to talk, but closed her eyes instead, smiling before opening them again. I dropped one of her hands and led her around the corner. I smiled when I heard her gasp. I'd arranged for a small table to be set up next to the Robert Indiana LOVE sculpture. It had always been one of my favorite sculptures. A few candles where lit on the table, and rose petals where laid out all around the table.

"Cale, oh my…I don't…this is beautiful. How did you? When?" She turned to me, her eyes filled with such a quizzical look that I couldn't help but chuckle.

"I'd originally planned for the restaurant, but it was so beautiful outside these last few days that I had a different idea. Lily and I walk by this sculpture all the time. It reminds me of you."

I led her over and pulled out the chair for her to sit down. She wiped away a tear and smiled. I moved and sat across from her as a young blonde in black dress pants and a light blue shirt poured us each a glass of champagne. I smiled and thanked her.

"My pleasure, sir. Would you like us to begin serving dinner?" she asked.

I peeked at Maddie and almost laughed. She still looked puzzled. Completely thrown for a loop. I was internally fist-pumping, having surprised her like this. The biggest surprise was yet to come.

I nodded, "That would be wonderful. Thank you." I reached across the table and took Maddie's hand. "Are you surprised?"

She grinned and nodded. "Very. I'm completely shocked that

you did all of this. How in the world did you get this place all to us?"

"A very hefty donation."

Maddie laughed and shook her head. The waitress brought us out our salads first. Maddie and I talked as we ate, mostly about Lily. She was our whole world. I was so glad Maddie had moved past not being Lily's biological mother. In my eyes, she had become Lily's mother the moment we both walked into her room and met her face-to-face for the first time.

The waitress came over and set down two plates. Each one had salmon and steamed vegetables along with a roll.

"I'm so glad I decided to rent my house out to Monica and Jack last year, before they got married." Maddie said as she took a bite of her salmon.

I nodded. "It's been great having them so close by. Have you noticed how Jack watches Monica with Lily? I mean like *really* watches her."

Maddie chortled and nodded. "Yes! I think Jack is getting the baby bug, which is so weird to me." She looked away for just a moment. "I was thinking…about um…maybe seeing if they wanted to buy the house." Her face blushed and she began playing with her vegetables. "I mean, it was just a thought."

I couldn't help but smile. "I think that's a great idea. I mean, unless you want it as an investment property. But if Jack and Monica are interested in buying, I say sell it."

She looked back up at me and smiled. "I think Jack and Monica would be perfect owners for the house.

I nodded and placed my napkin on the table. I motioned for the waitress. "Would you like dessert?" I asked.

Maddie licked her lips and pulled the corner of her mouth into a come-hither grin. "The kind of dessert I want I can't get from our waitress."

I squirmed in my seat to adjust my growing dick. The waitress set two cups down in front of us. They were filled with orange souf-flé, with a small, red heart in the center.

Maddie smiled and said, "Oh my gosh, orange soufflé? I love orange soufflé!"

Right about that time, the violinist I'd hired came toward us from behind Maddie. He was dressed in a tux and playing some classical song that he'd had to tell me the name of five times. I finally told him I was never going to remember it. When Maddie turned to look at him, I moved into position. I took the ring box out of my pocket and waited.

"Oh my God, Cale. This is so romantic."

Maddie was about to say something else, but she jumped, startled, when she saw me at her side, on one knee, holding the ring out.

She lifted her hands to her mouth and immediately began crying.

"I love you, Maddie. I want nothing more than to spend the rest of my life giving you moments like this. I want to start each day with your beautiful smile. I want to talk to you about our future, and our dreams. These last few months with you have been the most incredible months of my life. This journey I'm on…I want…no, I *need* you to be on it with me." I opened the box to reveal the solitaire, one-carat, round diamond.

"Maddison Nicole Powers, will you do me the honor of becoming my wife?"

Maddie dropped her hands and began nodding as she attempted to talk. I took the ring out and reached for Maddie's fingers. Her hand was trembling as I slipped the diamond onto her ring finger. I stood and pulled her up with me. She threw herself into me and began crying harder.

"Cale," she said. "I love you so much."

34

Maddie

I COULDN'T BELIEVE how I was staring at my engagement ring. I felt like a teenager who'd just had her first kiss. I was on top of the world. When Cale reached over and placed his hand on mine, my stomach dropped and I was overtaken with emotion.

"Cale, this ring is beautiful. This whole night has just been... beautiful." I glanced over and my smile grew bigger just seeing the expression on Cale's face. I closed my eyes and silently thanked God for bringing us back to together.

Cale pulled into the driveway of our house and put the car in park. When he looked at me, I found myself fighting to pull in air. I just couldn't believe he was mine.

He placed his hand on my cheek and whispered, "So beautiful." I smiled and placed my hand over his before he said, "I'm going to take you inside and make love to you all night, Maddie."

My heart raced at the idea of being alone with Cale all night. I licked my lips and attempted to talk. "I...um...Cale."

He smiled his panty-melting smile. "Tell me what you want, Maddie."

I unbuckled my seatbelt and lowered my head. I looked at him through my eyelashes and bit my lip. "You, Cale," I said. "I want you in every single way possible. And we have all night to make love. Right now, I want...more."

Cale quickly got out of the car and came around to my side.

Before I knew it, Cale had me up against the wall in our living room, tearing my clothes from my body. I loved how he couldn't seem to get to me fast enough, and my libido was cranked up as high as it would go. I unbuttoned his jeans and pushed them down. The moment his dick sprang free, I dropped to the ground and took him into my mouth. His long, hard shaft filled my entire mouth as I moaned.

"Yes," Cale hissed through his teeth. He placed his hands on my head, controlling the rhythm. "Fuck, I don't want to come in your mouth." He lifted me and in one fast movement, my panties where gone and Cale was moving in and out of me as he held me up and against the wall.

"Harder. Cale," I said. "I want it harder."

He held me as I wrapped my legs around him and he walked us over to the sofa. He pulled out of me as he set me down.

"Get on the floor, Maddie, and put your hands on the sofa. I'm taking you from behind."

I followed his instructions and, as soon as he slammed his dick into me, I screamed. The way he held my hips and moved in and out of me was building my orgasm. I loved being like this with Cale. It was raw and passionate. The sound of his breathing as he fucked me fast and hard had my body reeling with pleasure. I threw my head back and called out his name as my orgasm raced through my body.

"Feels amazing. Yes! Oh, God yes!" I shouted as I totally let go. If my mother could see me now, she'd be appalled. Cale and I had plenty of hot sex, but something about this felt so raw...heated...hot as hell. "Oh, Cale...yes..."

"Is...this...what...you...wanted?" Cale panted as he thrusted harder and faster.

"Yes!" I cried. "I'm going to come again! Fuck me harder, Cale! Faster!"

He gave me what I asked for and I was calling out his name almost incoherently.

"Maddie, I'm coming," Cale said as he dug his fingers into me. He pushed in one last time and grunted as he came. I could feel his warmth spilling into my body. I reached down and touched my clit, only to cause myself to fall into another orgasm. I screamed out in pleasure as Cale continued to move in and out of me until we both collapsed onto the rug, dragging in breath after breath.

"Holy...shit," Cale said, trying to catch his breath. "That wore the shit out of me."

I let out a laugh. His chest was heaving, and just the sight of him had me turned on again. But I was exhausted, and I knew he was even *more* exhausted.

"Hottest moment of my life...so far," I said, wiggling my eyebrows.

"Give me thirty minutes and I'll be ready to go again," he said.

I pushed him onto his back and crawled on top of him. I began grinding against him as I grabbed my breasts and played with my nipples. "Cale, you turn me on so much. I can never get enough of you."

He grabbed my hips and closed his eyes. "Damn it, Maddie. You're going to kill me. My dick can't possibly function right now."

I took my right hand and began touching myself as I dropped my head back. "Yes...ah...feels so good," I whispered.

I could feel Cale's dick getting harder and I smiled. "Why, Mr. Blackwood. You underestimated him."

Cale sucked in a breath and mumbled something. I began rocking more. The harder his dick got, the more it rubbed on my clit. I moaned as I felt my orgasm building. "Ride me, Maddie. Ride me hard and fast."

I lifted up some and sank down onto him and began moving up and down.

"Yeah baby," he said, "That's it. God, Maddie..."

"Seriously. You two fuck more than rabbits."

I stopped moving. I quickly looked around. I didn't see anyone. I mouthed to Cale, *Is someone here?*

He made a face and shrugged. "I don't know," he whispered. "Hello?"

"I'm in the kitchen."

My mouth dropped open. "I thought you took the key from them!" I said as I ran down the hall to our bedroom. Cale was right behind me. He quickly closed the door.

"Shit," he said. "I forgot to get it from them."

I shook my head. "Damn it, Cale. He can't keep walking in on us like that. Son of a bitch! I was about to have another amazing orgasm."

I stomped my foot like a five-year-old, and I didn't even care. Cale tried not to laugh, but I could tell he was holding it in. He walked over to his dresser and pulled out a T-shirt and a pair of sweatpants.

"I'm so sorry, baby. Let me go get rid of him."

I grabbed Cale's arm. "Don't be mean to him. Just forceful."

He nodded and gave me a quick kiss on the lips. "Be right back."

I watched as Cale made his way to kick his best friend out of our house. I sat down on the bed and waited. After almost fifteen minutes with no sign of Cale, I got dressed and headed to see what was going on.

Walking into the living room, I saw the back porch light on. Through the sliding glass door, I saw Cale and Jack sitting out there. Cale had his hand on Jack's back and appeared to be consoling him. I wasn't sure whether I should let them be or go out there.

I was just about to open the door when my phone rang. I ran over to my purse and pulled it out. Monica was calling me.

"Hello?" It was silent until I heard her sniffle. "Monica? Are you okay?"

"No! Jack and I had a fight. Our first fight. It was bad, Maddie. It was really bad."

I looked back toward the deck. "Um, Jack is here now," I said. "He's talking to Cale."

"Is he? He said he was going out, that he needed to get a drink. I was sure he went to a bar or club." She started crying harder.

"Monica, what happened?" I asked as I made my way into the formal dining room.

She tried to stop crying and talk. "I don't know! That's the whole thing. I told Jack about dinner at your place tomorrow night, and I said something about Lily. He rolled his eyes and slammed his hand down on the counter. It scared the shit out of me, Maddie. It brought back all those memories of my father."

I closed my eyes and shook my head. Monica's dad had never hit her, but he'd verbally abused the hell out of her. "Oh, no. Monica. Why was he so angry?"

Her voice was laced was sadness. "I asked him and he...he said he didn't know...then he said...he said...oh God."

My heart began racing. "What? He said what?"

Her voice cracked as she spoke. "He said marrying me was...a mistake."

I looked back out at the porch. My heart hurt for Monica. "No," I whispered.

Monica was crying so hard that she was slurring her words.

"Monica, please calm down," I said. "I can't understand you. Take in a deep breath."

After a few minutes of deep breaths, she was finally calm.

"I don't think Jack meant that," I told her. "I see the way he looks at you and I know he loves you. Maybe something else is wrong or...maybe..."

"It doesn't matter. I'm not going to be in the same type of marriage as my mother and father. I won't do that, Maddie. I packed a bag and I left."

I walked back out into the living room. That's when I saw it— Jack's shoulders shaking. He was crying.

"Wait! What? Monica, just take a deep breath and think about what you're doing." I started to panic, but I wasn't sure why. "Monica, Jack is here and he's…he's…honey he's crying."

Silence.

"Monica? Are you still there?"

I heard a faint sniffle. "What did you say?" Monica barely whispered.

"Um…Jack's crying. Monica, where are you? Can you come over here?"

"I…I can't, Maddie. What he said to me…I just can't."

I closed my eyes and prayed that she'd change her mind. There had to be a reason that Jack lashed out like that. I just couldn't see Jack acting that way toward Monica. He loved her so much. I opened my eyes to see Cale looking at me. I pointed to the phone and mouthed, *Monica.* Cale just stood there. He almost seemed stunned. What the hell was going on?

"Monica, Cale is coming back into the house, honey. Give me two minutes to talk to him. Just give me two minutes, I won't hang up."

Monica blew her nose. "Just call me back Maddie. I need to calm down and have a few minutes to myself."

I took in a shaky breath. "Okay, Monica. I'll call you right back."

I didn't like the way Cale was looking at me with worry all over his face. Something was wrong. Something was terribly wrong.

35

Cale

MADDIE ENDED HER call with Monica and asked, "Cale, what in the world is going on? Did you know that Jack told Monica marrying her was a mistake? Why would he say such a thing? She's leaving!"

"What do you mean she's leaving?" I asked, looking back outside at Jack.

"Just that. She said she packed a bag and left. She was hysterical. What the hell is happening?"

I ran my hands through my hair and let out a breath. "Oh, God. Jack is a drunken mess."

Maddie gasped. "He didn't drive did he?"

I shook my head. "No. He said he took a cab here, but he's a mess."

"Why? I mean, just the other day I watched him with Monica and Lily. Cale, I've never seen him look at her with so much love."

I nodded. "I know, but...something's happened and it's thrown Jack for a loop. He doesn't know what to do about it."

"What could possibly make him say such a hurtful thing?"

I took a deep breath and glanced back outside to where Jack was sitting with his head in his hands. "Jack can't have children."

Maddie's eyes widened. "What? Why? I mean…is he sure? Cale, oh my God. I don't even know what to think or say right now." Maddie turned and looked at Jack.

"Jack talked to his father right after the wedding about wanting to have kids right away," I said. "His dad told him about how he and Jack's mother had had a terrible time getting pregnant. I guess his father had a very low sperm count, but after a few years of trying they finally had Jack. So Jack had his sperm tested and they told him this morning his sperm count was too low to ever be able to have kids." I shook my head and took another deep breath. "Jack said he and Monica had both decided they wanted to have a baby right away. Today, when Monica came home, Jack had already started drinking. She mentioned coming over for dinner to watch Lily, and how they should maybe get in some baby-making sessions, and Jack lost it. I guess he slammed his fist down and scared Monica. He's feeling so guilty about not being able to give her a baby, Maddie. That was the only reason he said that about marrying her. He's devastated. He's been trying to call her and she won't answer. He went back to the house and she was gone."

Maddie quickly wiped a tear from her cheek and picked her phone back up. She hit a button and looked at me. "Monica, I think you need to come over right away."

I waited to see how she was going to get Monica here after what Jack had said.

"No, listen to me. It's not my place to say, so I need you let Jack talk to you. He's been drinking, but Cale's been giving him coffee. He's more upset than anything."

Maddie looked at me as she listened to Monica talking. "Do you trust me as your best friend? Then, yes, I think you need to come as soon as you can. Okay, we'll see you in about ten minutes."

Maddie hung up and smiled. "She's on her way. She hadn't gone far."

I pulled her into my arms. "I'm so sorry our evening was ruined. This was supposed to be about us."

She held me tighter. "Let's get our friends back together. Then you can make love to me all night long."

Maddie was always trying to help other people first and that was one of the things I loved so much about her. I leaned down and lightly kissed her on the lips. "I love you so very much, Maddie."

She gave me that smile that makes me weak in the knees. "I love you too," she said.

I glanced back out to see Jack pacing back and forth. "Should I tell him Monica's on her way?"

Shaking her head, Maddie whispered, "No, lets just let things happen on their own."

The doorbell rang and I let Maddie go so she could answer it. A few seconds later, Maddie was walking into the living room with a very upset Monica.

"Hey, Monica," I said with a slight smile.

She smiled back weakly and said, "Hey, Cale."

Monica looked outside at Jack. She looked so confused. When I turned to look, Jack was sitting with his head in his hands. It was pretty obvious that he was upset.

"Why did you have me come here, Maddie? Why?" Monica sat down and wiped her tears away. Maddie and I sat down with her, Maddie taking Monica's hand.

Swallowing hard, Maddie blinked slowly and began talking. "Monica, the last thing you need to do is run away. Jack received some news earlier today that really upset him. He didn't know how to process it. He started drinking this morning and, when you came home, he handled it all wrong."

Monica eyes widened in horror. "Oh, God, is Jack okay?" She turned to me. "Cale...is he okay? What's wrong with him? Oh, God."

I held up my hands. "No, no. Monica, Jack is fine. I mean...he's not fine, but he's fine. I mean, he's not sick or anything like that. He's not gonna die."

The moment the words came out of my mouth I wanted to

punch myself. *Fuck.*

Poor Monica looked so confused. "Die? Wait, what is going on? Why is Jack crying? Why is he so upset?"

"Honey, one reason is he hurt you. He never meant to hurt you. What you need to do is go out there and talk to him. Please, just go out there."

Monica began chewing nervously on her lip. "Um…"

"Monica, please. If you love Jack, go out there." I said as I stood, holding out my hand.

She placed her hand in mine as she nodded, barely saying, "Okay."

Maddie stood and smiled at Monica. "I'm going to make some more coffee."

I guided Monica over to the sliding door and opened it.

"Jack?" I said. He still had his face buried in his hands and I could hear his sobs. Monica placed both hands over her mouth and tried to hold back her own tears.

"I hurt her…oh, God, the hurt in her eyes."

"Jack?" Monica's voice was shaky.

Jack dropped his hands and jumped, spinning to face her. "Monica."

"Please tell me what's wrong," she said. "Please."

Jack pulled Monica into his arms. "I'm so sorry, baby. I'm so very sorry. I didn't mean it. I swear to God, I didn't mean it."

I took a step back to give them privacy.

"Jack why did you say our marriage was a mistake?" Monica asked between her sobs. Jack closed his eyes and opened them again. Tears were streaming down his face.

"I can't give you what you want. I'll never be able to give you what you want."

I watched as he fell apart again. But this time, his wife was there to catch him. As they both sank to the ground I walked back into the house, attempting to keep my own tears at bay.

36

Maddie

CALE AND I sat in the formal living room together. My heart was breaking for both Jack and Monica, who were still talking on the porch. The moment I saw Jack drop to the ground, falling into Monica's arms, I lost it.

I ran my fingers up and down Cale's arm. "Cale?"

He was holding me close, and my head was buried in his neck. "Yeah, baby?"

"When are you thinking we should get married?" I asked, closing my eyes and dreamed about walking down the aisle to him. I knew that his marriage to Zoey had been rushed—not a whole lot of thought went into the process. They'd gone to a justice of the peace, getting married right before Cale went out of town for work.

"I'll marry you tomorrow if you want," He said, taking my hand in his.

I giggled. "I'd love to get married at Jack's parents' house, on the beach where we first met. Just us and a few close friends and family. Keep it low-key."

"I think that sounds perfect," he said. "Low-key. I like low-key."

I smiled. "With Lily turning one in July, I don't want to overshadow her birthday. What if we did it the week after her birthday? I would feel more comfortable leaving her with your mom or Monica while we went on our honeymoon."

Cale smiled and I swear his eyes were sparkling. "I think that sounds like an amazing plan. I say we talk to Jack's parents, Craig and Diane, and see if that works for them."

I snuggled back into his body. I couldn't believe this was really happening. I looked at my engagement ring. I was going to marry Cale. We would officially be a family come July.

"Maddie? Cale?"

I sat up and saw Monica and Jack standing in the doorway. I jumped up and my heart began to beat faster. I silently prayed that they'd worked things out.

"Hey..." Cale and I both said at once.

Monica looked at Jack before telling us, "We talked. Everything's going to be okay."

I let out a small sob and made my way over to my best friend. We hugged, both of us in tears.

"Oh Monica," I said. "I'm so glad you worked it out."

I wasn't sure how long we were hugging, but I heard Cale say something to Jack, too. Monica pulled away and smiled, wiping her tears away. Jack wrapped his arm around her and smiled. "We're not going to give up hope on a miracle."

Monica's smile to Jack had my heart soaring. I firmly believed that love could do anything, and the kind of passionate love that Jack and Monica shared was capable of delivering a miracle.

Jack held out his hand and dangled our house key in front of Cale. I laughed as Cale grabbed the key and shoved it in his pocket.

"Thanks, guys, for letting me crash your...party." Jack said, wiggling his eyebrows. I smiled and looked down, heat moving across my cheeks. Monica chuckled and hit Jack lightly. When I looked back up, I saw that Jack's eyes were still red from being so upset.

"Come on," Monica said. "Let's leave and let these guys...

resume."

I grabbed Monica's arm. "Wait. I have news."

She tilted her head and smiled. "What kind of news?" she asked.

I held out my left hand. Jack and Monica both looked at my ring. Monica began jumping and so did I as we grabbed hands and squealed.

"For Christ's sake! Why do you guys scream like that?" Jack said, shaking his head. He wrapped Cale in a bear hug before slapping him on the back. "Congratulations, dude. I'm happy for y'all."

"Thanks, Jack. I appreciate it," Cale said as Monica hugged Jack.

Monica took a step back and smiled at me. "Have y'all talked about a date at all?"

I peeked over toward Jack and raised my eyebrow. "Well, we were kind of hoping to have the ceremony the week after Lily turns one, at your parents' place, Jack. You know, take it back to the beginning."

I glanced over to Cale and he was smiling from ear to ear. I knew he thought the idea of having the wedding there was perfect, and that just made me all the happier.

"That's a wonderful idea." Jack said.

"Oh Maddie! How romantic, honey. I can't wait to start planning it!" Monica jumped up and down. "Lily can be the flower girl!"

I let out a little scream and began jumping, too. Finally Jack pulled Monica away from me and they headed to the front door. "Come on, baby—we have some serious making up to do."

Jack picked up Monica, threw her over his shoulders, and slapped her on the ass.

Monica waved at Cale and me, then gave us two thumbs up and said, "Have fun celebrating!" She laughed as she and Jack made their way out the door.

Cale locked the door behind them and leaned against it.

"Wow. That was emotionally draining," he said.

I nodded. "It really was."

I glanced at the clock—it was after midnight. I pulled the T-shirt I was wearing up and over my head as I made my way to our bedroom. Cale's eyes lit up with desire as he followed me. I unclasped my bra and let it fall to the ground as Cale moaned. I slowly pushed my sweats off and stopped only long enough to kick them to the side. I was so glad I'd put on my new, black lace boy shorts. I might as well not have had panties on—they were totally see-through.

"Maddie, you turn me on with just your innocent smile, but this? This makes me want you, baby. So. Damn. Much.

I smiled and ran my tongue across my teeth as I sashayed into our bedroom. I could hear Cale right behind me. He turned me around and walked me back against the wall.

"Do you know how much you drive me wild?"

I shook my head. "I think you should show me."

It didn't take long for both of us to call each other's names out in pleasure. In bed, Cale pulled me up against him as he drifted off to sleep. I lightly moved my finger in a circle on the top of his hand as I listened to his breathing. I glanced at my engagement ring and smiled.

Finally. I felt like I was home.

37

Cale

"CAN I HELP you, sir?"

I turned to see an older sales lady smiling at me. I glanced back down to the jewelry case. "Um, I'm looking to have something made for my fiancée for Valentine's Day. I also would like something for my daughter."

She smiled bigger. "How old is your daughter?"

"Seven months old," I said with a proud daddy smile.

She chuckled. "I believe I can help you with your fiancée, but your daughter may be a little young."

I laughed. "I was thinking of starting a charm bracelet for her. I was going to give Maddie, my fiancée, both gifts to open."

"Did you have an idea of what you would like to get Maddie?"

I nodded. I reached into my pocket and pulled out the small bag. I set it on the counter and watched as she stared at it. "I'd like to have a necklace made with this in it."

She looked into my eyes and grinned. "Sand and tiny seashells? I take it the beach has a significant meaning for you?"

"Yes, ma'am, it does. I was thinking a small glass container with this inside of it. Do you think she'll like that?"

The woman picked up the bag and examined it. "I think this is one of the most romantic things anyone has done since I've started working here. I think I just fell in love with you."

I threw my head back and laughed. "I'll take that as yes."

"Yes. She is going to love it."

I opened the piece of paper that I'd drawn on at work with the help of James, Maddie's father. He'd left his wife, Nancy, almost a month ago, and I'd never seen a man so happy in my entire life. When he'd seen me doodling in my office, he'd asked what I was doing, then sat down and helped.

"We can certainly make this custom piece for you. Now, lets discuss your daughter. Did you have a charm in mind that you want-ed for her first charm?"

"Yes," I said, placing of the paper down. The saleslady picked it up as I said, "I was wanting this all to be white gold."

She looked up at me. "There are two drawings on here."

I nodded. "The first one is a crown, because Lily is my princess and always will be. The second one is an idea I had for a Mother's Day gift for Maddie." I pointed to my drawing. "That is a mother and father bird sitting on a branch. The small charm dangling down is a baby bird. I'd want the branch to be big enough to add one, maybe two other baby birds. Then the rest of the bracelet will be a charm bracelet for Maddie that I can add to each Mother's Day." I smiled at the saleslady. "So I guess I want three pieces made. I'll just hang onto Maddie's charm bracelet until Mother's Day."

The saleslady glanced back down and looked at my drawing. "You designed this?"

I shrugged. "Well, Maddie's dad, who happens to be my boss, helped me with it."

"I've...it's just...this is so sweet."

I grinned, nodding. "I hope she thinks so. She loves birds. I'm hoping she'll like it."

She smiled bigger and nodded. "Oh, she will. Excuse me for a moment while I run to the back and talk to the master jeweler."

I stood at the counter and waited for her to return when I felt a hand on my arm. I turned to see Monica.

"Tell me you're buying something for my best friend and I won't be forced to kick you in the balls and take pleasure in the pain on your face."

I was stunned into silence. Monica placed her hands on her hip and looked at me like she was my mother, waiting for me to confess what I had done wrong.

The saleslady returned. "Well, it looks like the jeweler can make both of Maddie's gifts, as well as the charm for your daughter."

"That's wonderful," I said. "Can he have the two done in time for Valentine's Day?" I asked as Monica patiently stood there, eavesdropping.

She nodded and gave me a thumbs-up. "He loved the idea of custom work and said he would start as soon as possible to get these done by the end of the week. But we would have to charge extra for rushing them."

I shook the saleslady's hand. "That's completely fine, I understand. You have no idea how happy this makes me."

She slid a piece of paper across the counter and I filled it out as she took the sand and seashells and placed them, along with the drawings, inside a large, clear envelope. She stapled the receipt to the bag and gave me a copy.

"Be sure to leave a good contact number so that we can notify you when these are ready to be picked up."

I slid the paper back to her, thanked her and turned to Monica. She was trying like hell not to smile. "Have coffee with me?" I asked as she smirked.

"You're lucky I like you," she said. "Come on, there is a new, darling little coffee shop that just opened around the corner."

I followed Monica out the door. We walked along in silence until we reached the coffee shop. I ordered a black coffee while Monica ordered a green tea.

"Cale?" Monica asked as we stood in line waiting for our order.

"Yeah?" I turned to look at her. She had tears in her eyes and I felt my heart drop. "What happened? Monica, what's wrong?"

The one tear that quickly escaped her eye had me wanting to track down Jack and beat his ass. If he'd hurt her again, I was going to kill him. Monica and I both startled when the girl behind the counter screamed our names. "Find us a seat," I said to Monica, "and I'll grab these."

Monica found a seat and sat down as she wiped tears from her eyes. A million terrible things were running through my mind.

I set her tea down and smiled weakly at her as I sat down. She looked away and closed her eyes. When she turned back to me, her tears were falling freely. I reached across the table and took her hand in mine.

"Who do I have to kill?"

She let out a chuckle. "No one. I'm sorry. I don't know why I can't keep my feelings under control. It's just, well, I just can't believe it. I mean…"

She was beginning to talk in circles. "Monica, take a deep breath and let it out. I can't understand a damn thing you're saying."

Monica took a deep breath. "Cale, you can't tell anyone. I mean *no one*. If you do I'll hang you from a tree by your nuts and take a baseball bat and beat you like a piñata."

I leaned back some and frowned. "Um…I'm not sure I really want to know now, Monica."

She grabbed my hands, pulling me closer. "Do you swear to keep this between us? I'm freaking the hell out. I'm experiencing emotions I've never experienced before. Do. You. Swear?"

I nodded. I wasn't sure if I feared for my life, or if now I was just curious as hell about what had her acting like this.

"I swear, Monica."

She closed her eyes, smiled and opened them again. Something was different about her. She seemed to be…glowing.

She swallowed and bit her lip before saying, "Cale, I'm two months pregnant."

38

Maddie

I SMILED AS Cale walked through the door. "Hey!" I called out.

He gave me a weak smile. "Oh, um, hey."

From the look on his face, I could tell something was wrong instantly. I stood up and walked over to him, checking on Lily, who was fast asleep in her playpen.

"What's wrong?" I asked as I stood on my toes to kiss him gently on the lips.

"I um...uh...nothing." He looked away and I couldn't help but smile. I used my finger to turn his face back to me.

"You're a terrible liar, Cale Blackwood. Spill it." I raised an eyebrow at him.

He shook his head. "What? No, I mean. I just got done picking out your Valentine's Day gift that's all."

He slipped his hand behind my neck and pulled me in for another kiss. His tongue sought entrance to my mouth and I easily granted it access. Soon, we were both lost in the kiss.

"Maddie, I want you," Cale whispered, his lips caressing the delicate skin behind my ear.

My whole body came to attention as I let him take control. Barely, I said, "Yes."

Cale pulled my shirt up and over my head. In one swift movement, he pushed my bra up and sucked on one nipple while his fingers pulled and twisted the other. I threw my head back and called out Cale's name.

"Maddie, I want to make love you," he said. I wrapped my arms around his neck as he picked me up and carried me to the sofa. "I want to bury myself inside of you and stay there forever."

"Cale," I whispered as I felt the love igniting between us. "I love you so much."

He kissed along my neck and up to my lips, saying, "I. Want. You. So. Badly."

My breathing picked up as Cale pulled off my pants and panties. He slipped his fingers inside of me and I could feel my body pulling him in. It never ceased to surprise me how he made my body come to life. He gently moved his fingers in and out of my wetness as I felt my orgasm begin to build. I grabbed a pillow from the sofa and moaned into it as my orgasm took control of my body. Before I even recovered, I felt Cale push inside of me. Our bodies became one and I dropped the pillow and looked into the eyes of the man I would forever love. Cale moved slowly in and out as I placed my hand on his cheek. He smiled and I felt tears building in my eyes as we experienced this strong emotional connection.

Cale pushed in and moaned as he poured himself into me. "Maddison, I love you so much," he said, and I wrapped my arms tightly around him.

I couldn't say how long we lay on the sofa wrapped up in each other as I watched Lily sleeping soundly.

I ran my finger along Cale's arm and smiled. "So are you going to tell me now what's wrong? I'm pretty sure it has nothing to do with you going and buying a Valentine's Day gift...although I'm curious about that, now."

I felt the vibration in his chest as he laughed. "You know me so well, Maddie. There is nothing I can hide from you."

I laughed and said, "Nope," popping the p.

Cale dragged in a deep breath. As his chest raised, so did my head; it lowered as he breathed all the air out.

"You have to promise not to say a word," he said.

I nodded as I watched Lily's sweet little back move up and down with each breath. "I promise," I said with a wide grin.

"Okay, here goes," he said. "Monica is pregnant."

My smile dropped and held my breath for a second, expecting him to say he was playing a mean joke on me.

"Did you hear me, baby? Monica is two months pregnant."

"What?" I asked. "How? I mean, when did you find out? How did you find out?" I pushed away and jumped up. "Oh my God. No. Please don't tell me she cheated and confided in you. Oh God!" I turned and began pacing, wondering why she'd confide in Cale like that. Wondering if it was someone we knew.

Cale's face dropped as he jumped up and pulled his boxer briefs back on. "What? Wait, Maddie. Calm down for a second. Please, just take a deep breath okay? Monica didn't cheat. The baby is Jack's."

I closed my eyes and shook my head. My mind was running rampant.

"Wait," I said. "So Monica didn't cheat, and it's Jack's baby… but I thought…I thought Jack couldn't…I mean, he said he couldn't have kids."

Cale smiled. "I know. That's what the doctors told him, but Monica said that they are telling her she probably got pregnant on their honeymoon."

I placed my hands over my mouth and attempted to hold back sobs as tears began to roll down my face. Then I dropped my hands and curled my lip. "Wait one minute," I said. "Why the hell would my best friend, who didn't think she would ever be able to get pregnant, tell you about this, and not me?"

Cale laughed as we both turned to Lily, who was now sitting up in her playpen, mumbling, "Dada. Dada. Dadadada."

Cale got dressed and scooped Lily up as I fumbled to get dressed. I hopped on one foot, trying to follow him. As he climbed the stairs, Lily smiled over his shoulder at me.

"Monica saw me in the jewelry store and came in."

I gasped and said, "I'm getting jewelry!"

"Fuck," Cale whispered as he disappeared into Lily's room. I pulled my shirt over my head and took the stairs two at a time.

I leaned against the doorjamb and watched Cale as he talked to Lily.

"How did you sleep, Princess? Did you miss Daddy?"

"Dada. Dadadada," Lily said, giggling.

Cale masterfully changed Lily's diaper and had her dressed within seconds. "Oh my, big girl. Daddy loves you so much." Lily's hair was growing in more and more—I couldn't wait to start putting it in little ponytails. Her blue eyes were beginning to change to a more blue-green color.

I cleared my throat and said, "Jewelry, huh?"

He shrugged and winked at me. "Do you want to know about Monica or your gift?"

"Monica!"

He picked up Lily and said, "So I ran into her and asked if she wanted to get coffee. I knew something was wrong when we walked in silence all the way to the coffee shop. Monica is never quiet. Before I knew it, she was breaking down crying and I was thinking the worst. I was ready to kick Jack's ass. Then she just busted out with the pregnancy news."

I put my hand over my mouth and shook my head. "Oh my gosh! How, though? When did she find out?"

"She'd just found out. I think that's why she was so emotional and couldn't hold it in," Cale said. "She had to tell someone. She wants to tell Jack before everyone else, but she honestly just seemed shocked. She asked her doctor how this could happen when Jack's doctors told him it was nearly impossible to conceive."

I wiped my tears away and asked. "What did they tell her?"

The smile that spread across Cale's face made me smile bigger.

"The doctor told Monica that nothing is impossible. Miracles happen every day."

I reached out for Lily as she began saying, "Mama."

"A truer statement could never be said," I sighed.

Cale kissed Lily on the cheek and then kissed me gently on the lips. "When can we try for our little miracle?"

My stomach dropped and my heart began beating harder in my chest. Carrying Cale's child was something I couldn't wait to make a reality. I held Lily closer. Having Cale's child would round out our little family. I would finally feel whole. I knew it was silly to feel this way. I just didn't feel like I was…complete.

I sighed and said, "I'd like to at least wait until we get closer to the wedding before we start trying. If that's okay with you?"

Cale's eyes lit up. I wondered briefly if it was the idea of the two of us making a child together. Lily would forever and always be my daughter, but I wasn't really her mother. No matter how much I tried to move on from that fact, I just couldn't. At least not yet. Zoey still held that one last thing over me.

Cale placed his hand on my cheek and smiled so tenderly. I'd never experienced the kind of love I felt with Cale. I fell more and more in love with him every day.

"Of course it's okay, Maddie," he said. "I'm ready whenever you are, baby."

I licked my lips as his eyes traveled down to my lips and he smiled. He leaned down and kissed me as Lily started laughing. Cale and I both chuckled as he took Lily from my arms.

"You want to go to JJ's for dinner tonight?"

I nodded and said, "Yes! I think Lily will love feeding the fish."

The rest of the day was spent at JJ's. By the time we made it back home, Lily was exhausted, so she went to bed earlier than normal. I was about to open up a bottle of wine when the doorbell rang. I set the wine down and walked to the door. When I opened it, my mouth dropped to the ground—Andre was standing there.

I tried to speak, but nothing came out. He smiled and looked me over from head to toe. "Bella," he said. "I've missed you so much."

I glared at him. "What are you doing here, Andre?"

His smile faded, his eyes turning from happy to angry in an instant. "I came to see if you were done playing house yet. I want you back."

I looked behind me, then turned and pushed him on the chest to back him up. I stepped outside and shut the door.

"Are you kidding me? Really? You have the nerve to show up on my fiancés doorstep and ask me something like that?" I asked. "I love Cale. I've always loved him and I will always love him. Now, if you don't mind, I'm asking you to please leave and never contact me again. I'm happy. Very happy and very much in love."

Andre looked over my shoulder. I turned to see Cale standing in the doorway. "I think you heard the lady," he said. "Leave."

Andre stood up taller and smirked at Cale. "I walked away from you once before, Bella, without a fight. I've returned to claim what is rightfully mine." He glanced over to Cale. "Fiancé or not."

My mouth dropped open as I stood there in a stupor.

"I thought maybe all you needed was time, so I gave that to you. I'm tired of waiting. I can give you…" Andre gestured toward Cale. "I can give you what he can't."

I closed my eyes. I couldn't believe this was happening. When I felt Cale push past me, I knew things were about to turn ugly. I opened my eyes as Cale grabbed Andre and pushed him against the side of the house.

"You motherfucker," Cale said. "You have some damn nerve showing up at my house and talking to my fiancée like this. I'm only going to tell you one time—stay the hell away from Maddie. If I so much as see you step a foot onto my property, I will beat your ass all the way back to New York."

Andre's breathing had picked up. I couldn't move. I finally got my wits together and walked up and grabbed Cale. "Cale, please, just let him go. It's not worth it."

I gave Cale a pleading look. He let go of Andre with a forceful push. He took a few steps back as Andre fixed his ruffed-up jacket.

"Andre," I said. "I thought I made it very clear to you about my feelings for Cale."

"We had something special, Bella. Do you not remember our time together in Italy?"

I felt my face flush. I didn't want Andre talking about us being together in front of Cale. "That's all in the past. I'm where I belong, Andre. I'm home. I'm in love with Cale; I've always been in love with him."

He shook his head and looked at Cale and then back to me. His eyes weren't filled with sadness, but with anger. I don't think Andre was used to not getting his way.

He held up his hands and made a face. "Fine. If this is what you really want, Maddison, then I will turn and walk away. Just know that if I leave, this is it."

"Oh, for the love of God. Do you not hear what she's saying, asshole?" Cale shouted.

I had to admit I never thought I'd deal with Andre again. In that moment, I wondered what I'd ever seen in him in the first place. He was arrogant, conniving, and selfish.

"Goodbye, Andre." I said, taking few steps back.

Slowly shaking his head, Andre said, "*Arrivederci*, Maddison." He turned on his heels and walked away.

I shook my head, turning to Cale. "I swear I haven't been in contact with him or anything. I have no idea what would make him just show up like that and—"

Cale quickly kissed me. The kiss was hungry and full of passion. It wasn't long before we were calling out each other's names as Cale exploded inside of me. A big part of me wanted to stop taking my birth control, but I knew it would be best if we waited until after the wedding.

I lay in bed, tangled up in Cale, as I thought about that first night. My mother had said you couldn't fall in love with someone so quickly, but I knew she was wrong. The feelings I'd experienced that night with Cale were magical, mysterious, and powerful. Something

I wasn't sure I would ever be able to explain. Those same feelings were beginning to stir again, but in a very different way. I felt loved, safe, and needed. For the first time in my life, I started to believe that I had finally found that missing piece. Cale was it. I needed him like I needed the air I breathed. That feeling excited and scared me.

Cale began to stir as I slowly slipped out from our web of love. I looked down at him and couldn't help but smile. I loved him, and there is no way I would ever be able to survive a day without him.

39

Cale

JACK SAT OPPOSITE me on the floor, watching Lily. Lily was now attempting to crawl.

Jack sighed. "Dude, she just gets up on all fours and rocks. When is she going to actually move?"

I smiled and shook my head. As soon as I told Jack on the phone that I thought Lily was about to crawl, he made an excuse to hang up, and the doorbell rang ten minutes later. He always acted like he didn't care, but he wanted to be here just as much as Monica did for this moment.

I chuckled and said, "Give her time, she'll do it."

Maddie sat down next to me as Monica joined Jack on the floor. Monica glanced at me and I smiled. She was about to tell Jack she was pregnant. She wanted to do it with all of us there. It meant a lot to her to have Maddie and me there when she told Jack, since we had both been there for them during their rough patch.

"Here's a cookie I helped Maddie make," Monica said as she handed the cookie to Jack. His eyes were focused on Lily, who was staring at him.

"She's eyeing me like she knows something's up." He said as he titled his head and looked at her. He reached for the cookie and looked down at it.

He looked up at me and frowned. "I think this one is for you."

I snapped my head back in surprise and asked. "Why?"

He looked away as he said, "It says 'Congratulations, Daddy.'"

Maddie grabbed my hand as Monica quickly wiped a tear away. I shook my head. "I don't think so. Monica?"

Jack turned to Monica. He dropped the cookie and placed both hands on the sides of her face. "Baby, what's wrong?"

Monica let out a small sob and said, "I made that cookie for you."

Jack looked down at the cookie before grabbing it. He was about to put it in his mouth when Monica and Maddie called out, "No!"

Lily startled, then squealed and giggled.

Jack dropped the cookie again. "Motherfucker. What the hell is wrong with you guys? You scared the shit out of me." He looked back at Monica and used his thumbs to wipe her tears away. "Monica, why are you..."

My heart began to beat faster as I looked at Maddie. Her smile was breathtaking and I knew this moment was big for her.

"Wait," Jack said. "You made that cookie for me?"

Monica nodded and whispered, "Yes. I made another one too."

She reached behind her and handed him another cookie. Jack read the writing on the cookie out loud. "Miracle baby on board..." His head snapped up. "What? I mean...what does this mean? Does this mean...are you?"

Monica began crying harder. "I'm two months pregnant. I'd like to think it happened on our honeymoon."

I watched as tears began to make their way down Jack's face as I fought to keep my own tears at bay.

"Monica! Oh, God." Jack pulled his wife close and they kissed.

I glanced to Lily and saw her inching toward the cookie that Jack had dropped. I nudged Maddie and pointed. "Look! Look at Lily!"

Maddie gasped. "She's crawling! She's crawling."

Jack and Monica stopped kissing, and Jack practically pushed Monica away. "That's right, baby girl. Come to Uncle Jack. Come on. Come on." Jack was clapping his hands as he tried to get Lily to come to him.

Monica snarled, hitting Jack on the arm. "She's not a dog, for Pete's sake." She grabbed the cookie and held it so Lily could see. Lily laughed, turning toward Monica.

"What the hell?" Jack yelled. He grabbed the cookie out of Monica's hand. "Lily, look at what a big girl you are, crawling! Come to Uncle Jack. I have two cookies."

"You prick!" Monica shouted. "Give me that cookie."

I looked at Maddie who was crying as she watched our daughter crawl for the first time. I glanced back and said, "Lily, Daddy has a cookie."

I reached for the cookie Maddie was holding and held it up. Lily stopped and looked at me. She smiled, and all I could see was the two little teeth that had broken through her gums. I couldn't believe how fast she crawled toward me with those blue eyes sparkling.

"Hey! That is totally not fair. She was coming to me first. You cheated!" Jack said.

When Lily crawled up to me and reached for the cookie, I scooped her up and kissed all over her face as she laughed.

Maddie jumped up and clapped and said, "Yay! Look at our big girl!"

Jack and Monica both stared up at us, smiling. I couldn't wait for them to experience all of this with their own child. I smiled at Jack as he nodded.

We spent the rest of the afternoon following Lily around as she crawled everywhere.

I looked over at Maddie and laughed. "Shit. I think our world just changed in a major way."

She giggled and nodded. "I think so too."

"MR. BLACKWOOD?"

I glanced up from my computer to see Katrina, my assistant, smiling at me.

"Yes?" I watched as she moved toward my desk.

I was going to have to talk to her about her work attire. It was getting tighter and tighter. I was pretty sure she didn't have a bra on today—her nipples were showing through her light blouse.

She stopped at my desk and leaned over. "Mr. Powers needs that presentation to be ready first thing in the morning. He asked me to stay late in case you needed anything."

I narrowed my eyes at her, then checked the time. *Fuck.* It was six-thirty already. I picked up my phone to see that I had a few missed texts from Maddie.

Maddie: *Hey! Are you working late tonight? I haven't heard from you all afternoon.*

Maddie: *You must be busy. Lily and I are going to the park with your mother. Call me.*

Maddie: *I'm guessing you're working late. Just gonna make something for me for dinner. Hope everything is okay.*

I ran my hand through my hair and sighed. I can't believe I hadn't even talked to Maddie at all this afternoon. I began typing her back a reply as I talked to Katrina. "Why are you here so late? And why didn't remind me of the time?"

"I knew you had this big presentation, so I just assumed you wanted to be alone to work on it. Then Mr. Powers asked me to stay, too. Would you like some dinner?"

In that moment, my stomach decided to answer for me. Katrina giggled and said, "It's a good thing I ordered Chinese, isn't it?"

I smiled. "Yeah, I guess it is."

Me: *Hey, baby. I'm so sorry, I didn't realize it was so late and my damn phone was on silent from a meeting earlier this morning. Your dad is expecting this presentation first thing tomorrow morning. I'll probably be at least another hour. I'm sorry.*

Maddie: *No worries. I'm just glad everything is okay. I was about to call Daddy.*

Me: *Why didn't you call my office number?*

Maddie: *I did, twice. Your assistant said she gave you the messages, but that you were working on a big presentation.*

I looked toward my office door. *Weird. Katrina never gave me any messages from Maddie.*

Me: *I never got any messages. I think Katrina needs to go. She's still here. Working late.*

Maddie: *Really? I called twice, once just a few minutes ago.*

Me: *I'll take care of it. Give me an hour and I'll be home, baby.*

Maddie: *We'll be waiting. Not sure the princess will be able to hold out that long. Her and Grandma had tons of fun today.*

I smiled as I thought about my mother and Lily playing. My mother had become a new person this year. Something about Lily had changed her, and we had never been closer. My father was happier too.

I looked up to see Katrina walking in. She had taken her hair down and was holding a bag of food. I had to admit—it smelled heavenly.

Me: *I'm glad they had fun. I'll try to hurry. I love you, Maddie.*

More than anything.
    Maddie: *I love you! Please hurry. I have something for you.*
    Me: *I love you, too, baby. I'm counting down the minutes. I'll be as quick as I can.*

She sent a photo, and I waited for it to load. When it did, I about dropped my phone. Maddie was standing naked in front of her full-length mirror. I licked my lips as I thought about all the dirty things I wanted to do to her tonight.

    Me: *Holy shit, Maddie. I'll wrap this up as fast as I can.*
    Maddie: *Don't rush. Just know I'll be waiting for you.*
    Me: *I'll text you when I'm heading home.*
    Maddie: *K!*

"Dinner's ready," Katrina said as she placed everything out on the table, then sat down on the sofa.

I had a huge office. A conference table and eight chairs were on the left side of my office, and a sofa, coffee table, and two chairs sat on the right side. I got up and walked over to the sofa. I was attempting to think of anything besides Maddie's naked picture and my rock-hard dick. I grabbed the food and made my way back to my desk.

"You're not even going to take a break and eat with me on the sofa?" Katrina asked.

I looked over my shoulder at her.

She licked her lips. "It's after hours, so I thought we could be a bit more relaxed."

I turned away from her. "It may be after hours, but we're still working."

I sat and went through the spreadsheets one more time. Everything was pretty much ready to go for the presentation, and I was just double-checking everything before I finished up. Since Katrina was here, I would send the file to James—Maddie's dad—and Katrina could send it to everyone else after she got it all in order. James just needed the data ahead of time. He didn't need it looking all pretty.

I was so deep into the power point that I didn't even notice Katrina get up and approach my desk. She placed her hands on my shoulders and I jumped.

"Relax. Let me take all your tension away, Cale." She messaged my shoulders and brushed her lips against my neck. "I can relax you in so many ways."

I stood and turned to her. "Katrina, I think it's best if you leave for the evening."

She smiled and tilted her head. "Is that what you really want, Cale?"

"It's Mr. Blackwood."

She bit her lip. "I do like a man who is in control."

I stared at her. Was she for real? I picked up my phone called security.

"Good evening, Mr. Blackwood. Is everything okay?"

I shook my head as I watched Katrina start unbuttoning her blouse. I held up my hand to stop her. "Yes. I need you to come to my office ASAP and escort Ms. Miller from the building. She is being terminated as of this moment."

Katrina's mouth gaped open as her hands fell to the side. "What? You're firing me?"

"Yes sir. Sending up Philip now, Mr. Blackwood."

"Thank you." I hung up the phone and walked to the other side of my desk. Turning to Katrina, I said, "I need you to gather your things. Security will be here any minute to escort you from the building.

"But...I thought. You're not interested in me?"

I ran my hand through my hair and shook my head. "I'm very much in love with my wife, and I'm pretty sure I never gave you any indication otherwise."

She quickly began to button her shirt as she headed out of my office, back to her desk. She stopped at my door and turned to me.

"I'm uh…I'm sorry. It's just that most men don't turn me down. Not even the ones who are happily married."

I put my hands in my pockets and looked at her. I felt so sorry for her. She needed to find someone who'd treat her with enough respect that she wouldn't feel like she needed to throw herself at men.

"If a married man slept with you, Katrina, he was not happy in his marriage, and he had zero respect for his wife."

She swallowed hard and headed to her desk. I heard Philip walk into the office and ask if she could hand him her badge.

After Katrina cleaned out her desk and gathered up her items, I walked out as they both made their way to the elevator. She turned to me. "What are you going to say?"

"I'm going to send HR the letter of resignation that you sent to me."

She looked confused, but then it hit her. "Thank you for not… well…you could have said what happened."

"Nothing happened, Katrina. Besides, it wouldn't do you or I any good in spreading it around, would it?"

She shook her head and slowly turned away. I returned to my office and picked up my phone. My first call was to James, and my second was to Maddie to tell her how much I loved her.

40

Maddie

I LOOKED UP from my book as Cale came into the living room. "Rough day?"

He nodded and threw his stuff down on the chair. "I had to fire Katrina tonight."

I sat up and set my Kindle down. "Oh my gosh, why?"

Cale sat down and pushed his hands through his hair. Taking a deep, he said, "She came on to me tonight."

Anger engulfed my body. "She came on to you? Is that why the bitch didn't tell you I called?"

Cale nodded. "I guess."

My voice cracked as I said, "What happened?"

"She didn't bother to tell me you'd called or even that your dad had called. I was so lost in Power Point that I didn't realize how time was flying by. She ordered dinner and brought it into my office and sat on my sofa to eat it. I took it to my desk and, the next thing I knew, she was massaging my shoulders and she…well, she came on to me."

I nodded and stood. "What did you do?" I asked as I sat down on the coffee table directly in front of Cale.

"I called security and had her removed from the premises. Then,

234

I called your dad and told him what had happened. Then I called you to tell you I was on my way home."

I gave him the same look I always gave him when he said something that just tickled me. "And to tell me you love me."

He grinned and pulled me onto his lap. He placed his hand behind my neck and pulled my lips to his. We kissed gently as I laced my arms around his neck.

"Thank you for telling me what happened," I said, looking into his emerald eyes. I couldn't believe how much I loved him. How much I needed to just be near him.

"I'll always be honest with you about everything, Maddie. Always."

I sucked his lower lip into my mouth and gently bit it. Then I stood and began to get undressed. "Make love to me, Cale."

Cale watched as I stripped out of my clothes and walked to our bedroom. He jumped up and tore his own clothes off as he followed me. I lay down on the bed and waited for him to move over me. I cupped his face in my hands and looked deeply into his eyes.

"I don't want to wait, Cale."

The smile that moved across his face told me he knew exactly what I was saying. I wanted to try for a baby. I wanted to feel a child growing in my womb. I wanted to feel *Cale's* child growing in my stomach. I wanted a piece of him.

Cale took my hands in his and pushed them above my head as he gently kissed me. He teased my entrance, building up my anticipation for sweet relief. He released one of my hands and twisted and pulled one nipple as his lips moved to my neck and slowly over to my ear where he sucked my ear lobe, then lightly blew in my ear. I arched my back to him, whispering his name, as he pulled back and looked lovingly into my eyes.

He leaned down and kissed me gently as his hand explored my body, leaving a trail of goose bumps in its path.

I love this man with my whole heart.

He pushed inside me as I moaned. As he gently pumped in and

out of me, we locked eyes. I could feel the love moving between us, and I was overcome with emotion. As a tear slowly made it's way down my cheek, Cale wiped it away with his lips.

"You're mine, Maddison."

I closed my eyes and whispered, "Always."

MAY

"BAH-BAH."

I smiled at Lily and giggled as I held her bottle up for her to see. "You want your bottle, baby girl?"

It was May, and I couldn't believe how big she'd gotten. She threw her hands up and down as she got more excited. "Mama! Bah-bah!"

I handed Monica Lily's bottle and said, "Aunt Monica has your bottle, princess."

Monica sat down as Lily crawled into her lap and settled in. "She's brilliant. You realize your daughter is brilliant don't you?"

I laughed as I sat and watched my two favorite girls. Monica was now five months pregnant, and her baby bump was adorable. A small ripple of jealousy raced through my body. I wasn't pregnant yet, and I was beginning to wonder if the stress of planning our wedding in two and half months had anything to do with me not being able to conceive.

"How've you been feeling?" I asked Monica.

She smiled. "Finally better. The morning sickness has really died down. I feel a little nauseous at night but, other than that, I feel good. We have a sonogram tomorrow."

I smiled and clapped as Lily did the same—Monica was holding Lily's bottle. I laughed and shook my head. "Are you going to find out the sex of the baby?" I asked.

Monica made a funny face, and I could tell she was excited. "I don't want to know," she said, "But I kind of do. Jack totally doesn't want to find out the sex. He says he wants to be surprised. Even if I decide that I want to find out, he still doesn't want to."

I laughed as I pulled my legs up and rested my chin on my knees. I was so happy for my best friend. Who could have known how much would change in a year? Last year her and Jack had just started dating. They'd both been free spirited when it came to dating and sex, but something must have happened that night when they first hooked up. They just fell right into place.

"I'd want to be surprised," I said, looking at Lily. Lily waved, almost as if she knew the silly doubts that were intruding my thoughts. I waved back. Each morning when we walked into her room she would wave and say, "Mama" and "Dada." Cale loved it. He loved Lily so much; I couldn't wait to have another baby. I looked down and sighed.

"It'll happen when it's meant to happen, Maddie," Monica said. "You guys just started trying. Give yourself a break, sweetheart. Just breathe."

The sliding door to the porch opened and Jack and Cale came walking in. They both had their shirts off and I had to ignore the urge between my legs. I licked my lips as I surveyed Cale's body with my eyes. He smiled and winked at me as he walked by, headed for the kitchen.

"Jack and I got the boat and the jet skis ready to go," Cale said.

I rolled my eyes. I hated the jet skis, and I hated the boat. I'd told Cale I wasn't thrilled with the idea of buying a boat, but all he and Jack ever talked about was fishing and waterskiing. They both loved to ski.

"This warm weather has me itching to get out there and ski," Jack said. "What about you, Maddie?" he laughed.

I rolled my eyes and looked back at Monica. I loved living on the lake, but you wouldn't catch me swimming in it. Nope. The moment I felt the little fish nibbling on my legs, I was done. I'd rather float in a pool where I could see what was around me.

"No thanks," I said.

Monica chuckled as she held Lily, who was sitting up and attempting to stand. Lily bounced with excitement in Monica's arms. She'd seen her daddy, and that was what she'd wanted.

Cale came into the living room and kissed me quickly before picking up Lily. "Come on, Princess," he said. "Let's go outside and enjoy the day now that you have a full tummy."

I watched as the two loves of my life walked through the sliding glass door and down the deck stairs, making their way down to the dock.

I turned back to Monica and tilted my head. "Why are you staring at me?"

She shrugged. "I just enjoy seeing you happy."

I smiled and scrunched my nose. "I wouldn't trade any of this. Never."

She stood up and placed her hand on her stomach. "That goes for me, too. Come on, let's go see what the two over-grown boys are up to."

MY PHONE VIBRATED in my pocket as I looked up from my Kindle. I was working in the library, but I'd tucked myself away in a corner to sneak in a bit of reading. I was reading one of my favorite series, the *Remembrance* trilogy, and Ryan was about to make me moan internally and wish for Cale's touch. I pulled my phone out. It was a text from Monica.

Monica: *Sonogram went great. I decided to not find out, but my husband broke down at the last minute and told them he wanted to know.*

I giggled and shook my head. I could totally see Jack changing his mind when he saw the baby on the screen.

Me: *LOL! Did you stay strong?*
Monica: *No!*
Me: *So?*
Monica: *So???*
Me: *Oh my gosh! Monica. Are you having a boy or a girl?*
Monica: *We'll tell y'all at dinner tonight. JJ's sound good?*
Me: *So wrong. So wrong on so many levels. Fine. JJ's at six.*
Monica: *Perfect! See ya then!*

I sent Cale a text letting him know that we were having dinner with Jack and Monica to find out the sex of the baby was.

Cale: *Sounds good. Miss your touch. See you soon!*
Me: *Same here. More than you know. Love you, see ya soon.*

I closed my eyes and thought back to last night when Cale and I had been alone. Mary had asked to keep Lily for the night, and Cale and I had jumped all over the chance to be by ourselves. I chewed on my lip as I thought about how hot it had been.

CALE HAD BEEN working with Jack most of the day getting the boat ready for summer when my father called and asked him to join a meeting. Cale had been on vacation, but he'd drop anything if my father asked—which was why my father hardly ever asked.

I'd been in the kitchen when saw him standing there, naked. The only thing he'd kept on was his tie. I couldn't believe how incredibly turned on I'd been at that sight.

I'd sent him a text saying his mother had picked up Lily for the evening and Cale had texted back to say that the meeting was over and he was on his way home. Monica and Jack had left with Mary, and I'd been cooking dinner. My cooking had improved as I'd branched out to try more things. Tonight was homemade sauce and pasta.

It was warm out, so I'd changed into a light summer dress. I'd been so glad I was wearing my new light blue lace bra and panties. Cale would go nuts when he saw them. He grabbed my breasts as he moaned.

"You look beautiful in this dress." He'd whispered, placing his lips on my neck.

"Um, thank you," I'd whispered back, my libido quickly took over. I'd begun to lose all my senses—except for my desire for Cale.

"Maddie," he'd said. "I'm going to make love to you all night. But, right now, I really want to fuck you, baby."

I'd dropped the pasta spoon to the floor.

"Yes," I'd said, flinging my head back. "Oh, God, yes." I'd whimpered as he'd pulled my dress up, pushing my bra down. My breasts had spilled out, and he'd taken a nipple into his mouth as I'd

grabbed onto the tie and called out his name. With my other hand, I'd held on to the counter. I'd always loved it when Cale was gentle and sweet, but sometimes I just wanted to be fucked senseless—he never disappointed me with that.

"Cale, I want you so badly. Please don't tease me," I'd said.

Cale's fingers had brushed across the light lace of my panties over and over as he'd sucked and gently bitten my nipple.

"What do you want, Maddie?"

"You," I'd panted.

He'd sucked hard on my nipple and used his other hand to rip off my panties, making me cry out. I'd hooked my leg around him as he'd pushed his fingers inside me.

"Jesus," he'd said. "You're so fucking horny."

He'd lifted me up and impaled me with his rock-hard dick as I'd screamed out, "Fuck me, Cale. Fuck me hard!"

"MS. POWERS? IS everything okay?"

I was snapped out of my sexy memory by the voice of the head librarian. I placed my hand on my cheek to attempt to hide the fact that I had just been daydreaming about being fucked and was turned on beyond belief.

"Uh, yes. I'm fine," I said. "It's a little hot in here don't you think?"

"Why are you in this corner?" she asked.

"I, um…I was just taking a break. I'm not feeling, um, quite myself right now."

She smiled sweetly and nodded. "I see. Well, darling, if you're not feeling well, head on home. I know Cale is off this week. Go spend some time with him."

I nodded and grinned. "You're absolutely right. I should totally go home and spend some time with him. We have some wedding details to discuss."

I gathered up my purse and sent Cale a text.

Me: *I'm heading home. Be prepared for a repeat of last night!*

41

Cale

I GLANCED DOWN at Maddie's text and wanted to moan. Memories of last night flooded my head. I had to bite the inside of my cheek to keep my dick from getting hard.

"Cale? Honey, are you listening to me?"

I jerked my head up and looked at my mother. She'd brought Lily home early this morning, since she'd had a business lunch with my father and a few of his associates. She hardly ever did that sort of thing anymore, but this was for a charity that was close to her heart—she wanted to make sure everything was set and ready to go.

I tried to look innocent and said, "Yeah, sorry, Mom. I was thinking about something."

She reached down to kiss Lily goodbye. Lily had been racing all over in her walker, and I knew that at naptime she was going to be out.

"I can't believe in less than two months our princess is going to be one," Mom said.

I laughed and nodded. "I know. Maddie is already making plans for the birthday party. I think she even ordered the cake already."

A look of pride washed over my mother's face. "I just adore Maddie," she said. A girl after my own heart. Marry her quickly before she gets away."

I laughed as I stood and jumped out of Lily's way as she raced by. I followed my mother as she made her way to the front door.

"Be sure to tell Maddie to give me a call," she said. "I want to help with all the birthday plans. And we still have to shop for a wedding dress. I've never known a girl to wait until the last minute to buy a dress. She was more worried about Lily's dress than hers. Monica is planning a surprise shower this weekend, so don't make plans, darling."

She raised her hand as she walked ahead of me. I smiled and shook my head. Sometimes the old Mom still showed through.

"I'm hosting it, so come up with something grand to do with Jack and Lily."

"Will do," I said. "Thanks for taking Lily last night, Mom. It was nice to be able to spend some time with Maddie."

She opened the front door and spun around with a huge smile on her face. "Oh, believe me, son—I know all about those moments."

My smiled dropped and my stomach turned. "Yuck. That was just gross mom. Did you have to give me that visual?"

She threw her head back and laughed before turning around on her heels and heading to her car. I shouted at her as she retreated away. "I can tell you what we did last night, Mom, if you want!"

She opened her car door and turned to look at me. "Doesn't phase me son...does not phase me at all. Love you!"

She got in, shut the door and took off. Lily rammed into the back of my legs over and over, in her attempt to get out the door. I turned and smiled down at her. "Legs up, princess! Daddy is going to spin you around. Let's head to the kitchen and make Mommy and us some lunch."

"Mama!" Lily screamed.

"Yep, Mommy is on her way home."

Twenty minutes later, Maddie walked into the kitchen. She leaned over and kissed Lily on the cheek, then smelled Lily's hair. I smiled as I watched her do the same thing she had done since the first time she held Lily in her arms.

Maddie looked up at me and gave me a smile that made me weak in the knees. *I wonder if she knows how much she means to me? How she lights up the entire space around me with her smile.*

"Hey," she said with a wink. "I was hoping to beat your mom home so we could have a repeat of last night."

I pulled her close to me. I slipped my hand up her skirt and pushed her panties out of the way as I buried my fingers inside of her.

"Cale, Lily is right…oh God…"

She was soaking wet. "Are you in need of some relief?" She bit down on her lip and nodded. I pulled my fingers out of her and turned around. I moved Lily's high chair so she was looking out the window to outside.

I spun back around and grabbed Maddie, turning her around and pushing her over the table as I unzipped my pants and began stroking my dick. "Fuck, Maddie."

She looked over her shoulder. "Okay," she said. "Sounds good."

I pushed myself into her, grabbing her hips as I fucked her hard and fast from behind. Maddie held onto the table and met me stroke for stroke as I pulled out and slammed back into her.

"Cale," she called out as I felt her tighten up around my dick. I was about to explode inside her when I heard Lily mumbling. I shook my head to clear my thoughts. Maddie reached down and began playing with her clit as she called out my name.

"Fuck yes. Maddie, I'm going to come."

Maddie was moaning incoherently as I moved in and out of her. My orgasm hit me hard, and I hoped like hell that—either last night or today—we had made a baby. I'd fucked Maddie last night hard and fast, but we'd also made love twice during the night—once in the shower, and then at four a.m. when Maddie crawled on top of me. Nothing felt as amazing as being one with her. But this…this was just sexy as hell, and I knew she loved it as much as I did.

"Birda…"

I closed my eyes and let every ounce of my cum spill into Maddie's body. I wanted nothing more than to give her the one thing I knew she wanted. A part of me. A baby. *Our* baby.

"Oh God, Cale that was amazing." Maddie said as I pulled out and grabbed a dishtowel to clean us up.

I wanted more of her. I wanted to taste her, but I wasn't sure how she'd feel about me doing that after what we'd just done. I dropped to the ground and began wiping her off. I lifted her leg more and placed it over my shoulder. One swipe of my tongue and she grabbed fistfuls of my hair and moaned. Soon she was riding out her orgasms against my tongue as she mumbled my name over and over.

"Birda…"

"What did you say, Cale?" Maddie panted. "I'm still trying to recover from one of the most mind-blowing orgasms ever."

I stood and smiled as I zipped my pants. I turned and washed my face off and leaned against the counter as I stared at Maddie. She was about to say something when Lily laughed and pointed to the window.

"Birda. Dada…birda."

My mouth dropped open and I looked back at Maddie.

"Oh my God," Maddie said. "Oh my God. Did she just say bird? Oh God, Cale. She said her first word while we were…" Her eyes widened in horror. "What kind of parents are we? We were…" she looked around and then back at me as she whispered, "We were fucking…while our daughter said her first word!"

I laughed and pulled Maddie close. "We are parents who are very much in love, and we're hot for each other. Does it suck that she said her first word while we were doing it? Yeah, maybe. But she said *bird*, baby. Not fuck."

Maddie slapped me and pushed me away, then turned Lily's highchair back around.

"That's right, baby girl," she said, pointing to the window. Maddie had put birdfeeders all around our house. "That *is* a bird! Good girl. Say 'bird.'"

Lily smiled her big, adorable smile and flailed her arms. "Birda!"

I sat next to Lily. "Bird. Say 'bird' for Daddy." Lily's hair was starting to get lighter and curlier, but her blue eyes seemed to be fading to a blue-green. When Lily's eyes met mine, something happened. It was as if she was looking into my soul. No one other than Maddie would ever make me feel the way Lily does.

She giggled and then said, "Dada…bird."

MADDIE CARRIED LILY as we walked up to the table where Jack and Monica were sitting. "Hey guys!" Jack said as he pulled out the highchair for Lily. Of course the big fabric thing had to go in first, but not until Monica wiped it down with antibacterial wipes.

Once Lily was settled with a bunch of Cheerios, Maddie and I sat down. We both looked at Jack and Monica. They just stared back at us, smiling.

"Well?" I asked.

Monica shrugged. "Well, what?"

Maddie sighed in frustration. "Don't play games. Boy or girl?"

Jack took a deep breath and said, "Both."

I stared at him. "Huh? What, do you have a mutant growing in ya?"

Maddie giggled, then said, "No."

Monica smiled and nodded. "Yes."

Maddie and Monica both jumped up and squealed as they jumped up and down. Lily got in on the action and tossed a handful of Cheerios in the air. I looked around at everyone, but couldn't figure out what in the hell was going on.

I looked at Jack, confused, as he laughed.

"Twins, dude. We're having twins."

I stood and reached across the table to grab my best friend.

"Congratulations, Jack. I'm so damn happy for you."

He pulled back and blinked his tears away. "It's a miracle." He shook his head. "It's a double miracle."

42

Maddie

WHEN MARY AND Monica walked into L'Fay Bridal, I stood outside the door feeling panicky. I couldn't believe I'd let them talk me into flying to New York City for a damn wedding dress. The Berta dress I'd found in a magazine was perfect, and Monica had made it her goal to get me that dress. I would have married Cale in a paper sack, to be honest. This whole show of buying a dress was just not me.

I pushed the doors open and walked into the ultra-modern boutique. The wood floors and white furniture made me want to take off my shoes and not touch a thing.

By the time they pulled the dress down and ushered me into the changing room, I was in a full-out panic attack. *I hate doing this kind of thing.*

"Deep breaths, Maddie. It's not that big of a deal."

My best friend was smiling as she rested her hands on her six-months-swollen belly. I shook my head.

"Monica. We've flown to New York City to look for a stupid dress I saw in a magazine. Do you know how much I could have saved by just buying something local?"

Monica shrugged and pushed me into the changing room. "Stop

being such a whiney bitch and try the damn dress on."

I forcefully pulled the curtains shut and turned to look at the breath-taking lace dress hanging before me. Stripping out of my clothes, I slipped on the dress. I looked at myself and gasped. I looked beautiful. Really, the dress looked beautiful. It fit me like it had been made for me. I turned slightly to see the sexy, low back. "Oh my," I whispered.

It barely covered anything—if it went down another inch, you'd see ass cleavage. The train hung low, adding just the right touch. The dress was romantic, sexy, and still classic looking. I pushed the curtain open. Monica and Mary both sat on a white bench talking to Suzie, the bridal consultant who was helping us. She was a tiny little thing. I bet she wasn't even five feet tall. Her dark, bouncy curls and dark-framed glasses matched her spunky personality. The three of them all looked up and stopped talking.

Suzie smiled and adjusted her glasses. "That is the dress, Maddison. The way it fits your body is perfect." She turned to Monica and Mary. "Ladies, don't you agree? This dress was meant for her."

Mary wiped a tear away. Monica grinned from ear to ear and cleared her throat. I knew she was choked up.

"You look beautiful, Maddie." Monica said. "Just beautiful."

I looked down at the dress and I chewed on my lip. I peeked back up and asked, "Yeah? You think so? Do you think Cale will like it?"

I picked up the train and turned around slowly. When they saw the back, Mary and Monica both gasped. My nerves were finally settling. It appeared I'd found my dress.

"Holy shit. I can practically see your ass! Cale is gonna faint." Monica said, fanning herself.

Mary giggled and said, "If you aren't already pregnant, you will be by the end of your wedding night."

I felt a blush moving across my cheeks as I looked down at Suzie. She winked and said, "It's perfect."

I nodded and said, "I'll take it."

Monica skipped and did a little fist pump. "Yes! Now let's go have lunch. I'm starving, and these babies must be having a rolling over contest in here."

We spent the rest of the afternoon discussing the details of the wedding. It was going to be small, very small. Only family and close friends. Craig and Diane, Jack's parents, had done an amazing job having an arch built for the beach.

I'd turned fifty shades of red when Cale said he wanted the arch to placed in specific location on the beach. My heart soared when he pulled me to him and whispered in my ear, "This is the exact location I first claimed you as mine." It took everything out of me not to beg him to take me again, right there on the spot.

"Is everything ready for Lily's party?" Mary asked.

I took a sip of tea and nodded. "Yep. I ordered the cake months ago. All the decorations are set and ready. Did Mitchel order the bouncy house?"

Mary rolled her eyes. Cale's father, Mitchel, had insisted on a bouncy house. Lily wouldn't be able to go in it without one of us with her, so I figured Mitchel secretly was using Lily's birthday as an excuse to get one.

"Yes, the damn thing was ordered weeks ago." Mary said, sighing.

Monica and I giggled, but Mary said, "Don't laugh, your father got all excited about it, too."

I almost choked on my tea as I busted out laughing. "Did you know Daddy has been dating?"

Mary waved me off like what I'd just said was old news. "Please, I set them up."

I gasped as Monica leaned in closer and said, "Do tell, Mary. Do tell."

She wrinkled her nose and said, "Well, I had a friend who just moved here from LA. She went through a terrible divorce a year ago. Her ex was starting to call and show up at her house, so she decided she needed some time away from California. She used to be a teacher, years ago, so I talked her into applying at the university. She got hired and she is loving it. She's also loves dating your father." She wiggled her eyebrows.

Who is this person sitting before me? The older Lily got, the more relaxed Cale's parents became. They'd even bought tickets for a train ride across Canada to celebrate their anniversary.

I rolled my eyes and looked away. "Gross."

My mother popped into my head and I was momentarily saddened by her not being with us. I pulled out my phone and went to send her a text message. She hadn't responded yet to the wedding invitation. Daddy hadn't wanted me to invite her, but I just couldn't do that. I didn't invite her to Lily's birthday party, though.

I looked closer at my phone.

Mrs. Jones: *Please contact me as soon as possible.*

I had a text from Zoey's mother. My heart pounded and I instantly felt sick. Why was she texting me? Why did she want me to contact her?

"Maddison? Honey, is everything okay?" Mary asked as she reached for my hand.

I felt tears building in my eyes as I looked up at her. "It's Zoey's mother. She wants me to call her."

Mary's face dropped. She reached for my phone. "What? Let me see that." She read the text, then took a screen shot of it and sent it to someone before picking up her own phone and making a call.

"Mitchel? I just sent you a screen a shot of a text that was sent to Maddison's phone. Okay, good. Call Jonathon and have him get on it. Yes. I know."

Monica looked just as confused as I was. I couldn't help but wonder why Mary was having Mitchel call their lawyer?

Mary handed my phone back to me as she continued to talk to Mitchel.

"What's going on, Maddie?" Monica asked.

I shook my head and whispered, "I don't know."

My phone rang and I jumped. I looked down to see it was Cale. I answered. "Hello?"

"Maddie? I need you to come home. Right away."

I jumped up, making the table jerk. Everyone looked over at us. "What? Why? What's wrong with Lily?"

"Nothing's wrong with Lily. It's Zoey's mother. She just served me with legal papers. They are seeking joint custody of Lily."

My entire world stopped. There was no way in hell I was letting that vile woman anywhere near my daughter.

CALE TOOK MY hand as we sat in the conference room full of lawyers. My father had his lawyers present. Mitchel had his lawyers, and Zoey's parent's had their lawyers.

Daddy's top lawyer stood up and faced Mr. and Mrs. Jones. "We are more than ready to take this to court. You have had zero contact with Mr. Blackwood since the death of your daughter. You've made no contact whatsoever to even try to see your grandchild. For you to approach my clients and say you want joint custody of her is insane. There is no judge on this planet who will even entertain this petition."

I swallowed hard as Cale squeezed my hand. Zoey's parents leaned over to listen to something their lawyer was whispering. He seemed totally caught off-guard when it was revealed that neither of Zoey's parents had ever laid eyes on Lily.

Mrs. Jones leaned back and shot me a dirty look. I smiled politely and she turned away. Their lawyer stood up and cleared his throat.

"My clients are willing to let the petition go, for now. They would, however, like to be a part of Lily's life.

Cale and I both said, "No," at the same time. Mrs. Jones snapped her head back and the look she gave me actually caused me to shudder.

"We have every right to see her." Zoey's mom said. I stood up and glared at her.

"How long did she have colic?" I asked.

Mrs. Jones looked at me like I was nuts. "Excuse me?"

"When did she cut her first tooth, or run her first fever? Does she like carrots? What was the first word she ever said? Has she taken her first steps yet? What's her favorite thing to have in her cereal? When she fusses at night, what settles her down?"

Mrs. Jones' mouth dropped open, but nothing came out. Zoey's father hung his head down, not even bothering to look at me.

"You can't answer a single one of these questions," I said, "because for the last year you have had zero contact with her. None."

The woman narrowed her eyes at me and slammed her hand down on the table, making me jump. "You. Are. Not. Her. Mother."

Cale went to stand, but I put my hand on his shoulder. I shook my head. "I'm more of a mother to her than you would ever be. Even if Zoey *were* alive, you and I both know she'd never have stayed. She'd have left Cale and gone back to her single, carefree life."

Mrs. Jones stood up. "You don't know that."

"She didn't even think Lily would live. She never even bothered to set up the nursery. She didn't buy a single thing for Lily. Not even a crib. You know, you weren't even around when your daughter was pregnant. You abandoned her, just like you abandoned Lily the day she was born."

Mrs. Jones squared her shoulders and held her head higher. "Well, I'm ready to be here for my granddaughter now. You are *not* her mother. You will *never* be her mother."

I locked eyes with her. I was not backing down from this fight. Lily was my daughter, and I would stop at nothing to keep this woman away from her.

I laughed gruffly, looking down at Mr. Jones. I had the feeling he wanted nothing to do with this fight. Why Zoey's mother had decided to pull this shit now was beyond me.

"I'm going to find out why the hell you are suddenly so interested in our daughter. And, as far as me not being Lily's mother, and you getting visitation rights? You can go fuck yourself."

I pushed my chair back and walked out of the room. My hands were shaking and I felt sick to my stomach. I covered my mouth and made a beeline for the restroom.

After I threw up everything in my stomach, I sat down, finally letting my tears fall.

"I'll never let her have my daughter. *Never.*" I whispered.

43

Cale

I PACED BACK and forth outside the bathroom door. I was about ready to go in when Maddie came out. I quickly pulled her into my arms. When she broke down in tears, I wanted to go back and pound the shit out of Zoey's mother. I had never hated anyone in my entire life, but I hated that woman with everything I had.

"Shh, baby, don't worry. They have no legal rights to her."

"Surely no judge in their right mind would grant her anything. Right?" she said.

I held her tight. "No, with zero contact, there is no way. Dad seems to think there is something else fueling Zoey's mother. Whatever it is, we are going to find out and put a stop to it so she never bothers us again. The lawyers are also drawing up the papers to have you legally adopt Lily."

Maddie wiped her eyes and looked up at me. Her beautiful, green eyes were so bloodshot from crying, and mascara streaked down her face. It broke my heart. "Come on," I said. "Let's go home and see our daughter."

She slipped her arm around my waist as we walked out of the courthouse. I glanced over and nodded at my father's lead council. He smiled and gave me a thumbs-up. I'd given him the phone number to Jack's private investigator. I knew that guy would get to the bottom of this. There had to be a reason Zoey's parents were showing up out of blue.

We'd driven in silence for twenty minutes when I finally asked Maddie a question. "Did you find your dress?"

For the first time since she'd flown in yesterday, she smiled. "I did," she said, wiggling her eyebrows. "And I'm pretty sure you are going to faint when you see it."

I raised an eyebrow. "Really? Will I want you out of it?"

She nodded and giggled. "I even know what I'm wearing underneath it."

I felt my pants getting tighter and I adjusted my growing dick. "Damn it, Maddie. You're going to make me pull over and take you in the car."

She laughed. "I like that you get so horny for me," she said. "Just so you know, I don't plan on wearing any panties when we get married. I want you to think about me wet for you during the entire ceremony and reception."

I hit the brakes and quickly pulled down a side dirt road.

"Where are we going, Cale?" Maddie asked, laughing.

I had no clue where the hell I was going. I drove a bit further until I saw another small road. Turning, I drove about a mile. I parked, jumped out and walked to Maddie's side where I opened her door and pulled her out.

"Cale, we are on someone's property, what are you doing?"

I unzipped my pants and pulled them down as I reached up her dress. I yanked her lace panties and they fell apart in my hand. I loved that she wore such delicate panties.

She smiled and placed her hands on my shoulders. I knew that Maddie loved it when we made love—slow and sweet. But I also knew she loved when we did things like this—spontaneous, raw, passionate sex.

Picking her up, I placed my dick at her entrance. She dropped her head back and moaned as I entered her. I pushed her against the car, taking us to heaven and back.

MADDIE WALKED THROUGH the door and into the kitchen. Monica looked up and smiled. "How did it go?"

"She's such a bitch." Maddie said, whispering the word "bitch." Continuing, she said, "I hate her. She's never going to get within a foot of Lily."

Maddie picked up Lily, who smiled and said, "Mama, bird!"

Maddie walked to the sliding glass door and out onto the deck. She was smiling as she talked to Lily and pointed up to the birds. She sang to her as she danced with Lily.

I let out a long sigh and turned to Monica. "Jesus, I hate to see Maddie so upset. But, I have to tell you, I almost yelled out, 'Hell, yeah' when Maddie told Zoey's mother to fuck off."

Monica covered her mouth as she started to laugh. Jack came over and slapped me on the back. "I always did like that girl".

I threw my head back and laughed.

"How about some dinner?" Monica asked as she stopped and put her hand on her stomach. "Oh God…Oh God…"

Jack and I both looked at her and said, "What?"

Jack rushed to her and said, "What's wrong, Monica? What's the matter?"

She looked down—something was moving across her stomach.

"Holy shit," I said as I walked over and placed my hand on her stomach. I looked at Jack as Monica grinned from ear to ear.

"What was that?" Jack asked.

Monica laughed. "I don't know. Maybe a tiny foot or something? Oh, shit. One of them is kicking big time." She grabbed both our hands and placed them under her stomach. Sure enough, someone was going to town in there.

"God, this is the most amazing thing ever," I said.

Jack nodded. "These are the greatest moments of my life. Nothing like feeling your child moving inside your wife's body."

I looked to my right and saw Maddie standing there, holding Lily. She was staring at us, as we had our hands on Monica's belly. She had a wounded expression on her face.

"The um…the babies were really kicking," I said, facing her.

She smiled slightly as she nodded and set Lily down.

"Look," she whispered as she let go of Lily's hands.

Lily wobbled for a few seconds before she started walking toward me. I dropped to the ground and held out my hands as she walked right into my arms. I held her as Maddie clapped and praised Lily. I glanced back up and saw tears in Maddie's eyes. Monica and Jack started clapping as Lily clapped and, yelled out, "Bird!"

I WALKED OUT of the bathroom to find Maddie already asleep in bed. I'd wanted to talk to her all evening. I wasn't sure if she'd been happy about Lily walking, or upset about Monica and the babies. I couldn't read her, but I knew something was off. Monica had told me that Maddie was starting to worry because she hadn't gotten pregnant yet. As much as I reassured her, she still seemed to be falling deeper into a depression.

I crawled under the covers and pulled her body into mine. She mumbled something as I kissed her shoulder. "I love you, Maddie," I said. "I'll love you and Lily for as long as I live."

When she rolled over, her green eyes looked so sad. "What if I never get pregnant?" she asked.

"Maddie, you have to stop stressing. Please. It will happen when it's meant to. Let's get through Lily's birthday and the wedding. Then we'll have our honeymoon. A week alone. We'll do nothing but relax and try to make a baby."

She gave me a weak smile. "What if—"

I placed my finger to her lips. "Shh. Stop thinking that way. Now, I need you to do me a favor."

She nodded. "Anything."

"Let me make love to you."

She sat up and pulled her T-shirt over her head as she crawled on top of me and rocked against my dick. I rolled her over and placed her hands over her head as I pushed myself into her and began to slowly make love to her. We didn't need to say anything. Just gentle kisses and one whispered I love you as we both came together. My body was overcome with so much love. Soon I would be marrying the woman of my dreams.

44

Maddie

JULY

LILY'S BIRTHDAY HAD finally arrived. I laughed as I watched my father and Mitchel, Cale's father argue over whose turn it was to take Lily back into the bouncy house. I called to them both, "She's going to get sick if you guys keep bouncing her around like that!"

My father turned and waved, like I didn't know what I was talking about. I laughed and turned my attention to Cale. Biting my lip, I placed my hand on my stomach. I couldn't wait to be alone with him. I'd wanted to talk to him as soon as I got home from my doctor's appointment this morning, but everyone was around.

I closed my eyes and thought back to when I received the best news of my life.

MY DOCTOR HAD just walked into the room and given me a sweet smile. Internally, I'd rolled my eyes, thinking she was about to tell me I had the flu. I didn't have time to have the flu. I had a birthday party today and a wedding next week.

"I knew it, I have the flu. Shit. Can you give me something to make me feel better? Oh, God. What if Lily gets sick before the wedding? We won't be able to go on the honeymoon."

Doctor Jacobs laughed, as she sat down and shook her head. "I don't think you have to worry about any of that, Maddie. You don't have the flu."

I looked at her, confused. "What's wrong then? Can you give me something to make me feel better?"

She inhaled quickly and let the breath out just as fast. "I'm afraid not."

The nurse had walked in and smiled, setting down a plastic bin that had a needle and two vials in it. "What are you doing?" I asked.

"Taking your blood," she replied.

I turned my head quickly and looked at Doctor Jacobs. "Oh, God. Do you think something is wrong with me? Why is she taking blood?"

Doctor Jacobs stood up and walked over to me and placed her hand on my arm. "Calm down, Maddie. Everything is fine. I'm having her drawn blood to double-check the results from your urine sample."

My heart dropped. "What kind of results?"

She smiled bigger and tilted her head as she looked at me like I had just said the sweetest thing ever. "A positive pregnancy result."

I let out a breath. "Oh...that's it." I closed my eyes and then snapped them open again. "Wait, what?"

"Congratulations, Maddie. You're pregnant."

I JUMPED WHEN I felt someone touch the side of my face. I looked up and was greeted by the most beautiful green eyes.

"Jack and I are headed out on the boat with a few others. We're gonna get in some knee-boarding and skiing. You wanna come?"

I looked back at my father and Cale's father. They were taking turns bouncing with Lily. I smiled and shook my head. "Nah, y'all have fun. But don't stay out there too long. We're going to be singing 'Happy Birthday' to Lily soon, and cutting the cake. She's going to be really tired, and I don't want her staying up too late especially since she's missing a nap today."

Cale leaned down and kissed me on the lips. I loved how gentle his kisses were. At the same time, they were so powerful.

"Okay," he said. "We'll just do a few rounds. I love you, Maddie. You look so beautiful and happy today, baby."

I placed my hand on his cheek. "I love you, too. When we get a moment to be alone, I have something important to tell you."

He stood up, concerned. "Do you want to talk now?"

I chuckled. "No, it can wait until after everyone leaves and we're alone."

He tilted his head and asked, "Are you sure?"

I stood and placed my hand on his chest. "I'm positive. Go have fun, but be careful."

He took my face gently and gave me a quick kiss. "Always, baby. Always."

He turned and jogged down to the dock. The way our house sat on the lake, we had a flat area just above the dock where we were having the party. The bouncy house was set up next to the new swing set that Jack and Cale had put up last week. We had a walkway that led from the deck down to the yard area, and another crushed granite walkway that led to the dock. I looked across the lake to what use to be my house. *What are the odds of Cale and me buying houses so close to each other?* I turned to my best friend. Monica was now seven months pregnant—and huge. Poor thing. I couldn't imagine being pregnant with twins. Monica and Jack had ended up buying my house, and they had just finished building an addition. They added a guest bedroom with a private bathroom and one other bedroom. With Jack and Monica both able to work from home, they wanted to have two designated offices for each of them.

"You're the one who made her throw up, James."

I turned to see Mitchel and my father approaching me with Lily. She had something all over her shirt. "What happened?" I asked.

"She spit up a little." My father said with an innocent smile.

I looked at Lily's shirt. It was covered in what looked like the carrots and noodles she'd had for lunch.

"Gross, Dad," I said. "Here, let me have her. I'll go change the princess and get her dressed in something new." I was making my way up to the house when I called over my shoulder. "We're going to be singing 'Happy Birthday' and cutting the cake soon!"

"Do you need help, sweetheart?" My father called out.

I held up my hand and waved it. "I got this, Dad."

I stopped in the living room for a few minutes to talk to Mary and Michelle. Michelle was Daddy's girlfriend, and I adored her. She'd had no clue for the first two months they dated that my father owned one of the biggest communications company in the U.S. She liked my father for who he was. They'd just gotten back from a weeklong camping trip. I smiled as I looked at her. Her hair was pulled up into a ponytail and she had on capris and a T-shirt that said, "I stop at all fishing holes."

As I changed Lily, I started talking to her. "Mommy has a big surprise for Daddy."

Lily smiled. "Dada."

I laughed. "Yep, Daddy is going to be over the moon. If I tell you something, can you keep it a secret?" I whispered as I kissed her nose. She giggled and kicked like crazy. "Mommy is going to be giving you a baby brother or sister."

Lily smiled bigger. Almost as if she knew what I was saying.

"Oh Lily, Daddy is going to be so happy."

"Daddy."

My jaw dropped. "Yes! Daddy! Can you say Mommy now, big girl? Mommy."

"Daddy...bird...moon."

"Oh my gosh. When did you start saying moon? Oh my gosh! Oh my gosh, Lily. Daddy is going to freak!"

I helped Lily sit up as she started clapping her hands. "Yes! Yay! Lily said Daddy. Now say Mommy."

Lily grinned at me. "Mama."

I laughed and picked her up, hugging her. I glanced out the window to the lake. Lily had the best view of the lake from her bedroom. I saw that Jack was driving the boat and Cale was kneeboarding. There were an unusual amount of boats on the lake today. It was a crazy-hot July day, so I wasn't too surprised to see that many boats.

Jack's cousin Tim was in the boat with him. He'd just moved here for a job with Mercy Hospital. I was about to turn and leave when I saw another boat heading toward ours. The driver was looking back at a bunch of girls.

"Hey, how is the little birthday girl doing?" Mary asked as she walked up and took Lily from me.

As Mary took Lily from my arms, I whispered, "Oh God."

Jack quickly jerked the wheel, just barely missing the other boat, but Cale was still moving toward it. The moment I saw Cale hit the side of the other boat, my world felt like was moving in slow motion. I screamed, spun around, and ran out of the bedroom.

"Maddie, what's wrong?" Mary called out after me.

I ran so fast that I almost fell down the stairs. Michelle stood up as I ran by her toward the back sliding door. I pushed it open as she yelled out, "Maddie! My God, Maddie...what's wrong?"

I screamed out Cale's name as I saw Tim in the water with him, pulling him back to the boat. Jack was bringing the boat back around to where Tim and Cale were in the water. I ran onto the dock and was about to jump into the water when my father grabbed me.

"Daddy!" I shouted. "Daddy, let me go!"

I watched Cale's father swimming out. Cale looked like he was passed out. He was limp and...oh God...oh God. Please don't take him from me.

"Cale!" I screamed out as my father held me closer. I could barely see him through my blurred vision. "Daddy...please *do* something. Let me go. Please."

"Baby, it's okay. Tim is out there, and he's a trauma doctor. Just take a deep breath."

I kept staring out over the water. They were now scrambling around the boat. "What are they doing? Why is he not moving? What..."

I tried to suck in a deep breath. "He hit the side of the boat. He hit the side of the boat!" I screamed out.

I barely heard Monica talking on the phone. She was saying something about what had happened. For them to please hurry. I watched as Jack ran back to the steering wheel and began to bring the boat to shore.

I grabbed onto my father. "Is he okay? Dad, can you see him?"

"I can't see him, honey. I can't see anything. I need you to calm down."

Everything started to fade away. All the voices sounded like they were in tunnels. I heard crying. Lily was crying. Sirens. Monica was crying. The boat's motor as it grew closer to us. More sirens, closer.

As Jack brought the boat up to the dock I could see Tim doing CPR on Cale. I threw my hands up to my mouth. "No! No! Cale!"

I tried to run to the boat, but my father held me back. "Maddison," he said. "I need you to calm down. Please."

I pulled on his arms. I needed to get to Cale. I needed to be there for him. "He needs me," I shouted. "Daddy, let me go."

Two men in uniforms ran by me. Everything was happening so fast. I looked around and saw Monica crying as she stood next to Mary. Mary didn't have Lily. I panicked at not knowing where my daughter was.

I spun around and saw Michelle pacing back and forth trying to soothe Lily, who was crying. When I turned back to the boat, I saw that they had Cale's head turned the side. He had blood all over his face. I could barely recognize him. My father held onto me tightly as I tried to make my way over to him.

"Baby, let Tim and the paramedics do what they have to do," he said.

I stood there helplessly as they worked on Cale. I glanced over to Jack who seemed stunned. Out on the lake, two police boats flanked the boat that had hit Cale.

"He's breathing. Let's move," the paramedic shouted as they carefully lifted Cale onto a stretcher.

Another man walked by quickly talking on a radio. "Dispatch we're going to need StarFlight to go ahead and land."

StarFlight? I grabbed onto my father's arm. "Daddy?"

"Roger that. There's a cul-de-sac in front of the home. Roger. We'll be transporting the patient in less than a minute."

That's when I saw the helicopter. I looked at my father. "Please let me go," I said. "I'm calm, but I need to know what is going on. Dad. Please."

He nodded and let me go as I approached the paramedic. "Please tell me what's happening. I'm his fiancée. *Please.*"

He took my arm and led me up to the house. I turned back to see them carefully carrying Cale. Jack and Tim were helping the other two paramedics.

"Ms...."

"Powers," I whispered.

"Ms. Powers, your fiancé has sustained a head trauma. He has a compound fracture of his leg and possibly some broken ribs. The doctor who was out on the lake with your fiancé said he passed out on impact. He wasn't wearing a life jacket."

I closed my eyes and held back my sobs as best I could.

"Your friend got to him rather quickly and began CPR in the boat. He's breathing now and, since there could possibly be internal bleeding, it's best to transport him to Mercy by helicopter."

"Can I go, too?" I asked.

"I'm sorry, ma'am I can't let you ride with him in the helicopter. But you can ride with me in my vehicle and I'll get you there as fast as possible.

I nodded as I looked up to see a helicopter landing in front of our house. The wind blew leaves and small branches around, and people were ducking.

As the paramedics walked by, I ran over to Cale. "Cale! I love you!" I shouted. "I love you!"

Three other people jumped out of the helicopter and helped to get Cale in. Jack stepped back as Tim jumped in. Jack came over and held me close to his side.

"Tim! Please don't let...don't..." I covered my mouth and began crying.

Tim nodded. "I won't leave his side, Maddie. I promise."

I SAT CURLED up in the chair as Mary gently played with my hair. Cale had been in surgery for three hours. Tim was in the operating room with the surgeons. No one could really tell us anything. When

StarFlight landed, they took Cale in for a CT scan and then immediately into surgery.

I looked across the waiting room and saw Mitchel. He was leaning with his elbows on his legs. My father was on one side of him and Michelle was on the other. He was crying. My heart broke as I closed my eyes. I didn't have any tears left to cry.

Mary gasped as I looked up to find Zoey's mother standing in front of us. She had a smile on her face as she stared at me.

"Looks like I'll be getting custody of the child after all," she said with an evil grin.

I stood and looked her in the eye.

"You will never, ever, with God as my witness, get custody of my daughter. You won't be allowed within fifty feet near her."

She gave me a once-over. "If he dies, she's mine."

I wasn't sure how I found the strength, but I pulled my arm back and punched her as hard as I could. Michelle and Mary both screamed as my father and ran to me.

Mrs. Jones stumbled backward and grabbed a chair to keep from falling.

"How dare you! I'm going to sue your ass for hitting me."

Monica came and stood between us, holding up a video on her phone.

"I suggest you leave now," Monica said. "Once a judge sees you saying that you want your granddaughter's father to die, you'll never be allowed anywhere near Lily."

Jack walked up to Mrs. Jones. "I also think the judge would be very interested in knowing that Zoey took out a life insurance policy while she was pregnant. When she died, Lily became the sole beneficiary. It's a pretty big number I might add."

Mrs. Jones' jaw dropped and she stared at Jack, incredulous. "How did you...?"

Jack shook his head and took another step toward her. "How did we find out about the insurance policy? It was rather simple, really. Oh, one more thing." Jack smiled as he said, "Cale and Maddie's lawyers should be alerting your lawyers of Maddie's adoption of Lily any day now."

Zoey's mother straightened up and squared her shoulders. Security came rushing in and surveyed the situation. "What's the problem here?"

I shook my head. "There's no problem. Mrs. Jones was just leaving."

Zoey's mom glared at me, then turned and left. I watched as she walked to the elevator, escorted by a security guard. The moment the elevator doors closed, I hit the ground and began crying. Jack picked me up and carried me back to the chairs.

"Why is she doing this?" I sobbed "Why?"

Mary sat back down with me and Jack squatted on the floor in front of me.

"Don't worry about her," Jack said. "She'll never be able to take Lily away. Ever."

I looked into Jack's eyes. All I saw was fear. Fear of the unknown. I shook my head. "He can't leave me, Jack. I can't breathe without him. I don't want to be without him. He's my entire life." I cried as Jack placed his head in my lap and cried with me.

Pain that shot through my abdomen caused me to immediately stop crying. *Oh God, I thought. The baby.*

"Don't do this to me," I whispered. Jack looked up, confused. I repeated myself: "Don't you take this from me."

Jack was about to speak when the doors to the waiting room opened and Tim came walking out. Everyone jumped up and made their way to him.

Tim looked at me, nodded, and smiled before turning back to Mitchel and Mary.

"Tim, please tell us what's going on," Mary said as she wiped tears away.

Tim took a deep breath before speaking. "He's in a medically-induced coma."

I closed my eyes briefly and silently prayed.

"There's some swelling in his brain, and they're not sure if there has been any brain damage." Tim looked at me and then at Mitchel and Mary. "To allow the swelling to go down, and allow faster healing the doctor's feel it's best to take this approach. I'll let them talk to you more about that. He broke his left femur, along with three ribs. Cale also suffered a splenic rupture. The doctors were able to repair it without having to remove the whole spleen."

Mary let out a small sob as she said, "Oh, thank God."

Mitchel cleared his throat. "How long will they keep him in the induced coma?"

Tim shook his head. "That will be up to his doctor. They will schedule him for a CT either first thing in the morning or possibly even later this evening. He'll talk to you about all of that."

Jack walked up to Tim and reached for his hand. "Jesus, dude. I don't know what we would have done if you hadn't been on the boat with us."

Tim smiled weakly. "I'm glad I was there." He walked up to me. "May I talk to you in private, Maddie?"

"Sure," I said as I followed him down the hall to the elevator. He sighed and pushed his hand through his hair as we stepped in. We stood in silence until the doors opened and we walked to the cafeteria where he ordered a cup of coffee and a bottled water.

When the girl looked at me, I smiled and said, "Just a bottle of water for me, please."

We sat down at a table and I tried to smile, but he was scaring me. *What if he didn't tell Cale's parents everything? What if something else was terribly wrong?*

"You're starting to scare me," I said.

He frowned and said, "I'm sorry. Shit. I didn't mean to scare you, Maddie. I just didn't want to ask you this in front of everyone."

I stared at him. "Okay. Ask me what?"

He looked down at his coffee, then back up at me. "Are you pregnant, Maddie?"

My jaw dropped. "How did…how did you know?" I asked. "I

just found out this morning."

He smiled and nodded. "The way you kept touching your stomach today. The flush on your cheeks. My wife did the same thing when she found out she was pregnant. When they say you glow... you really *do* glow. Cale had told me something was different about you today. He said you were so happy. I overheard you telling him you wanted to talk to him alone. I wasn't being noisy, I just overheard and figured it out."

I smiled and felt heat move across my face. "You have a child?"

"Almost. She's due in two weeks," he said, sitting up taller.

"I didn't know. Congratulations!" I said, looking away. He reached to take my hand.

"What is it?"

I chewed on my bottom lip and I fought like hell to keep my tears at bay. "A little bit ago, I felt a pain. A sharp pain, like a cramp. What if..." A sob escaped my throat and I sniffled loudly. "What if I lose the baby?"

He shook his head. "Maddie, cramping is normal, especially in a first pregnancy. Don't stress about it. Stress is the worst thing for..." He stopped talking and looked away. "Well, shit. Just try not to stress about Cale. I promise, he's going to be okay."

I let my head hang as the tears began to fall. "What if he has brain damage? Or he can't remember me or Lily?"

He squeezed my hand tighter. "Have faith. Pray hard and keep positive."

I nodded and said, "I will, yes. I will, for sure." I saw Monica and Jack approaching us. I smiled as Jack helped Monica to sit down.

"Man, before you know it, I'll need to be lugged around by a cart or something." Monica said. She looked between Tim and me. "Is everything okay? Tim, were you holding something back up there?"

"No. I just wanted a few moments alone with Maddie. Just making sure she's okay and all that." He turned to me and winked. I smiled and mouthed, *Thank you.*

I spent the rest of the evening convincing Mitchel and Mary to go home to shower and change. Jack and Monica were picking up Lily from my neighbors' and were planning on staying at our house so that Lily would be more comfortable. My heart hurt for her—I'd left with her so upset.

When they finally got Cale into an ICU room, and everyone had left, I made my way to his room. I sat at the side of his bed and took his hand. The nurse told me that Cale could hear everything I said. I'd tried to stay strong and positive, but I couldn't. I lost it and began crying.

"Please don't leave us. Please, God. Please don't take him from the kids or me. Please."

45

Cale

MY BODY HURT everywhere. I tried like hell to respond to Maddie. Was I just dreaming she was talking to me? She kept crying. Asking me not to leave her. But I would never leave her.

Jesus it felt like I had been hit by a bus. Where was I?

"The swelling is completely gone," a voice said, "and all scans show normal brain activity. We just need him to wake up now."

I didn't recognize whoever was talking. His voice was deep, and I didn't know it.

"Why isn't he waking up?"

Maddie.

"Just keep talking to him. He'll wake up when his body is ready."

I felt someone touch my hand and warmth spread through my achy body.

Maddie.

"Cale? Baby, please wake up now. Lily keeps asking for you. She's been saying 'Daddy.' Not 'Dada,' but 'Daddy.'" She sniffled, faintly crying. "I really need you. Please. Please come back to me. I can't live without you. I can't lose you."

I forced my eyes open. Everything was blurry. I looked around and my head was pounding. I'd never had such an awful headache in my life. I tried to take a deep breath and stopped almost immediately.

Oh, fuck. I'd hit the side of that boat. It was all coming back to me. I'd turned my body as best I could, but my left leg hit first. I remembered hearing a cracking sound. I'd closed my eyes before the rest of my body slammed into the boat, and that was the last thing I remembered.

I was pretty damn sure my ribs were broken, since it hurt to breathe. My left leg hurt like a son of a bitch.

Maddie had her eyes closed and she was holding my hand. I wanted to just look at her before I said anything. When I saw a tear slide down her face, my world about fell apart. *Our wedding.* I'd fucked up our wedding.

I tried to talk, but nothing came out. Maddie dropped her head onto the bed as she cried. I lifted my fingers some to show her I was awake and could see and hear her.

Nothing.

Swallowing hard, I forced myself to talk. "Maddie…" It came out barely a whisper.

I moved my hand more and she lifted her head and looked at our hands.

"Maddie…" I whispered again. She snapped her head up and looked at me. Tears streamed down her face as she jumped up.

"Cale? Did you say something?"

I nodded. "Maddie," I whispered, hoarse.

The smile that spread across her face lit up the entire room. "I love you so much." She started crying harder, but she also laughed. She gently kissed my lips. When she pulled back, her eyes searched my face. "We're selling the boat."

I laughed, then quickly stopped and groaned. "Ribs…so sore."

"Oh, God. I'm so sorry." She kissed me again before hitting the call button. A few seconds later, a voice spoke.

"May I help you, Ms. Powers?" a nurse said.

She grinned bigger. "He's awake."

"I'll page the doctor now."

Maddie's smile faded as she wiped away more tears. "You scared me, Cale."

I shook my head. "I'm so sorry. I would never do anything on purpose to hurt or scare you. I hate knowing that you've been so upset." I remembered the wedding. "What day is it?"

She closed her eyes and shook her head as if she, too, had lost track of the days. "It's Tuesday."

"Tuesday? What? The wedding is in three days. How long...holy shit. I've been out since last Thursday?"

She nodded. "Yeah. They had you in an induced coma for a few days so your brain swelling could go down and your body could heal a bit before you began moving around. Your spleen tore, but they repaired that, too."

Jesus. All the worrying and pain I'd put her through. I hated myself. "My ribs...are they broken?"

She cleared her throat and gave me a sad look. "Yes. Three broken ribs, and the femur in your left leg."

Son of a bitch. "Yeah. I remember hearing something in my leg crack when it hit the side of the boat."

She grimaced. "Oh, Cale." She leaned down and kissed me. "I...love...you...so...much." She kissed me after every word, then sucked in my lower lip and began kissing me more passionately. When the door opened and a male voice cleared his throat she pulled away.

I smiled and winked. "Well I know one thing that isn't broken."

Her face flushed and she stood, taking a few steps back as she continued to look at me with nothing but pure love in her eyes.

I SMILED AS my mother walked in holding a tray. I inhaled the best I could and said, "Oh, man, Mom. That smells good."

She smiled and set the tray down. There was fresh, cut-up fruit, two whole-wheat rolls, and a huge bowl of chicken and dumplings.

"Well, hell. If I'd known breaking a few bones would get you to cook like this, mom, I'd have done it years ago."

Mom sneered at me. "Funny. I didn't make it though. Your bride to be made it."

I pulled my head back and looked down at the chicken and dumplings. "Maddie made this? My Maddie?"

She giggled as she pulled up the side chair and sat down. She grabbed the remote and put the TV on some stupid reality show. "Yep. Your Maddie."

I spooned up some of the soup and a dumpling and blew to cool it off. The moment it hit my tongue, I was in heaven. "Damn. Mom, did you have some of this? I had no idea Maddie knew how to make chicken and dumplings."

She nodded. "Yep, it's really good."

"It's delicious. Where the hell did she learn this? The dumplings are homemade."

My mother laughed and looked at me. "She's an amazing woman. She loves you so much, Cale. It practically pours off of her."

My heart slammed in my chest. "I love her so much, too." I took another bite. "Hey, Mom, can I ask you something?"

She changed the channel to some show where people were rushing around and making cupcakes. "Or course you can, Cale," she said. "You can ask me anything."

"Why do you think Maddie hasn't gotten pregnant yet?"

She picked up the remote and turned off the TV. She turned her whole body to face me. "Cale, I know how badly you both want a baby. I'm thinking right now it's probably a good thing Maddie isn't pregnant. I can't even imagine what the stress from the last two weeks would have done to her and a baby."

I nodded. "It's been five months since we started trying. *Five*, Mom. Damn. Zoey practically got pregnant the second I touched her. It isn't fair."

She narrowed one eye and looked at me. "Do you regret Lily?"

"What? No. My God, I could never, ever regret her. She's my life."

She nodded and looked away for a few seconds. "What Maddie needs is to not think about it. She needs to relax, and just know that it will happen when it happens."

I took another bite of my dumplings. "I think she's given up."

"What? Why would you say that?"

I shrugged. "I don't know. She hasn't talked about it lately. I mean, I know she got busy with planning the wedding, and Lily's first birthday. But these last few days…she seems so happy. Like she's content with everything. But I'm far from being content. We should be married now. We should be on our honeymoon right now and working on that baby. Now she's home, cooking dumplings."

"Maybe she enjoys this lifestyle. Maybe she likes being home and taking care of you, cooking your favorite things. By the way, she made lemon cheesecake."

I licked my lips and moaned. Lemon cheesecake was my ultimate favorite thing.

My mother smiled and said, "I've never met anyone like Maddison. She's strong, but willing to lean on others. She's smart as hell. I swear, though, sometimes the girl lacks common sense."

I chuckled, trying not to move much.

"She's probably the best mother I've ever seen. Far better than I ever was. I watch her sometimes and wonder why I was never that way with you. I make excuses, of course. I was too young when I had you. I wasn't really ready to be a mother. I got caught up in a world I really didn't want or need to belong in—"

"Mom," I said. "You weren't a bad mother…always."

She made a face at me. "Ha, ha. The bottom line, Cale, is that girl would walk over hot coals for you. The only thing she truly needs in this world is your love and Lily's. If you're meant to be blessed with another baby, it's in God's hands."

The door to the bedroom opened and Lily came walking in. "Daddy! Bird!"

My heart broke that I couldn't spend much time with my girl. "Hey, Princess."

Monica came in behind Lily. "Peanut missed her daddy and threw a pretty massive fit to get into this room."

I smiled as my mother picked up Lily and brought her to the other side of the bed. She set her down and Lily looked at my dumplings. "Nummy!"

I chuckled and then groaned when pain shot through my side. I put some of the soup on my spoon and blew on it to cool it off. Lily had her mouth open and ready for some yummy goodness.

"When did she start saying that?" I asked, putting another spoonful in her mouth.

"About a minute ago," Maddie said as she leaned against the doorjamb, watching me feed Lily between my own bites.

"Well, the kid sure is smart." I said with a wink. "Takes after her father, that's for sure. Knows a good, home-cooked meal when she tastes one."

Maddie laughed and came over to kiss me on the forehead. "Do you like it?"

"Like it?" I said. "I love it. Where did you learn to make it?" I took another bite and Lily pulled on my arm for more.

"Michelle has been teaching me. Today's lesson was lemon cheesecake." She wiggled her eyebrows and I moaned.

Mom stood up and picked up Lily. "You know what your father

and I need? We need time with the little princess here. How about if I take Lily for tonight and most of tomorrow? That gives y'all a bit of time to just relax. Maddie made enough chicken and dumplings to last five days."

Maddie laughed as she watched my mother. "Mary, are you sure? I know I could use a day of sleeping in."

I'd been home from the hospital for a few days, and my parents had been here ever since the accident. Monica and Jack had practically camped out in our house for the last three days, and I was pretty sure Maddie was ready for everyone to leave.

"I'm positive. You're probably sick of seeing Mitchel and me. And I need my own bed again." She started to walk out of the bedroom as she talked to Lily. "Come on, Princess. Let's go pack an overnight bag and plan our slumber party."

Thirty minutes later, the house was cleared out and it was just Maddie and I. Except I had no clue where Maddie was. I was about to call out for her when I saw her standing at the door. She was wearing a light blue corset and her hair was pulled up in a messy ponytail. She looked hot as hell. My eyes trailed up and down her body and I licked my lips, taking in the thigh-high stockings that were help up by a matching powder-blue garter belt. She had on white pumps.

"I'm pretty sure I just died and went to heaven." I said as she ran her tongue along her lips.

"I figured that your broken bones didn't mean I couldn't show you what I'd planned to wear on our wedding night."

I closed my eyes and moaned. I wanted to bury myself deep inside of her. "Fuck. Maddie, you're killing me here."

She put her finger in her mouth and then pulled her hand out from behind her back. I chuckled as I watched her put the nurse's hat on. She slipped two hairpins in and winked at me. "Nurse Maddie is here to take care of you, Mr. Blackwood. Are you finished with your lunch?"

I looked down at the empty bowls. I'd eaten everything my

mother had brought in. Maddie took the tray from me. She turned and started out the door, but not before looking over her shoulder and saying, "I'll be back to give you a sponge bath after I take this to the kitchen."

I pulled the covers away to reveal my favorite pair of sleeping shorts. I looked around. No way I could take them off by myself with this damn broken leg and my messed up ribs. I yelled out the bedroom door, "Maddie! Bring scissors with you when you come back."

She poked her head around the corner and gave me a puzzled look. "Why?"

I pointed down to my shorts.

"Your shorts?" she asked.

I nodded. "Yeah. I want you to cut them off."

Maddie came back and stopped in the doorway to our bedroom. She slowly began to walk over to me. The come-hither look on her face instantly had my poor dick jumping in anticipation. I wondered how the hell were we going to have sex when I had so many broken bones.

"Did you bring scissors?" I asked.

She moved to the right side of the bed and crawled onto it slowly. We had a Tempur-Pedic mattress, thank goodness. I didn't feel Maddie moving on the bed.

"Oh, ye of little faith," she said. "I've got this." She slowly moved up and gently kissed me on the mouth.

I smiled against her lips. "I love you, Maddie."

She pulled back and looked adoringly into my eyes. She didn't have an ounce of makeup on and her brown hair was beginning to fall down from her ponytail. She'd never looked so sexy. "You're so beautiful. You steal the air from my lungs with just a look."

She began to chew on her lip.

"Maddie, I wish like hell we could have sex, but…" I looked down at my leg and placed my hand on my ribs. "I can't move without something hurting."

She began to gently slide down my sleeping shorts. "Don't move. The nurse at the hospital showed me how to do this, and I watched the nurse here the last few days."

My parents had insisted on having a nurse come help for a few days. I couldn't take the babying and sent her home earlier today. Maddie skillfully removed my shorts, and I hardly moved an inch. The worst part was moving my torso, because of the broken ribs.

Maddie got up and walked into our closet and came walking back out with a bag. "What's in the bag?" I asked as I raised my eyebrows in an expectant manner.

"A welcome home gift," she said as she began to slowly strip out of her clothes.

She stood before me naked, and I began stroking my dick as best I could. I closed my eyes and moaned. I heard her pull something out of the bag and then I heard a buzzing sound. I snapped my eyes open to see her holding a vibrator in her hand.

"I'm going to take care of you first." She wiggled her eyebrows as she took off the nurse's hat. "Then I'm going to let you take care of me."

I swallowed hard as she moved back onto the bed. She was on the right side of my body and she placed one hand on the bed next to my leg and the other hand on my shaft. She leaned over and took my whole dick in her mouth, moaning. I fought like hell not to move. One small jerk on my part had my ribs telling me to settle down.

I watched as she worked her mouth slowly up and down as I ran my hand through her hair. I leaned back against the pillows and let out another long moan. "Feels so damn good, baby."

She picked up the pace and I could feel the buildup. It wasn't going to take me long. I glanced at the vibrator on the bed and pictured Maddie working it in and out of her pussy. *Oh, fuck.* I began panting, which my ribs were telling me to stop doing, but I didn't care. It felt so damn amazing. She let her teeth graze along my dick and I turned again to see the vibrator. "Maddie, baby, I'm going to…oh God!"

I moved. Bad idea, but she'd begun to suck harder on my dick. She did something with her hand along my shaft. "Ah…" I cried out as I came in her mouth. She continued to move as she took in every ounce of me.

When she finished, she sat back on her knees, smiling as she wiped her mouth. "I've been practicing on a cucumber."

I wanted to bust out laughing—she seemed so damn proud of herself.

"Your mother almost walked in on me giving head to one in the kitchen. I bit into it and told her I was craving cucumbers."

I started laughing and then groaned. "Damn ribs."

She sat next to me, holding the vibrator. "Can you lean a little on your right side?"

I didn't have any broken ribs on that side, so I rolled over a little. Maddie lay next to me, smiling. "Can I rest my leg on your good leg?" she asked with a scrunched-up nose.

I nodded and held out my hand. She was lying down, but close enough that I didn't have to bend or really move much. She reached down and began pushing the vibrator inside her. When she pulled it out and pushed it back in, my damn dick started jumping again. I looked down and he wasn't up, but he was sure as hell putting up a fight.

"Oh God, Cale."

Her eyes were closed and I was hoping like hell she was picturing me moving in and out of her. I moved a bit more and felt the pain shoot through my ribs and left leg. *Fuck.* Watching Maddie work the vibrator in and out I knew she was close. I wanted to lean down and kiss on her nipple so bad.

Screw this. Pain or no pain, I'm going to be the one holding that thing when she comes.

I took the vibrator from her hand and began working it in and out faster. I had to bite down on my cheek to keep the pain at bay, but it was worth it to see the pure pleasure on my girl's face. It didn't take long for Maddie to scream my name. It must have been one hell of an orgasm, because she kept saying she couldn't take any more. When she finally came down from her orgasm, and I pulled the vibrator out, she sat up and took deep breaths.

"Jesus. I must have needed that," she giggled.

I raised my eyebrow and adjusted myself into a more comfortable position. "I'd say. I'm pretty sure Jack and Monica heard you screaming from across the lake."

She narrowed her eye at me and said, "Very funny."

She got up, put the nurses hat back on, and sashayed into the bathroom. She came out with a hot washcloth and began cleaning me off, naked. I couldn't help but think I'd died and gone to heaven.

THE DOOR TO the bedroom opened and I lifted my head to see Maddie walking in with a tray. I attempted to sit up some as I smiled at her.

"Dinner time," she said, all chipper.

The smell of steak filled my senses and I moaned. She set down the tray, revealing a plate with a T-bone steak, a fully-loaded baked potato, and steamed broccoli on it. She also had a hot roll and a tall glass of tea on the tray. I licked my lips as I eyed the food.

"Wow," I said. "You have all my favorites on here, baby."

She grinned from ear to ear. "I even grilled the steak out on the deck. Let me go grab mine." She hustled out of the room. I impatiently waited for her to return. Once she walked through the door with another tray, I began to cut into my steak.

She sat on the bed and faced me. I looked up and saw she had candles on her tray. I smiled as I grabbed the lighter and lit them.

"Are you sore or anything from earlier?" She asked, blushing.

I chuckled softly. "Nope. The pain pills kicked in. I was dozing when you walked in. I heard the door open and I smelled steak."

She smiled and took a bite of her baked potato.

I took a bite and sighed. "Man, Maddie this is delicious."

"Thank you. I'm glad you like it. Your mom wanted to order us something to be delivered, but I wanted tonight to be special."

I nodded my head as I took another bite. That's when her wedding dress caught my eye. It was hanging on the back of her closet door. Why had I not noticed that before? My heart instantly broke in two. Maddie must have noticed me staring, because she turned to look, too.

"I hung it up earlier while you were sleeping," she said. "Monica had it at her house and thought that I might want it here."

I closed my eyes. "I'm so sorry, Maddie. I knew you didn't want us messing with the boat on Lily's birthday, and I didn't pay attention to what you wanted. God, I'm so sorry I ruined our wedding."

She shrugged and cut into her steak. "I'm just glad you're alive and the only thing wrong is a broken leg and a few ribs. I don't know what I would have done if I'd lost you, Cale. You're my whole life."

I swallowed as I attempted to hold back tears. "I asked the doctor about when I could walk down the aisle. He told me to take it one day at a time."

She gave me a warm smile and nodded. "I agree with him." She pulled an envelope from under her plate. She ran her fingers across it and rapidly blinked her eyes.

Oh shit. I bet it's our marriage license. Damn it.

"I thought I could wait until we'd eaten and had dessert, but I can't wait a minute longer. The day of Lily's party, when I came home from the doctor, I had something I needed to talk to you about, but everyone was already here. Then the accident happened, and your parents and Monica and Jack practically moved in. We haven't been alone long enough for me to show you this."

She handed the envelope and I set my silverware down. "What

is it?"

She sucked her lower lip in and sniffled. "Just open it. I wanted us to be alone for this. I wish I could have made it more…special."

I looked at her, confused. Turning the envelope over, I opened it. I pulled out the folded piece of paper and began to open it. There was another paper wrapped up in it. A sonogram picture. I just stared. I couldn't pull my eyes away from the tiny peanut in the middle of the picture. I looked up and Maddie had tears falling down her face.

"Maddie…are we?"

She nodded and wiped away her tears. "Yes. We're about eight weeks along."

My eyes stung with tears as I felt the emotions build. My lips quivered and my heart did the same crazy-ass thing it did the first time I ever laid eyes on Maddie. *Pregnant. Maddie is pregnant with our child.*

A sob escaped my lips and I didn't even care that my ribs were screaming in pain. "Maddie. We're gonna have a baby? This is our baby?"

She laughed. "Yes. I'm so sorry you weren't there for the first sonogram. The doctor wanted to do it as soon as possible. I haven't told anyone else, since I wanted to tell you first. I kind of think Jack knows, but he hasn't said anything. Tim knows. He figured it out the day of your accident." She looked at me with such sadness in her eyes.

"Baby, it's okay. I'll be there for everything else, I swear. Now, will you please move these trays so I can kiss the mother of my children?"

Maddie froze. Something moved across her face…an emotion I'd seen before, but slightly different. She stood and set her tray on the dresser, then reached for mine and did the same. She crawled back onto the bed and was about to kiss me when she stopped just short of my lips and smiled the biggest smile I'd ever seen.

"I could never in a million years tell you how that just made me feel. I love you, Cale Blackwood. I love you so much."

Placing my hand on her cheek, I brushed away a single tear before sliding my hand behind her neck and pulling her lips to mine. Our kiss was passionate, and full of love.

She pulled away and giggled. "Our dinner is getting cold."

I smiled and whispered, "Let it get cold. Where is that vibrator?"

46

TWO MONTHS LATER

"**Y**OU KNOW, YOU really can't do that anymore."

I turned to see my father standing in the doorway of the baby's room, shaking his head. "If Cale saw you standing on that ladder, he'd be furious."

I laughed. "Help me down?" I asked as I held out my hand. My father held my hand as I stepped off the small ladder. "Daddy, you know I was only two steps up?"

"Doesn't matter. Just because you're not really showing, Maddie, doesn't mean you're not pregnant. If you need something done in the nursery, just ask one of us to do it, sweetheart."

I saluted my father. "Yes, sir."

He kissed me on the forehead as he chuckled. "Where is my granddaughter?"

I looked around the nursery and smiled. We'd decided to use the guest bedroom downstairs as the new nursery. I had no clue if I was having a girl or a boy, but I had a feeling that it was a girl. So I'd started decorating in a French country theme. Cale thought I was crazy, but something in my heart told me I was having a girl. Plus, I had been insanely sick the first three months, and Mary assured me that meant it was a girl.

"She's with Cale and Mary," I said. "They took her to the park so I could rest, but I couldn't sleep, so I started messing with the baby's room."

"How are the plans for the second wedding going?" My father asked, walking out of the nursery and toward the living room.

I slapped at his arm as I passed him by to sit on the sofa. "You're so mean. How's your wedding plans coming along with Michelle? You know, Mom called me the other day and was asking all kinds of questions."

He sat in the recliner and rolled his eyes. "I hope you didn't tell her anything. With the amount of money I gave her in the divorce, I figured she'd just stay in Paris forever."

I giggled. "Daddy, that's so mean."

He had a serious look in his eyes when he asked, "You don't agree with me, Maddison?"

I held up my hands. "Now, I didn't say that! I wasn't surprised when she took off for Paris. She always loved it there, and said she wanted to live there."

He let out a gruff laugh. "Well, she can stay there forever as far as I'm concerned."

My cell phone rang and my father jumped up and grabbed it from the sofa table behind me. When he handed it to me, I saw that it was Jack. My heart beat faster.

"Hello?"

Jack yelled, "Her water broke! Her water broke!"

I stood up quickly. "What?"

"Her. Water. Broke. They're coming. Finally!"

I smiled at my dad and gave him a thumbs-up. "Okay, Jack, calm down. Where is Monica?"

I could hear Monica in the background talking. "I'm heading on out to the car. Honey, grab my makeup bag, will you?"

"I don't know what's wrong with her, Maddie. She's too calm. She's about to give birth to twins and she is so chill. She walked to the bedroom, changed her clothes, grabbed a towel and told me to meet her in the car. And she wants makeup. Why does she want makeup?"

I tried to hold back my laughter. Monica was so ready to give birth to the twins. She was nine months pregnant and they'd told her she'd deliver earlier. She hadn't, and she'd been one pissed off pregnant woman the last three weeks.

"Jack, just grab the makeup bag and head to the car. Did you call the doctor yet?"

"Fuck! I forgot. Son of a bitch."

Then my phone beeped. I pulled it away and looked at it. "He hung up on me," I said to my dad. "He didn't even say goodbye. He just hung up. What the hell?"

I heard Mary and Cale come in through the front door. "Maddie!" He yelled.

"I'm in the living room with Dad."

Cale came rushing into the living room. I could tell he was still having a bit of trouble with his leg.

"She's in labor," Cale said. "We have to go."

He walked back down the hall and all I could hear was Cale rummaging through the hall closet. I looked over to my father and then to Mary who was holding Lily. She set her down and Lily quickly made her way to me. I kneeled down and took her into my arms. She smiled at me and then gave me a slobbery kiss.

"Mom, James? Can one of y'all watch Lily while we go to the hospital?"

I stood up and Lily screamed excitedly and pointed to Cale. I stood there, staring.

"What the hell is that?" Mary asked as my father laughed.

Cale was holding a camel. A giant camel.

"Wait, where *was* that thing?" I asked as I walked over to him. He frantically looked around. He pointed and said, "Your purse. Maddie, get your purse. We have to go."

I shook my head. "Right now, I'm more curious about the giant camel in your arms."

He looked at me like I was crazy. "The camel?" he asked, surveying the room.

I placed my hands on my hips. "Daddy, up. Up!" Lily said, pulling on Cale's jeans.

"Yes, Cale. The camel. What's the story with the camel?"

He looked down at Lily and smiled. He dropped the Camel to the ground and she laughed and crawled all over it. "Well, it's kind of a joke," he said. "Er, um, well…not a joke I care to share right now."

I raised an eyebrow. "Cale…"

"Really, Maddie now might not be…"

"Oh just tell the joke, for Christ's sake," my father said.

Cale ran his hand through his hair and sighed. "Fine. The first time Jack ever saw Monica, he made a joke. She was wearing these tight pants…and, well..."

The moment he said it I was taken back to the night we meet Cale and Jack. "I think we should go now." I blurted.

"Oh no, I want to hear this joke now." Mary said.

Cale sighed. "Jack looked at Monica and said, 'To hell with kissing that girl under the mistletoe, I'll kiss her camel toe instead.'"

I closed my eyes and shook my head as my father and Cale's mother both laughed. "You are *not* bringing that to the hospital. Are you insane?"

"What? He'll never see it coming." Cale said with a smile.

My phone buzzed, notifying me of a text message.

Monica: *Please tell me you're on your way. I'm about to kill my husband.*

Me: *Same here. Leaving now. Don't worry. It will all be okay!*

I looked at my father and Mary. Mary smiled. "Go. I've got Lily. Go be with Monica and Jack."

I bent down and kissed Lily. "Mommy loves you, Princess."

Lily waved bye-bye and I waved back. Her light brown, curls

fell to her shoulders and her green-blue eyes lit up as I waved back. She was the spitting image of Cale.

Cale went to grab the camel when I pulled him away from it by the arm. "No, Cale."

"Aw, Maddie. Don't be such a killjoy." Cale whined.

I walked out to the car and got in first, followed by Cale. He started the car then told me he'd forgotten something. He jumped out of the car and ran back into the house. When he came back out with the camel, I rolled my eyes. I'd clearly lost this fight.

I COULDN'T BELIEVE how insanely beautiful the twins were. Monica and Jack named them Craig and Lucy. Craig had been named after Jack's dad and Lucy was named after Monica's grand-mother. I glanced up and saw Cale holding Craig. I looked down at Lucy and smiled.

Lucy yawned and made the sweetest sound. My heart slammed in my chest as I thought about the child growing in my own stomach. "Hey there, little one," I whispered. Welcome to this crazy world."

Jack came into the room and smacked Cale on the back of the head. "Get that damn camel out of this room. Now."

Cale laughed as Monica asked, "What's with the camel any-way?"

Cale went to explain, but Jack stepped in front of him and said, "Don't even think about it, Cale Blackwood."

I giggled and shook my head.

"How are you feeling, Monica?" I asked.

She adjusted herself in the bed and said, "I feel great. I really do. It's nice to have my body back. I wouldn't trade a minute of any of it though."

I smiled warmly at my best friend. She looked beautiful. She didn't have an ounce of makeup on. Jack was still asking why he'd had to run and get the makeup if she wasn't even going to wear it.

"I can't wait for Lily to meet Craig and Lucy. She is going to have so much fun with them." Cale said as he stood and rocked a cranky Craig.

I also stood and walked around with Lucy in my arms. She was so tiny, and I couldn't get enough of her smell. I kissed her head before I placed her back in her bassinet. "How long do you have to stay here?"

Cale placed Craig, now asleep, in his bassinet, too. He stood, staring at both babies.

"I'm hoping I'll be home in the next day or two," Monica said. "Everything went great with the delivery, and the twins are as healthy as can be. I think we'd all be more comfortable at home." She looked up and Jack smiled. He leaned down and kissed her.

"I love you, Monica," he said. "Happy Mother's Day, baby."

I watched as a tear rolled down my best friend's cheek. I couldn't help but stare at the two of them. The way they looked into each other's eyes, it was clear how much they loved each other. I pulled my eyes away and saw Cale watching me. He smiled and I smiled back. He pulled me into his arms. Cale's lips moved across my neck, sending a chill from my head to my toes. When he found his way to my ear, I had to grab onto his arms to steady myself.

"I want to make love to you, Maddie," Cale whispered as he kissed around my ear, which always drove me mad. His voice was laced with desire, which only blossomed my own want.

"Okay," I whispered back. He stepped back and grabbed the camel.

"I'll take this home and keep it safe for y'all, then bring it over once you get home."

Jack shot Cale a dirty look. "Bastard."

Cale threw his head back and laughed before giving Monica a kiss on the forehead. "We're gonna let you rest now, sweetheart. The babies are beautiful, like their mother."

Monica smiled and nodded. "Thanks, you guys, for coming and staying with us. You're next!"

Monica pointed at me. I placed my hand on my stomach and giggled. I kissed Monica goodbye, and then Jack.

"We'll be back tomorrow! Love you both!" I called out as I walked out the door.

Driving home, I couldn't stop thinking about our baby.

Cale reached for my hand and squeezed it. "What are you thinking about?"

"The baby." I glanced over and smiled weakly at him. "I'm... scared."

He looked at me, concerned, before quickly looking back at the road. "What are you scared about?"

I shrugged. "Oh, I don't know. Am I going to be able to do this? Is it going to hurt? Will I know what to do with her?"

Cale smiled. "Her huh? You still sure we're having a girl."

I nodded and chuckled. "Yep."

Cale took my hand and brought it to his lips. He gently kissed it. "Maddie," he said, "you're going to be wonderful. Look at how you just took over with Lily. Baby, you're going to be the best mommy ever. And I'm sure our little princess at home will be itching to help out."

I laughed and nodded in agreement. "Oh, I'm sure she will be. Let's just hope that our Lily isn't the jealous type."

I WALKED INTO the living room and attempted to sit down on the sofa with some sense of grace. When I plopped down, I sighed. Monica laughed as she placed Craig into his swing. Lucy was sound asleep in her swing as it moved back and forth.

"I can't believe the twins are five months old already," Monica said as she stood and gazed at her two kids.

I jumped when my little kicker gave me a good one in my ribs. "Oh, God. When will this baby come?" I asked as I leaned back on the sofa. "It's snowing like hell outside. I just want to go for a walk, and I'm stuck in the house…with you."

Monica placed her hands on her hips. "Hey!"

I waved my hand to brush off Monica and looked up at Cale standing in Monica and Jack's living room, looking all hot and shit. I couldn't believe how horny I'd been during this pregnancy. I licked my lips as I looked over his body.

He looked at me and asked, "You ready to head home Maddie?"

I grinned and replied, "Yeah, I think so."

Lily came running by as Jack chased her. "Jack Rembrandt, you hush up this second!" Monica called out. How the twins slept through everything was beyond me.

Cale helped me stand up. Pain shot through my abdomen and I let out a little gasp. I'd been having small pains since around six in the morning. At first, I thought maybe there were just Braxton Hicks contractions. Now I wasn't so sure, since they were slowly getting stronger.

"Jesus, she finally sat down and now you're making her get up and leave?" Monica said. "I swear, Maddie, if I didn't know better, I'd say you were having an elephant."

I glared at her. "You're such a bitch."

"Bitch!"

I covered my mouth and Monica busted out laughing.

"Bitch, bitch, bitch!" Lily repeated as she ran around Cale and me.

"Great," I whispered.

Cale tried not to laugh as he scooped up Lily and we made our way to the car.

Five minutes later, Cale was telling Lily a story in her room before putting her down for a nap. I made my way into the kitchen and sighed. I was nine months pregnant and felt like a beached whale. Cale would tell me at least five times a day how beautiful I was.

I opened the refrigerator and peered in. I needed something spicy to get this baby out. I pushed things around on the shelves, looking for something to kick-start my labor.

Nothing. I turned and headed into the living room and down the hall. I walked past our bedroom and into the guest room, which was now the nursery. Inside, I stopped as I felt the baby moving.

I placed my hands on my stomach and watched as an elbow moved across my swollen belly. I smiled and shook my head. "I think you're too comfy in there. It's time to come out and meet your big sister, Lily. Mommy needs her sleep back, little one."

I felt Cale's presence as he walked into the nursery. He came from behind me and placed his hands on my stomach. The baby must have just repositioned herself. "Is he moving a lot today?"

I smiled to myself when Cale called the baby a he. We'd never found out the sex of the baby. The French country theme could go either way. I glanced around at the finished nursery. All it needed was our baby.

Cale, his dad Mitchel, and my father, had all painted the nursery in one day. The walls were painted my favorite color, Sea Salt from Sherwin Williams. It was neutral enough to go with either a boy or a girl. The country cottage, distressed, white furniture looked beautiful in the room. We'd bought a crib, a wardrobe, and a changing table. There was a light blue chair in the corner that had belonged in Lily's room when she was a baby. I'd spent weeks making a canopy for the crib. It looked beautiful.

Cale rubbed my stomach as he said, "This room is truly breathtaking, Maddie. You did a wonderful job on it."

I smiled and nodded. I glanced up and looked at the blue ceiling and the white, puffy clouds that Monica and I had made together. It truly was a beautiful nursery.

"I just wish *she* would make an appearance soon. I can hardly sleep anymore and *she* seems to be the most active at night. I think *she's* confused."

Cale laughed. "I think it's because during the day you rock *him* to sleep. At night is when *he* wakes up to party."

I turned around and smirked. "I'm telling you, Mr. Blackwood, it's a girl."

He shook his head. "Boy."

"Girl."

Cale's eyes moved over my body and I saw the lust in his expression. I was instantly turned on. "I know a way we can try and speed up your labor."

I raised my eyebrows and smiled. "Lead the way. And I hope you've come up with a good position, 'cause I can't move!"

Cale took my hand and led me out of the nursery and into our bedroom. He quickly stripped out of his clothes and I followed. I stood before him completely naked and was shocked by what I saw. "Cale, do you have…tears in your eyes?"

He cupped my face with both hands. "You're so beautiful. I don't think I've ever in my life seen a woman so breathtaking. You stomach swollen with our child turns me on more than you could ever imagine, Maddie. I desperately want you right now." Cale kissed me softly on the lips. "Marry me. Now. I don't want to wait until the baby is born. I want to make you mine."

I closed my eyes as he moved his lips across my neck. "Cale," I whispered. He moved his lips down my body to my nipples. I felt a sharp pain in my stomach as I held my breath. *Shit. My body must be reacting to him in different ways.*

"I love you, Maddie."

Soft kisses covered my body and threw my libido into overdrive. I wanted to have an orgasm so badly that I thought I might cry. When Cale dropped to his knees and lifted my leg over his shoulder I hissed out, "Yes." One swipe of his tongue across my sensitive bud had me moaning like a crazed woman. "More. Give me more." I pulled on his hair and buried his face between my legs. Dropping one hand. I reached out and held onto the bedpost as Cale began to suck and lick.

"Yes. Yes. I want it so bad, Cale."

Cale let out a moan that vibrated through my entire core. I began to feel the familiar build up. "More! Give me more!"

When I felt his hand move up and behind onto my ass I knew what he was about to do. My body began to shake with anticipation. He slipped a finger inside my ass and I lost it. I began calling out his name as an orgasm ripped through my body. I gasped as the pain shot through my stomach again. *Oh no.*

Cale stood up and looked at me with hungry eyes. "Lay down on the bed on your side Maddie. I'm going to take you now."

I swallowed hard. I slowly made my way onto the bed and lay down. Cale positioned himself as he lifted my right leg and slipped his dick inside of me. The relief I felt when he entered me was heavenly. As he moved in and out, I let myself go.

"Maddie, I'm going to come, baby."

I called out his name softly as he called out my name again. Cale didn't move for the longest time. I was about to say something when I felt another pain. At that point, I knew it couldn't be anything else – it was a contraction.

Cale pulled out. "Hold on baby, let me get a washcloth to clean you up.

I inhaled deeply through my nose and slowly blew the air out my mouth. I looked over at the clock and made a mental note of the time. I didn't want to tell Cale just yet. I wasn't sure why. I was pretty sure it was because once I told him; it would all become real. I was scared to death.

After Cale and I got dressed, we headed out to the kitchen to start dinner. Lily had gone down for her nap later than normal, and I knew she would be starving. I started to pull out chicken for Cale to put on the grill.

"Cale, will you start the grill?" I asked. He laughed and I turned and looked at him. "What's so funny?"

He looked at me with a confused look. "Baby, it's snowing hard outside. I'm not going out there to grill."

I placed my hands on hips and glared at him. He knew how much Lily and I loved grilled chicken.

"I'll use the indoor grill if you want," he said as he smiled and winked at me.

I smiled and nodded. As I made the salad, I heard Lily singing over the monitor. I smiled and placed a hand on my stomach. I picked up the glass bowl and turned to set it on the island and a contraction hit me hard and fast. I dropped the bowl and watched as glass shattered everywhere. "Fuck," I said as I glanced at the clock.

Cale came running and stopped when he saw the glass. "Maddie, are you okay?"

I nodded. "I um…I dropped the bowl."

Cale ran to the laundry room and began cleaning up the broken glass. Lily was crying like crazy. She must have heard Cale call my name. "I'll go get Lily," I said.

Cale bent over and swept glass onto the dustpan. "Okay, I'll get this mess cleaned up and will make another salad in no time. Don't worry, baby."

I went up to Lily's room. When I opened the door, she smiled and said, "Mama."

I got her out of her crib and brought her over to the changing table. I changed her diaper, then helped her walk down the stairs into the living room. I retrieved one of her favorite toys and set it in front of her. I knew the toy would occupy her for at least fifteen minutes while I helped Cale finish dinner.

I pulled the rosemary potatoes out of the oven and placed them on top of the stove. I was about to take out our plates when another contraction hit me.

"Oh shit!" I said, starting to breathe like they taught us in

Lamaze class. The contraction lasted longer. I looked at the clock. "Oh gosh," I whispered.

I turned to see Cale on the floor playing with Lily. They were both laughing at the sounds the game made. "Um, Cale?"

"Yeah?"

"I think...well no, I know for sure...I'm having contractions."

He was making a silly face at Lily. "Is that right?"

I rolled my eyes. He clearly wasn't paying attention to me. It must of hit him, though, because he jumped up, turned and looked at me. "What? What did you say?"

47

Cale

I STARED AT Maddie. She was rubbing her hand across her stomach, smiling. "I said I'm having contractions."

Shaking my head I said, "No, you can't."

She shrugged. "Oh, yes I can…and I am."

I placed my hands on Maddie's upper arms. "Maddie, there is a blizzard outside. You're not due for another few days. You can't have this baby."

Her face turned red. I instantly dropped my hands and took a step back.

"I don't care that there is a blizzard outside, or that I'm not due for another few days. I *do* care that I've been having contractions all day and now they are about thirty minutes apart. I'm having this baby, Cale Blackwood. Now."

I swallowed. "Now? Now? Like right this second?" I looked at her stomach and turned around in a circle. "Holy shit!"

Lily jumped up and spun around as she repeated what I'd said. "Shit! Shit, Daddy!"

I looked back at her and nodded. "I know, Lily! Daddy knows." I took Maddie by the hand and led her to the sofa. "Hold on," I said. "Let me see how bad the weather is."

I sprinted to the front door and heard Lily running behind me. I slid to a stop at the door and turned. Lily was running as fast as her little legs could go, laughing. I bent down and held out my arms and scooped her up as I stood and ran back into the living room. "Mommy needs lovin', Lily. You baby brother…"

"Or sister," Maddie said with a smirk.

I gave Maddie a look and set Lily down next to her. "Your baby brother or sister wants to come out of mommy's tummy now to play with you."

Lily smiled and Maddie clapped her hands as Lily followed.

"I'll be right back," I said, taking off again.

"Where are you going, Cale? We have to call the doctor!" Maddie called after me. I threw the door open and ran outside. I wasn't wearing anything but a T-shirt, sweatpants and my socks. I stopped right at the edge of the front porch. All I could see was snow. It was falling from the sky in a full-blown blizzard. "Why? Why today of all days?"

I pulled my phone out of my sweatpants pocket. I found Jack's number and called.

"Are you missing me, bro?"

"I need your truck. I mean, I need to borrow your truck right now."

Jack laughed. "Fuck no! You're not driving my truck in this weather. Jesus, Cale, it's a damn blizzard outside."

I felt my breathing pick up. I was freezing my ass off, but I didn't want Maddie to hear the panic in my voice.

"Dude! Listen to me. I don't have time for this. Maddie is in labor. I *need* your truck. It's a four-by-four, and the only thing that will get us to the hospital."

"Maddie's in labor?" Jack asked as I heard Monica yelling in the background. I heard some noise and then Monica's voice.

"Cale, how far apart are her contractions? I knew something was off with her. I knew it!"

I took a deep breath and looked back at the front door as I

jumped around to warm up. "She said thirty minutes."

"Okay. Jack is on his way over. Call the doctor first and let them know. Then call your neighbor and ask them to come stay with Lily—you can't bring her to the hospital. Then call your parents and Maddie's dad and Michelle."

I nodded. "Got it." I turned to open the door and ran smack into it. "Shit. I locked myself out."

I rang the doorbell as I listened to Monica tell me all the things I needed to do. I kept jumping around to warm myself up. I rang the doorbell again. "Damn it. Maddie isn't answering the door. What the hell? Oh God. Oh, no—what if something happened to her? Fuck! Fuck! Fucker! Suck a dick!"

"Um, yeah I don't want to ask about that last outburst. Bang on the door."

I banged on the door and kept ringing the doorbell. "Monica, I'm freaking out. She isn't answering." I banged louder and rang the doorbell again and again. I put my ear to the door. When I hit the doorbell, nothing happened. Then I heard music. Loud music.

"She's playing music. Like really loud."

"Huh?" Monica asked.

I ran my hand through my hair as I blew out a breath. "She's dancing with Lily, I bet. Lily loves the music up as loud as we can get it, and they dance. The doorbell is fucking broken and she can't hear me banging on the door."

Monica laughed. "Is it cold out?"

"I really hate you right now, Monica." I hung up my phone and looked out over the front yard.

I stared at the falling snow. It really *was* beautiful. The white snow blanketed the area, making everything look new. This was it. This was the one thing I'd been waiting for. The moment in time I'd been dreaming about for years.

The front door opened and Maddie laughed. "Jesus, Cale get in here!"

I spun around and ran into the house. I pulled Maddie into my arms and gently brought her lips to mine. "Thank you," I whispered.

Her breathing was rapid as her eyes searched mine. "For what?"

"For loving me."

She smiled bigger and whispered back, "Always."

MADDIE WAS HAVING another contraction when Jack finally pulled up to the ER. "I'm really going to have to thank James for calling the cops." he said with a chuckle.

Maddie groaned. "I'm…going…to…kill…my…oh God!" Maddie took quick breaths as she worked her way through the contraction.

She let out a breath. "Father…I'm going to kill my father for this police escort."

I jumped out of the truck and ran into the ER, slipping twice. Just as I was about to reach the door, I slipped again and fell. Two nurses came running out to help.

"Are you okay, sir?"

I pointed to the car as I kept doing that stupid breathing exercise from Lamaze class. "My wife. Contractions."

I looked back and Jack was walking slowly with Maddie up to the doors. They all walked past me and sat Maddie in a wheel chair. I brushed off the snow as I followed them in, ignoring the incredible pain in my left leg.

"Cale! You're limping. Did you hurt your leg again? Wait, stop!" Maddie attempted to get out of the wheel chair, but the nurse stopped her.

I caught up to Maddie and kissed her lips. "I'm okay, baby. I promise." Tears filled her eyes and she nodded.

She grabbed my hand. "Cale, I'm so scared."

"Don't be scared, Maddie. I'm right here with you, baby. I won't leave your side. I promise."

We got Maddie checked in and they brought her up to her labor and delivery room. The room was decorated in neutral colors. The nurses all wore scrubs patterned with kid or baby themes. Some were in bright pink, some in baby blue. Maddie's nurse was wearing some with rubber ducks on it. I laughed as the memory of cleaning Lily after the shit fiasco came back to me.

Maddie had decided to have a natural birth. I was pretty sure she was regretting her decision. Especially when she grabbed me by the T-shirt and pulled me down. "I can't take the pain anymore. Do something. Cale do something!"

My eyes widened and I looked around. The nurse smiled and winked at me.

Maddie let me go and let out a moan. "Please can I have an epidural? *Please*."

I turned to the nurse and gave her a look. She nodded and said, "Let me get your doctor in here, sweetheart, and we'll see how far you're dilated."

I sat next to Maddie as her doctor examined her. He turned and said something to the nurse and she rushed out the door. Doctor Green walked to the side of Maddie's bed. "Maddie," he said, "you've been a trooper, but we can't give you an epidural."

Oh shit, I thought. *This poor man is about to die at the hands of Maddie.*

"What? Why not? Please, Dr. Green. *Please*." Hearing Maddie beg nearly killed me.

Doctor Green took a deep breath. "Maddie, the baby is breach. You're dilated too far for us to give you an epidural. We need to get in there and get the baby out. Her heart rate is starting to drop."

My knees almost gave out. "What?" both Maddie and I said at the same time.

More nurses walked in as Dr. Green kept talking. "Cale, you can walk with us down to the OR, but you can't come in."

Maddie sobbed. "No. Cale has to be there. Someone has to be there for our baby."

The nurse grabbed Maddie's hand and said, "Maddison, I promise you, Cale will be the first person outside of the OR to see the baby. I promise you."

They moved Maddie out of the room and I followed along with her. Everything was happening so quickly. She held my hand so tight that it felt like she was breaking my fingers, but I didn't utter a word about it. I just kept telling her how much I loved her.

"Maddie, baby I love you so much," I said. "I'm so proud of you. I'll be right outside the doors. I swear."

She looked at me as I wiped her tears away. "Please, Cale, please don't leave. You promised me."

My heart broke as I let my tears fall freely. "Never, Maddie. I'll be right here."

They pushed her through the doors and she held my hand as long as she could.

Dr. Green stopped and put his hand on my shoulder. "Everything will be fine, Cale. I promise. Maddison will be out for about forty minutes. As soon as possible, the nurse will come and get you."

I nodded. "Take care of them, please. I can't live without her."

He nodded and smiled as he turned and walked through the doors. I raked my hands through my hair and walked over to the small waiting area. I sat down in the chair leaned back against the wall as I thought about the day Lily was born. Zoey had pretty much given up the fight. For months, I couldn't get it out of my head— why Zoey did what she did. I'd finally asked Jack for the name of Zoey's cousin, and I'd called and arranged lunch with her.

I closed my eyes and was brought back to the day I meet Zoey's cousin, Lori.

I WALKED INTO the restaurant and looked around. A young girl with blonde hair stood and waved. I smiled and nodded as I made my way over to her. I reached out my hand.

"Hey, Cale," she said. "It's nice to finally meet you."

"Likewise, Lori." We both sat down and the waiter arrived almost immediately. "What can I get you to drink?"

I took a deep breath. "A root beer, please."

He nodded his head and turned to leave.

I couldn't help but notice how much Lori looked like Zoey. I told her so.

Her smile faded and she looked down and played with her fork that was sitting on the table. "Yeah, people used to tell us that all the time. Zoey liked to live a more...carefree life though."

I nodded. "Lori, listen, I'm just going to cut to the chase. You knew Zoey better than anyone. Hell, I didn't even know you existed until right before Zoey died. I can't stop going over in my head why all this happened. Why would Zoey get pregnant knowing that it could possibly take her own life?"

Lori stopped spinning the fork and looked into my eyes. "I'll never forget the first time Zoey talked about Maddie. It was as if she'd found a kindred spirit. Maddie was nice to Zoey, when others weren't. Zoey was a bit of a...bitch."

I let out huff and grabbed my root beer, taking a sip. I needed to remember this was still Zoey's cousin.

She grinned weakly. "Zoey quickly became obsessed with Maddie."

"What do you mean?"

Lori shrugged. "She basically wanted to be Maddie. She wanted her life, her looks, her personality. Her health."

My heart dropped and now it was my turn to play with my fork.

"She told me how Maddie had mentioned this guy. She had talked about you, I guess, to her best friend and to Zoey once or twice. Zoey loved the idea that there was something that Maddie wanted so desperately. The day she met you in the coffee shop and heard your name, she figured it out. After you took her home and fuh..." Lori blushed and cleared her throat. "Um, after y'all had sex, she called me and was so excited that she could hardly talk. She kept saying that she'd found and taken what Maddie wanted. At first, I had no idea what she was talking about. Then it dawned on me."

I closed my eyes and shook my head. "She lied about the pregnancy. Why?"

She slowly nodded. "She knew you didn't have feelings for her. But she was obsessed with keeping you. She came up with this twisted idea and convinced herself that she was doing the right thing. All that fueled her at that point, Cale, was taking something that should have belonged to Maddie. She wanted to be Maddie, and she thought this was the way. She wasn't thinking clearly. When she realized what she'd done, she talked about getting an abortion and telling you she'd lost the baby."

I instantly felt sick. "Thank God she didn't." I barely whispered.

"Well, one night, when we were at a bar, she broke down crying. She said that Maddie still had everything. A rich and powerful boyfriend, a job she loved, and friends who cared about her. She even talked about trying to hook up with Maddie's boyfriend after having the baby."

I leaned back in the chair, trying to take it all in. I knew most of this already, but hearing it from Zoey's cousin just made it all so real.

"So Zoey was never in love with me." I said. "She just wanted me because Maddie wanted me. She got pregnant out of fear that I would leave her. I get all of that. But how long was she going to keep

this all up? Didn't she think about her own life when she came up with this whole pregnancy thing?"

Lori shrugged. "I don't think she thought it through. The further along in her pregnancy she got, the more she pulled away from me. She told me once that she didn't think she was going to make it through the entire pregnancy. She really didn't think the baby would, either."

I sighed as I dragged my hands over my face.

"Cale, the only reason she did any of this is because she wanted what Maddie desired. What Maddie dreamed and fantasized about. Once she found out you where the Cale Maddie had been talking about, she was going to stop at nothing to make you hers. To hell with her own health or other people's feelings. She wanted to take you and keep you from Maddie. But the only thing she ended up doing was taking her own life."

I CAME OUT of the memory when I head a female voice clearing her throat. I opened my eyes and saw the nurse standing in front of me smiling.

"Are you ready to meet your daughter?"

My heart beat rapidly in my chest. *My daughter. Our daughter.*

48

Maddie

M Y EYES FELT heavy as I forced them open. I could hear Cale
talking, and it sounded like he was talking to our baby. My
eyes opened and focused as I saw Cale standing there holding
our baby. I instantly started crying. Cale glanced over to me.

When a tear rolled down his cheek, I covered my mouth with
my hand and tried to hold my sobs back. The nurse came in and
asked if I was feeling okay. I was sitting up just a bit, as I looked
around the room. I nodded and Cale came closer. When he turned,
all I saw was the most amazing, beautiful, perfect, precious face staring back at me.

"Say hello to Mommy, Paige Evelyn." Cale smiled. To me, he
said, "She's been waiting patiently for her mommy to wake up."

A girl. We have a girl. I could no longer hold back my emotions.
As Cale placed our daughter in my arms, I began crying like a baby.
I could hardly see her through my tears. I pulled back her blanket
and checked all her toes and fingers.

"She's so beautiful and perfect," I said.

Cale ran his fingers through my hair and kissed my forehead.
"Yes she is," he said. "Just like her mother."

I looked up at him and I couldn't believe how my heart felt. It was as if this was the moment I'd been waiting for since that day I first walked away from him.

My journey home was finally complete.

TWO MONTHS LATER

"MADDIE, STOP TURNING around and checking on Evie, she's fine."

I chuckled as I spun back around and looked out the window. It had been two months since she was born, but I couldn't help myself. "I thought we were going to pick up Lily from your mom's?"

"Mom decided to bring Lily to Crystal Bridges to play outside. Since it was such a beautiful April day and all. You know how much Lily loves the flowers there."

I smiled and nodded. I'd stopped by the library last month with Evie and introduced her to everyone. I'd quit my job when Cale had his accident and had loved being home, but I did miss it sometimes. I glanced down and looked at the charm bracelet Cale had given me last year on Mother's Day. I spun it around on my wrist as I thought back to the moment he gave it to me. I hardly ever took it off. Cale had added another bird to the charm to represent the birth of Evie.

We pulled up and parked at the front and Thomas, one of the gardeners, greeted us. "Cale, Maddie, how are you both?"

I stepped out of the car and smiled. "Wonderful! How are you doing?"

He chuckled and said, "I can't complain. The flowers are beautiful right now. Mary and Lily are down playing by the large field."

"Great. Thanks, Thomas." I turned and looked at Cale. "You're not leaving the car here are you, Cale?"

"Um…"

"Let me park it for you," Thomas said. "I have nothing else to do right now and the three of you can head on down."

I gave Thomas a huge grin. "That is so sweet of you."

Cale handed Thomas the keys and winked. "Thanks so much. For everything."

I gave Cale a funny look as he reached into the back and took out Evie's car seat. He held out his hand and we started our way over to one of the paths that lead to the trails surrounding Crystal Bridges. I was instantly brought back to the night that Cale had asked me to marry him next to the LOVE sculpture. Cale and I chatted about Lily's first official Easter egg hunt next week. She would be two in July, and last year she hadn't been walking enough to do any kind of hunt at Easter. This year, she was ready. My father's company was planning a huge event for all of the employees and their families. I smiled as I thought about how different my dad had become. But my smile faded when I thought about the letter I'd sent to my mother telling her about Evie. She'd sent me a reply that simply stated, "Congratulations on the birth of your first child." That was it. I ended up sitting on the back deck with Monica and burning it in a small trashcan as we toasted to not being like our mothers. Then we both got drunk. I was pretty sure I'd had amazing sex with Cale that night, too.

"What are you so deep in thought about?" Cale asked as we walked along the trail. The smell of the flowers was washing over my senses—it had such a calming effect.

"Last month, when Monica and I got drunk. I'm pretty sure we had some hot sex and it kind of pisses me off I don't remember it."

Cale smiled and nodded. "Oh, I remember it. Believe me, it was fucking amazing."

I hit him on the shoulder and laughed. We rounded the corner and I gasped as my hands came up to my mouth. "Oh my. Cale, I…it's…"

There was a beautiful white arbor sitting in front of the LOVE sculpture. White lilies were everywhere as my father, his wife Michelle, Cale's parents, and Jack and Monica all stood to the side. Lucy and Craig were now seven months old and they were both sitting in a playpen. Lily was running around the playpen, making Lucy laugh.

Lily was wearing a darling, light green dress that matched Monica's. I moved my eyes over each person. Jack was dressed in jeans and a dress shirt and light green tie. Mary was wearing a long, flowing dress that was a shade darker than Monica's. Mitchel was wearing jeans and dress shirt with the same tie as Jack. I looked at my father and he was dressed the same way. Michelle's dress matched Monica's. It all hit me.

"Our wedding," I said as Cale walked up and set Evie's car seat on a chair. He cupped my face with both hands and brought my lips up to his. When he pulled away, he looked lovingly into my eyes.

"Maddison Powers, today I will make you officially mine."

I started to cry as Cale wiped my tears away with his thumbs. Before we'd left the house, he'd insisted I wear a long white dress that his mother had bought for me. I couldn't figure out why he was being so insistent, but when he said his mother had been feeling down and that it would cheer her up to see me in it, I didn't think twice about changing. It was now that I realized my white dress matched Monica's and Michelle's.

Cale was wearing jeans and a white button down shirt, and I hadn't even questioned it. Mitchel walked over and handed Cale a light green tie. He put it on, the whole time keeping his eyes on me.

I finally found the strength to speak. "We're getting married?"

He nodded his head and reached for Evie. "Yes, we are." He took my hand and led me to where Pastor Leonard was standing. Monica handed me a bouquet of white lilies.

I looked back and saw Mary ushering Lily to stand next to me. She tugged on my dress and said, "Mommy? Up, peese?"

I looked at Cale who smiled and nodded. I turned and picked up

Lily, holding her as Pastor Leonard began the ceremony.

Lily was perfectly quiet. When I turned around, Mary was holding Evie and feeding her a bottle. My heart almost exploded. Cale's mother had been such a huge part of my life over the last two years. She was the mother I'd never had, the mother Cale had never known, and a grandmother who loved our children with every ounce of her being. I mouthed, "I love you" to her and she mouthed it back as she wiped away a tear. I turned back around and listened to Pastor Leonard. Cale and I exchanged vows as we both stared into one another's eyes. When I thought Pastor Leonard was going to pronounce us husband and wife he paused, pointing.

"Maddie, Cale would like to present you with two gifts." I let out a sob and attempted to wipe my runny nose in a ladylike manner.

"Princess, can Mommy set you down for a few minutes?" I asked. "Maybe you can go sit next to Grammy and your baby sister?"

Lily nodded and bounced on over to sit with Mary.

I focused on Cale as Jack handed him a jewelry box. I couldn't help but look down at my charm bracelet and smile. If I knew Cale, he was about to give me a charm, and probably a bracelet for Evie.

He stepped closer, took my left hand, and began playing with my charm bracelet. "I've been holding onto this charm, trying to decide when to give it to you. I had it made a week after the birth of Evie, and was just waiting for the right time to give it to you. Then it hit me. A wedding present. I would give it to you as a wedding present. That meant I had to throw a wedding together with the help of our best friends and our parents. I know you really wanted to get married on our beach…"

My cheeks flushed and I looked down briefly.

"And, someday, we'll have that beach wedding. But this felt so right. I hope you agree."

I sniffled and nodded. "It's…perfect."

His grin grew bigger—he was so happy. He opened the box and pulled out a charm bracelet. "First gift goes to our beautiful daughter, Evie."

Mary walked over with Evie. Cale clasped the bracelet onto Evie's wrist and kissed her. I smiled as Mary turned and sat back down. Lily held up her own charm bracelet to show Evie. I couldn't help but giggle at the sweet, innocent act.

Cale cleared his throat and smiled. "Now, for your gift."

He reached back into the box before handing it back to Jack. When he turned around, he held up the charm for me to see. I gasped as I looked at three interconnecting hearts. The bigger heart had Lily's initials in it. The smaller heart had Evie's initials and the middle heart had Cale's and my initials on it.

"I thought it was fitting to make this charm all about hearts," he said. "You stole mine the moment you spoke to me. Then Lily..." Cale's voice cracked and he closed his eyes. "Lily healed my broken heart. And Evie...she brought together all of our hearts and bound them together to make us a family. The road we traveled to get to this very moment was a winding one, for sure." I grinned and wiped a tear away. He continued, "But when two hearts combine, and they travel that road together, it leads to something even greater. It leads to home. To a love so great it makes your heart burst. Maddie, my heart will always belong to you. You are, and will forever be, the love of my life."

I sobbed as Cale placed the charm in my left hand and closed my fingers around it tightly. "I love you, Maddison Nicole. I love you so much."

"I love you so much, Cale. I'll love you forever and for always."

Cale pulled a small box from his pocket. He turned to face Lily and bent down, motioning for her to come to him. She jumped up, brown curls bouncing as she hopped over to him. He opened the box and Lily smiled.

"Oh purty, Daddy," she said.

I tried to hold back my sobs as Cale placed a necklace with a dolphin, Lily's favorite animal, around her neck. He kissed her and whispered something in her ear. She wrapped her arms around his neck and I watched as a tear fell from his eye. Lily let go and hopped back over to Mary. Cale stood and wiped his eyes as he winked at me.

Cale turned to Pastor Leonard and nodded.

Pastor Leonard cleared his throat and took a step forward. "I now pronounce you, Mr. and Mrs. Cale Joseph Blackwood. Cale, you may kiss your bride."

Cale cupped my face in his hands and gave me the biggest, most panty-melting smile ever. I couldn't help but smile back. "Finally," We both whispered.

He leaned down and kissed me gently at first before pulling me closer and making the kiss more passionate. All I could hear was Jack and Monica whooping and hollering. Lily ran up and pulled on her clothes. "Me too! Daddy me too!"

Cale bent over and picked up Lily as we both kissed her on each cheek. I had never been so happy in my entire life. I looked around and everyone was clapping. I turned back to Cale and our eyes locked.

He brushed his lips against my ear. "Please tell me you still have that corset."

I smiled as I pulled back and raised an eyebrow. "I'm thinking a do-over is in order for this evening, Mr. Blackwood."

His eyes widened and he nodded his head. "I completely agree, Mrs. Blackwood."

EPILOGUE

Maddie

FIVE YEARS LATER

LILY CAME RUNNING up to me with a concerned look on her face. Her green-blue eyes held my eyes attention. "Mother. You will not believe what Father did!"

I tried like hell not to start laughing. Especially when I noticed Monica snap her head back and stare at Lily.

"One can only imagine what he did." I said as Monica's head jerked to the left to look at me.

"He…oh my gosh I can't even say it."

Monica shouted, "Say it! Please, I must hear you say it."

Lily took in a long, deep breath and slowly let it out. "He said I had to play soccer with him and Uncle Jack."

I let out a gasp and held my hand to my chest. "No!"

Monica leaned over. "Wait. You love soccer. I'm so confused."

Lily glanced at Monica. "Yes! Can you even believe the audacity of him?"

Monica started choking and Lily and I both busted out laughing. Lily held up her hand and I high fived it. "I'm really impressed you used that word correctly." I said.

Lily smiled. "I know, right? Aunt Monica, are you okay? Did the baby kick you too hard?"

I glanced down at Monica's seven-month swollen belly. "Um… your behaving like a twenty-five year old is what made me choke," Monica said.

Lily giggled. "I'm taking an acting class. I'm going to be an actress someday. Part-time, of course. My singing career will take center stage, but only on weekends. When I'm not working at my vet clinic."

Cale called out for Lily. "Lil, we're getting ready to start. Come on!"

Lily kissed me on the cheek and then kissed Monica's stomach. "Got to go kick Dad's butt at soccer. Later!"

She turned and started running toward Cale. We were at an office picnic for my father's company and Cale and Lily loved organizing the soccer games. Lily was a natural and loved to play.

"Holy crap, Maddie. I hope you guys are socking away money for that kid. She has her whole life planned out. I do like how she's planning on keeping the vet clinic her number one focus, instead of the acting and singing, though."

I threw my head back and laughed. "She definitely keeps us on our toes." I smiled at Monica. "How are you feeling?" I touched her stomach and the baby decided to kick right at that moment. We both laughed.

"I've never in my life been so happy, Maddie. I know Jack and I thought the pregnancy with the twins was our miracle, but to be blessed with this baby as well? I just…I'm…I'm so happy."

I pulled her into my arms and held her for a few minutes. "I'm so happy for you two. I really am."

Monica wiped away her tears and rolled her eyes. "Oh, God. Pregnancy emotions." She took a deep breath. "What about you, Maddie. Do you ever want another one? I mean I know Cale got his balls cut off and all."

I slapped my best friend on the arm and laughed. "Shut up. He didn't get his balls cut off. It was a small incision."

"Uh-huh. He got his balls cut."

I rolled my eyes. "No, Cale and I are happy with the girls. I couldn't imagine my life any different."

We both looked out and saw Evie, Lucy, and Craig all making mud pies. Lucy and Craig both had blonde hair and the bluest of blue eyes. Lucy favored Monica and Craig favored Jack, especially his personality.

"I think Evie has a crush on Craig." I said, looking at my younger daughter. Her brown hair was pulled up into a ponytail. She looked so much like me—it was unreal. She even scrunched her nose like I did.

"Shut up!" Monica said. "Craig totally has a crush on Evie."

Cale and Jack came over and I heard Cale gasp. I glanced over at them and Jack was smiling while nodding. "That's my boy, nothing but a ladies man."

Cale looked at me with nothing but pure horror in his eyes.

"No. Oh, *hell* no."

Jack reached into the cooler and grabbed a water bottle before taking back off toward the soccer game. "Just think dude, we could be in-laws someday!"

Cale's mouth dropped open as Monica and I busted out laughing. I watched as my husband slowly walked away, mumbling something about locking up his youngest spawn until she was twenty-one.

I giggled as Evie laughed at something Lucy was holding. *Oh no. Not the camel.*

I heard Cale yell out. I glanced over to see Cale and Lily both high-fiving each other—Lily had apparently scored a goal. I yelled, "Go Lily!"

Lily looked over at me and smiled as she gave me a thumbs-up.

Monica hit me in the arm and asked, "Hey, is that the camel Cale brought to the hospital the day the twins were born?"

Evie and Lucy were playing with the giant camel as Jack walked over to them. "Where did you guys get that?" he asked.

Lucy pointed to Cale and said, "Uncle Cale gave it to us!"

Jack spun around and took off running after Cale. "You bastard!"

Monica sighed. "Some things never change."

I laughed and shook my head. "Nope. I wouldn't want things any other way."

THE END

THANK YOU!

Darrin – Thank you for all that you do to support me. Thank you for your help, your patience when I'm sitting at my computer sometimes until after midnight, and for your inspiration! I love you, Darrin, so very much. You are my everything. Always and forever.

Lauren – I thank God every day for you. You're my breath of fresh air every single day. Even when you're rolling your eyes at me, talking back to me, staring at me like I'm an idiot, telling me you already know something I'm trying to explain to you… when I know for a fact you don't know, cleaning your bathroom and bedroom….oh wait…I'm still waiting for you to do that. I love doo so very much!

Kristin Mayer – Thank you for always being my friend first and foremost. You'll never know how much it means to me to have you read along as I write. I love how we throw ideas off each other and you totally get me! I'm so blessed to have you in my life and as my friend.

Ari Niknejadi – You make me laugh all the time with your one liners. I can't wait to start writing the book using them all! LOL! I'm still waiting on you to find your RFB. Thank you for being an amazing friend and a wonderful mother. I also wanted to say thank you so much for taking the beautiful photo that I used for the cover of this book. It says more than I could have ever hoped. Love you girl!

My beta readers – Kristin Mayer, Heather Davenport, and Laura Hansen, thank you both so much for taking the time to beta read for me. I appreciate it more than you will ever know.

Nikki Sievert – Thank you for EVERYTHING you do for me. You are the last eyes on my each of my babies and for you to take time out of your busy life to help me…I can only say thank you thank you thank you! Girls trip with you, Kristin, and me to NYC!

Lisa Wilson – I can never begin to express how much I love this cover. You did an amazing job and I cannot wait to work with you on more projects. This is by far one of my favorite covers.

Kelly's Cowboy Chasers – I just adore all of y'all. Thank you for making me smile on days I really needed it. Thank you for your support and love as well!

Kelly's Most Wanted – Thank you for being such an amazing street team. I don't think words could ever express my gratitude.

My HIPAA girls – Thank you! Thank you! Thank you! You are amazing friends and I'm blessed to have known you.

Kathy Bankard – You do so much for me and I hope you know how much I appreciate it. You're the best! Love you girl.

To my readers/friends – I wake up every morning and feel so blessed and it's because of your love and support. I hope and pray that I can continue to keep writing the stories that pull you in and have you longing for more. Thank you for allowing me to follow my dreams. Without you….none of this would be possible. Thank you!

Mom – Thank you for raising me to the person I am today. The journey of life sure is hard as hell and I really wish you were here to help on some of these steep hills…but then again…you are here. I love you.

Patty – I love you. Thank you for being there for me and being the best big sister ever.

Last but certainly not least. Thank you, God, for the blessing you have bestowed upon me. I'm in awe of your grace and I pray I never let a day go by where I do not close my eyes and thank you.

OTHER BOOKS BY KELLY ELLIOTT

WANTED SERIES

Wanted
Saved
Faithful
Believe
Cherished
A Forever Love
The Wanted Short Stories

BROKEN SERIES

Broken
Broken Dreams
Broken Promises (coming December 2014)

JOURNEY OF LOVE SERIES

Unconditional Love
Undeniable Love (coming spring 2015)

FOR UPCOMING BOOKS AND MORE INFORMATION ABOUT
KELLY ELLIOTT, PLEASE VISIT HER WEBSITE.

www.kellyelliottauthor.com

FOR EXCLUSIVE RELEASES AND GIVEAWAYS SIGNUP
FOR KELLY'S NEWSLETTER AT

http://eepurl.com/JoKyL